MW01065966

CARROLL & GRAF

INTIMATE MEMOIRS

INTIMATE
MEMOIRS

ANONYMOUS

CARROLL & GRAF PUBLISHERS, INC.
NEW YORK

First Carroll & Graf edition of *The Intimate Memoirs of an Edwardian Dandy Volume I* 1994
First Carroll & Graf edition of *The Intimate Memoirs of an Edwardian Dandy Volume II* 1994
First Carroll & Graf edition of *The Intimate Memoirs of an Edwardian Dandy Volume III* 1995

Carroll & Graf Publishers, Inc.
19 West 21st St., Suite 601
New York, NY 10010-6805

ISBN: 0-7867-0497-7

Manufactured in the United States of America

Contents

INTIMATE MEMOIRS

VOLUME I

Introduction

RUPERT MOUNTJOY'S FASCINATING autobiography tells the story of a wealthy young Englishman whose adolescence and early adult life was spent first in the depths of the country and then among the cream of London Society around the turn of the century. It permits the present day reader to look backwards in time to when scions of the leisured aristocracy were able to devote their days and nights purely in pursuit of pleasure. Rupert Mountjoy sets down details of his own sybaritic life-style in frank, unexpurgated detail that gives weight to the arguments of those social historians who claim that a powerful current of sexuality surged beneath the repressed public morality paraded during these years.

Certainly we now know that it was members of the upper classes who ignored the almost hysterical thundering by the Church (then a more powerful social force than now) about the perils of sexual experience. From Rupert's diary (which would appear to have been kept as far as possible on a contemporary basis with the entries written down as soon as possible after the events described took place) we read, for example, of how the school chaplain Reverend Clarke railed against the harmless practice of masturbation. Interestingly enough, Rupert and his friends ignored these and other dire warnings about the Sins Of The Flesh and his memoir shows that a strict straight-laced public morality was challenged at both the top and bottom ends of the social scale.

Rupert describes his hedonistic life-style – enjoying huge luncheons after lazy mornings, followed by unhurried afternoons spent leafing through sporting magazines at the club, to be rounded off perhaps by a formal dinner party or by an evening at one of the popular West End theatres where outside, to complete matters, he and his cronies would visit one of the *maisons privées* to take their pick of the pretty girls available as bed-mates. This may well appeal to members of the vast majority of young men of Rupert's age living almost one hundred years later who have neither the time nor money to enjoy such a comfortable existence!

This is not the first publication of the Mountjoy adventures. Shortly before he was forced to decamp to the Australian outback by his irate father after a disastrous speculation involving the purchase of three racehorses in the late autumn of 1913, he wrote to his solicitors, the fashionable firm of Godfrey, Allan and Colin, instructing Sir David Godfrey 'to make the best financial use possible of my scribblings'. Sir David, himself known in London's clubland as a man of robust sexual proclivities, promptly sold Rupert's manuscript to the editor of an illicit magazine published by the notorious Cremornite fraternity for a sum that appeared to satisfy the most pressing of Rupert's creditors.

The Cremornites were a semi-secret band of rakes which included such well-known *roués* as the financier and friend of King Edward VII, Sir Ronnie Dunn; Max Dalmaine the writer and artist; Captain Alan Brooke of the Guards; and the suitably named Dr Jonathan Letchmore who appropriately enough makes a brief appearance in this narrative, which makes one wonder whether Ruper Mountjoy was not himself at least associated with the group in some way. Incidentally, this charmed clique took its name from the infamous old Chelsea park of Cremorne Gardens, which was closed down in the 1880s after many complaints about the rowdiness there that often ended with free fights spilling over into the Kings Road, after the bars closed. It was also one of the major venues for prostitutes to meet their clients, on a par with Leicester Square and Piccadilly Circus. Ostensibly, the Cremornites simply ran a dining society, but in fact their Mayfair headquarters was a known haunt for upper class men-about-town where discreet privacy was offered to participants in several recorded orgies that took place there in the presence of some of the highest personages in the country.

Rupert's personal confessions were serialised in the quarterly Cremornite journal through till 1917. Copies that were smuggled out to the trenches must have brought back wistful memories of happier days to the officers and men who faced the terrible slaughter of the Great War.

Luckily for Rupert, he was many thousands of miles away from the terrible conflict which was to spell the end of the kind of sybaritic luxury that we associate with the Edwardian era. From his letters to friends and family, it appeared that our author was in fact keen to enlist but was wisely prevailed upon to stay at home. He was influenced, one might surmise, by his fiancée, Nancy du Boute, to whom he was introduced shortly after his arrival in Australia. Also, the wheel of fortune turned in his favour in Sydney, even though his father, Colonel Mountjoy, had cut him off with only a second class one-way ticket to the New World and a cheque for £2,000 Rupert promptly invested this money in the establishment of a gentleman's club, the Odd-bods, in an elegant mansion just off Pitt Street, in the heart of Sydney. From all accounts it was based on very similar lines to the Cremornites' gatherings and, within a few years, Rupert was able to charge a hundred guineas a year as a membership fee. Nevertheless, the Club had a long waiting list of would-be members.

A few months after the Armistice in November 1918, a second unauthorised publication of Rupert's early diaries was printed in Manchester by the Society of Venus and Priapus, a circle about which little is known. In fact, scholars now speculate that the Society may never have actually existed but that it was simply a front for the spectacularly rude booklets printed under its name, probably by Oswald Knuckleberry of Didsbury, a great-nephew of Ivor Lazenby, the Victorian writer and publisher of such under-ground erotic classics as *The Pearl* and *The Oyster*.

In 1921 Rupert and his family (he married Nancy in 1915 and they produced three children, twin boys and a girl, within five years) emigrated once more to a new home, this time to a palatial ranch house in southern California. In a letter to his old friend, Sir David Godfrey, Rupert complains bitterly about the officers of the Sydney police force who he said were becoming too rapacious for the turning of a blind eye to the raunchy happenings at the Oddbods Club. And the Mountjoy family lived quietly in the sunny climes of California, with both Rupert and Nancy living to a ripe old age not far from the ultra-fashionable area of Beverly Hills.

There may be some who find Rupert Mountjoy's uninhibited writing somewhat shocking even today. But as Webster Newington, one of our foremost authorities on turn-of-the-century British erotica, has stressed, 'It must be noted that the underground publications of this time show that there existed a persistent questioning of the taboos which then existed and this sceptical attitude helped lead to the more relaxed self-understanding and enlightenment concommitant with the multiplicity of views on sexual relations which exist in the 1990s.'

Authors such as Rupert Mountjoy set themselves firmly against the authoritarian notion that mainstream sexuality was an area which had to be stringently controlled by the ruling Establishment, and it is timely that his writing has survived the years to be republished almost one hundred years later to provide an unconventional, irreverent insight into the manners and mores of a long-vanished world.

WARWICK JACKSON
Birmingham
February, 1992

I am fully aware that my youth has been spent,
That my get-up-and-go has got up and went.
But I really don't mind when I think with a grin,
Of all the grand places my get-up has been!

RUPERT MOUNTJOY
London
September, 1913

CHAPTER ONE

First Stirrings

LITTLE APOLOGY IS NEEDED – OR WILL BE made – for putting into print my frank, uncensored memoirs. For why should I not publish my diary? It may be of interest to both present and future generations of readers for many famous people are named in its pages. Here at the very start, however, I will freely admit to the alteration of certain names and places and the omission of a number of events, for nothing could induce me to embarrass or offend the sensibilities of any lady, from the parlourmaid positioned in the lower classes to the high and mighty London hostess who claims pride of place at the very apex of Society.

I trust you will appreciate my concern, dear reader, though let me hasten to assure you that the above *caveat* notwithstanding, I also confirm in clear type a matter of importance which I have stated verbally on numerous occasions to my close friends, whilst placing in order the many and tidying recollections from the disordered files of memory. I refer, of course, to the fact that every gentleman whose name appears in my memoir has happily granted permission for his nomenclature to be revealed. Several letters have reached me from old acquaintances of both sexes who, despite having been warned of my intention to write a candid and undisguised account of my recent past, have expressed their pleasure to hear of the project. Indeed, they have urged me not to leave out their names in my manuscript, whilst not hesitating to remind me of jolly times enjoyed together at St Lionel's or sampling the varied and often exotic delights afforded to gentlemen of means domiciled in the heart of Belgravia and Mayfair, surely the most propitious areas in London for those like myself whose chief interest lies in *l'art de faire l'amour*.

To complete these introductory words, may I cordially thank all who have assisted me in the compilation of what has turned out to be, according to my dearest chum Harry Price-Bailey: 'the horniest book of licking and lapping, sucking and fucking I have ever had the pleasure to read'.

So without ado, let us turn back the years to the summer of 1898 when I was a lad of just fifteen years of age, living with my parents at the family seat of Albion Towers, which lies near the sleepy little village of Wharton on the edges of the Forest of Knaresborough in Yorkshire. Few areas of Britain are so rich in beauty and interest as this part of the country. There are moors to hike across, several wooded valleys through which flow lovely streams with glittering falls, grand ruins of castles, abbeys and historic houses and many fine buildings which show few signs of the passage of time – all these and many other features of appeal are to be found on every hand.

This is why my father, Colonel Harold Elton Fortescue Mountjoy, late of the Indian Army, so enjoyed coming back to the home country after long service on the North West Frontier, for Yorkshire has an insistent appeal to all who delight in open-air pursuits, while the bracing air is unrivalled in England Whilst the Pater busied himself with looking after our estate and taking every opportunity to go hunting, shooting and fishing, my Mama occupied herself with other ladies from the best families in the county. As surprisingly few houses were yet connected by telephone (I should add that we were an exception to this rule for though Father could be a bit of a crusty old buffer now and then, he was extremely interested in scientific progress and was the proud owner of one of Monsieur Lumière's cameras that could take moving pictures, but more of this anon) Mama spent much of her time writing letters regarding social events in our neighbourhood, from dinner parties for the gentry to trips to Harrogate with Lady Scaggers, The Hon Mrs Boote and other close friends

We returned from India four years ago, leaving my elder sister Barbara in New Delhi where she lives with her husband, Lord Lisneigh, Deputy Governor of the North East Territories However, though to all intents and purposes I was an only child, I rarely suffered from the pangs of loneliness. Although I had no companions of my age locally, I was at home only during school holidays for my education was conducted at the grand old school of St Lionel's College for the Sons of Gentlefolk far down south in the beautiful county of Sussex There I made many pals including some like Harry Price-Bailey, Terence Blacker, Clive Allingham and Frank Folkestone who have remained firm friends throughout the passing years. During our vacations we frequently visited each other's homes, and as Mama was always more than pleased to extend hospitality to my school-fellows, I spent few days without someone to pass the time with.

Nevertheless, I begin this excursion down the lane of recollection on one of these rare days. It was a glorious morning in early July 1898 and I looked forward to welcoming Frank Folkestone, the captain of the Upper Fourth at St Lionel's, to Albion Towers. Frank was spending the first week of the summer vacation with his parents at their home in St John's Wood before taking the train up to Harrogate where Papa and I would meet him. But what I hoped would turn out to be a highly satisfactory day opened on a gloomy note with the arrival of a telegram from Lady Folkestone, stating that Frank was suffering from a heavy summer cold and so she was postponing his trip up to us for twenty-four hours.

'It's only one day, Rupert,' said my Mama, trying to lift my spirits, 'and the weather looks so fine, why don't you spend the day out of doors? Perhaps you would like to join your father and Reverend Hutchinson who are fishing at the river on Mr Clee's land? I'll ask Mrs Randall to make you up a packed luncheon and I'm sure it will be in order for you to borrow one of your father's rods.'

But I declined the offer, for I have never possessed the patience to wait for a fish to take the bait at the end of the line. Still, the idea of spending the day out of doors appealed to me. An idea struck me – Mr Pilcher, the senior teacher of natural history at St Lionel's, had fired my class with the notion of starting a birds' eggs collection [*a practice now heavily discouraged – Editor*] and I thought that today would be as good as any to begin making up a set. I mentioned this to Mama who conveyed my request for roast beef sandwiches and a bottle of ginger ale to Mrs Randall in the kitchen whilst I went upstairs to change into an athletic vest and football shorts as the weather was uncommonly warm and I planned a three-mile hike to Knaresborough Woods.

So this is why, on that never-to-be-forgotten July morn, I went striding out of our front gates, my rucksack on my back filled with food for my *al fresco* luncheon and a woollen jersey to slip on in the unlikely event of a change in the weather. It was just after ten o'clock when I left home to walk through our grounds and as I walked briskly along, I had a vague sensation that someone was dogging my footsteps. Yet when I turned round to look behind me, which I did several times, the road was clear and I was apparently alone. I must be imagining it, I said to myself, yet there was no shaking off the feeling that someone was keeping pace for pace with me. The sensation of being followed is most disagreeable and I began to wonder whether some vagabond tinker was waiting to pounce upon me, though such crimes of petty robbery were so rare in the locality that any news of such a happening would warrant substantial coverage in the weekly *Harrogate Chronicle*.

Yet I could not rid myself of the notion that I could hear the patter of light footsteps that were not my own. But soon the path was clear of trees and though I was still a mite apprehensive, I was now also slightly ashamed of my first concerns. After all, the Queen's Highway was free to all and I was probably just being tracked for fun by a young son of one of the farmworkers whom my father employed to till our arable fields.

If anything, the sun now shone even more brightly. Soon after I crossed the meandering country lane that led to the Harrogate road I sat down to rest for a moment or two on a mossy bank. It stood on the verge of a meadow owned by our neighbour Doctor Charles Wigmore, whose sixteen-year-old daughter Diana was a girl whose beauty struck me tongue-tied and left me awkwardly attempting to remember my manners on the few occasions when we had found ourselves together in company. Momentarily a picture of the delightful Diana flashed across my mind as I allowed my rucksack to rest along the slope of the hillock and I stretched my arms and yawned, at peace with the world. I sat for a minute or two and then heaved myself up again – only to hear the quickening approach of another traveller behind me.

I turned to see that standing only some twenty yards away was none other than the lovely Diana Wigmore herself, also dressed for the heat of the summer in a white linen blouse and a similarly coloured dress which barely reached more than a couple of inches below the knees of her uncovered legs. She really looked the acme of feminine perfection, being a lovely rosy-cheeked girl with a gay twinkle in her bright blue eyes. She wore her tresses of light ash blonde hair gracefully pinned up around her graceful neck, and young and inexperienced though I was regarding the fair sex, her saucy little nose and pouting lips, together with the clearly visible heaving of her proud young breasts as she recovered from her sudden exertion, set my own heart pounding at a fair rate of knots

'Good morning, Miss Wigmore,' I said shyly, congratulating myself on for the first time speaking to this gorgeous girl without stuttering or blushing furiously with nervousness. 'Have you been running to catch up with me? I thought there was someone on my trail but you kept yourself invisible every time I looked around to see who my mysterious follower could be.'

This time it was Diana whose face coloured up with genuine embarrassment. 'Oh Rupert, I do apologise – I know I should have called out to you at least a mile back. You looked deep in thought, and I thought it would be rude to disturb you.'

'I wasn't meditating about anything more important than how best to begin collecting birds' eggs for my collection. I haven't even started yet and I was only thinking as to whether I'd find anything in the nests at this time of the year.'

She smiled and a delicious dimple appeared on the side of her face. 'I don't know much about the habits of birds,' she said. 'Is your quest for schoolwork or simply for your own entertainment?'

'It's not very important at all – I just thought it a good excuse to get out of doors on such a fine day. I could have gone angling with my father

15

but, between ourselves, I find the sport boring though I know that many people derive much pleasure from the pursuit.'

Diana sighed and said: 'You are a lucky boy, Rupert. I have some holiday work which must be finished by the end of the vacation. As we are going on the Grand Tour next week [*a favourite summer trip by English families to Italy that usually encompassed Venice, Florence and Rome – Editor*] I must complete my portfolio to gain the certificate in art which I need to go on to further studies at college next term.'

'I didn't know you were an artist, Miss Wigmore.'

'Oh please call me Diana, Rupert. All my friends do – and you are my friend, aren't you?'

'I would love to be,' I said boldly, 'and I just wish there was something I could do to help you in your work. But I can hardly draw a straight line and I know very little about painting!'

'But there *is* something you can do, Rupert, though I hardly dare ask you,' she burst out.

'Well, if we are friends, you should be able to ask anything of me – all I can promise is to do my best to oblige. But if I cannot help I will just say so and nothing is lost.'

'You *are* a sweet boy. Very well then, I will take up your offer but promise me you won't be too shocked and that, whatever happens, you will keep this conversation secret,' she demanded.

'I give you my word,' I said, puzzled by the earnest look on her pretty face. 'This must be a matter of very great importance to you. So again, how may I be of assistance?'

Diana slowly expelled a deep breath. 'Rupert,

you might know that I attend Nottsgrove Academy, a progressive institution which believes in the equality of opportunity for women in both political and cultural matters. As far as art is concerned, Mrs Bickler, our art mistress, firmly believes that painters are often forced to suffer varying degrees of injustice from financial problems. This is due to a misunderstanding or dislike of their finest work by patrons or the ruling artistic establishment. For women, there has always been a further prejudice against which to battle which is why so few women have made any serious headway in this field.'

I listened patiently for even at this early age I had already realised the uselessness of interrupting when someone has climbed upon a hobbyhorse – and, anyhow, I enjoyed looking at this pretty girl who obviously cared passionately about her subject.

'There is still a bar against women at meeting places such as clubs or, heaven forbid, a genuine studio! Even at this early stage, I cannot find a subject for my figure studies.

'This is where I need your help, Rupert,' she added bluntly. 'I will not beat about the bush – I want you to pose for me whilst I make some charcoal sketches.'

'But that hardly seems an onerous task,' I declared, slightly puzzled by her words. 'Why, I'm truly flattered to be asked and I'd be delighted to help out. Look, I'm free this very minute if you would like to begin work straightaway.'

Her beautiful blue eyes sparkled. 'Oh Rupert, what a kind offer! Well, if you really mean it, just a half mile or so through that stile there is a

17

perfect place where I have set up my easel. On the ground lie my pencils and brushes. I've also brought along a small hamper, but Cook always packs too much and there'll be more than enough food for both of us.'

'It doesn't matter as I also have some sandwiches and a bottle of ginger pop in my rucksack '

'Well, that would seem to settle it. You really mean it, Rupert? Shall we really start here and now?' she asked eagerly, seemingly surprised that I made so little of the matter.

'Why not?' I said gallantly and gestured for her to lead the way. As Diana had promised, we did not have far to walk before finding ourselves in one of the numerous interesting copses on her father's property through which ran several shady footpaths hidden from the view of any passer-by. Sure enough, she had set up her equipment on a blanket spread out on a level piece of ground where I dumped my rucksack.

'Here we are then,' she called out. 'It's such a pleasant day and the light is quite superb just now Gosh, I can hardly wait to begin. Are you ready Rupert? Yes? Jolly good – we won't be disturbed in such a quiet spot I suggest you get undressed over here and put your clothes on the blanket.'

I could not believe what I had heard and I looked at her in astonishment. 'What the deuce do you mean, Diana? Take off my clothes, did you say?'

She looked at me with a trace of impatience in her gaze 'Yes, of course, my love, how else would I be able to sketch the male figure if not from an uncovered form?'

So this is why Diana was at first diffident about asking for my assistance! And why she was so happy to hear me consent to model for her without any fuss! I had assured her of my aid and it would be dishonourable and cowardly to break my word. I will readily admit that I could not bear to appear foolish in front of this gorgeous creature who, if I backed away from this challenge, would probably never deign to speak to me again! So I took a deep breath and said: '*All* my clothes, Diana?'

'Yes, dear,' she said steadily. 'Otherwise I would be unable to do either of us justice. So do be quick about it and then I'll show you just how I would like you to stand.'

I hesitated still. Sensing my modesty, she added encouragingly: 'Come on, Rupert, there's really nothing to it. Look, if it makes you feel any easier, I'll kick off my shoes and take off this blouse and skirt. It's so hot that I'll feel far more comfortable just dressed in my chemise.'

I closed my eyes, for the dreadful thought flashed through my brain that if I even took the most fleeting of glances at the sight of Diana Wigmore clad solely in a chemise, it would be impossible to prevent my penis from instantly betraying my secret sensual desires. As it was, like all boys at this difficult age, I had little enough control over my prick which would swell up sometimes for no good reason and which demanded the attention of my closed fist at least three times a day. Still, I had no avenues of retreat, so I sat down on the stump of a nearby tree and removed my shoes and socks.

Then, drawing upon every ounce of valour in my body, I turned away and slipped down my shorts and drawers together and wriggling out of

19

them, stood with my flapping white athletic vest covering just the upper part of my backside. I exhaled slowly before raising my arms and pulling off my remaining garment to stand totally naked in front of this amazing girl

To her credit, Diana appeared to be unconcerned about her first sight of my bare body. 'Rupert, would you just lean back against that tree at a slight angle to the sun, but facing me full on. Good, that's absolutely how I want you. Lay your hands on your thighs and raise your head to the sky, no, not too much – there, that's right, can you hold that position? Are you comfortable? Now please keep as still as you can.'

I complied with her request and surprisingly soon the fact that I was standing in a state of complete nudity began to fade in importance Diana chatted away as she worked, saying: 'Your body is well suited to a classical study, Rupert You have the physique and more important, perhaps, the confident pose of a youth capable of surmounting all the obstacles which might occur in your life – not only through your undoubted physical strength but also by the sheer force of your personality. Now I have the talent, I want to capture that pensive look along with a clear-cut profile of your face with that proud look of determination stamped upon your brow.'

Her comments were perhaps slightly above my head but I felt flattered by all this attention and when, after half an hour or so, she suggested that we allowed ourselves a ten-minute break, I could hardly wait to pad over and see what she had committed on canvas. But before I could come round she placed her hand on my chest and said:

'Please, Rupert, wait till we have finished. You might not like what you see and whichever way you feel may adversely affect the way you pose for me afterwards. You don't mind, do you?'

'No, of course not,' I stammered, all too conscious again of my unclothed state and of the cool touch of her slender fingers upon my skin, especially when she let them trace a circular pattern around one of my nipples. 'You are so well proportioned for such a young lad. Why, you're almost as muscular as Roger, Lord Tagholm's son. My friends and I all much admired his manly torso when we saw him at the football club's gymnastic display last Easter.

'Naturally enough we never had a chance to see his powerful frame in such a glorious state of freedom, unburdened by superfluous vestments,' she murmured throatily, looking directly down at my perceptibly stiffening penis which was still dangling down but swelling inexorably, its ruby head already only semi-covered as I tried to prevent it jumping up to its full length. But despite all my efforts I felt my cock rise higher and higher, now fully uncapping the red-topped helmet as my shaft swelled up to its full eight and a half inches, standing smartly to attention against my belly.

My face turned bright crimson, for there was no way that Diana could have missed the swift rise of my tumescent tadger. Now a further shock awaited me, for I was certain that the lovely girl would toss her blonde tresses in disgust and at best walk silently away from me or, at worst, castigate me violently for being so rude.

I braced myself for the onslaught but to my

21

amazement, Diana moved her hand downwards to seize my shaft, and her long fingers, working as though they possessed a will of their own, started to frig my throbbing tool, rubbing it slowly, which made me almost swoon from the delicious sensations that coursed around my entire body.

Diana was delighted by my response and she said, really talking to herself: 'My goodness, what a splendidly proportioned penis for a mere lad. It looks so scrumptious that I would like to kiss it. But no, no, I must not let myself be so roused by this handsome boy and his immensely big prick. I really am very naughty to even touch it but I cannot help myself.

'Ah, how lewd,' she muttered as she drew back my foreskin, making my knob leap and bound in her hand. With her free hand, Diana unbuttoned her chemise and freed the uptilted, bouncy globes of her bosoms to my excited view. Now, I had peeped at French photographs of undraped females in the pages of *The Oyster* which Clee kept in his locker in our dormitory back at St Lionel's, but never before I had seen in the flesh the breasts of a pretty young woman. How tempted I was to touch those two proud beauties! And how well they were set off by the two cheekily pointed nipples, themselves each capped by the pink circles of the aureoles. The sweet girl groaned with unslaked passion as I plucked up enough nerve to move my hand up and gingerly tweak one of her engorged strawberry-like titties.

'Stop, Rupert, stop, you must be a good boy, she murmured but I was in no mind to heed this plea and continued to feel her erect tittie with my fingers. No, I mean it, please stop that. I like it very much but we must get back to work. First, however, I'll finish you off which will give you some relief,' she gasped, gripping my twitching shaft even tighter.

Reluctantly I obeyed but she was as good as her word, as increasing the pace of her frigging, she rubbed my cock so sensuously that in a matter of moments the creamy froth shot out of my tool all over her fingers and splattered out over her chemise.

'Oh dear, I'd best take off this chemise and wash it in the stream. I'll have to do the same with my knickers, as they are already wet with my juices. If I don't, our laundrymaid is bound to gossip with the other servants about the state of Miss Diana's underclothes,' she said lightly. The thought of seeing this exquisite girl strip off her remaining garments set my truncheon standing up to attention again from its state of semi-erectness it had subsided into when Diana had finally relinquished her grip.

'Now, now, Rupert, behave yourself!' she grinned, ordering me back to my tree with an imperious wave of her arm. I sighed but trudged back obediently as Diana called out: 'I tell you what, my family only sent you a boring old book for your birthday last month. If you will try to stay as still as you can, in the same way as you managed before, I'll give you a very, very nice late birthday present before lunch which we'll both enjoy even more that we did just now.'

A late birthday present, I mused to myself as I leaned back into my old position – what the blazes could she mean by that? Genuinely, I had not the slightest idea and even the sight of her licking her upper lip with the tip of her tongue failed to provide the clue to unlock the puzzle for me. Meanwhile, I had to concentrate both mind and body on holding my pose for this sweet lass, *la bella donna della mia mente** for Diana was a truly industrious worker and she stuck to her task, looking up and pausing only occasionally to ponder now and then for artistic inspiration. The minutes ticked away but I stayed as still as could be. To pass the time I thought of all the fun Frank and I would have after he arrived to stay with us tomorrow. I could just see his face when I told him about this current adventure! Wouldn't he just be green with envy when I told him about how Diana had wanked my cock! No, that's an unworthy thought I decided as, feeling weary, I shifted my weight from one foot to the other. On the other hand, I could tell him all about it without mentioning her name and ever letting on even if she and Frank were to meet at some later date

'Okay, it's time for lunch,' sang out Diana, breaking into my reverie. I stretched my arms out and walked across to her, my excited gait showing her that I was ready and waiting for this special treat she had previously mentioned. She gave me a dazzling smile as she put her hands on my shoulders and said: 'Would you like your birthday present now, Rupert, or would you like to wait until after we've eaten?'

'May I have it now, please?' I asked humbly and she nodded her head. 'Yes, you deserve a nice present as you've been a very good boy and not tried to make me go further than I wanted.' Again, I was at a loss to understand her words

* The beautiful girl of my memory

24

though now, of course, I realise that what she meant to convey was that I took heed of her request to let go of her tittie when it became plain that she really meant what she said.

Diana took hold of my arms and put them round her back, at the same instant moving forward so that we were now sweetly crushed together. She lifted her arms up to cradle my neck and bring my face to hers and our mouths met to join together in what was the very first kiss of passion I had ever experienced. I was totally engulfed in a torrent of idyllic bliss that swept in waves over me. I heard nothing, saw nothing and felt nothing but the ravishing excitement of this first embrace. Far from discouraging my roving hands, she herself moved them to her breasts and as I caressed the firm, rounded globes, she slid the straps of her chemise off her shoulders and I thrilled to the touch of her naked nipples that rose up like hard little bullets to greet me. My prick had already stiffened up to stand powerfully upright, as hard as a rock, my knob already burst free from its covering as the luscious girl grabbed hold of my straining shaft.

We were swept off our feet by this fierce outpouring of frenetic energy and we sank to the ground, still joined by our mouths with my right hand cupped around the jutting orbs of her breasts and Diana's fingers gripping my prick, ardently rubbing my shaft and now tonguing my mouth so vehemently that I could feel the boiling juices already fermenting in my balls.

The prudent girl sensed that I was nearing a spend and she swiftly withdrew from my mouth and rolled me over onto my back. Then suddenly her tousled blonde tresses were between my legs and her lips were upon my cock as she kissed the unhooded helmet, lapping up the blob of liquid that had already formed there and licking my purple mushroomed crown with her pink little tongue. She opened her lips wide enough to encircle my knob and instinctively – for of course my young penis had never before been placed in such a sublime haven – I moved forward to push my excited tadger even further into her mouth 'A–h–r–e, A–h–r–e, A–h–r–e!' I panted as her magic tongue travelled wetly all over my tool. I thought I might even pass out from the unbelievable pleasure that scorched every fibre when her teeth scraped the tender flesh of my knob as she drew me in again between those luscious lips, sucking my shaft slowly from top to base, with her every sweet suction transporting me to even higher peaks of Elysian delights.

I groaned as I felt my balls hardening for I only wanted to continue this marvellous game. Diana looked up at my contorted face as I tried desperately to hold back the flow of sperm. The understanding girl promptly solved my dilemma by immediately freeing my twitching tool from its heavenly prison and she also withdrew her hand from my throbbing shaft.

Then with a saucy glint in her eyes she said: 'Well, you've unwrapped your birthday present, so to speak – let's see if you are old enough to know how to play with it.' And without further ado she climbed on top of me with her knees on either side, pulling open her love-lips with her fingers and massaging her pussey back and forth across the tip of my cock. I bucked and heaved, wanting above all to slide my rampant rod into her cunt. She teased me for a moment or two but then she lifted herself before crashing down on my pulsating pole, tightening the walls of her cunney as she held me in place, rocking backward and forward, slicking my shaft with her juices as she rocked with ecstasy. This was simply too much to bear and as I pushed upwards once more I felt the white frothy spunk burst out of my cock. Diana screamed with joy as she too climaxed as the hot creamy spunk flooded into her and she shuddered with glee as I pumped jets of jism into her flooded crack. She leaned forwards, my now shrivelling penis still snugly inside her slit, and kissed me on my mouth. 'Well done, Rupert! That was a really splendid fuck,' she whispered in my ear as we lay panting with exhaustion.

As we rested, bathed in the bright sunlight, now entwined in each other's arms, I proudly mulled over the fact that I had now crossed the Rubicon and hopefully there would be many more opportunities to make further journeys with Diana. Naturally, like all of my contemporaries in the Upper Fourth, I enjoyed a daily five-knuckle shuffle. But I could never have imagined that real fucking could be so exciting and wonderful; it had surpassed all my expectations. Here I was lying on Nature's bed of grass, having made passionate love to the beautiful naked girl now in my arms. Or to be more accurate, having just had her make love to me! The tenderness of this first engagement will never fade from my memory. As the poet says, *me tamen urit amor; quis enim adsit amori.**

* Love consumes me yet – for what bounds may be placed on love?

Once we had regained our senses, we ate our luncheon with gusto, for the worship of Venus and Priapus fuels the appetite better than any medicine. 'I suppose you want to continue your drawing.' I said with a sigh as I collected up the detritus of our picnic and placed it in my rucksack.

'No hurry, my dear,' twinkled Diana as she took hold of my prick as I passed by, stroking the limp shaft until I felt the first stirrings of an erection.

'I don't know whether I can do it again,' I confessed, though the way my prick was swelling under Diana's ministrations appeared to leave little doubt.

'Just lie back, Rupert, and leave the rest to me,' advised my love with a gay smile.

Slowly at first she gently stroked the sensitive underside of my still-stiffening penis, allowing her fingers to trace a path around and underneath my balls which instantly made me tingle all over with an electric gratification. After a while she closed her finger and thumb around the shaft, sliding them along its length as her head dived down and, like a magic serpent, her tongue slid around and around my stiffstander until it was as hard as a poker and fairly bursting for action.

'M'm, I think you are now more than ready for the fray,' she murmured huskily, disengaging her lips from my pulsating prick as she rolled over on her back and motioned me to scramble up in front of her. I was on my knees in a moment, my cock just inches away from the gaping lips of her cunney that thrust through the silky mass of her blonde bush. I brought my straining stiff to the

28

charge and to our joint squeals of delight, fairly ran it through into the sopping depths of her warm, willing cunt until my ballsack swished against Diana's bottom. We lay quite still for a few moments as Diana's pulsing pussey squeezed my cock so exquisitely that for the second time I almost swooned away from the sheer pleasure of it all She then heaved up her *derrière* and I responded to this move with a mighty shove of my own and we commenced a most exciting fuck. My rock-hard staff fairly glistened with her love juices as it worked in and out of her sheath, whilst the lips of her cunney seemed to cling to it at each time of withdrawal as if afraid it would lose its delectable sugar stick.

Our movements now locked themselves into a furious rhythm. Diana was transformed into a wild animal, screeching uninhibitedly as she writhed uncontrollably under me with the force of an approaching orgasm. I fucked her at an even greater speed until, with a little wail, she slumped backwards, her thighs clenched around my waist as her body shook in a rapid drawn-out series of spasms. Her cunney squeezed my cock even tighter and the pressure led very soon to me shooting off a further libation of sticky white seed inside her saturated love channel that drained my prick of every last drop of its precious elixir . .

I have heard it said so many times that one's introduction to the joys of love-making can often be a traumatic experience and certainly it is a stepping stone into adulthood that one rarely forgets. First love can be tremendous – or absolutely disastrous. This usually depends upon the circumstances, on the partner of one's choice and to a very great extent, upon ourselves. I was naive, slightly shy and, at first, frankly bewildered by my first voyage along the highway of love but I was fortunate enough to be accompanied by a sophisticated girl who took the trouble to care for and cater to my every need.

Indeed, my heart was bursting with gratitude to Diana for her kindness and I leaned over to kiss her and said: 'You've been so good to me. I've never had such a marvellous time. Did you enjoy making love as much as I did, Diana?'

'Oh yes, it was a dreamy fuck,' she replied as I rolled off her soft body to lie beside her. 'That's the second time I've spent. Who have you fucked with before, Rupert? Did one of your horny servant girls teach you about how to pleasure a pussey? Or was it an assistant matron perhaps at St Lionel's? I've heard all about some of the goings-on in such places!'

'No, I've never ever done it before,' I confessed timidly, feeling the colour rise to my cheeks. Would the divine girl laugh at this intimate personal revelation?

But no, far from it – she clasped her hands together happily and said: 'You were a virgin and I was your first conquest? Oh, what an honour! Let me kiss your lovely cock, Rupert, he deserves every praise for his performance.' Yet even as she planted her lips upon my shaft, which now dangled flaccidly over my thighs, I realised that I still had much to learn about fucking if I wanted to become such a cocksman as the merry young men-about-town whose exploits I had read about in Clee's naughty magazine. I resolved then and there to devote my life to the study and appreciation of *l'art de faire l'amour*.

But I must return to my story – Diana and I worked on assiduously after this feast of fucking and when she showed me the result of her labours, I was most gratified to see myself immortalised through her perceptive artistry. She had sketched a most lifelike portrait of my face in bold sweeping lines, capturing the essence of my likeness and though I thought she flattered my physique (especially by the very prominent bulge under the fig leaf she was forced to paint over my cock and balls!) I told her in all candidness that for what it was worth, there could be little doubt that one day her work would hang on the walls of the Royal Academy in London.

'Do you really think so?' she said as she carefully packed up her materials and folded up her easel.

'Well, I don't suppose my words mean much to anyone but I'm going to ask you here and now to paint my picture again when I leave St Lionel's,' I said with genuine feeling.

'That's a deal – my very first commission,' she laughed 'I won't charge you more than twenty guineas.' [*Twenty-one pounds or about thirty-five US dollars.*]

[*Diana Wigmore's later canvases, completed after her studies at the Slade School of Art, did in fact hang in the Academy's Summer Exhibitions of 1902, 1903 and 1908 and her paintings enjoyed a reasonable amount of critical and popular acclaim, especially when one of the most distinguished European connoisseurs, Count Johnny Gewirtz of Galicia, started to collect her work. Most unfortunately, many of her best pictures, which were in the Count's collection at Allendale House in Belgravia, were destroyed by enemy action during the*

31

London Blitz in 1940.

However, we will meet the attractive young artist again in Rupert's diaries for she was to be invited to join many a country-house party at the express invitation of King Edward VII. Diana first met the King at a reception given in his honour six years later in 1904 by the Lord Lieutenant of Yorkshire which was attended not only by Rupert's father, Colonel Harold Elton Fortescue Mountjoy but also by our author himself, who penned an account of the secret shenanigans that took place afterwards in the royal suite of the Grand Hotel and which will appear in a later volume of Rupert's reminiscences – Editor.]

There was ample time for us to sit on the banks of the lazily flowing nearby stream as Diana had not forgotten her self-appointed task of washing her knickers and chemise which lay drying on the sun. She had slipped on her blouse and skirt and I had also dressed myself, for though the sun still blazed down, there was the remote possibility of some hobbledehoy of a farmworker or one of Mrs Wigmore's domestics passing through the Wigmore's property on their way to work.

I threw a pebble into the water and said somewhat hesitantly to Diana. 'Don't think me nosey but when did you first, er –'

'First fuck?' she interrupted brightly, for she could see that I was still too unsophisticated to speak in vernacular terms. 'I don't mind telling you about it. Let's snuggle down together and, whilst my underwear is drying, I'll tell you all about it.

'I suppose I'd always been attracted to my brother Humphrey's best pal, Ronald Greyfriars. Ronald and Humphrey both row for Cambridge University and they spend much of their vacation time together catching up on their studies as during termtime both spend too much time on the river and not enough in the library, especially for a difficult course such as law which they were both reading at Trinity Hall. As fortune would have it, Ronald was staying with us during last year's Christmas vacation and naturally, both he and Humphrey were invited to my birthday party on December 8th. You were invited, if you remember, but had to refuse as your parents had made arrangements for you to go down to London with them on a family visit to your Uncle, the one who sits in Parliament.'

'You mean Uncle Edmund, the Liberal member for West Bristol,' I said gloomily. 'Yes, I was dashed upset at the time but my parents insisted I joined them as he thought a tour round the House of Commons would be most instructional and improve my understanding of politics. It was quite interesting but I would far, far rather have been at your party!'

'Never mind, there will be other parties – anyhow, it was only a small affair with local friends. There was no dancing but we played parlour games after dinner and I think we all enjoyed ourselves. After my guests had left, Papa and Mama went to bed and suggested that I do likewise. I did go to my room but I wasn't sleepy even though it was quite late. I looked at myself in the mirror and thought I looked rather fetching in the new dress Miss Foggin from Harrogate had made up for me. It was an evening gown in décolleté style and I insisted that it was cut as low as Mama would allow. She had insisted that it should be fringed with lace. I stepped out of the dress and took off my bodice. It was easy to unpick the fringe and when I slipped the dress back on, the cleft between my breasts was clearly visible now in the mirror when I leaned forward. I could see the swell of my breasts which were now only barely covered. The tips of my fingers passed lightly over my nipples and I thought how marvellous it would be to have Ronald's hands there in place of my own.

'As I said, I was too wide awake to sleep so I walked quietly downstairs to the library where I thought I would read the evening newspaper which I had not scanned. No-one seemed to be around although the lights were all burning, but then Armstrong rarely locks up until midnight so I was not alarmed when I thought I heard somebody moving in the drawing room. I opened the door and was pleasantly surprised to see that Ronald was still there, reading through one of his textbooks.

' "Hello Ronald, are you burning the midnight oil? It's more than Humphrey would care to do," I said.

'He rose from his chair and grinned. "Humphrey's worked harder than me or he'd be down here too to cram for these bally examinations. But golly, young Diana, you look spiffing. Wait a moment though, there's something different about you. What is it now, let me see ... By thunder, I have it, you've altered your dress. What's happened to that fringe of white lace?"

'I was not in the least embarrassed by his question and I replied: "Well, if you must know, I thought my figure was much nicer to look at than a frilly piece of material."

'He put down his book and moved closer towards me. "My God, I should say so," he said thickly. "I remember when your chest was as flat as mine." "But no more," I said, touching his arm with my hand. "I'm sixteen years old now and fully developed." His handsome face betrayed his struggle to keep his composure as I deliberately leaned forward to expose even more of my breasts to his excited gaze.

'He took a deep breath but said nothing, though I could see that this show of the snowy white globes deeply affected him. I looked steadily at his deep brown eyes and said softly: 'Why don't we sit down for a minute on the Chesterfield and talk?'' [*a large tightly stuffed sofa, usually upholstered in leather, and very popular in wealthy Victorian and Edwardian homes – Editor*].

'Still without speaking, he took my hand in his own and we adjourned to the aforementioned couch. I knew full well that Ronald was simply dying to touch me but he needed some further sign of encouragement so we chatted quietly about this and that. After a while I decided that I would have to make the first move so I put my hand on his shoulder and let it rest there. This did the trick! Indeed, I had not expected him to be so forward for suddenly he spun me around, turned my face up to his and kissed me passionately on the lips.

'A surge of excitement coursed through my veins for there was something about this kiss which made it impossible for me not to respond. "Diana, you have always epitomised the very quintessence of female beauty," he muttered.

"Goodness me, that's quite a little speech,

could you not speak plainer?" I said, though I knew well enough what his convoluted words were attempting to convey

Ronald swallowed hard and said: "I mean, my darling girl, that I have an overwhelming desire to make love to you "

"You have never mentioned this to me before," I said with a small smile, stroking his flushed cheek.

"No, because you are the sister of my best chum and in any case I would never take advantage of a girl of tender years," he replied hotly.

"Your candour does you credit," I said firmly. "However, I am not totally without experience of the joys of sensuality, though I have never actually made love yet – but now would be an appropriate time to remedy this, for as the country folk say around these parts:

> *When roses are reddest they're ready for plucking,*
> *And when she's sixteen, a girl's ready for fucking!"*

'Ronald smiled at my rude verse and his hand slid gently from my shoulder down underneath my arm as he positioned me to receive a further intimate embrace. Now, as our lips crushed together in a burning kiss, I felt his hand close gently over my breast. At the same time his tongue sank inside my mouth. Then I could feel his hands lift out my naked breasts from their scanty covering and he toyed with them so excitingly, tracing circles around my hardening nipples with the tips of his fingers and then rubbing them deliciously against the palms of his roving hands until they stood up in salute like small red bullets.

'But my lips could not satisfy his ardour and

soon he was passing his mouth over my cherry titties, kissing and sucking my nipples so sensually that I felt my pussey beginning to moisten. I was putty in the hands of a master builder for at this stage he leaned down to take hold of my ankle and began to caress it lovingly. I knew what was in Ronald's mind but I made no attempt to stop him as his hand worked its way up my leg and inside my thigh. A strangled cry of exultation escaped from his throat when his fingers reached inside my new pair of minute French knickers, a *sub rosa* purchase I made in Paris on my last visit to the Continent, and soon they became enmeshed with the silly hair of my pussey. Even at this stage, I was still just in control of my senses but I had no wish to end it all just yet. Ronald's fingers played exquisitely with my thatch and when he began to roll down my knickers, I assisted his efforts by raising my bum so he could more easily pull them down. Once the tiny garment was over my feet, I stepped out of them and said: "Ronnie, did you know that the hair of my bush is as blonde as the hair on my head?"

' "Nothing would give me greater pleasure than to see for myself," he panted, moaning softly as with a deliberate carelessness I let my own hand brush against the prominent vertical bulge in the lap of his trousers.

'Without further ado I unbuttoned my dress and let it slide to the floor. I stepped out of it towards him totally nude, the first time I had exposed my naked body to a man. Feeling slightly decadent, I draped myself across his clothed body on the couch, and my pussey ached with excitement as Ronald began to tear off his clothes.

His muscular frame gleamed in the light afforded by our newly installed electric lamps. His face too looked so adorable, set off by his large eyes with their thick lashes whilst their dark brown colour matched so handsomely with his tightly curled hair. But the *pièce de résistance* was of course his lovely prick which I now saw for the first time. It was exquisitely fashioned, bobbing out in front of him like a curved scimitar and his burgeoning erection had already partially pushed back the foreskin over the beautiful pink crown All thoughts of control fled from me as I reached out and encircled his shaft with my hand, pulling down the foreskin to completely bare the full helmet of his cock which was already glistening with a blob of pre-spend that had emanated from the tiny "eye" on the tip of his knob.

'We fell back on the couch and Ronald stretched me out on the big sofa. He knelt alongside me and fervently kissed my breasts and belly – and when he placed his head lower I clutched it lovingly, moaning my approval as he pressed his lips against my silky blonde thatch. The sensations were simply divine and when I felt his tongue begin licking my pussey I almost screamed with unalloyed delight.

' "You have the most delicious cunney ever, Diana, and I could feast on it all night," he said, raising his head for a moment before carrying on his sweet sucking of my cunt. These lewd yet complimentary words raised me to an even higher pitch of excitement when he parted the lips of my love chink with his wicked fingers and started to lap between my cunney lips. He relentlessly continued this thrilling stimulation, sinking his fingers into my moistening slit, making me tremble with expectation as he eased them deeper and deeper inside my pouting pussey crack.

'His tongue and fingers were delighting me to new peaks of pleasure that I had rarely before been able to climb. My clitty was now tingling with an intense excitation as he cupped it between his lips and nibbled furiously at the erect little miniature organ of ultimate pleasure. He twisted his fingers around inside my cunney as I writhed wildly, clamping my legs around his neck, and holding his head pressed even harder against my now dripping pussey with one hand whilst the other flew from one nipple to the other, tweaking them up to attention as I felt an approaching spend begin its journey. Ronald must have sensed it too for he licked even harder at my clitty and his finger sped even faster out of my dripping slit and this fabulous pressure kept me at the highest pitch of ecstasy for what seemed to be a blissfully long time. He was a natural cunney sucker who clearly enjoyed eating pussey and I am sure that his devotion to this art – so shamefully neglected in this country although not, I am assured, by our American cousins – will always assure Ronald of an inexhaustible supply of women ready and willing to be fucked. Indeed when my climax juddered through my body, satisfying though it was, I was still more than keen to continue.

'I pulled him upwards over me and his thick stiff cock now was hovering between my thighs. But to his everlasting credit, Ronald somehow dragged himself from the point of no return and whispered: "Are you certain you want me to carry on, my darling? Say now if you want me to stop because I can scarcely hold back as it is and in a few seconds it will be too late. But if I do continue, I'll be careful not to come inside you."

' "Yes, I want you to fuck me, Ronald," I replied softly. "It will soon be my time of the month, tomorrow or probably the day after so you can shoot off in my pussey. Besides, I want to feel you come inside me."

'I laid my head back and relaxed as I watched Ronald take his cockshaft in his hand and gently insert the tip of his tool in my cunney. He pushed it in so slowly that I could feel the ridge of his cock scrape past the folds of my inner channel. Ronald felt so big inside me as my cunney muscles gripped his cock, the first penis ever to have passed through the lips of my love-channel. He pulled back almost as slowly as he had entered my virgin hole and then pushed in and out again at a slightly quicker pace.

'He looked up at me enquiringly: "I am not hurting you?" he asked anxiously. There was a slight discomfort at the very commencement of my début fuck but that very soon passed. This was doubtless due to the solitary frigging I had practised at school and perhaps too to the bouncing up and down on the saddle of my pony. Oh, do not look so shocked – do you think that only boys know how to play with themselves? But for whatever reason, I experienced no pain as Ronald's proud prick rammed in and out faster and faster and deeper and deeper inside my suppurating cavity. He now began to pump into me with great swinging thrusts as I raised my pelvis to allow him to clutch my cheeks of my pert little backside. We fucked away like a couple possessed and my body squirmed with joy as I came again and again as Ronald's cock slammed in and out of my saturated cunt. Ronald, too, was now reaching the point of no return and I could feel his prick throb inside me as his hairy ballsack banged against my thighs which were now wet with my virgin spendings of love juice and a tiny amount of blood. As he shuddered to a crashing climax, I felt a rush of liquid fire coat the back of my grotto as spasm after spasm of jism shot into my very vitals and I achieved a further spend as wave after wave of pure, unadulterated enchantment enveloped me from head to toe.

'He raised himself on his hands and knees and withdrew his cock which squelched out, still almost as stiff as when he started to fuck me, but covered now with a mix of our love juices which was tinged with the claret of my virgin emission. I must have appeared concerned for Ronald smiled and said: "Do not be concerned, the next time there will be no blood, I can promise you." He reached down to the floor and brought out a handkerchief from his trousers with which he tenderly wiped my pussey and his own cock clean. He put the handkerchief back into his pocket and said that he would treasure the ensanguined linen as a loving remembrance of how I had so gallantly surrendered my virginity to him.

' "Ah, that was a magnificent fuck. Yet I fear that all is not well for, unless I am much mistaken, I thought I noticed a frown of disappointment flicker across your face?" he asked as I turned my head slightly to one side.

' "No Ronald," I replied truthfully. "I thoroughly enjoyed making love with you. If there is any disappointment it is only because we have finished so soon and I am still feeling randy!"

' "Is that all, dearest?" he exclaimed delightedly. "Oh, but this is a situation easily rectified." He took my hand and cupped my fingers halfway round his sticky pole. "Just rub my cock up and down and watch it swell up ready to fuck you again."

This turned out to be no idle boast for it took only a few moments of frigging before he raised himself above me and this time he let me guide his knob between the squishy lips of my infatuated pussey. Once he was settled inside my welcoming quim he needed no further urging and I eagerly lifted my hips to salute his thrusting tool. His cock was very thick and I was in heaven as he pumped his throbbing prick to and fro and he played with my breasts, tweaking my titties as they bounced back and forth, moving in perfect rhythm with the movements of his cock. My cunney was still soaking with Ronald's jism and my own love juices but it was still gloriously tight and when he increased the tempo, slamming the entire length of his shaft inside me, I thought I might expire with happiness. Oh, how the fiery currents surged through my pussey and crackled their way through every inch of my frame. In no time at all I was twisting and rolling around like a crazed animal and I shouted out: "Fuck me! Fuck me! Fuck me!" in sheer uninhibited lust.

' "Shush, shush, my precious, you'll wake up

the whole house," he breathed as he reamed the furthest niches of my cunney with his rampant rod. Our mouths melded together in a luscious French kiss and as we wiggled our tongues wetly in each other's mouths, he jetted his powerful emission of hot, creamy spunk just as I too reached the dazzling peaks of a truly magnificent spend.

'Well, that is the story of my first experience of the joys of love-making. As you can imagine we continued to fuck until Ronald simply had no more strength. I sucked his cock back to erection three times more that night before we crept back to our beds just as the first rays of the sun began to break through the darkness of the night sky.'

Here Diana ended her tale and after giving me a grateful nod of thanks she drank deeply from the glass of lemonade which I had poured out for her.

'Did you see him again?' I asked, wriggling around to try to accommodate my bursting cock which had naturally stiffened up to full erection whilst I listened to the stimulating story of Diana's sexual awakening.

'We did manage one more night of bliss. Alas, there were to be no other opportunities for us to indulge ourselves in any further fucking as Ronald and my brother had arranged to spend some time with Professor Aspis, one of the world's leading authorities on bats, who was staying with our friends the Grove-Radletts, who live on the Kentish coast near Herne Bay.'

'Bats?' I echoed in astonishment. 'For God's sake, what's so interesting about bats?'

'Not a great deal as far as I am concerned, but Professor Aspis is paying the boys ten pounds each to assist him in catching a certain kind of bat which can only be found in caves around that area. Ronald has become quite fascinated by these little creatures, which ignorant folk think are sinister and demonic. But, as Professor Aspis has shown, they play an important part in nature and are very helpful towards us as they eat many harmful pests. In tropical climes, there are bats which feed on fruit and many trees are entirely dependent on bats to pollinate their flowers and disperse their seeds.'

'So if it weren't for the bats shifting the seeds –'

'– there would be a lack of wild species of dates, figs, guava and others,' finished Diana.

So not only had I fucked my first girl but I had also learned something of the habits of the bat – material I would make good use of when Mr Pilcher, our science teacher, set us an essay on a subject of our choosing. But my thoughts were still centred around matters connected with human biology – namely, whether the beautiful Diana would allow me to fuck her again before we parted. I even made so bold as to ask but she shook her pretty head and said: 'No Rupert, I really don't have the time. But meet me tomorrow afternoon around half past two in the old barn next to our stables and we can enjoy ourselves again there.'

Her reply brought a gleam of pleasure to my eyes but suddenly my face fell – tomorrow morning I would be playing host to my chum Frank Folkestone. 'Drat it!' I exclaimed as I spelt out my predicament to Diana. 'No, don't worry yourself – bring Frank along and I'll ask my friend Cecily Cardew to join us,' she cried. 'We'll have some real larks, I promise you, if your friend can show her a good-sized stiffstander.'

My heart leaped with joy. 'I'll say he can – Frank's prick is the biggest in our dormitory. When he gets a hard-on his shaft rises so high that the tip is on the same level as his belly button.'

'That's something Cecily and I will really look forward to seeing – goodbye, Rupert, and thanks again for posing so patiently. When I've finished all my work, I'll frame my study of your body and give it to you for Christmas. See you tomorrow in the old barn.'

We kissed each other fondly on the cheek and I walked home briskly to arrive just in time for tea.

CHAPTER TWO

A Whoresome Foursome

THE SUNLIGHT WAS ALREADY BEAMING THROUGH MY BEDROOM curtains when I awoke early the next morning. As usual, my sturdy young penis was as hard as a brick and, as was my regular habit, I gripped my smooth shaft in my right hand, frigging it slowly up and down as I closed my eyes and dreamed with lustful anticipation of what might be in store for me that afternoon. The previous evening I had tossed myself off twice thinking about how Diana Wigmore had sucked my cock and then later had allowed me to fuck her. It occured to me that I should not spend this morning if I wanted to perform properly in the afternoon. But there was no way I could resist rubbing my prick in my closed fist until I had spent copiously all over my pyjamas. In my haste I had forgotten to reach out for the spunk-stained handkerchief I kept hidden in my bedside drawer! I have always enjoyed a good wank and take issue with those foolish folk who warn against the practice for supposed reasons of health or morality. On this occasion, though, after the riches of genuine fucking, the joys of self-induced simulation were but limited. I cursed silently as I leapt out of bed and unknotted the cord of my pyjama trousers. I put them in my laundry basket and hoped that the sticky stain would be undetected by the servants before the offending garment was washed.

I looked at my watch. As it was only just after six-thirty, I decided to polish up some verses I had composed when I returned home after my fateful meeting with Diana. I sat at my desk and, after poring over an exercise book, pronounced myself satisfied with the following poem of praise to my new-found love:

> Oh when I shall behold, my love,
>   Your merry eyes, your fair-skinned
>   face
> I cannot wait until my arms
>   Enclose you in my tight embrace.
>
> Yet though I've sworn so many times
>   The world no sight can show,
> To match your locks, your lips divine,
>   Your bosoms' hills of snow.
>
> For sweeter now is what I have seen,
>   Two lips have I beheld
> And lovelier on a happy day,
>   A mound which does excel.
>
> Your breasts can boast no swell as fair,
>   No teats that these eclipse;
> Your lovely face can scarce compete
>   With such enchanting lips.

For now I've seen your hairy mount
Where all your favours centre,
Yes! I have fucked your juicy cunt
And wish again to enter!

'Well, it might not stand up to a Shakespearean sonnet, but then neither should it be thrown back in my face,' I muttered to myself as I then jotted down the draft of a covering letter:

Dearest Diana,

I dedicate these verses to you – I can think of no better way to express my heartfelt love and gratitude for the way you initiated me into the joys of coition. I will never forget our glorious love-making as long as I live.

Your ever affectionate friend,

Rupert

I put the exercise book safely away (or so I thought at the time!) in my bedside drawer, resolving to copy out the poem carefully in my best writing and give it to Diana with a bunch of flowers which I could obtain from Stamford, our ancient head gardener, who had been employed at Albion Hall for the last thirty-five years. I then ran a refreshing cool bath. Doubtless because I could not clear my mind of the promised joys to come, my prick refused to lie down until my soapy face flannel had travelled up and down the shaft to provide the necessary manual relief.

My father had already taken an early breakfast and left the house when I arrived downstairs, for the local petty sessions began today and he had sat on the bench as a senior magistrate since the family had returned home from India. My mother was also preparing to leave as she had a committee meeting of the Liberal Association to attend that morning. (Much to my father's chagrin, I should add, for he was a crusty old Tory. To his credit, though, it must be added that he simply accepted the fact that Mama and later myself were both wedded to a progressive political philosophy, even when we both staunchly supported the Suffragette Movement which demanded the right of women to vote.)

'Would you please pass my apologies to Frank, dear, as I doubt if I shall be here to greet him when he arrives,' said my Mama as she passed me the morning newspaper. 'This meeting will probably drag on until mid-afternoon as we have to choose our candidates for the forthcoming county council elections and for some reason there are more budding politicians than ever. Now your Papa has commandeered the motor car to drive to court and I shall need the Brougham [*a large four-wheeled carriage – Editor*] so I suggest you go with Wallace in the landaulet to the station and meet your friend there. His train arrives at Ripley Valley station just before a quarter past eleven. Remember to leave in good time as it's market day and the roads are likely to be congested.'

If anything, it was even warmer than the previous day and I closed the folding hood over the passenger compartment as Wallace, our second coachman, drove at a steady pace through Ripley, a pretty village whose main street is prettily shaded with trees. Its fifteenth century church has marks on the outside of the east wall that are attributed to bullets fired by Cromwell's soldiers – some say, when shooting prisoners taken at Marston Moor during the English Civil War. I made a mental note to take Frank on a walking trip round these parts as history is his favourite subject and he would be fascinated to see the house in the village of Scotton where Guy Fawkes lived as a young man.

We arrived ten minutes before Frank's train was due so Wallace and I sat sunning ourselves on the platform whilst we waited for the train. It arrived punctually and Frank jumped out eagerly to greet me. 'Hullo, Rupert, how smashing to see you,' he said, heartily shaking my hand. 'My mother gated me until I was over this poxy chill but I'm fighting fit now and ready for anything. I know that you're not that keen on cricket but tennis is all the rage in town these days. I've brought up a couple of rackets and some balls so we could have a game – it'll be great fun especially in this weather. Your neighbour, Doctor Wigmore, laid out a court if I remember rightly – if you haven't fallen out with him perhaps he would let us play on it.'

I grinned as Wallace collected Frank's cases and we walked over to the exit. 'I haven't seen Doctor Wigmore since the Easter vacation but I met his daughter Diana yesterday,' I said with a grin.

'Fine, perhaps she would also be keen to play? How about this afternoon if the weather stays fine?'

I was sorely tempted to reply: 'I'll say, but at a much better game than tennis!' But I held my tongue until we were seated in the coach and Wallace had driven us out of the station yard.

Once we were on our way I turned to him and said: 'Frank, I like playing tennis and though you'll probably beat me hollow I'll do my best to give you some sort of a game. But I've already made other plans for us this afternoon which, as it happens, involve Diana and one of her girl friends.'

'Well, that's all right, we could play doubles.'

I gestured impatiently. 'Listen, old boy, forget tennis for a moment. How would you like to play a game you've dreamed about since you've had hair growing round your cock?' As I expected, this startled him into an astonished silence! 'You heard,' I repeated. 'I'm not joking, no really I wouldn't jape about something so important. Just play your cards right, young Folkestone, and you'll be fucking a pretty girl this afternoon just like I did yesterday! It beats tossing off any day of the week, I can tell you!'

'I don't believe it, Rupert, you're having me on, aren't you?' he said, half-afraid perhaps to accept such wonderful news and then be brought down to earth with a hefty bump when he learned that I was only teasing him.

'Honestly, I'm not joshing, Frank, I swear I'm not,' I earnestly assured my pal. I went on to tell him of my great adventure into manhood and how Diana and her friend Cecily would meet us at the old barn that very afternoon for some further frolics.

'This sounds too good to be true,' he breathed. 'Why, the very thought is already making me feel terribly randy!' He wriggled uncomfortably in his seat and I could clearly see the bulge in his lap.

'Ha! Ha! Ha! That's made you forget all about

tennis, hasn't it?' I laughed. 'Well, Diana wanted to know if you were ready for your first fuck and, from the size of your stiffstander, I don't think she and Cecily will be too disappointed!'

'They won't be disappointed at all,' he said with mock indignation. 'Haven't I got the thickest prick in our dormitory? Look, I'll show you, I bet you can't match this for size!' He ripped open his fly buttons, releasing his big red-headed cock, which stood up stiffly as he frigged it up to its fullest measure.

He then helped me pull out my own stiff truncheon which, though not so massive an instrument, was still substantial enough to have satisfied Diana Windsor – as I hastened to remind him. We were now so fired up that we handled each other's tools in an ecstacy of anticipatory delight, and the proceeding ended by a mutual tossing off, aiming each other's emissions of gluey white jism onto the newspaper which luckily I had brought with me to read on the way to the station.

'Well, I hope no-one wants to read *The Times* any more today,' I quipped as we entered our carriage drive. 'I'll hide it in my jacket and chuck it in a bin when we get indoors and if anybody asks for the paper, I'll say I left it on the platform by mistake whilst helping you down with your luggage.'

Goldhill, the new butler Mama had persuaded to our household from Lord Mozer's establishment, was ready to greet us at the front door. As instructed I dutifully passed on Mama's message to Frank and Goldhill asked me at what time Mrs Randall should serve luncheon. 'Oh, one o'clock will suit well enough, only do tell her that we will require only a very light meal – I would suggest perhaps one of her famous cheese omelettes with fried potatoes and a green salad with a fruit *compote* to follow.

'Would that suit you?' I asked, turning to Frank. 'Absolutely spot-on,' he replied with a grin. 'We don't want too much to eat if we're going to take some strenuous exercise this afternoon.'

Goldhill nodded. 'Very good, Master Rupert. Might you young gentlemen be playing tennis later, for I noticed that Master Frank has brought his tennis rackets. Your equipment is in the games room and I'll get one of the maids to bring it downstairs for you. Will you also require balls?' With a great effort my chum stifled his laughter as I gravely replied: 'Yes, we'll need our balls this afternoon, Goldhill. But I'll help you unpack, Frank, and we can take our tennis togs with us in my games bag.'

Now as you may imagine, dear reader, Frank and I hardly did justice to Mrs Randall's tasty fare. We bolted through our luncheon and stuffed our tennis clothes – white short-sleeved shirts and thin white cotton trousers – into two sports bags. 'Pack all your stuff in one of your own cases, Frank. I've just remembered a couple of things to take that we'll find very useful.'

We were in so much of a hurry that Goldhill had to remind us to take our rackets! 'You won't play very much tennis without these, young gentlemen,' said the old retainer with a grave smile. 'With luck we won't be playing with them at all!' muttered Frank under his breath.

When we were on our way down the drive he turned to me and said: 'Rupert, I don't doubt your sworn word but I'm still frightened that this is all a lovely dream and that in a minute I'll wake up in bed with an aching stiff prick!'

'Have no fear, the girls will not let us down,' I reassured him, although I too could hardly take in our good fortune. We reached the old barn ten minutes before the appointed hour and I spread out on the clean wooden floor the eiderdown I had packed in my bag. '*Voilà*, this should make for more comfortable fucking,' I said with satisfaction.

'Yes, so long as the girls arrive,' said Frank, nervously moving his weight from one foot to the other.

'Why don't we change into our tennis outfits?' I suggested. 'It will help pass the time and we won't have so many clothes to take off when we begin our fun.'

'What a good idea,' he agreed and we took off our shoes and socks and then our trousers, taking care to fold them neatly before placing them in our valises.

We had both just taken off our shirts and were standing solely in our drawers when the door opened and the forms of our two frisky young fillies stood framed in the sunlight. Never before nor ever since have I clapped eyes on two such superb contrasting examples of female pulchritude. The blonde beauty of Diana was marvellously complemented by the equally pretty Cecily's wavy brown hair, her graceful Grecian face of rosy cheeks, large dark eyes and lips as rich and red as midsummer cherries. The exquisite girl was deliciously proportioned with large, heavy breasts covered only by a cream-coloured blouse, of such fine silk that it was almost transparent. Frank and I could easily make out the shadow of her swollen nipples that pressed so invitingly against the softness of her clothing.

'Goodness me, were you two boys planning to begin the proceedings without us?' said Diana brightly. 'Cecily, I do hope that these two boys have not been seduced into the ways of Oscar Wilde and the homosexualists!'

The other girl chuckled, showing pearly white teeth which we were to see frequently exhibited in a later succession of winning smiles that were rarely to leave her charming face. 'It would mean that we will have wasted our afternoon, but they might just be changing their clothes to prepare themselves for our visit.'

'Indeed, that this precisely what we were doing,' I grinned back. 'Frank, I have the honour to introduce Miss Diana Wigmore. Miss Wigmore, this is Frank Folkestone, my best friend at St Lionel's.'

'How do you do?' said Frank, shaking hands with the cool blonde beauty.

'Very well thank you – what a funny experience being introduced to a boy unclothed except for his drawers! Still, I will give you both the benefit of the doubt as to why you are both so scantily clad and introduce my best friend, Miss Cecily Cardew of Harrogate. Mr Folkestone, Mr Rupert Mountjoy, Miss Cardew.'

The formalities over, I asked the girls if they would care for some refreshment. I flourished an ice-box in which stood a bottle of champagne that

55

I had sneaked out of our cellar before luncheon. 'There are even four glasses inside it,' I explained as I opened it up. 'My Uncle Gilbert gave it to me for Christmas last year, isn't it a useful gift?'

We rapidly finished off the bottle of Krug '87 and, though we were far from being blotto, the bubbly fizz certainly loosened our tongues. We were very soon engaged in a most relaxed and friendly conversation. Earlier in the morning Diana had also brought a quilt into our secret hide-out on which she and I sat, whilst Frank and Cecily lolled together on the duvet I had taken from one of our spare bedrooms.

'We had a good fuck yesterday, didn't we, Rupert?' said Diana chattily.

'It wasn't good, it was magnificent!' I responded, putting my arm around her waist. 'I can't wait to fuck you again.'

'All in good time, you randy boy, all in good time,' she riposted. 'But what I really would like first is to see Frank fuck Cecily – we have presumed that, like Rupert, Frank has never before made love and Cecily has a great urge to rectify this sad situation. Haven't you, my dearest? Despite being only seventeen years old, she is far more experienced than I, having tasted the fleshpots of London with Sir David Nash and all the other young rogues of Belgravia.'

'Not *all* of the others, if you please, Diana, though I could tell you a tale or two about Lord Andrew Stuck and his friend Matthew Cosgrave! Still, I will admit, dear Frank, that the idea of fucking your virgin prick very much appeals to me. In fact, I have quite a fancy for it right now. How do you feel about the matter?'

Frank gulped and said: 'I'd like nothing better'. But we could see that he was nervous and I knew how he must be feeling – I too had butterflies in my tummy just before I made love to Diana, and that was without any spectators to witness the event!

'Go on, Frank, don't mind us,' I said to try and help my friend. 'We're going to kiss and cuddle as well, don't you know.'

Cecily stood up and let her tongue pass sensuously over her lips as she slowly unhooked the tiny buttons of her blouse. With feline grace she opened the garment to reveal the luscious swell of her large breasts topped by nut-brown nipples, already as hard as little sticks, sticking out at least a whole inch in length. She cupped these exciting globes in her hands and, kneeling down in front of Frank, she rubbed the palm of her hand against the bulging erection hidden in his drawers.

'Dear me, Frank, it was just as well you began to undress before Diana and I arrived – I do so hate wasting time with unnecessary preliminaries. Now, is that a cucumber you have hidden in your pants or are you really excited by my bare titties?' she asked with a mischievous glint in her sparkling brown eyes. Alas, poor Frank was so overcome by his emotions that, though at school he was rarely lost for words, the thrilling sight of this exquisite half-naked girl left him completely tongue-tied and he could not find his voice to make a reply to this amusingly rhetorical question. Indeed, the poor chap was so overwhelmed that he made no attempt to help Cecily when she took hold of his undershorts and tried to tug them down.

'Frank, old fellow, lift yourself up,' I urged. This did the trick, for he recovered his composure and raised his arse so that Cecily could slide his drawers under his bum. She then lifted them over his stalwart staff which was standing as high as a flagpole. Diana craned her head forward for a closer look at his tremendous erection – for it was no idle boast that Frank had made earlier on our way home from the station when he laid claim to be the proud owner of the thickest prick in the Upper Fourth form at St Lionel's – and the two girls admired the tumescent proportions of Frank's cock. 'What a whopper for such a young sport!' cried Cecily, stroking Frank's throbbing tadger with the tips of her fingers. 'It *is* one of the biggest I've ever seen,' agreed Diana. 'My sweet Cecily, I wonder if you will be able to accommodate such a monster.'

'Just watch me,' Cecily advised her friend. 'I have not yet come up against a prick that is too big for me to suck.' Both Diana and I admired her dextrous technique as she began by clasping Frank's plump penis with both of her small hands, and massaging his gigantic tool up to bursting point. She then leaned over and took the mushroomed head of the purple bulb between her lips, jamming down his foreskin and lashing her tongue around the rigid shaft. She tickled his helmet with the tip of her pink little tongue and then she opened her mouth to take in almost half his enormous erection whilst her hands played with his hairy ballsack. She swallowed hard and then somehow managed to take in almost all of his swollen stem. Diana and I watched in fascination as her tongue flicked out to lick the soft underfolds of skin along the base of Frank's shaft. She sucked lustily upon his succulent cock, sliding her lips along the rock-hard rod, gulping noisily as the helmet of his smooth skinned knob slid against the roof of her mouth to the back of her throat.

'He'll spunk too soon if she's not very careful,' Diana whispered to me as her hand slipped inside my under-shorts to grasp my own pulsing organ, which had already ballooned up to stand stiffly upwards. The soft touch of Diana's fingers soon set my tool twitching with excitement.

Cecily had also surmised this probability and she pulled her head up and said to Frank: 'Here it comes, Frank – your very first fuck. Lie down on your back and let me take charge.' He did not have to be asked a second time as he lay back, his thick prick poking up in salute as she swiftly pulled off her skirt. My cock throbbed uncontrollably at the sight of the curly brown bush that surrounded the visible lips of her pussey cunney lips! Now totally nude, Cecily straddled Frank and took hold of his yearning tool and placed it at the gateway of her cunt. 'Ready, steady, go!' she cried as she slid down his cock until it was totally engulfed in the warm, wet walls of her cunney. As soon as it was lodged deep inside, she swayed back and forth. Frank frantically arched his body up and down and his face reddened and his breathing quickened until, as we expected, he shot his sperm right up inside her.

Cecily raised herself off Frank's prick which now glistened with their liquid libations. She grasped hold of his sperm-coated shaft, which was still almost as stiff as when she had first sat on it, and after a few quick wanks, his cock was back up to its full majestic height. 'Now it's your turn to call the tune!' she said gaily as she lay down and pulled his sinewy body over her Frank's shaft slid joyously into her hungry pussey and, with barely a pause to take breath, he started to pump up and down in a steady rhythm, his arse quivering with every movement of his hips.

Looking back on this erotic event, I must say that although this was his first fuck, Frank had a natural understanding of what was required of him. He did not rush in and out like a man possessed – perhaps because Cecily had cleverly decided to get his first spunking out of the way as quickly as possible – but he thrust home steadily, taking his time as he withdrew and then re-entered the juicy haven of her cunt. This pleased Cecily, who began to toss and turn as she gasped: 'Oh, lovely, really lovely, Frank, you big-cocked boy – ram in harder, you won't hurt me! Ah! That's the ticket! I want to spend as well, you know!'

Her bottom ground and rolled violently as she threshed madly under his renewed onslaught. She clawed Frank's back and he grasped her shoulders and began to ride her like a cowboy on a bucking bronco. Her legs slid down, her heels drumming a tattoo on the quilt as she arched her body upwards, working her cunney back and forth to meet the fierce thrusts of Frank's powerful tool.

'I'm coming, yes, I'm coming! Yes, there I go!' screamed Cecily as Frank shuddered, his penis sheathed so fully inside her cunt that his balls nestled against the luscious cheeks of her bum. With one last mighty shove in and out of her pulsating pussey, he sent the trembling girl right off into the sweet ecstasies of a superb spend as his prick squirted jets of glutinous white sperm exploding inside her cunney, on and on until the last dribblings oozed out and he sank down on top of her, his weight pinning her to the ground as the last delicious throbs died away. Cecily manoeuvred him to her side and they lay together in each other's arms, panting heavily to get back their breath, but with blissful smiles of fulfilment upon their faces as they sensibly let their exhausted bodies enjoy a well deserved rest.

This first-rate fucking had so galvanised both Diana and myself that her hand travelled faster and faster up and down my own hard stiffstander and almost immediately after Frank had shot his load, my own trusty tool also sent a fountain of spunk high into the air and I spent copiously, sending blobs of jism over the sleeve of Diana's dress!

I apologised profusely, saying with some embarrassment: 'Oh dear, I am so sorry, that's the second time I've spent over your clothes.'

But Diana refused to blame me and said: 'No, please don't apologise, the fault was all mine. I should have taken off my clothes before I started to toss you off. Let's both undress now – I far prefer to fuck naked anyway and we won't have to worry about any further accidents.'

We stood up and I pulled down my pants as Diana threw her dress over her head to reveal that the naughty girl had already dispensed with her underclothes. Her beautiful bare breasts, with their jutting red nipples and the abundant thatch of silky blonde hair between her legs fired me with the most urgent desire. My penis gradually swelled up to its former height and hardness and suddenly her tousled blonde hair was between my legs as she kissed my now rampant cock. Her tongue flicked out and washed my unhooded helmet and when she opened the lips wide and encircled my staff, instinctively I moved forward to push my prick even further inside her mouth Her wicked tongue lapped all over my knob, savouring the blob of juice which had already formed around the top, and her teeth scraped the tender flesh as she drew me in between her luscious lips, sucking in all of my shaft and sending shivers of pure pleasure racing from my thrilled tool throughout my entire body. She circled the base with her hand and started to bob her head in the most sensual of rhythms as she sucked away with gusto. Then she let my cock fall from her mouth to nibble and slurp her tongue upon the soft wrinkled skin of my ballsack. This sent me into fresh paroxyms of delight. Finally, she filled her mouth with saliva and again palated my prick as I plunged my raging shaft between her lips. Very shortly afterwards I let out a great bellow and spent copiously, filling her mouth with the hot gush of sperm that cascaded out of my throbbing tool. She gulped down my spend with obvious enjoyment, drinking me dry as slowly but inevitably my sated shaft shrank down to dangle down flaccidly between my thighs.

Diana led me back to our eiderdown and I sank down, quite *hors de combat* after this strenuous erotic engagement. Diana stood over me and sighed: 'Oh Rupert, your poor little cockie looks so forlorn. I suppose it needs a rest.'

I nodded dumbly as Cecily called out: 'I'm

afraid that I have the same problem with Frank's cock, Di – look, it just flops around all over the place.' And to prove her point, she took hold of his limp penis and rested it in the palm of her hand. She squeezed his shaft and rolled back his foreskin to uncover his knob, but his recalcitrant rammer stayed obstinately in a deflated state.

'Please, just give us a little more time to recover,' Frank begged with heartfelt vehemence. Cecily cocked her head to one side and then snapped her fingers as a new plan of action suggested itself to her. 'I have just thought of the solution to all our problems,' she exclaimed, rising to her feet. 'Frank, you go over there and sit down with Rupert. Diana, you come and lie down here and we will show the boys how well we can manage without their silly pricks.' Now remember, friendly reader, that Frank and I were the merest novices in *l'art de faire l'amour*, so do not be surprised when I say that whilst we readily obeyed Cecily's request, we truly had no real inkling of what was in her lewd mind.

Frank scrambled to his feet and came across to join me. Meanwhile, to our amazement, Diana had taken his place in Cecily's arms. They kissed like sisters at first, their lips meeting in a tentative brushing that gradually deepened into a firmer urgency. Then their mouths opened and Cecily slid her hands up and down Diana's back until the blonde beauty was shuddering in her arms, thrusting her breasts and pussey forward as her own hands slid down to squeeze the plump cheeks of Cecily's dimpled bottom. The two young women were now kissing and cuddling with great affection, and Frank and I watched in astonishment as they ran their hands around each other's breasts and thighs, squealing with delight. Cecily pushed Diana backwards and began to tongue her ear with rapid little flicks of her tongue. This brought moans of joy from the blonde girl who squeezed her legs together and murmured her encouragement as Cecily pressed her long nipples between her fingers before substituting her tongue, drawing circles all around Diana's titties before dipping her head downwards over her white belly towards her golden fluffy nest. She kissed all around Diana's honey-coloured bush before she separated her folds with her fingers to coax out the first dribbles of love juice from her pretty pussey. Diana opened her legs even further apart and all three of us could see the red crack of her cunt.

'Oooh, I'm so wet, get your fingers in me quickly!' she pleaded. Cecily immediately obliged, inserting one, then two fingers inside her squelchy cunney, rubbing and playing with the gaping crimson slit, working her fingers in and out slowly at first and then faster and faster as Diana's cunney became wetter and wetter. She found the stiff button of her clitty and frigged it by twiddling the little rosebud with her thumb and forefinger whilst with the other hand she played with Diana's nipples, rubbing them against her palm which made Diana shriek with delight as she spent all over Cecily's questing fingers.

'Now it's my turn to repay the compliment,' said Diana when she had recovered her composure. 'My pussey is more than ready to receive you,' replied Cecily, stretching out languidly like a spoiled contented kitten. Diana pulled herself on top of the dark-haired girl, positioning herself so that their pussey mounds ground together and then she leaned forward first to nibble Cecily's chewy, rubbery nipples and then working her mouth all over her gorgeous breasts, her flat white belly and inexorably downwards to her curly brown muff. Cecily had clipped her bush around her cunney lips and the pressure of Diana's lips around there was very soon sending her wild.

Now at the beginning of this two-girl exhibition, the sight of the two tribades making love to each other had filled Frank and myself with a new surging lust. By this stage in the proceedings both our pricks had risen up to a vigorous erectness.

'By Gad, I'd give anything to be there with them,' I murmured as I smoothed the tips of my fingers along the smooth underside of my knob.

'Do you think they'd mind?' Frank muttered, his hand now also gripped around his thick cock, capping and uncapping his swollen helmet which bulged over his clenched fist.

'Well, I suppose we ought to wait for an invitation, though I'm sure they would not be offended if we asked. Let Diana finish sucking Cecily's pussey and then I'll say something.'

Not long afterwards, my judgement was vindicated by the lewd girls, both of whom very much enjoyed playing with each other as an occasional change – for as Cecily was later to remark, as in most all other activities, variety is the spice of life – but their main preference was for throbbing stiff pricks in their cunnies.

We did not have to sit on the sidelines long, for Diana was soon hard at work – though work is hardly the correct word for she kissed Cecily's large nipples before saying: 'What a pretty girl you are, darling! Such firm, proud breasts and as for your pretty pussey, just looking at those pouting lips and the red crack between them makes my own cunney wet! If only I were a man, I would like nothing better than to stick my big hard cock in your cunt and spend all day pleasuring your pouting pussey. Damn, I don't even have a dildo here to push in and out of your slit! Never mind though, let's see if I can bring you off with my tongue. After all, I haven't failed to do it yet, have I?'

When she ascertained that Cecily's cunney was ready for the attack, she grasped the quivering girl's bum cheeks, one in each hand, and gently kissed Cecily's dampening slit, her mouth probing against the yielding fleshy lips, nuzzling her face against the curly brown hairs of Cecily's love-mound. She rubbed the brunette's heavy breasts, making the titties stand out like two dark little bullets, as she softly repeated her rude plan of action to make Cecily spend, about how she was going to slip her tongue into Cecily's cunt and rub her mouth all around it as she sucked her clitty.

These lewd musings fired Cecily's fancy and she cried 'Do it, yes, do it!' as Diana plunged her face into her muff and passed her tongue lasciviously around the cunney lips. Cecily yelped as the clever minx found her clitty almost at once and began teasing the erect little rubbery flesh which now projected out from Cecily's crack.

'Oh Diana, you are the best cunney sucker in the world!' she screamed, her legs now drumming against the ground as the other girl continued to work her face into the sopping cleft between her thighs. Diana sucked harder and harder with increasing ardour, rolling her tongue round and round, lapping up the aromatic love juices which were now freely flowing from Cecily's cunney. Within less than a minute, this relentless stimulation achieved its desired effect as Cecily cried. 'Ooohl Aaaahl A-h-r-el Yes, I'm there, I'm there!' She started to spend as her hips bucked, her back rippled and then with a final little scream her cunney spurted its final tribute, splattering Diana's face and filling her mouth with the tangy essence which she greedily lapped up. Cecily shuddered into limpness as her delicious crisis slowly melted away.

By now, Frank and I could scarcely contain ourselves and it was with great joy that we heard Diana call out: 'Come on, you two – your cocks should be rock-hard by now.' Indeed they were, and in a trice we were at their side. 'Lie down beside me, Frank,' ordered Diana who immediately clamped her red lips around Frank's prick and began sucking it with unashamed relish. Cecily then heaved herself up and told me to also kneel down. She encircled her hands around my throbbing staff and began to play with it, hugging it and pressing it against her gorgeous big breasts, squeezing it between them, pressing it against her cheeks, gently rubbing it with her hands and taking my bared helmet between her rich, full lips, softly tantalising it with her wet little tongue. She now sucked on my truncheon in earnest, lashing her tongue around my pulsating pole, and drawing my shaft inside her hot, wet mouth.

The sensation was unbelievably grand but a short throaty cry from Frank made me turn my head to one side, just in time to see him spend. Diana was fucking his huge cock so voluptuously with her mouth that he could no longer delay his spend. He shot off his spunk with a final thrust as she milked his agitated penis of sperm, noisily emptying his tightly scrunched-up balls and gulping down his copious emission of sticky white jism as his twitching tool slid forwards and backwards between her lips.

An apprehensive whimper escaped my lips as Cecily decided to pull back her mouth from my own palpitating prick and substituted her hand which was tightly grasped around the base of my shaft. 'Oh, please don't stop sucking, Cecily, it was so delicious. I was just about to come in your mouth!' I pleaded unsuccessfully, for she had hauled herself up to sit pressed against me

'Never mind, darling, instead just look at Diana, the saucy minx – don't you agree that she possesses the most succulent backside you could ever wish to see! Doesn't the brazen hussey enjoy showing it off! Well now, so far you've fucked her juicy cunney, Rupert, and in return she has sucked your sturdy stiff prick. Now perhaps you are ready to perform a further service for her.' She breathed sensuously in my ear and, as Frank sank back on his haunches, Diana wriggled her body around to present me with a full view of her rounded bum cheeks. Cecily continued her lewd whispering: 'Now feast your eyes on the lovely globes of her bottom, Rupert, and just think of how exciting it would be to slew your thick prick between those luscious beauties she is flaunting shamelessly in front of you?'

These lewd thoughts fired my imagination but still I hesitated. 'Perhaps so,' I questioned. 'But how can you be so certain that Diana would like me to do what you propose?'

'Ask her yourself if you must, but I know well enough what she wants,' replied Cecily, nipping my ear-lobe with her sharp little teeth. But I had no need to take this matter further for Diana turned her head round and looked up to us. She suggestively thrust her pert bottom upwards and said, smilingly: 'She is right, Rupert, I really would enjoy having your cock up my arse! But first, dear Cecily, would you be kind enough to anoint Rupert's penis with the pomade [*a popular perfumed hair oil of the era – Editor*] you will find in my bag? He has such a thick shaft that it will need the extra lubrication.'

'Of course, Diana, it will give me the greatest pleasure to smear the pomade upon his sturdy stiffstander,' cried Cecily, rising to perform the errand demanded by her lovely friend. She rummaged through Diana's bag and triumphantly brought out the bottle of oil. She slicked a liberal amount upon my throbbing cock so sweetly that my cock threatened to release a libation of spunk before even beginning its planned libidinous journey between Diana's quivering buttocks.

To prevent such a dreadfully unfortunate occurrence, I gritted my teeth and somehow cast my mind to a subject so tedious that it would send the sperm reversing back along its channel to my balls. So I concentrated upon the conjugation of the dullest irregular Latin verb to prevent myself

69

sending a gush of jism all over her hand. By this titanic effort, I managed to hold back the flow of semen that had already been manufactured in my balls. I must mention, incidentally, that I have used this stratagem ever since. Without a shadow of doubt it has benefitted my command of the majestic language of ancient Rome and – which is of far more importance – has indubitably heightened my ability to hold back flooding my partner's pussey until she too is ready to release the tangy liquid elixir of her own spend.

However, on this occasion, Diana leaned forward to raise even higher the chubby white cheeks of her arse. Cecily carefully positioned my knob between them. 'Push forward slowly but firmly,' advised Cecily, realising that I was new to the sport of bum-fucking. I parted Diana's buttocks to open up her wrinkled little bum-hole that beckoned me in so invitingly. Then I followed Cecily's advice and pushed forward steadily as instructed. Despite my worry that I might injure dear Diana, I was able to shove forward without any problem until my prick was completely ensheathed in her bottom, with my balls touching the backs of her inner thighs. I rested a moment and then slowly began to pull my penis backwards and forwards. It was obvious from the high-pitched little yelps from Diana and the wriggling of her delicious arse that she was enjoying it as much as I was, and she grabbed my hands and took them to her front saying: 'Wrap your arms around my waist and frig my cunt.' This I was naturally more than happy to do. Her cunney expelled a veritable little rivulet of love juice as I twiddled her clitty and the tingling contractions of her rear dimple soon brought a torrential discharge of jism crashing out from my cock into her back passage.

'Oh yes, yes, what a lovely big spend, my God! Frig my clitty, Rupert, I'm coming too! Aaah! What lus – lus – luscious pleasure!' She almost fainted away as, with last maddened writhe, she spent copiously all over my hand as I furiously pumped out the final milky drains of sperm into her bottom.

'My God, look everybody, my prick's ready again!' called out young Frank, stroking the swollen shaft which stood up proudly between his legs.

'Well, don't let's waste it,' cried Cecily. 'Let's have some action rather than mere words!'

This spurred Frank to cover her mouth with a burning kiss and the randy girl responded by reaching out for his stiffened staff, holding it firmly between her long, tapering fingers.

Gad! At this tender age we could fuck like fury and still have stiff cocks after several spends. As my friend (for I had the privilege of meeting the great writer on many occasions and I refuse to condemn his artistic works simply because the chap was a sexual deviant) Oscar Wilde has said: 'Youth is wasted upon the young.' [*Most modern readers would applaud Rupert's staunch defence of Wilde, himself a former Cremornite and the author of such classic plays as* The Importance Of Being Earnest. *He was shunned by the vast majority of people after being jailed for homosexual offences yet was lionised by Society before the scandal broke out – Editor*]

Cecily groaned with pleasure as Frank slid his hand between her legs, running his fingers

71

through her hairy mound and, as they rolled together on the eiderdown, he opened her tender cunney lips, sliding his fingers into that dainty crack that was already moistening to a squelchy wetness. He continued to frig her with one, two and then three fingers as she took hold of his throbbing tool with both hands. Wriggling herself across him, she bent her face forward to receive the bared purple domed knob between her eager lips. She sucked at the mushroom helmet, her soft tongue rolling over and over it as she slipped her hands underneath to cup his tight hairy ballsack. She palated his pulsating prick for a little longer before rolling on to her back, her eyes closed, her mouth open.

She was ready to be fucked and Frank was more than ready to oblige. He positioned himself on top of her, balancing his weight upon the palms of his hands as Cecily took hold of his straining cock and placed it between her yearning cunney lips that opened like magic to receive it. 'Let me have it all!' urged Cecily as Frank thrust forward, burying his penis deep inside her willing love channel. She wrapped her legs around his waist as she bucked vigorously, her buttocks coming off the soft quilt as she gyrated from side to side. She began to moan, her breathing increasing to short, sharp pants as Frank's pounding quickened to a crescendo and then the surging cries of fulfilment burst forth from their throats as they began to orgasm together, with Cecily milking Frank's thick cock which was pistoning in and out of her sopping cunt. 'Keep going! Keep going!' she screamed as she arched her hips to welcome the approaching spend and happily Frank was able to continue to squirt his spermy white tribute inside her as she shuddered to a wonderful climax.

The young couple sank back exhausted into the happy reverie that follows the opening of the gates of love and my own cock was now standing as stiff as a poker as Diana stood in front of me with a pensive look in her eyes. We kissed and as our bodies crushed together she slid her hand down to my backside and without warning slipped a finger into my arse-hole. I gasped with the shock and my shaft responded by butting forward blindly against her silky blonde muff. She released her finger from between my clenched buttocks and guided my cock to her pouting cunney lips. An exquisite sensation spread over my shaft as the hairy dryness of her bush gave way to the damp promise of her wet cunt.

Rubbing herself up against me, she continued to urge my bursting knob inside her ever-opening crack. Then, with the easy grace of a ballet dancer, she lifted her right leg and hooked it around my waist. At once my member slid at least halfway inside her cunt and, as I pressed myself deeper inside her salivating cunney, she carefully linked her hands behind my neck and swayed back to look at me at arm's length. 'There you are, Rupert, fucking can be a most artistic affair when performed by an agile couple. Now, please hold me very tight.'

As I did so, the graceful girl pulled herself towards me and raised the other leg, locking both her legs now around my waist and impaling herself completely upon my delighted prick.

Clinging to me, she nipped and nuzzled my neck as I clasped her to me. She gave a small sigh and wriggled as if to take up a more comfortable position. I clung on to her waist as now she swayed back again but this time let go of my shoulders so that her body was arched backwards with her arms hanging loosely and her fingers trailing on the eiderdown.

Then, as I supported my delicious burden, she slowly pulled her body back up to me, and I could feel the muscles of her back ripple under my hands as she repeated the movement. But this time, as she clung to me again, she lifted herself slightly, taking her weight now on her arms and pressing down but not too heavily upon my shoulders. With her legs still locked around my waist, this enabled her to smooth her cunney in an almost teasing way along my cock. I felt the butterfly touch of her erect little clitty as it rubbed its way exquisitely on my shaft which was made even more slippery by her free-flowing juices.

Diana then began to rotate her hips and we began the inevitable journey towards our climax. I felt her cunt grip my cock even harder as we entered the final stages. She shivered and trembled as she first reached the desired haven and seconds later I too started to spend, spurting my hot jet of love juice inside her and Diana gurgled with joy as the frothy white cream filled her cunney and she shuddered with ecstacy as she milked my twitching tool of every last drop of sticky essence.

We collapsed in a heap on top of Cecily and Frank and we stayed there in a tired but contented tangle of naked limbs. But the girls were not yet sated! Frank and I dug deep into our reserves of strength and produced two fine fresh stiffstanders and we developed an excellent fucking chain with Cecily on her knees, leaning forward to gobble my cock whilst Frank pushed his prick into her cunt from behind whilst he frigged Diana's pussey as the blonde temptress exchanged the most passionate of French kisses with me and I fondled her erect raspberry nipples that were as hard as miniature pricks as I rubbed them between my fingers. To conclude this afternoon of lechery, the two girls lay down again and played with each other's pussies, each fingering the other as Frank and I knelt down to have our cocks sucked, mine by Cecily and Frank by Diana.

So ended Frank's first fuck and for both of us, a valuable lesson in *recherché* fucking. We learned much from this lusty joust, not least perhaps, the necessity to experiment until one finds one's way to best please both oneself and one's partner. This is a most important maxim which I gladly pass on to budding cocksmen both young and not-so-young who may be reading my carnal confessions.

CHAPTER THREE

A Night To Remember

ALL GOOD THINGS COME TO AN END, AS my dear mama was wont to say, and to the chagrin of Frank and myself we only managed one further hectic bout of fucking with Cecily and Diana before the girls were whisked away unexpectedly only three days later by Cecily's parents, Sir Jack and Lady Cardew, to spend the rest of the summer at the sumptuous villa of Lord Zwaig, in the heart of the Dordogne region of southern France. We cursed our luck as we were looking forward to a summer holiday like no other, spending our days exploring the multifarious joys of love-making. However, this was still to be a vintage vacation for my sturdy young cock, for the very same morning that we heard the gloomy news about the impending loss of Cecily and Diana, the weather changed as it so often does in this country and the rain fairly howled down, leaving us no alternative but to spend the entire day indoors. Frank leafed through a copy of *Country Life* whilst I idly explored the books in a cabinet usually kept locked but which, on this afternoon, was unaccountably open.

I picked out a thick volume covered for some reason not with a cloth or leather binding but by a plain wrapping of brown paper. My curiosity was aroused and when I opened the book to my great surprise I discovered that I had chanced upon my father's bound copy of *The Oyster*, an anthology of stories from the most salacious of illicit magazines. I had never actually seen the publication myself but Hammond, the captain of cricket at St Lionel's, once obtained a copy from a sporting acquaintance of his father. Alas, it never reached beyond the exalted studies of the sixth form landing before it was confiscated by our housemaster, Mr Prout, after Hammond had carelessly left it folded inside his Latin text-book. Even more surprising to me was the fact that the book began with a special introduction 'on the delights of good fucking' penned by a frequent visitor to our house, one of my father's oldest and closest friends, that famed traveller of the Indian sub-continent, Professor Grahame Johnstone of Edinburgh University.

[*Not too surprising actually when one considers that Professor Johnstone wrote an erotic novella for* The Oyster *in 1891, a piece very different from his well-known books on various aspects of life in late Victorian India – Editor.*]

'Frank, you must come and look at what I've found here,' I called out excitedly to my friend. 'I can hardly believe it but my pater has been keeping a copy of something really fruity in this bookcase.'

'You don't say,' he said as he ambled over to see for himself. 'Gosh! What kind of book is this?

77

I've never seen anything like this in my life!' he exclaimed as he riffled through the pages and stopped at a fully coloured illustrated photographic plate. We pored over the picture which had, as its background setting, the inside of a cobbler's shop. In the foreground, in full view of a shocked-looking clerical gentleman peering through the window, an attractive girl was shown on her knees, her breasts bared, pleasuring a happy young fellow whose trousers and drawers were round his ankles and whose veiny cockshaft was being lustily sucked by the comely red-haired miss. The caption under the lascivious photograph was: *'She was only a cobbler's daughter but she gave the boys her awl'*, a jocular play on words made even more amusing by its very rude complementary illustration.

There were several other such photographic plates, all artistically hand-coloured by Michael Harper [*a Scottish-born painter and a highly respected member of the Royal Academy whose services were in great demand during the late Victorian and early Edwardian years and who deemed it prudent to emigrate to the United States in 1906 after his supposed involvement with the Duchess of Cornwall and King Edward VII in an orgy at the home of Elizabeth Thomson, a popular music hall artiste of the Edwardian era – Editor*]. We sat engrossed by this truly superb collection of coloured plates which showed girls and boys in the nude, both singly and together, enjoying themselves in a variety of love-making positions. Even more surprising was the fact that we were certain that one of the models was Mr Newman, the former games master at St Lionel's, who left the school only the year before to take up a similar post at Eton College. If it were another gentleman, I would have been amazed for the likeness to Mr Newman was to the tee, even down to the small appendectomy scar on his stomach.

Frank's cock had now hardened in his trousers and he pulled out his bursting prick to relieve himself by a quick wank. 'Well, well,' I commented, laying my hand around his hot, throbbing shaft. 'What a size yours swells up to these days. It seems to have grown even bigger since your first fuck with Cecily the other day.'

'I do believe you're right, Rupert. I think it's probably about another half inch longer and probably a bit thicker too.'

We then jumped out of our skins as a merry female voice suddenly broke into this lewd conversation. 'So it's Cecily Cardew who you've been having fun and games with, along with Diana Wigmore! I wondered if you'd found a partner for your friend, Master Rupert, or whether Miss Diana would be asked to share her favours!' We looked up to see who was so knowledgeable about our secret – thank goodness it was only Sally, the prettiest of our parlour-maids, whose shapely curves had been in my thoughts during many a tossing-off since she joined our household the previous November.

Sally was a real smasher and I had thought that a great many of our male visitors thought so too – from the vicar, Reverend Lavery, and old Doctor Attenborough, our local medical practitioner, to my Uncle Algernon (Lord Trippett) who always seemed to find some trifling excuse or other which would involve Sally taking something up or bringing something down from his bedroom and always, come to think of it, when my Uncle was in there by himself! One could hardly blame Uncle Algy, for Sally was more than a cut above the ordinary. Her fair-skinned features were well set off by a hint of pretty freckling around her nose. Her light blue eyes sparkled gaily and her tresses of blonde hair were pinned up underneath her black maid's cap. She was perhaps taller than the average and her firm curvaceous figure promised delights galore, especially as she always wore her white blouse with the top buttons open, giving a delicious view of the swell of her proud white breasts.

I was aghast though that Sally appeared to know far more than she should about what Frank and I had been up to over the previous few days. But what could I say? Frank too was similarly tongue-tied, and I must say that he did look rather funny, standing there with his hand round his prick which still stood high and mighty despite the interruption. It was left to Sally to break the ice. Walking towards us and casting an admiring eye on Frank's tremendous tadger, she said: 'So, Master Frank, you think that your cock has grown since you fucked Miss Cecily? Well, you do have a big one for your age, that's for sure – now how would you like me to finish you off?'

Frank found his voice at last. 'I should say so!' he exclaimed as Sally ran her fingers along his visibly palpitating prick. 'Fair shares for all!' I cried, unbuttoning my flies and bringing out my own substantial shaft for her inspection. 'M'm, that's a nice-looking tool as well, Master Rupert, even though it's not quite the size of your friend's. But then, size isn't so important. It's how you put to use what the Lord has blessed you with, as the vicar is always telling me. After all, your father's pal Algy Moncrieffe hasn't got a very big cock at all, but he's probably the best fuck I've ever entertained between my legs, and that's the honest truth.'

With these wise words Sally grasped our two throbbing tools. Poor Frank was already so excited that he spent almost immediately. Sally was only nineteen but this did not prevent her saying regretfully: 'Ah, what a pity, but you young boys can't last out like older men.' However, I did manage to hold on a little longer than Frank before my prick also jetted out a prodigious stream of spunk all over one of Mama's favourite Chinese rugs.

'Damn, how on earth are we going to clean up the carpet?' I wailed but Sally was not flustered by the problem. 'Don't worry, boys, I'll fetch a bottle of Dr Stanton Harcourt's cough medicine and rub in a few drops. Mr Goldhill showed me how to take out sperm and cunney juice stains out of my sheets after he fucked me the day after I joined the staff. You know all butlers have their way with the girls, given half a chance, and I didn't mind obliging – especially as I can always wangle an extra day off here and there from him if I promise that I'll suck his prick some time afterwards!'

So our starched old retainer was another in our household not above enjoying a good fuck, I mused as Sally continued: 'Yes, the mixture's quite marvellous at removing all traces of love-making. It's quite a good weed-killer too, which is worth remembering! Now, take off your trousers so you'll be ready for when I return.'

We not only took off our trousers but also our shoes, socks, shirts and vests so we were both stark naked when Sally returned with the bottle of Dr Stanton Harcourt's magic liquid. 'Oooh, how nice,' she said as she carefully locked the door behind her. 'I'll be with you both just as soon as I've attended to this carpet.'

When she had completed her chore she unbuttoned her blouse completely and shrugged off the garment. She was wearing nothing underneath and we gasped at the sight of the curvy *rondeurs* of her uncovered breasts. How firm and proudly they jutted out and how stalky were her rose-red nipples that she tweaked up against her palms as she lifted the nude beauties as if offering them up to us for closer inspection. What lovely nipples they were, well separated, each looking a little away from each other and tapering in well-proportioned curves until they came to two crimson points set in the pink circles of Sally's aureoles. These taut titties acted as magnets to my hands as I fondled these succulent spheres, rubbing her rubbery red nipples until they were as hard as my stiff cock which was pressing up against her flat tummy.

'Quick, I want you to fuck me before you spend,' she said urgently. She stripped off the rest of her clothes and turned round, bending over so that her glorious bum cheeks were only inches away from my straining knob. She stood with her legs apart and my hands trembled as I parted the chubby soft cheeks, as white as alabaster. I paused for a moment to savour the sight of her pouting cunney lips as they stretched open to reveal the flushed inner flesh of her cunt.

I leaned over her and Sally whimpered as she felt the smooth crown of my cock wedge itself between her buttocks. Before fucking from behind with Cecily and Diana I would have certainly been too shy to attempt a fuck in this fashion but *experientia docet* and she turned her head round to look at me with her limpid blue eyes and murmured: 'Go on, Rupert, fuck me in whatever way takes your fancy!' What a wonderfully open invitation but, as afore-mentioned, I did not attempt to cork her winking little bum-hole. I propelled my prick, which was now as hard as rock, as far forward as I could manage and Sally wiggled to enable my shaft to enter the supple, glistening crack of her cunt. Fiercely, I pushed onwards, burying my cock to the very hilt so that my balls banged against her backside as I pulled back a little before plunging in deep inside her welcoming cunney.

I began to fuck the delicious girl with a quickening pace, my ballsack now slapping against her arse as she cried out with delight, her whole body rocking in rhythm with my cock as it slithered in and out of her juicy pussey which squeezed open and shut like a slippery fist as we thrilled each other with our bodies. I held her round the waist with one hand and leaned round to rub the nipple of one of her magnificent breasts with the other, which excited her greatly. I felt Sally explode into a series of peaks of pleasure as I continued relentlessly to pump in and out of her pussey. Her cunt was incredibly tight and wet and her love-channel clung to my cock as I rode her to the very limit. Again and again I drove home until I felt the familiar surge building up in my balls. At the same time Sally screamed and shuddered to a superb climax as I gushed a torrent of hot spunk into her crack. What a blissful fuck this was and I withdrew my still semi-stiff shaft, which was gleaming with its coating of Sally's pussey juice, and the cheeky girl turned round and chuckled: 'Ten out of ten, Master Rupert, I told you that the size of a prick is relatively unimportant '

I stroked my penis proudly and Sally took hold of it with both hands and rubbed it between her palms until it regained its full length and strength and rose as hard as iron against my belly. 'Can you carry on for another fuck?' she asked anxiously. When I nodded my assent she gave my sturdy staff a frisk final frigging before laying herself down on a nearby couch. She then told me to come over and lie on top of her and to straddle her body with my legs. I did as I was told and Sally took hold of my pulsating cock, pulling me forwards and I assumed that she was going to suck my throbbing tool But no, she placed the sticky shaft in the cleft between her breasts and squeezed them around my pole. 'Go on, Master Rupert, fuck my big titties!' she whispered and I began a further lesson in the delights of *l'art de faire l'amour*. I was not over-sure as how best to continue but instead let nature take its course. I rocked my hips to pump my rigid rod up and down the snug cleft of Sally's breasts. It was extraordinarily sensuous, especially when she leaned her face forward and took the crown of my cock and began licking and lapping it as it moved to and fro between her breasts.

'I'm coming! I'm coming!' she wailed, one hand

now dipping between her legs to finger her pussey and the other teasing my balls and arse. 'Oh yes, yes, yes, you're making me come by fucking my titties!'

She threw back her head as she continued moaning and her white teeth gleamed as her lips parted and her eyes closed in ecstasy as she spent profusely. Her blood was still up, though, and the last thing she wanted to do now was to stop this grand sport. But would my now tiring cock be able to continue with this now frenzied fucking? As I now know, there is no strong performance without a touch of fanaticism in the performer. I held on as I found new strength to slide my pole backwards and forwards. She clamped her lips around my knob and sucked hard, sending little electric currents along the shaft. Then she released my knob from her mouth and pushed my shoulders upwards and told me to be still.

Who was I to disobey such a sweetly spoken command? So I lay back and let Sally clamber over me. First she made herself comfortable, sitting astride me and trailing those magnificent breasts up and down my torso as she leaned forward so that her tawny nipples flicked exquisitely across my skin. Then she lifted her hips and crouched over my truncheon which stood high in the air with her cunney directly above my knob. She took hold of my staff and encouragingly rubbed the pulsating pole before cleverly positioning my uncapped helmet so that it pressed directly against her clitty. Rotating her body, she edged forward slightly to allow my rigid rod to enter her. Ever so slowly she lifted and lowered her sopping pussey and each time she sank downwards my cock went deeper and higher inside her until our bodies simply melted away in sheer delight as she lay sated upon me, my prick so fully ensheathed inside her cunt that our pubic hairs were enmeshed together.

I heard Frank draw in his breath sharply and turned my head to see my friend sitting on the edge of his chair, his big prick visibly swelling as he frigged it up to its fullest stiffness. 'Go on Rupert, fuck her juicy cunt,' he muttered. 'And when you've finished perhaps I can have a go!'

Our senses were now at fever pitch. My upward strokes excited her into taking up a fresh, fierce little fucking rhythm as she thrust down to meet my movements to cram every inch of hard cock inside her cunney. Now we both felt the first unmistakable tremors of an approaching spend. Shudder after shudder ran through Sally's quivering body as she half sat back again so that I could best cup her plump breasts in my hands. She gave a choking cry and began to ride up and down on me with a renewed vigour, forcing herself down even harder on my cock. It even crossed my mind that her cries might attract attention from outside the library!

Then I felt that magical first stirrings as my spunk began to force its way up my distended shaft. Sally sensed this and immediately she ceased all movement, her cunt now halfway down my cock as she reached down to kiss me. Twice more she arrested our spends until she was fully ready for her own orgasm. She moved up and down with shorter, faster thrusts and I responded with similar upward jerks. Her mouth was open and she was gaping and moaning as we reached the very brink of ecstacy. Suddenly her cunney muscles tightened about me in a long, rippling seizure that ran from the base to the very root of my cock. Three times more this clutching spasm travelled the entire length of my shaft and then just as Sally screamed out: 'Yes, Yes, Yes! I've come, I've come! Now shoot your spunk, young Rupert!' in a near-delirium, grinding her pussey against me as the frothy jism forced its way out of my knob, hot and seething into every nook and cranny of her cunt.

As we slowly subsided, panting and near collapse, we lay entwined in an intimate jumble of bare flesh. Though I could hear a series of rapid knocks on the door (thank goodness Sally had locked it!), a warm wave of fatigue washed over me and I just could not bring myself to even answer the insistent unknown caller

Fortunately Frank was still *compos mentis* and I could not help smiling as he heaved himself out of his chair and padded naked across to the door, stiff frigging his stiff cock which was raised as high as a flagpole against his tummy. 'Who's there?' he asked. 'It's Goldhill, sir,' came the voice of our old butler. 'I'm sorry to disturb you but I have a message to give to Master Rupert from his father.'

Even at the early age of fifteen and a half, Frank was one of the most quick-witted chaps I have ever known. With only a brief pause, itself covered by a clearing of his throat, he replied: 'Ah, well, Goldhill, I'm afraid Rupert's just fallen asleep and I don't really want to disturb him which is why I locked the door. You see, he was complaining about having a slight headache and hopefully he'll sleep it off.'

'I distinctly thought I heard noises coming from the library.'

'So you did,' said Frank. 'Rupert was talking in his sleep and I think he must have been having a nightmare! Is the matter of great urgency or can you come back in ten minutes?'

So thanks to Frank's fast-thinking we had time to dress ourselves and for Sally to sneak out of the library, undetected by Goldhill or any of the other servants. When Goldhill made his second appearance ten minutes later as requested, I made a great show of yawning and stretching out my arms. 'Frank has told me that you have a message from Papa,' I said. 'I hope that it wasn't too urgent as I had a beastly pri–, I mean, headache and needed forty winks. But I'm all right now, thank goodness.' I added though I noticed that this had not prevented the butler from shooting me a suspicious look.

'Yes, Master Frank told me about it. I am glad you have recovered so quickly. The Colonel and Mrs Mountjoy are attending the annual general meeting of the Yorkshire Society For The Promotion Of Science in Harrogate and they have asked me to tell you that they are expecting a visitor to arrive here early this afternoon. On their behalf, they ask you to extend every hospitality to this gentleman as your parents do not expect to return until about half past three as they are taking luncheon today with Lord and Lady Beasant in Bilton. Our new guest, who will be staying here for a few days, is a Mr Frederick Nolan, an American gentleman from California. You may be interested to know, Master Rupert, that Mr Nolan will be bringing with him one of these new-fangled cinematographs. If you know what I mean, sir, these are the machines that take moving pictures.'

'Moving pictures,' echoed Frank. 'Well, what a coincidence! I was reading about them in the *Manchester Guardian* only this morning. Is this Mr Nolan going to give us an exhibition of his work?'

'Yes, sir,' intoned Goldhill. 'Indeed it was Mr Nolan who wrote the article you read in the newspaper. He is in Yorkshire to make a film on the Dales which he intends to show to audiences in America.'

'Wow, perhaps we can be in it?' said Frank excitedly. 'Wouldn't that be great?'

'I doubt it as the sight of your face would crack the camera lens!' I replied with a laugh.

'Ha, ha, ha – well, you can laugh but I'm jolly well going to ask him if I can help in any way,' responded my chum. 'Goldhill, is there anything we must prepare for Mr Nolan's arrival?'

'No, sir,' said the butler. 'I will be sure to let you both know when Mr Nolan arrives.'

Goldhill did not have to carry out this task, for we were so keen to meet Mr Nolan that we bolted through luncheon and when the doorbell rang just after two o'clock Frank and I raced to the front door to welcome our American guest in style.

I opened the door to a handsome gentleman in the prime of life, perhaps a mite shorter in height than the average, dressed in a snappy summer suit and carrying a silver topped walking stick. 'Good afternoon, sir. You must be Mr Nolan, the cinematographer. Welcome to Albion Towers.'

'That's right, young man, Fred Nolan at your service, all the way from the USA. And who may you be?'

'I'm Rupert Mountjoy, sir, the Colonel's son. And this is my friend, Frank Folkestone.'

'Glad to meet you, Frank,' said the genial stranger, beckoning to his driver to unload the cart which contained his luggage and two large chests which no doubt contained all his cinemato-graphic equipment

'I'll have someone bring in all your cases, sir,' I said.

'Well, thank you, my boy, but I'll supervise the operation, if you don't mind. My cameras must be handled very carefully.'

After we had helped Mr Nolan to settle in, he gratefully accepted the offer of some refreshment. Goldhill brought in a large whisky and soda and Mrs Randall provided a platter of cold roast beef sandwiches and a pot of hot black coffee. I apologised for my parents' absence but Mr Nolan waved aside my words: 'No need to apologise, you've done me proud, young man, though I look forward to meeting your parents. Now before they come I'd very much like to take a walk around your estate whilst the rain holds off.'

'Are you planning the scenario for a film?' I asked.

'Yup, that's the idea. My boy, motion pictures are in their infancy and the three-minute film will, I predict, soon be overtaken by full-length plays which will be shown in special movie theatres,' he replied.

We must have looked dubious for Mr Nolan continued: 'I see you doubt me. Well, boys, I'll go further, I will go so far as to predict that motion pictures will in your lifetime be seen in colour and you'll be able to hear the spoken word coming out from the screen! Ah, I see you smile – well, we shall see, we shall see. Just remember that people laughed at Mr Edison's idea for a phonograph [*or gramophone as the British called the early record-players – Editor*].

'But that probably won't happen until the dawn of the new century. Right now, how would you like to come out with me to look for a suitable location for my film?'

'I should say,' said Frank with alacrity, 'especially if we could later watch you make your film '

'Of course, of course,' said Mr Nolan cordially. 'If you like, you may even appear in it!' The promise of such a treat was more than enough to get us out of doors and we tramped round our garden until Mr Nolan stopped and said: 'This looks like the perfect spot. I want to take a shot of the house before pointing the camera at a tea-party taking place on the lawn. If the weather is good enough and your parents are amenable, we will made a start directly after breakfast.'

My parents arrived home soon afterwards and, like Frank and myself, they thoroughly enjoyed the company of the gregarious American who regaled us with a flood of anecdotes about his fascinating life. Mr and Mrs Harbottle and their daughter Katie had also been invited to dine with us and I could see that Katie, a slim, attractive girl of twenty-one, who was sitting next to Mr Nolan, was especially taken with his recounting of his adventures. It seemed that Mr Nolan's late father was one of the railway magnates back in America and being the sole heir to a very considerable fortune had enabled his son to travel the world at his leisure.

'You must find it very dull here after New York, Rome, Paris and London, Mr Nolan,' sighed my Mama who unlike Papa, enjoyed the bustle of town life, having been brought up in London.

He shook his head. 'Dull? Not a bit of it, ma'am, it's a real pleasure to be able to enjoy the peace and quiet of the country. Why, in New York, or in any great city, I don't think it is possible to secure even six hours of undisturbed sleep. I certainly never achieved this last week in London. I can't blame anyone for the choir of cats that decided to hold a concert on the roof of my hotel but I could have cheerfully strangled the two cabbies who careered down Marylebone High Street shouting imprecations to each other that I cannot repeat here!'

As he paused to take a glass of champagne from Goldhill, I bent under the table to retrieve my napkin which had fallen to the floor. And what a shock I had as I looked across to see that Katie Harbottle, who was sitting opposite Mr Nolan, and who was a most pleasant but quiet and shy girl in company, had taken off her right shoe and was running her stockinged toes up and down Mr Nolan's left leg! Yet the American continued this little tale as if nothing untowards was happening even though Katie's foot, hidden from general view, was now caressing his inner thigh and was rising higher towards his groin with every stroke!

I could hardly remain under the table but, as I straightened up, Mr Nolan continued as if nothing untoward was happening: 'Then one has to cope with the rumbling thunder made by the dustmen's carts, to say nothing of the infernal row made by drunken revellers pouring out of the clubs. Oh, I could think of a hundred other sleep-preventers as well.'

'I can think of a better sleep-preventer than all that – Sally the parlourmaid sucking my cock!' muttered Frank, who was sitting besides me. I dropped my napkin, deliberately this time, and when I bent down to pick it up, I drew a sharp breath to prevent an exclamation of amazement escape from my lips. Katie was still rubbing one foot down Mr Nolan's leg, but now he had brazenly opened the buttons of his flies, and this was allowing Katie to wriggle the toes of her other foot inside his trousers, stroking them against his naked rampant penis which stood up stiffly out of his under-shorts.

With difficulty I suppressed the urge to succumb to hysterics, though I wondered wildly how the two of them would extricate themselves from this compromising situation. Surprisingly enough, it proved far less awkward than I envisaged for when the time came for the ladies to retire, Katie simply slipped her shoes back on and left the room together with the two older ladies. Mr Nolan did not rise fully as the ladies left the table but crouched over his chair, hastily buttoning his trousers as Goldhill came in with a tray of liqueurs.

'Do you belong to any clubs here in England, Mr Nolan?' asked my father, as Goldhill poured out cognac for us all (Frank and I were allowed a small measure as a special treat) and Mr Nolan nodded his head. 'Yes, I belong to the Reform and the Travellers and my club in Washington, D.C., the Beesknees, has connections with the Jim Jam in London.'

'The Jim Jam,' said my father thoughtfully. 'I don't think I've ever heard of that establishment.'

93

Mr Nolan looked quickly at Frank and myself and hurriedly changed the subject: 'I don't get there very often, Colonel. Tell me now, how do you occupy your time since you left the Indian Army?'

[*It is hardly surprising that Mr Nolan had no wish to elaborate further upon his membership of the Jim Jam Club, a semi-secret gentlemen's* maison close *situated in Great Windmill Street, Soho. The uninhibited revelries that took place there (King Edward VII was a frequent visitor in his younger days as Prince of Wales) were commented upon with relish in several underground magazines of the era including the notorious* Intimate Memoirs of Dame Jenny Everleigh *recently republished by Sphere Books, London – Editor.*]

'I'm enjoying the life of an English country gentleman,' replied my father. 'Plenty of hunting, shooting and fishing, you know.'

'Are you keen on country pursuits, Mr Nolan?' asked George Harbottle, Katie's father and the local squire who was perhaps the best shot in the entire county, a fact that was best kept from Mr Nolan whose only pursuit this evening was fucking the squire's daughter!

'As an American I'm always at ease in the great outdoors, sir, and have always been extremely fond of the country,' said Frederick Nolan with a smile.

'Well, it's true that he's extremely fond of cunt!' I said softly to Frank.

'Why, what are you talking about?' my friend whispered back. I quietly explained what I had seen going on underneath the table, which made Frank choke with laughter.

'Let us all in on the joke, boys,' said my father genially.

Frank again showed his uncanny ability to manoeuvre his way out of a tight corner by explaining that the cognac had 'gone down the wrong way' and we sat quietly whilst the others finished their liqueurs. 'Shall we join the ladies?' said my father, rising from his seat and as neither guest had taken up my father's previous offer of a cigar, we trooped into the drawing room. Not surprisingly the conversation came round to Mr Nolan's films and Frank and I exchanged a knowing glance when Katie Harbottle said: 'I'd very much like to see your equipment, Mr Nolan.'

'Ah, that creates a slight problem,' said the cunning cinematographer, 'You see, I have set everything up in my room and it would be rather difficult to bring it all downstairs.'

Katie looked disappointed but Mrs Harbottle said: 'I don't see why you could not go up to Mr Nolan's room and see his equipment there.'

'I say, Enid –' spluttered her husband, but she imperiously waved away his protest. 'Really, George, by refusing Katie permission to go with Mr Nolan you are, unwittingly of course, insulting them both! Do you feel that Mr Nolan or your daughter would behave improperly just because they would be alone for fifteen minutes?'

I wondered who was silently cheering Mrs Harbottle's progressive views – my Mama, who had persuaded Mrs Harbottle of the justice of the Suffragette cause (much to the squire's disgust!), or Katie and Frederick Nolan who I knew would like nothing better than to find themselves together in a private place and especially a bedroom!

So the young couple made good their escape and at the same time Frank and I were given leave to go and play ping pong [*table tennis – Editor*] on the new table my father had bought me for my birthday last February. On our way to the games room, I suddenly remembered that the other day I had noticed that the bats were missing so I said: 'Come downstairs, Frank and we'll find Goldhill He'll know where the blinking bats have been put away.' Everyone on duty must have been in the kitchen as there was no member of staff to greet us at the foot of the stairs. However, we heard a girl giggling and then a short murmur coming from a room in front of us. 'That sounds like Goldhill,' I said so we followed the sounds and pushed open the door of the servants' sitting room. I don't know who was the most embarrassed, Frank and myself or Goldhill and Polly, the scullery maid. For the dark-haired girl was sprawled naked on the large sofa with Goldhill, who was still in uniform (except for his trousers and drawers which were lying over his ankles) slewing his prick in and out of her hairy pussey. At first we stood unseen as the butler's lean bottom cheeks pumped up and down while the couple rocked in time with their amorous exertion. Then Polly let out a little scream as she saw us standing there, gaping at this lewd scene.

'Don't mind us, old fellow,' Frank called out 'We'd much rather wait until you've finished before attending to us.'

'Yes, attend to Polly first, Goldhill,' I said, rather enjoying the butler's discomforture though I noted that Polly seemed little put out by the interruption. 'Her need is greater than ours.'

Polly giggled. 'Come on then, Mr Goldhill, let's take up where we left off!' And to encourage him she turned over to lie face downwards, reaching across for a soft cushion to insert under her belly so that her hips and chubby rounded bum cheeks were raised high in the air. The butler shuffled between her legs and nudging her knees part, took his sizeable stalk in his hand. 'Are you ready then, Polly?' he asked and after receiving a quick nod of assent, he carefully guided his gleaming weapon into the crack between her bum cheeks, his knob brushing up against her cunney lips before sliding through them into the warm wetness of her welcoming cunt.

I must say that Goldhill was no slouch when it came to the mark. As soon as his prick was safely ensheathed in Polly's pussey the butler began to fuck her at a slowish but regular pace and leaned forward so that his chest lay on Polly's back. He reached round to fiddle with her large tawny titties, holding them in thrall as he continued to slew his cock in and out of her sopping slit. Her backside slapped enticingly against his surprisingly muscular thighs as she slipped into the rhythm of fucking that he had established and he increased the pace, now forcefully pounding away as Polly wriggled in delight.

As you may imagine, friendly reader, the sight of his thick, veined member see-sawing in and out of her willing cunney made Frank and I extremely horney, especially when the rude girl reached behind to grab hold of his swinging ballsack as it slapped against her bum. Sensing that she was waiting for him, Goldhill increased the speed of his fucking once more and he croaked: 'Here it comes, Polly, brace yourself!' as his torso went rigid and his twitching tool expelled its emission of frothy jism into her seething crack. Polly yelped with glee as the glorious sensations of her own impending orgasm swept like magic throughout her body. The butler collapsed on top of the delighted maid who twisted her bum lasciviously to draw out the last drains of sperm from Goldhill's now exhausted cock.

'Now that was a marvellous fuck, let's do it again,' said Polly brightly but our old retainer looked disconcertedly down at his shrunken shaft and shook his head.

'I'm sorry, but I'm not up to it, my girl. Besides, I've got to do some work for Master Rupert,' he said as he pulled up his trousers.

'Oh dear,' wailed the gorgeous girl. 'Is there not a single stiff prick in the entire house?'

This question was immediately answered by Frank who fairly ripped open the buttons of his fly to bring out his huge naked cockshaft. 'Will this do?' he enquired, bringing his giant tool closer for Polly to inspect, making the purple knob leap and bound in his hand.

'Oooh, that looks good enough to eat,' said Polly, sliding down on her knees from the sofa and weighing Frank's meaty staff in the palm of her hand. 'What an enormous penis for a lad as young as you!' she exclaimed. I was now getting a little miffed at hearing all the girls say this as soon as Frank showed his cock to any female either upstairs or downstairs!

'Would you like me to suck it or would this mean you wouldn't be able to fuck me afterwards?' she asked.

'Do put it in your mouth, I'll come twice without

any problems,' he answered eagerly and on hearing such good news she popped his swollen helmet into her mouth. I could see that Polly was a brilliant *fellatrice*. She worked on his knob with her tongue, easing her lips forward to take in a little of his shaft. She encircled the base of his cock with one hand and with the other, she began to work the pink, velvety skin up and down, her head bobbing as she sucked away with undisguised relish, taking as much of his rigid pole as she could manage between her lips. Her warm breath and moist mouth sent Frank into the seventh heaven of delight and the feel of her wet tongue slithering around his tingling tool soon brought my chum to the brink of a spend. His tadger jerked uncontrollably as she now moved her hands from his cock to grasp the firm, muscular cheeks of his bottom, moving him backwards and forwards until with a final juddering throb he spurted a lavish stream of sperm into her welcoming mouth. She swallowed his emission joyfully, smacking her lips as she gulped down his tangy jism.

'Now, Master Frank, is your young cock still up to the mark as you promised it would be?' gasped Polly as she cast herself back on the sofa, her legs wide apart to expose her pouting pussey and the receptive red slash of cunney flesh which made my already swollen prick strain even more unmercifully against the material of my trousers. I must confess that I wondered whether Frank could fulfil his boast after squirting his spunk so powerfully down Polly's throat but my doubts were quickly assuaged as Frank, his cock waggling, clambered upon the girl's rich curves with hardly a pause. A moan from them both signalled that his knob had slipped between her cunney lips without any preliminaries. He withdrew and then pushed in again slowly and I saw how, parting slowly to his push, the velvet lips appeared to draw him in as their mouths met in the most passionate of kisses. The bold minx jerked her bottom to absorb more of his slippery staff and in a trice, with a cry of bliss, he was fully engulfed inside the sweet prison of her cunt, his hairy ballsack dangling against her plump backside.

Frank's slim, smooth body moved in rhythm, faster and faster until the naughty pair were rocking furiously as he now pounded his thick, rock-hard prick into her willing juicy love channel. Polly twisted in veritable throes of ecstacy, panting and grunting with delight as she slipped her hands down Frank's back to grasp his bum cheeks, eagerly lifting her hips to welcome the thrusting shaft that was sliding so deliciously in and out of her sopping cunney.

'Oh yes, what a glorious fuck! What a strong young cock you have! Faster, faster, I want all that lovely jism in your balls, fill me up with it, flood my cunney!' she gasped.

Quite berserk, the lewd couple rolled around on the sofa as Frank's delighted penis slewed joyously in and out of her honeypot. 'There I go!' she squealed, and Frank tensed his frame as with a cry he crashed down one final time upon Polly's quivering body, his cock jetting spasms of spunk streaming inside her slit as she squeezed her thighs together and milked every last drop of jism from his spurting stalk. She showed no signs of releasing him until his penis started to deflate and only then did she allow him to pull it out of her drenched cunney.

I would have liked nothing better at that moment then to have fucked Polly myself especially as I could see that her eyes were looking directly at the bulge between my legs as my stiffened prick twitched uncomfortably in the confines of my trousers. But Goldhill cleared his throat and murmured: 'I suggest that we all leave here as soon as possible, the other servants will be returning at any time ' We could not ignore his warning so Polly and Frank began to dress and I turned to Goldhill to ask him where the table tennis bats might be found. He told me that they were kept with a bag of ping pong balls in a cupboard on the landing just outside the games room

'Do you still fancy a game, Frank, or are you now too tired?' I laughed.

'No, no, I'll happily play with you,' he said, buttoning up his fly buttons, 'although I'll tell you now that it won't be as much fun as playing with Polly!'

'No, I bet it won't,' I said sourly. 'I would have liked to have judged the difference myself.'

'Now, now, Master Rupert, don't be jealous,' smiled Polly. 'Look, I tell you what, I'll come up to your room at eleven o'clock tonight and we'll all have some fun.'

'All have some fun?' I queried.

'Oh, yes,' she said gaily. 'Master Frank must be there or I won't come. He has the most amazing prick –'

'Yes, yes, I know, it's so big for a boy his age.' I

said heavily, but I wasn't really too put out at yet a further compliment given to Frank's huge penis. After all, my friend's cock was paving the way for my own prick to find its way between Polly's legs and so far, none of the girls who I had so far fucked – Diana, Cecily nor Sally – had made the slightest disparaging remark about the prowess of my cock and had indeed praised highly its abilities whilst performing *l'art de faire l'amour*.

This incident first showed me how important it is to know that there will always be a fellow with more notches on his cockshaft than yours; just as there will always be bigger pricks and heavier ballsacks than yours to be seen in the sports club's changing rooms. But at the same time, there will always be those with tinier tadgers and it must be stressed that there are even some young men blessed with members the size of cucumbers who would gladly give their all to have taken part in the number of sexual experiences that you have enjoyed. Of course, I did not fully appreciate this maxim fully at this early stage in my sexual education but I do so now *in toto* and urge its acceptance to all gallant gentlemen.

In fact, it turned out that I had only a couple of hours to wait until my carnal appetite was totally sated by the exquisite Polly Aysgarth who, I will tell you now, dear reader, left our service shortly afterwards to take up a position in Lord Borehamwood's establishment down in London Roger, his Lordship's youngest son, became infatuated with the sensuous parlourmaid and proposed marriage. Rather than attract the publicity that would be certain to occur if Polly went ahead with a breach-of-contract suit, his Lordship settled the affair by giving Polly four thousand pounds and sending the Honourable Roger off to Australia. Happily, all worked out for the best as Polly settled down in an admittedly unconventional form of marriage with the Russian *roué* Count Sasha Motkalevich and Roger is now one of the most prosperous sheep farmers in New South Wales.

Back however, to my story – on our way upstairs Frank and I heard the sounds of giggling coming from Mr Nolan's quarters and it sounded as though Katie Harbottle was enjoying her private view of Fred Nolan's equipment. However, being gentlemen, we did not eavesdrop and marched on through to the games room. False modesty is just as foolish as overweaning pride, so I will not disguise the fact that I easily vanquished Frank at table tennis, even though he was the best all-round sportsman in my form. We played snooker for a while but neither of us were good enough to make a game of it so we decided to wander back to the drawing room. We met Fred Nolan and Katie just coming out of his room and he looked somewhat flushed of face whilst she was busying herself doing up the buttons of her dress.

'Did you find Mr Nolan's equipment of interest, Miss Harbottle?' I enquired as we approached them.

Without batting an eyelid, she replied sweetly: 'Oh yes indeed, I was quite overwhelmed by the sight of his accoutrements.'

'I'll bet she was, the naughty girl,' I murmured to Frank as we passed by them. The Harbottles left shortly afterwards and Frank and I retired in good time for my chum to be able to dash unseen into my room after changing into his pyjamas.

'I've only cleaned my teeth as I thought I could take a shower after we've fucked Polly,' he said, taking off his dressing gown. I was already eagerly anticipating Polly's arrival and was sitting naked on the bed. Frank decided to slip off his pyjamas, too, as the night was very warm When we had waited for Diana and Cecily I had been totally confident that they would appear but for some reason I had a nagging doubt as to whether our lusty parlourmaid would keep her word. But I need not have worried because on the stroke of eleven there was an urgent tap on the door. I leaped down and opened the door a fraction – yes, it was Polly, also clothed simply in a dressing gown and looking anxiously up and down the hallway to make sure that she had not been seen.

'Quick, come inside!' I whispered and after she had slipped in I closed the door behind her.

She sat on the bed and looked at Frank and myself. 'Well, boys, here I am and I hope that you two are good and ready for a good night's fucking because I feel very, very randy!' she said, letting the dressing gown fall from her shoulders to slide gracefully down her body. What a wonderful creation the human form is, I marvelled as, very deliberately, Polly traced her hands over her plump yet firm breasts before letting her fingers find their way around her belly and towards her dark, glossy pussey bush. Polly smiled knowingly as she rubbed her thumb against her pouting lips and flashed a saucy smile at us. 'Well, boys, do you approve of the goods on display or do you wish to return them to the manufacturer?' This was a somewhat rhetorical question for already both our cocks were standing smartly to attention and Polly inspected them critically. She was a happy, chatty kind of girl and she prattled away cheerfully as she took our two stiff pricks in her hands and rubbed them up to bursting point.

'M'm, these are two very good-looking cocks. I must admit, and I'm going to enjoy fucking and sucking them. But which one should I start with? Frank, yours is the biggest but size isn't everything. After all, Mr Goldhill hasn't got a very big one either but he always manages to bring me off time after time which is more than your Uncle Martin did, Master Rupert, last time he was at Albion Towers. As Captain Luton down in the village – you know him, I believe, the old sailor who keeps the Fox and Feather Inn – is fond of saying, "It isn't the size of the ship that matters, it's the motion of the ocean!" So I think we'll start off with your prick, Master Rupert, and see what it tastes like. But don't fret, Master Frank, I won't leave you out of it!'

And without further ado she swooped down, clamping her luscious lips around the red mush-roomed crown of my cock whilst she grasped Frank's massive shaft at its base and started to wank the rigid rod as she sucked lustily away at my uncapped helmet, washing her tongue over the sensitive knob until I thought I would faint away with the pleasure of it all. I groaned and pressed her curly-haired head downwards until her lips enclosed almost all my throbbing shaft and she dipped her head up and down with a regular motion that sent waves of pure ecstasy rolling out from my groin.

I saw Frank's hand snake out towards Polly's pussey as she continued to rub his stiffstander. She wriggled across so that his fingers could play in her shiny muff. 'Well done, that's the way!' she gasped as he nudged his forefinger against her cunney lips and entered her moist cunt. He pushed first one and then two fingers deeper inside her love-box as she raised her hips up, panting breathlessly as he began to establish a rhythm. Her head continued to bob up and down over my twitching tool until I felt a great shudder of pleasure run through me and I shot a stream of hot spunk down her throat. Polly milked my prick expertly, sucking out every drop of frothy white essence out of my cock whilst Frank continued to play with her juicy cunney as she gripped his hands between her thighs and squeezed it hard against her dripping crack.

Polly smacked her lips and said: 'Master Rupert, your jism is less salty than your friend's, so even if his prick is bigger, your spunk tastes sweeter. There, does that make you feel better?'

Then without waiting for a reply, she turned her attention to Frank for she must have realised from the throbbing of his tool that he would soon shoot off if she carried on masturbating his manly pole. So she lay back on the bed and parted her thighs as Frank clambered on top of her to press his purple knob against her cunney lips. I took hold of his giant shaft and guided it home, sliding the head of the veiny rammer. He sank into her cunt with a grateful sigh of relief.

Once his cock was totally enclosed in her channel Polly closed her thighs, making Frank open his legs and lie astride her with his penis well and truly trapped inside her pussey. 'I love doing this,' Polly panted lewdly. 'Now you just fuck away, young Frank, and let me feel your big prick rub against the sides of my cunt!' However, Frank could scarcely move his cock as the muscles of her cunney were gripping his shaft so tightly but he was happy enough as Polly began to grind her hips round, massaging his prick as it throbbed away inside her cunt which by now was dribbling its love juices down her thighs. I was now desperate to join the fun and games but my cock was still hanging limp. Then suddenly I had a bright idea and slid my hand under Polly's backside and inserted my forefinger in her bum-hole. My precipitate action surprised but in no way upset Polly, who wiggled delightedly upon my finger and squealed: 'You naughty boy, Master Rupert, who's been teaching you about bum-fiddling then!' For some reason this set off Frank and so Polly shifted her thighs and eased the pressure around his raging prick. My chum began to drive wildly now, in and out, in and out like a steamhammer, fucking at such intense speed that I knew he would soon send his gushings of foaming sperm flying out into Polly's sopping slit.

Meanwhile, Polly was being brought off all the time, building herself up to a tremendous orgasm as the fierce momentum of Frank's fucking made her pussey disgorge a veritable rivulet of love juice. She brought her legs up against the small of his back as I continued to jab my finger in and out of her arse-hole. Frank now bore down on her yet again, his body now gleaming with perspiration, fucking that juicy pussey faster and faster, the rippling movement of his cock sliding at breakneck speed against the glistening skin of her cunney. Then with a groan he spurted his seed, drenching her cunt with his jism as Polly quickly closed her thighs together again as he released his entire copious emission, not releasing him until his tool lay still, shrinking back to its natural flaccidity inside her.

Polly wriggled up and rolled the unresisting body of Frank on to the side. 'Now, now, boys, we've only just started! Master Rupert, your cock looks just about ready for another game!' She took hold of my burgeoning prick which was by now stirring anew and it swelled up to its full proud proportions in her fist. She then lay back and drew her legs apart to expose the mark as I took my place on top of her. I glued my lips to hers and clutched her swelling breasts in my hands as she kept firm hold on my cock, ready to place it in position – but she had no need to do so, for the combination of her own and Frank's juices had prepared the oven for the dish, so to speak, and had made her pussey so slippery that my cock immediately slid right in deep inside her cunney without any preliminaries whatsoever. As soon as I felt my cock ensconced in her wet, throbbing sheath I began to heave and shove to our mutual enjoyment. Through the intensity of the sucking off she had previously given me, I was able to prolong the ride, bringing the trembling girl off twice before I added my own sticky liquid tribute to the pungent blobs of love juice that had formed all around her pussey lips and in her furry tuft of cunney hair. I slicked my still stiff shaft in and out of her willing cunt until Polly said: 'Hold hard, Master Rupert, it looks like Frank's cock is rising up again. I think we can now all three play together now, won't that be fun?'

'I should say so,' said Frank, brandishing his erection in his hands and offering up the tip of his prick for Polly to suck. She slurped her lips over his bare red knob, liberally coating it with spittle before saying: 'I want you to fuck my bottom with that big cock of yours, Master Frank.'

She leaned over so that both Polly and I were lying on our sides, for I was still threading her juicy pussey whilst the above conversation was taking place, but this new position allowed her to thrust her chubby buttocks out as I bucked my way into her cunt. Frank then grasped her bum cheeks and parted the rounded globes so that the tiny wrinkled brown orifice between them was fully exposed. He manoeuvered the glowing knob of his proud cock between the adorable cheeks of her ripe derrière and eased it blissfully within the puckered rim of her rear dimple.

'Aaah! Oooh! Aaaah! It's going in! You've filled me up, you randy little fucker!' she cried as Frank urged his cock majestically upwards and inwards into her willing bottom. Polly twisted in delicious agonies as her backside yielded to this attack, grinding her cheeks against Frank's boyish flat belly. At one stage we both pushed our cocks in together and I felt my own staff rubbing against Frank's with only the thin divisional membrane of Polly's cunney and bum-hole running between us. I came first, pumping jet after jet of frothy white spunk while Polly and Frank continued to writhe in new paroxyms of pleasure as Frank corked her bottom, stirring her blood so hotly that she spent copiously as she panted out: 'Come on, Frank, shoot your sperm up my bum. Ooh, that's right, work your shaft in and out whilst you rub my titties!' Frank rammed away in earnest whilst her bottom bounced upon his belly and his sturdy cock eased back and forth between her tightened cheeks until he deluged her little bum-hole with his spoutings, letting Polly climb once more to the very summit of the mountain of love in a final tremulous orgasm.

We continued to revel in such voluptuous delights until our pricks were simply incapable of further use to the insatiable wench, even when she crammed both of our stalks into her mouth and attempted to suck them up again to fresh erections. Ye Gods! What a fizzling fucker was young Polly Aysgarth, a girl who taught me that to fully enjoy the pleasures of love-making, it is necessary to cast aside all mental restraints, for man was made for woman and woman was made for man and as for the parsons and other do-gooders who can only cavil at mutual enjoyment of 'The Sins Of The Flesh', well, the more fool, they!

Polly left us shortly after two o'clock in the morning to sleep away the rest of the night in her own room. I was concerned that she would be reprimanded for not working well the next day, for she would have to be up at six o'clock sharp if not before, and less than four hours' sleep is insufficient for a hard-working servant. But Polly informed us that she had already arranged with Mr Goldhill that if he would not disturb her until noon, she would suck his cock as soon as she had woken up, which sounded a most equitable arrangement to my way of thinking.

Frank was too tired even to put on his pyjamas, let alone to retire to his own room, so we snuggled up together, quite nude, under the eiderdown. I was the first to wake, and though my balls had been emptied more times than I could remember the night before, miraculously they were full again and my cock was standing up majestically to attention. I looked down and saw that Frank's truncheon was in the same fine condition. He was still half-asleep when I took his hand and brought it down to my stiffstander, and he moved his fingers in compliance once I had moved them up and down my tingling staff. I then grasped hold of my pal's tremendous tadger and pumped away with my fist. Simultaneously we spent together, our cocks spurting their gummy essence over the sparse covering of hair around the bases of our shafts and onto our bellies.

'Damn, we've made the sheet sticky,' said Frank. I peered down and said: 'I wouldn't worry, old boy, look how stained the sheet is from last night cavortings!' But before Frank could reply, there was a brisk knock-knock at the door and in came Sally with my early morning cup of tea.

Frank dived beneath the bed-clothes as she put the tray down and went over to the windows to pull open the curtains. 'Good morning, Master Rupert,' she said cheerily. 'Wake up now, it's gone eight o'clock and it's time to get up.' She moved across to the bed and of course immediately saw through Frank's inadequate camouflage. 'Who's that in bed with you, then?' she asked brightly. 'Let's have a look.' And before I could prevent it, she threw back the eiderdown to discover that it was Frank cowering besides me and that we were both naked.

'Dear me, I would have thought you two were old enough and experienced enough to prefer real fucking to playing with each other,' she said reproachfully.

'We are too,' muttered Frank, 'but I was too sleepy from all the fucking last night to go back to my room.'

'Well, it's just as well I came in here first,' commented Sally, 'for if I had gone into your room and found that the bed had not been slept in, I might have raised the alarm and then goodness knows what might have happened.'

'Thank goodness you didn't, Sally, we're very grateful.' I said, covering Frank and myself up with the eiderdown.

'You don't have to be shy! she said. 'I've seen what you've got to offer before, remember? I'm a bit miffed, though, that you didn't tell me that there was some fucking going on because I would have loved to have joined in. Who was with you? It couldn't have been Katie Harbottle because I saw her leave with her parents and anyhow she fancies that spry Yankee gentleman Mr Nolan.'

You can't keep anything secret from the servants, I thought, but when Sally asked me again which girls had been sharing our bed I shook my head. 'You wouldn't like it if it had been you and someone else had asked the next day,' I said reprovingly.

'You're quite right, Master Rupert. It's a right

good maxim for both boys and girls never to tell your friends who you're fucking, unless they pass on the clap in which case you must tell everybody who'll listen to you.' She may have only been a humble servant-girl but her pithy, blunt words should always be remembered by those engaged in any kind of fucking.

Sally looked again and saw that some of the spunk stains on the sheet were fresh. 'Have you two just been tossing each other off? What a pity, I'm sure you would have enjoyed it even more if you'd have let me do it for you.'

'I'm sure we would have done, Sally,' agreed Frank with a touch of sarcasm in his voice as he tried unsuccessfully to rub his tool up to its former stiffness for her approval. 'But then we didn't know you would be bringing us early morning tea let alone providing any hand relief.'

'Oh yes, I wank any gentlemen guests at Albion Towers who request my services,' said Sally as she sat down on the bed. 'I would have seen to that American Mr Nolan but he was taking a bath when I knocked on his door and he didn't ask me to do anything for him except to shut the door behind me when I left his room.'

I looked at her in disbelief. 'What about Mama's cousins, the Reverend Horace Dumpole, who stayed with us for a week earlier this year? You're surely not telling –'

She laughed heartily at my naivety. 'The Reverend Horace? Surely you must be joking, Master Rupert. Why, he was one of the gamest boys I've ever seen. After he found out what I would do for him, every morning regular as clockwork he'd be lying naked on his bed waiting for me, fondling his shaft as if he could hardly wait. Mind, he was shy at first,' she added thoughtfully. 'What happened was that on the second day of his visit I took him his tea and when I leaned over to put down the tray, I made sure he got a good look at my breasts. I'd kept the top buttons undone, you see, and my chemise was cut so low that he could easily hardly fail to see my titties when I bent over him. I could see how excited he was because his hands were shaking so much when I gave him his tea that he spilled most of it into the saucer! Anyhow, I took the cup away and told him to take off his nightshirt as he'd spilled tea all over it and it would be best if I put it in the wash straightaway.

'He protested at first but after a little persuasion off came the nightshirt. But as he handed it to me you will never guess what I noticed lying on the bed – it was a copy of *The Intimate Memoirs Of Jenny Everleigh*! "My, my," I joked. "I would have thought that this was rather a rude book for a Man of the Cloth." He blushed a deep shade of puce and said: "Ah, yes, er, yes, well, the truth of the matter is that I borrowed this book to illustrate to my flock what kind of unsuitable material there is available at certain bookshops and how careful good people must be not to buy such publications in error when for example they might wish to purchase *The Recollections of Reverend James Everleigh*, the former Bishop of Swaziland, which is a very different volume indeed, I can assure you."

' "I'm sure it is, your Reverence," I giggled, "and I'm sure it is a very worthy book as well but it wouldn't give rise to spunk stains on your sheets."

"There aren't any spunk stains, I always use my handkerchief," said Horace indignantly and then he clapped his hand to his mouth for he realised that he'd given the game away!

' "Now, now, don't be a silly boy, there's nothing wrong at all with taking yourself in hand once in a while," I said soothingly and lifted up the eiderdown to look for myself at what this ecclesiastical gentleman had to offer. I was pleasantly surprised to see a fine-looking specimen hanging over his thigh, while resting on the sheet below his shaft lay a very heavy pair of balls. I passed my tongue hungrily over my lips for it had been three days since I had any canoodling. Goldhill had been busy seeing to Polly as usual and my boy friend Jack the blacksmith's son had been laid up with influenza. So I took off my blouse and skirt and sat down on the bed clad only in my chemise.

' "My child, what in the name of heaven are you doing?" stammered the Reverend Horace Dumpole.

' "I thought you might like to hear my confession. I've got quite a few juicy stories to get off my chests," I said.

' "Surely you mean *chest*," he corrected me.

' "Oh no, chests, both of them," I chuckled, quickly slipping off the chemise and pressing my bare bubbies together which made him gasp. His trouser snake began to stir under the bedclothes. "Would you like to hear my confession or not?" I demanded, climbing up on top of him.

' "I would love to, my dear, but you see I am not a Catholic," he said regretfully.

' "Well, neither am I but you can still listen to

115

them if you like!" I said, as teasingly I dangled my breasts up and down his body, just grazing his skin with my tawny titties. Moving down, I could see his erect cock throbbing with excitement so I lowered my nipples on to his knob and just brushed it. I knew he wouldn't last long and I only had to repeat this three more times before he shot an immense white fountain of sperm up over his belly. His cock twitched so powerfully that a few flying drops of spunk caught me on my breasts. Oooh, this did make me feel randy especially as I let my titties slide in the little pools of jism on his tummy. I lifted my nips up and licked up the sticky cream as best I could.'

Of course, by now, Frank and I both sported capital stiffstanders and Sally took hold of them in her hands as she continued: 'He was a nice chap, old Horace, and after what I have just told you about he always left me half a crown on the bedside table each morning as a tip for bringing in his early morning tea to his room.'

'And of course, for his daily wank!' I commented.

'Oh no, Master Rupert, I didn't rub his prick every day,' said Sally.

'You didn't?'

'No, occasionally I would suck him off!' she chuckled. 'He gave me a ten shilling note for that [*fifty pence or about eighty cents — Editor*] which I thought was very generous. On his last morning when I came in he had already taken his bath and was sitting on the bed in his undershorts. He must have been thinking about me because I could see the purple knob of his prick had reared up above the waistband of his drawers. I set

116

down my tray and without a word undressed until I stood naked except for my chemise. With trembling hands he pulled down the shoulder straps and caressed my titties until my pussey was as moist as anything. I pulled off his shorts and his stiff veiny shaft sprang free and I kissed the uncapped helmet whilst fondling his huge balls.

'He leaned forward and kissed my neck and he lifted me across to the dressing table. I sat on it and opened my legs and buried his face between my unresisting thighs. He sucked up all the love juice that was trickling down from my cunney and then his tongue found its way further until it found my clitty. He chewed on it which almost sent me off then and there but with a groan he carried me back to the bed and I lay on my back, my swollen sex lips waiting for his swollen tool. He groaned and then thrust his shaft straight in my cunt without the least difficulty. His heavy ballsack slapped against my wet bum as I wrapped my legs until he spurted his juicy froth inside me in a marvellous mutual spend.'

'That was surely worth more than ten bob,' said Frank, panting slightly as Sally was now wanking both our cocks by rubbing our shafts against the soft velvety skin of her inner arms.

'You're right there, Master Frank, he pressed a pound note into my hand after we had both dressed,' she said complacently.

'You must be quite a wealthy young miss,' I said laughingly.

'Not really,' said Sally. 'I enjoy sucking and fucking but would never do it just for money. I wouldn't even have taken the presents Horace and other gentleman have given me but I'm helping my brother Tom through college. He won the Sir Louis Baum Scholarship to Oxford University last year. But he always needs money for his living expenses and there are so many books that he has to buy.'

'What is he studying?' I said, breathing in heavily as Sally had now changed her style to tossing us off more slowly by making a circle with her forefinger and thumb and rubbing up and down the length of our cocks, barely touching the skin but chafing deliciously against the ridges of our knobs.

'He's taking a degree in Politics, Philosophy and Economics. Tom's a fervent Socialist and wants to become a Member of Parliament.'

'Never mind about those members, here's a member which is about to spout cock juice!' interrupted Frank as my own prick started to jerk uncontrollably in Sally's hand. We spunked almost together and Sally leaned forward to lick one cock and then the other, licking and lapping the jism that flew out of our bursting shafts.

Alas, we did not have time to repay the compliment though both of us would have appreciated a lesson in muff-diving from the gorgeous girl. But, hopefully, this would come at a later time. 'By the by, Master Rupert,' said Sally as she walked to the door. 'I couldn't help reading that lovely poem you wrote to Miss Wigmore which I saw in your exercise book. Now I don't want any money from you or Master Frank but I'd be very happy if you wrote a few verses for me to put in my scrapbook. Would you do that for me?'

As I said just before, you simply cannot keep anything secret from the servants! I should have reported her to Mr Goldhill for looking in my bedside drawer, but she had more than repaid this trifling wrongdoing! And her request for a keepsake was hardly a bothersome imposition.

'Very well, Sally, Frank and I will spend the morning composing an ode to you, on the condition that you don't show it to all and sundry in the servants' hall downstairs,' I said with a grin.

'I promise I won't, Master Rupert, never fear,' she replied as she opened the door. 'Shall I tell your Dad that you'll be down for breakfast in half an hour? You know how shirty he gets if you aren't at the table by half past eight and it's nearly twenty past eight already!'

Sally was right about my father's mood when Frank and I finally came down to breakfast. 'What sort of time do you call this?' he demanded. 'Young Folkestone, I'm sure your house has finished breakfast at this late hour.' Frank nodded weakly as he helped himself to tea and toast. 'Is that all you're having? There's bacon, eggs, sausages, kedgeree [*an Edwardian breakfast favourite of cooked flaked fish, rice and hard-boiled eggs – Editor*] and Mrs Randall will cook you a steak if that takes your fancy.'

'No thank you very much, sir, I rarely eat a cooked breakfast,' replied Frank politely.

'H'rumph, well, you must keep your strength up,' remarked my father and I muttered to my chum that he could have said that at least one portion of his anatomy was being kept up without any problem! My mother, who had been perusing the *Manchester Guardian*, looked up and said: 'Have you two boys forgotten that Mr Nolan is making a film this morning? He left a message to say that if you are interested in seeing him at work he has gone to Knaresborough Castle. Your father has provided him with a horse and cart and he left here about an hour ago '

Great Scott! In all the excitement of our late night and early morning escapades I had forgotten all about our American film-maker. 'Fred Nolan's a damned fine horseman,' grunted my father. 'I offered him the choice of a motor vehicle or the services of one of our coachmen but he declined, saying that he preferred to take the reins himself. But then he spent a year down in Texas as a cowboy so I suppose that's where he became such an expert.'

'Can we ride over there?' I asked.

'Certainly not, it's only two miles and you're best to hike it. I daresay you can travel back with Mr Nolan but a brisk morning constitutional will do you good. You both look a bit pasty round the gills this morning. Mind, I don't know why either of you should both look so tired, neither of you took any exercise yesterday.'

Little did he know!

CHAPTER FOUR

Captured On Camera

F REDERICK NOLAN WAS A FORTUNATE MAN, because the fickle English climate decided to greet our visitor from America with a morning of brilliant summer sunshine. Not even a hint of cloud could be seen in the morning sky as Frank and I trudged up the high road to Burbeck Field, whence Mr Nolan had been directed by my parents. Although the walk was not of a great distance, most of the journey was uphill, for Knaresborough stands on the summit of a hill overlooking the River Nidd. When we reached the outskirts it was easy to see why Mr Nolan had been recommended to use this location, for the luxuriant woods by which the little town is surrounded, the winding river at its foot, the venerable cottages, placed tier above tier on the face of the rock, the ruined castle and the old church combine to make up a most beautiful picture.

'Take the footpath just a hundred yards up the road on our right and Burbeck Field is behind the grove of silver birch trees you can see from here,' I said to Frank as we marched up Knaresborough

Road. 'The field itself is private land owned by Diana Wigmore's father. It is marvellously shielded by the trees, so one has a glorious view of the castle with the benefit of almost complete privacy.'

We made our way through the trees and we soon saw our horse and trap. Standing in his shirtsleeves behind a camera set up on a tripod was Mr Nolan and in front of the camera was none other than Katie Harbottle, dressed or rather undressed in a flowing white gown through which one could clearly see the curved outlines of her figure. She was standing in a classical stance, with one leg moved slightly forward and with her arms outstretched arms, a pose which pressed her breasts against the fine covering and her nipples showed up darkly through the finely spun cotton where her breasts bulged against the almost transparent material. Frank and I exchanged a knowing glance – so this was how Mr Nolan made moving pictures of the beauties of Yorkshire!

Surprisingly, the couple did not seem embarrassed in the least by our presence. In fact, Mr Nolan greeted us with a hearty 'Hi, fellows, what's been keeping you? Katie and I have been here for nearly two hours already.' He went on to explain that he wanted to make the first *tableau vivant* movie [tableaux vivants *were common in late Victorian years. In these shows actresses dressed in body stockings or even in the nude, could pose in dramatic classical or historical scenes on the strict condition that they never moved. The ban on nudity in the British theatre, except for bare-breasted girls who had to remain stock still, was not lifted until the*

*abolishment of stage censorship in the late 1960s —
Editor*].

'Shall we rehearse once more, Fred?' suggested
Kate. 'It will certainly help to have an audience.
Although you tell me I must always look at the
camera, if the boys stand with you, I can see
whether they are enjoying my performance.'

'Great idea, kid,' he replied, diving behind a
black cloth and making the final adjustments to
the focus mechanism. 'Try it one more time and
then we'll commit you to immortality on
celluloid. I need the strong sunlight for a
satisfactory exposure. You see, the showmen are
becoming more fussy and won't now accept dark
prints.'

'What do you mean by that, Mr Nolan?' asked
Frank. 'Who are these showmen you mention?'

'I'll tell you later,' he promised. 'Okay, Katie,
let's try it one more time.'

On his command Kate swirled around, dancing
nimbly around the relatively small area of the
field which was in the range of Mr Nolan's
camera. Then she slowed down to stand just six
feet away from us and teasingly, tantalisingly let
slip her robe to stand stark naked in front of us.
What a voluptuous beauty was Kate and how we
drank in the delights of her nudity. Her face was
finely formed with dark silky hair falling down in
curved ringlets onto her shoulders. Her breasts
were luxuriantly large, hard and firm, as white as
snow and tipped with delicately small nipples,
that were already raised like two pink bullets.

What a perfect picture of female pulchitrude
she made! We stood gaping whilst Fred Nolan
reloaded his camera and Katie let her hands fall to

brush her nipples softly and then passed them upwards to turn through her hair. The movement made her breasts lift and the flushed circles of her aureoles which ran around each nipple heightened in colour, framing the juicy tittie at the centre as if they were bulls' eyes on target boards.

Frank and I were not alone in wriggling uncomfortably as our erect cocks battered against the material of our trousers. Frederick Nolan, however, was already one step ahead and was busy tugging off his braces. 'Now look here, Rupert,' said the American moving picture pioneer hurriedly, as he sat down to remove his shoes and socks.

He ripped open his shirt and continued: 'Here's the chance of a lifetime for you to make moving picture history! I've put a new magazine of film in the camera and I want you to come over here and keep the camera pointing at the action whilst you wind this handle at a steady pace. Like this, do you understand? Now, Frank, you hold the camera steady and point the apparatus forward if Rupert asks you to when he will have to point the lens to the ground. When we begin filming, look at your watch – you have a second hand on it don't you? Good, now three minutes after Rupert begins turning the handle you call "cut". Rupert then knows we have come to the end of the picture, so I will reload the camera. Get it? Good boys, I know you won't let me down.'

We were still somewhat dazed by the rapid-fire instructions but we took up our positions as the movie-maker rapidly completed undressing and ran over naked to the trap, pulling out a yellow blanket which he brought back for Katie to stand on. His swollen penis stood up high against his stomach like a marble column and Katie gasped with satisfaction as she arched her hips forward to feel the proud throbbing against her flesh. She was almost the same height as Mr Nolan but she bent her knees slightly so that she could experience the delicious feel of his hard prick more directly against her pussey. She tilted her head to receive his mouth upon her full, red lips. He pulled away for a second to shout: 'Start, rolling, Rupert!' before he returned his attention to Katie and covered her mouth with a burning kiss.

I cranked the camera as Fred caressed the silky smoothness of Katie's back, his hands stroking deeply into her shoulders and down along her spine. Katie began to lean away from him, drawing him down on to the blanket and Fred lowered his body on top of hers with one of his legs dangling between her thighs. Then he heaved himself up to sit across her thighs, his legs gripping her hips as he cupped her quivering breasts with his hands, letting his fingers trace patterns across them as he gently tweaked the ripe strawberry nipples that were now as erect as could be.

Frank had moved the camera as directed and I concentrated on catching the expression on Katie's face as Fred moved the tip of his upwardly curved diamond hard cock towards her mouth. She opened her lips to receive the purple-domed crown and took hold of his pulsating penis in a firm yet tender embrace, looking admiringly at the delicately blue-veined rigid shaft before moving her mouth along it, lapping, licking, sucking, moving faster and faster as her hands now clasped his tightening hairy ballsack.

'Not so fast, young lady, not so fast,' growled Nolan who realised that he was in danger of releasing his sperm too quickly under this exquisite palating of his prick. 'I don't want to spend before we have to change the film.' So he took out his gleaming staff from her mouth and laid it between the firm swell of her breasts. Katie lay back and I let the camera focus upon her soft white belly and upon the mossy tuft of curly black hair between her legs and the superbly chiselled crack with its pouting lips which she parted with her fingers to reveal the glistening red gash of her cunney. 'Lick my pussey out, Fred,' she asked the American. He smiled his assent as he athletically sprang up and took up a new position, kneeling in front of her parted thighs.

'Cut!' yelled Frank and, momentarily startled, the couple looked towards us. 'Oh well, we could have found ourselves just beginning the paradise stroke,' sighed Mr Nolan, as he heaved himself up to effect the necessary mechanics. It took only a few moments and I waited until he was back between Katie's legs before shouting: 'Ready when you are!' and began to display what turned out to be his considerable pussey-eating talents for the camera.

I have kept a copy of this film in a locked compartment in my secretaire ever since and I understand that Dr Radlett Horne, the aptly named specialist in sexual dysfunction, also possesses a print of Mr Nolan paying attention to Katie Harbottle's pussey which he screens to patients and students alike as a perfect example of how to perform cunnilingus.

Mr Nolan started by letting his tongue travel down the length of her velvety body, stopping briefly to lick around her navel before sliding down to her thighs. He was still kneeling when he parted the crisp curls of her thatch to reveal her damp, inviting cunney lips which opened like a lust-hungry mouth, eager to welcome the tip of Fred's questing tongue. He worked his face down into the cleft between her thighs. Even through the viewfinder of my camera. I could not help but notice how appealing her pussey looked. Doubtless Fred Nolan was even further stimulated by the delicate aroma of cunney juice that had already drifted across towards Frank and myself.

Now he was down on his belly, between Katie's legs with one hand under her gorgeous backside to provide additional elevation and the other reaching around her thigh so that he was able to spread her pussey lips with his thumb and middle finger. She began to purr with pleasure as he then placed his lips over her swollen clitty and sucked it into his mouth, where the tip of his tongue began to explore it from all directions. Katie became very excited and thrashed about as he increased the vibrations of his tongue, wrenching out little yelps of excitement from the trembling girl who was now near to coming off. She wrapped her strong thighs around him and buried his head in her bush as he slurped noisily, varying the sensations for his partner by taking time out to lick the insides of her labia, kissing and sucking until her pussey must have been a veritable sea of lubricity.

'Aaah, that is heavenly! More! More! Oh Fred,

you've sent me off!' cried Katie as she twisted and turned whilst her paramour sucked up the flow of love juice as she shuddered into a body-wracking orgasm.

Mr Nolan scrambled up to lie on top of Katie and he slipped his hands around her back to clutch the plump cheeks of her warm bottom. He chuckled and said: 'I'm so pleased that I was able to bring you off with my tongue. Sucking off can be hard work for a man but it's so gratifying when the girl achieves a spend. But now, Katie, I am going to fuck you. Would you like to know just how?'

'Oh yes, please, do tell me.'

'Well, first I shall mount you and then I'll decide just how we will take our pleasure. But for now, I'm going to lie upon your belly and inset my long, thick cock into your wet little snatch. Then I'll feel the velvety clinging muscles of your cunney as I move my shaft in and out of your juicy cunt – and we'll see what happens from there.'

He moved surprisingly quickly, smoothing his hands over her breasts again which sent her into fresh raptures of delight. Then he was on top of her, hungrily searching for her mouth as they exchanged a burning kiss, moving their thighs together until their pubic muffs were rubbing roughly against each other. Fred's stiff prick probed the entrance to Katie's exquisitely formed crack and he lifted himself up on his hands and knees so that I was able to obtain a marvellous close-up shot of his swollen knob forcing its way through her pussey lips into the squelchy wetness of her cunney.

Like a steel bolt, his cock rode thickly through the moist channel, separating the folds of gluey skin and fucking higher and higher, only pausing when it was prevented from further progress by the jamming together of their loins.

'What a wonderfully juicy cunt,' panted Fred, as his body rose up and down, thrusting his sinewy shaft in and out of her yielding vagina. 'Katie, I do believe that you'd fuck day and night if you could.'

'Oh yes, yes, yes. Fuck me, Fred, fuck me – no more talking, just ram that big tadger faster, oooh, that's the way!' she gasped in reply.

Her eyes were shining and moist and a beautiful colour bloomed in her cheeks – such a shame that this could not be captured on celluloid, I thought, cranking away until Frank suddenly shouted: 'Cut, we're running out of time.' Alas, this meant that Mr Nolan had to scramble up, his erect cock glistening with cunney juice, and change the film once again before rushing back to place his prick back in its moist, warm haven of Katie's cunt.

'I'm ready when you are,' I called out and he took up where he had been forced to leave off. He moved his hands around her gorgeous curves with practised ease, squeezing her firm breasts, rubbing the big red stalks of her nipples against his palms as she took hold of his magnificently gleaming stiffstander and guided it back into her yearning cunney. Katie wrapped her arms and legs around Mr Nolan's lithe frame and urged him to make it 'hard and fast, Fred – I want to feel every inch of your big fat cock when you spunk into me.' She clamped her feet round his back and drummed her heels against his spine as he pounded his penis into her soaking little nookie. She took up the rhythm of his thrustings and this was too much for poor Frank. He let go the camera and tearing off his trousers, started to wank his enormous prick, frigging it up to bursting point.

'Join in, join in!' cried Katie, so he shuffled over to them, his trousers round his ankles, his cock in his hand. She took hold of his pulsing tool and pulled his knob into her mouth, lashing it with her tongue as she sucked noisily away. Frank shot a fierce jet of love juice between her lips just as Fred drenched her eager cunney with a flood of frothy sperm as Katie's hands clasped his bum cheeks, pushing him deeper and deeper inside her as she brought herself off into a tremendous spend.

'More! More! More!' she cried out, desperate to prolong the grandeur of her fulfilment. Gamely, Fred drove on and I could see the copious quantities of spunk overflowing from Katie's cunt and running down the crevice of her bum. One last spasm wracked their bodies and they fell back exhausted though Katie still had the strength to suck up the last remaining milky drops of Frank's sperm from the 'eye' on his now softening helmet.

'M'm, that was a splendid coupling, gentlemen,' said Katie, as she recovered her senses. 'Dear Fred, you really are one of the best fucks I've ever had, and Frank, dear boy, what a delicious *bonne bouche* your sweet cock made during it all.'

Fred smiled his thanks. 'Thank you, Katie, and

may I truthfully say to you that for me that you have one of the most magnificent cunnies it has ever been my pleasure to encounter. My prick will ever be at your service whenever you require it.'

After the participants had dressed themselves, Mr Nolan carefully put away the exposed film which we would have developed at Ramsay's Studios near Paddington Station in London. I still have a good copy of the print and often amuse myself and occasionally house guests these days by showing them this erotic little moving picture.

[Alas, no copies of this film have survived. An interesting aside here is not just that Rupert Mountjoy acted as cameraman on the first ever British blue movie. For this was not the first European sex film – this honour goes to Le Tub, a movie made a year earlier in 1897 by the French pioneer Georges Meliès using the newly developed techniques of the Lumiere brothers – Editor.]

But then, to my discomforture, I heard the unmistakeable sounds of the rustle of clothes behind us. I turned my head and to my horror saw that we had been joined by the Reverend Campbell Armstrong, a curate from Farnham, a little village close by, and Barbara, the second daughter of Major Dartland, the Squire of Farnham, a man of choleric disposition who my mother detested because of his antediluvian political views that would not have disgraced Ghengis Khan!

For how long had they been watching us? Oh well, I would just have to brazen it out ... 'Good morning, Rupert,' said Reverend Armstrong in his soft Scottish burr. 'Is the weather not glorious?

Ah, I believe you are acquainted with Miss Dartland.'

'Good morning, Reverend,' I replied. 'May I introduce Miss Katie Harbottle of Harbottle Hall near Wharton? This gentleman is Mr Frederick Nolan from the United States of America and this is Frank Folkestone, my best chum who is staying with me during the holidays.'

He beamed a bright smile at us. 'So pleased to meet you good people. I am Reverend Armstrong of Farnham and this is Miss Barbara Dartland whose father is the Squire of our little community.'

'Good morning,' said Barbara shyly. 'Mr Nolan, are you the owner of this moving picture camera?'

'I am indeed,' said our American guest. 'Would you care for me to explain the workings of the machine?'

Barbara smile. 'Oh no, that won't be necessary, for I was shown such a camera by my Uncle William whilst he worked with Mr Edison in your country.'

'Your Uncle William – good heavens, you don't mean Will Dickson, by any chance? But what a coincidence! He and I are the greatest of friends. Why, I was one of those who advised him to leave Mr Edison three years ago and join Biograph. He is a great pioneer of our industry.'

[*W.K.L. Dickson was indeed a truly important player in the production of the first moving pictures. He worked with Edison and then moved to the inventor's great rivals Biograph in 1895 and constructed a very different kind of camera which avoided Edison's patents. He helped build the first Biograph studio which was situated on the roof of the Hackett-Carhart Building on Broadway in New York City – for the only real source of power for the early film-makers was the sun! – Editor.*]

'I could not help observing that you were filming your actors *au naturel*,' said Reverend Armstrong genially. 'Was this an educational film, perhaps, for students?'

'You could say that,' agreed Mr Nolan, as I looked more closely at Barbara who I had only seen a handful of times before on formal occasions. She was an attractive girl of perhaps twenty years, somewhat sallow of complexion with dark brown hair over a rather low forehead but with a most pleasing expression of face. Even at this early stage in my career as a cocksman, it occurred to me that her large sparkling eyes promised sultry pleasures and it was not too long before I was proved right in this assumption.

After a few minutes conversation, Barbara said: 'Why don't you join us for a drink before luncheon? We have brought an ice-box with us. Campbell, perhaps you would be kind enough to bring the pony and trap over here?'

'With pleasure,' replied the young Scottish cleric and he walked off to fulfil her request. Barbara confided to us that Campbell was a terribly sweet young man. 'It is just as well that my Papa doesn't know that Campbell is one of those clergymen who hold progressive views, or he would forbid me to see him,' she confided.

'So I presume that Campbell has no objection to the consumption of alcoholic beverages,' commented Katie Harbottle.

'Certainly not, and being of Scottish stock, you will not be very surprised when I tell you at times

133

he can be a liberal imbiber,' replied Barbara with a slightly furrowed brow.

'But something troubles you, I can see,' Katie continued.

'Well yes, and seeing your film was very appropriate in the circumstances. You see, although Campbell may drink, he does not fuck.'

'Does not fuck!' gasped Katie in horrified astonishment. 'Surely such a masculine-looking young man is not of the persuasion favoured by Oscar Wilde?'

'Oh no, Campbell is no homosexualist. Indeed, he would very much like to fuck me but his religious belief forbids him to do so. I would not mind so much – for I respect his sincere religious conviction – but he really does not know how to pet properly and so I don't even get to enjoy a good kiss and cuddle.'

'This is bad news, but I have an idea,' said Katie. 'Let's all have a drink first and I'll tell you what I have in mind later.'

Campbell returned with the pony and trap and Fred helped him bring down the ice box and a large hamper. 'Why do cooks always provide enough food for an army?' he asked good-humouredly. 'It is uncanny how they know we will share our meal with friends.' How true, I thought, for we were almost in the exactly same situation I had found myself a few days before with Diana Wigmore.

Barbara was spot on target about her ecclesiastical friend's indulgent attitude to the two bottles of chilled white wine. Frank and I preferred lemonade but Campbell, Fred, Katie and Barbara had no problem in polishing off the

Chablis by themselves.

After our *al fresco* luncheon, Fred, Frank and Campbell decided to take a short stroll in the woods. I decided to remain with the two girls and lay in the long grass, using my jacket and rucksack as a pillow. Although my eyes were closed I could easily overhear the conversation between Katie and Barbara and their heart-to-heart chat certainly made my young prick stiffen up pretty smartish!

Barbara began it all by saying: 'I do envy you, you know, Katie dear, for you seem to have achieved total liberation if your love-making just now is anything to go by. If only I could enjoy such freedom, for not only my parents but also my gentleman admirers are so fuddy-duddy in their thinking that I do believe I shall go quite mad if I have to exist in this state for very much longer.

'It isn't so much my Papa, who is known for his old-fashioned obstinacy but dear Campbell who causes me such grief. I mean, he is so inhibited! We have exchanged kisses, many quite passionate and I have seen the swelling outline of his cock straining against his trousers. I have even brushed my hand against it once as if by accident of course, but the dear boy is so backwards in coming forward that I despair of his ever even caressing my breasts whilst we are engaged in an amorous embrace.'

'My dear Barbara! How extraordinary! It appears to me that you have a quite beautiful pair of bubbies. Any lad worth his salt would give his right arm to cup them in his hands and squeeze them,' said a shocked Katie.

'Thank you, Katie, I would have thought so –

my previous beaus have always tried as soon as possible to unbutton my blouse and caress my bare breasts. Oh Katie, I would like nothing better than to have Campbell's hands on my naked nipples. But he has never plucked up the courage to go further than a passionate kiss although I have now managed to make him put his tongue inside my mouth! I think he is frightened that he will upset me if he takes further liberties. You see, I am a virgin and do not feel ready just yet to enjoy the fullest delights of sexual play but I really would like to experience the joys of petting. I would greatly value your advice on just how to proceed as I feel very frustrated.'

'I'm hardly surprised to hear that,' said Katie kindly. 'Frankly, I am just astonished that any man could fail to be overwhelmingly aroused by your feminine charms. However, if I were you I should sit Campbell down somewhere and tell him before your lips touch his that he need not fear to let his feelings show, because you do not wish to let matters progress to their natural conclusion. Now, I do not believe for a moment that Campbell would turn out to be a cad, but just in case he does become over-excited once you begin the proceedings, I would keep a glass of cold water handy. I have found that either thrown in the face or down into the lap, a glass of cold water proves an ideal weapon against a too-ardent suitor.

'It's extremely doubtful that you will need any such protection with Campbell. Mind, he may become a different man once you have stroked his cock – men do, you know! Mind, I do not think that prick-teasing is a suitable sport for a lady. Once you begin you must continue until he obtains relief one way or the other through ejaculation, either with your hand or with your mouth.

'But first things first; come over here and sit next to me. Now let's pretend that I am Campbell and we are about to kiss.' Obediently, Barbara moved over to sit down next to her companion. Katie wrapped her arms around her and murmured: 'Now I think what would happen next is that he would take off your blouse once you had put your tongue inside his mouth.'

And through my half-shut eyes, for I was still feigning slumber, I saw the wicked little minx unbutton Barbara's blouse and opened her chemise to reveal an absolutely delightful pair of soft rounded globes, each tipped with large aureoles and hard, pointed nipples which Katie immediately covered with her hands. 'Is that nice?' enquired Katie as she found the opening to the other girl's skirt and quickly unleashed it so that Barbara was clad solely in white frilly knickers and stockings.

Whether by accident or design, I am unsure, but Barbara's legs were already slightly parted when Katie's hand slyly insinuated itself between them and began to rub her mound through the semi-transparent material of her drawers.

I only feasted my eyes on this lascivious scene for a moment because Barbara let out a little scream, saying that she could see the others returning from their walk in the woods. Reluctantly, Katie said: 'Oh, then put on your skirt and blouse but leave the top buttons undone so Campbell can see the swell of your lovely breasts. Gosh, he is a lucky man! If I were he, I would nibble upon your luscious red titties and bring you off by frigging your juicy cunney.'

'Katie! How could you be so rude!' said Barbara reprovingly but from her tone of voice I could see that she was not really offended by Katie's blunt country speech. She had plenty of time to prepare herself by the time the men returned and I stretched my limbs and let out a huge yawn as if I had just woken up from a deep sleep. When the others reached us Fred Nolan announced that he would be taking his camera to a picturesque location they had discovered during their walk.

'Come on, Rupert, we'll take the pony and trap,' said Frank.

'Do you mind if I stay here, I've got rather a headache coming on and I'm going to sleep it off,' I fibbed, and Campbell and Barbara also demurred.

'As you like,' said Fred Nolan. 'We'll be back in about an hour and half.'

As they left, I rolled over and pretended to go back to sleep, leaving Campbell and Barbara together nearby. Sure enough, as soon as the coast was clear, they fell to kissing and cuddling in the most passionate fashion. Yet Campbell forbore to let his hands move towards Barbara's bosoms even though she had left the top buttons of her blouse invitingly open as Katie had instructed. There was only one way forward, she must have thought, for she took hold of Campbell's hands herself and cupped them firmly around her magnificent breasts.

'Don't you like my titties?' she asked plaintively.

'Oh yes, yes,' he groaned, 'but I fear that if I let my hands stay there they might be tempted to stray elsewhere!'

'Don't fret about it, I would have no objection,' she told him as she opened the remaining buttons of her blouse. Even this highly disciplined young clergyman could not be unmoved by the sight of her bare breasts as she shrugged off the garment and opened her chemise. Her dark hair, now fully undone and hanging in long tresses, veiled yet highlighted her firm, bouncy breasts. The swell of those superb orbs acted as magnets to Campbell's hands as he squeezed the milky white globes and let his fingers play with the tawny, taut nipples which had risen up to greet him.

This stimulated the pretty girl so much that she let her hand run down to his lap from which bulged an alarming protuberance. As their lips crashed together once more she opened the buttons of his trousers and out sprang his huge stiffstander, sturdily rising upwards. Barbara took hold of his swollen shaft and I must say that this holy son of Hibernia had been blessed with an enormous prick. It stood up, blue veined and as stiff as a board, jutting out at a slight curve. Barbara pulled back his foreskin and exposed the giant bulbous knob. She started to rub her hand up and down the giant staff but this set Campbell off into a wild frenzy. He almost ripped off Barbara's knickers in a frenzy of lustful desire and her thickly matted brown triangle of pussey hair came into view, with the little pink labia already fluttering out in anticipation of the joys to come. He then pushed her legs apart and separated her cunney lips with a questioning forefinger, letting it run up and down the full length of her exquisitely fashioned crack.

'Ooooh, Ooooh! Oh, Campbell, at last!' panted Barbara, as the curate continued to let his finger slide along the edges of her pouting slit. 'Now work it in and out of my cunt, there's a dear man.' He looked shocked at her frank words but as they engaged in yet another almost bruising kiss, he let one and then two fingers dip in and out of Barbara's honeypot. She purred with pure lust as she continued to rub his prick up to a stupendous height whilst by now Campbell was sucking and slurping away on one enlarged brown nipple and flicking and teasing the other between his fingers at a great speed. When Barbara reached down and handled his balls, the curate's body visibly shook and a fountain of sticky white cream spurted out from his cock. Barbara was by now trembling with the force of her own orgasm which rippled through her just as the last dribblings of spunk oozed out of Campbell's cock. In her delight she bent forward and lapped up the last dregs of his spend and the curate looked shocked. But she simply smacked her lips and said: 'There's nothing wrong in swallowing sperm, Campbell. I do so enjoy the salty taste of spunk. It is the most invigorating of tonics and it enables me to remain a virgin whilst bringing us both to the summit of the mountain of love. And come to think of it, I am making sure that you are guiltless of the sin of Onan who let his seed fall upon the ground. [*See Genesis 38:9 – Editor.*]

Campbell was not without a sense of humour and he said: 'I'm not too sure about the theology, my love, but the main reason is good enough for me. What a pity though that you only managed to lick up a morsel.'

'Ah, well I'm sure we can see if the well has not dried up,' said Barbara, dropping to her knees and taking the now shrunken helmet of his prick in her hands. She stroked his soft, hairy ballsack and took his entire limp shaft into her mouth, rolling it around her tongue until in a very few moments she took it out the transformed tool, now hard as rock again! She kissed the top of this massive red topped truncheon and sucked lustily on the uncapped ruby crown. Barbara had to stretch her jaw to cram in Campbell's big stiffie and continued to lick and lap away whilst frigging his shaft which brought on his climax very quickly. With a throaty moan, he shuddered and the first creamy jet of spunk came hurtling out of his cock. The first jet hit Barbara's nose but then she opened her mouth wide and gobbled furiously upon her sweetmeat, swallowing quickly to keep pace with his tangy libation. Then, as his spend passed its peak she took his entire shaft back into her mouth, sucking for all she was worth to extract the very last milky drops of love juice from his pumping prick.

As they lay together, exhausted by their frenetic passions, I would have given anything for the opportunity to give myself some much-needed hand relief. But the lewd pair were looking almost directly at me and I could hardly move or they might guess that I had been watching them all the time!

Barbara was the first to stir from their reverie. 'Campbell, did you enjoy yourself? I'm ready for more larks if you are.'

141

'I'd like to carry on but though the spirit is willing, the flesh is weak,' he sighed ruefully, flipping his limp penis with his hand

Barbara looked sorrowfully down at his turgid cock and said: 'Never mind, you don't need a stiff prick to release a lady. How would you like to kiss my pussey? I'd really be happy if you would. Have you ever done it before?'

He blushed and replied: 'Back in Dundee there was a wee lassie named Lizzie who liked to have her cunney kissed. I'm not sure though that I was any good at it as she used to say that only my friend Eddie could bring her off with his mouth.'

'I'd like to find out for myself,' said Barbara, looking around to ensure that they were still alone. She unbuttoned her skirt and wriggled out of her knickers. She smoothed her hand between her parted thighs, letting her long fingers run through the thick tuft of curly brown hair through which I could just about see her cunney lips poking invitingly through their hirsute covering.

The curate heaved himself up to kneel before her and I could see that though there was now a crimson flush of excitement on his face, his prick still dangled flaccidly between his legs Gingerly, he bent his head forward and planted a chaste kiss on her hairy mound. Then he kissed her furry bush again, this time with more feeling, and then again and again until he rained a veritable deluge of kisses upon her cunney. Now he was lying on his belly, his mouth tightly affixed to Barbara's pussey which, though hidden from my view, must have responded to his attentions. Very soon Campbell was sucking and slurping her love juices with uninhibited abandon. This set Barbara off, for she clamped her legs around his head as he paid court to her cunt whilst his hands reached up and grabbed her breasts, rolling her titties around in a circular motion. I heard Barbara breathe: 'Oh yes, finger-fuck me, darling,' as Campbell continued to pleasure her pussey as her hips moved up and down with increasing vigour until finally, with a convulsive tremor, she shouted out with great passion and came off, drenching his face with her love juices as she writhed in the delicious agonies of her orgasm.

'Was that good for you?' enquired Campbell somewhat unnecessarily as he raised himself up on his knees.

'Lovely, that was really lovely,' she sighed. 'Campbell, you tongue pussey beautifully and though I have yet to experience it, I cannot believe that your cock could be a very much more powerful organ. I adored the way you began with a light flicking motion on my clitty and then how you switched to cover the length of my crack from the clitty to the arse-hole. Oh darling, I so want you to make love to me!'

He looked down and I saw that his once-turgid cock had now stiffened up into an enormous erection that poked up between his thighs like a flagpole. 'I would give anything to fuck you, Barbara, my sweet, and I fear that if we continue to carry on this way, this will happen as surely as night follows the day.'

'Then let us do it! I am tired of the stealthy hidden kisses, the furtive fondlings and clandestine meetings,' she declared, holding his throbbing tool and pressing it to the cleft between her gorgeous breasts. And who knows, perhaps

Barbara would have lost her virginity then and there if the sound of the pony and trap had not been heard in the distance. They hastily broke away from each other and dressed themselves in record time so that all was seemly by the time Fred Nolan stepped down from the driving board and said cheerfully: 'Hello there, you two! The sun has gone behind the clouds so until it reappears we thought we would come back and keep you company.'

Campbell smiled weakly and I am sure that Barbara would have been lost for words but I saved the situation by giving a loud yawn and saying: 'Ah, what a difference forty winks can make. My headache has totally vanished and I'm quite fit again. What shall we do now?'

'Alas, I must be off as I promised to chair a meeting in the village hall this afternoon,' said Campbell. 'Actually, it's of the local Sports Club Er, I don't suppose you would care to join us, Mr Nolan. Yours is such a fascinating profession that I am sure the members would be greatly interested in anything you had to day.'

'Members are usually more interested in which pussies they can slide into,' muttered Frank quietly as Fred Nolan shook his head.

'Thank you for the invitation but I must be getting back and start developing my film which will keep me busy for some time. Katie, boys, would you like to stay here or go back to Albion Towers with me?

'Oh do stay,' begged Barbara. 'These meetings can be tedious but they don't last too long and then if you have time we can go back to my house for tea and crumpets. I can always arrange for

Connor to take you back in one of our carriages.'

No doubt because Mr Nolan would be busy in the darkroom, Katie promptly accepted her invitation but Frank decided to go back home with Fred Nolan as he genuinely did feel the beginnings of a headache coming upon him (in later life poor Frank – or Sir Frank Folkestone to give my oldest friend his proper present-day nomenclature, for he inherited the family baronetcy in April 1912 when his father perished at sea, being a passenger on the ill-fated *Titanic* – has suffered badly from severe migraines, the pains of which can only be mitigated by lying down in a darkened room and when possible, having his prick sucked by a willing naked maidservant though I doubt whether his physician prescribed this latter treatment!).

'What a shame! After we have concluded the few items of business our little gathering is to be addressed by the hypnotist Dr Glanville Porterfield and it could prove to be a very interesting affair as he will offer to hypnotise members of the audience,' she said with regret.

'Oh, I'd like to come and see Dr Porterfield in action, if I may,' I piped up.

'Certainly, Rupert, do join us,' said Campbell and so I asked Frank to instruct Goldhill to send Wallace our coachman back with the pony and trap to Farnham Village Hall at five o'clock sharp. 'Katie, Wallace can take you back to Harbottle Hall,' I added.

So we made our way to Farnham Village Hall where fifty or so ladies and gentlemen of the local gentry were gathered. The main business of the meeting was to thank those ladies and gentlemen who had taken part in the croquet, cricket and lawn tennis matches played by Farnham against other localities.

Most of these matters were only of minimal interest but I will record the words of one Mr Anthony Cheetham, the captain of Farnham cricket team, which so far that season had vanquished all before them, winning eight matches and drawing one, and that only because rain stopped play when Farnham were poised for victory. He asked that despite past successes all members of the side should keep their noses to the grindstone. Mr Cheetham's wise advice was reproduced later in the week by our county newspaper and, being a keen cricketer myself, I reproduce them here – American readers of my journal may well consider that they apply equally to baseball, a sport which I also enjoy in the summer months. He said: 'It is related of the Hon. Peter Forbes-Hornby, one of the best-known old Yorkshire gentlemen sportsmen, that whenever he had an unoccupied half hour, he used to set up a stump and bowl at it. It is to be wished that there was more of this commendable practice. Bowling is much more of dogged perseverance than of initial skill and many more players would stand a chance of distinguishing themselves by their bowling than by their batting.' Mr Forbes-Hornby also said: 'A good cricketer will always keep a ball perpetually about him; to be always tossing it and throwing it so as to get thoroughly used to the feel of it.'

Perhaps this is how Mr Forbes-Hornby achieved his sensational throw of more than one hundred and twenty yards with the cricket ball which was witnessed and attested to by Mr Cheetham though it was impossible to ascertain the distance with absolute accuracy for the ball struck the trunk of a tree some four feet from the ground.

Once all these affairs had been completed, we settled down to listen to Dr Porterfield's address. He began by explaining just what hypnotism is – an artificially induced state of semi-consciousness characterised by a greatly increased susceptability to suggestions made by the hypnotist. 'There is nothing supernatural involved despite the warnings of some ignorant and irresponsible journalists in the popular press,' said Dr Porterfield, a plump, distinguished-looking gentleman who, though almost as bald as a coot, nevertheless sported a full black beard. 'Although the science of hypnotism probably dates back to ancient times, it was the Austrian physician Friedrich Mesmer [(1734-1815) – Editor] who first used hypnosis in a medical capacity, proving that by imposing his will upon that of his subject, he could treat his patients and at the same time spare them much pain.

'On the music hall stage, there are hypnotists who put members of the audience in a trance and make them perform strange acts. Frankly, this concerns me as I believe that hypnotism is a serious business and should not be popularised purely for the purposes of amusement.'

His speech was interrupted by a snort of disapproval from a lady sitting in the back row. The Reverend Armstrong, acting as Chairman, frowned and cleared his throat as he stood up, presumably to ask for order, but Dr Porterfield waved his hand. 'No, my dear sir, I think it obvious that the lady at the back has a point to make. Madam, would you like to say something?'

The lady concerned rose to her feet. She was a not unattractive woman in her early thirties, with a haughty expression on her rather sharp features. 'That's Mrs Robinson. She's a real martinet of the same ilk as my Papa,' whispered Barbara to us.

'I don't believe a word of all this mumbo-jumbo,' said Mrs Robinson firmly. 'I'd like to see somebody try and hypnotise *me*!'

'Well, rest assured, Madam, it is extremely difficult for even the most expert practitioner to hypnotise somebody against their will,' said Dr Porterfield.

'Stuff and nonsense! That's just an excuse – I've seen a so-called hypnotist at work at a house-party and he pretended to make a gentleman believe he was a duck and go quacking all round the room. He made a lady say "Please do not touch my nose" to another lady five minutes to the second after she came out of her trance and performed other parlour tricks.'

Dr Porterfield spread out his hands. 'These may have been parlour tricks, but I assure you that if the hypnotist was genuine then these tricks, as you term them, were genuine enough and had not been planned beforehand by those concerned.'

'I find that hard to accept and would need further proof,' she said, shaking her head in disbelief.

'Then come up to the front and I will hypnotise you here and now,' said Dr Porterfield. 'On the condition that you will not fight against me, I will prove to you and the ladies and gentlemen present, that I am not trying to perpetrate a gigantic confidence trick.'

'Very well,' said Mrs Robinson and made her way up to the stage to an excited buzz in the audience. Campbell Armstrong gave her his chair and she sat down, looking directly at Dr Porterfield. He called for silence and then took out his pocket watch and dangled it on its chain in front of her.

'Just look at this watch,' he said, 'and follow its progress as it moves from side to side. There, you are feeling sleepy, very sleepy. Your eyes are drooping and now, on the count of three, you will be asleep, one, two, *three!*'

The audience watched fascinated as Mrs Robinson's eyes closed as she sat slumbering in her chair. 'Raise your right arm,' commanded the hypnotist and she immediately obeyed. 'Now when I tell you to do so, you will try and rest your elbow on your lap. But your arm is so light, as light as a balloon so though you want to bring it down, you find you cannot do so because it flies up again straightaway. Now, on the count of three, try to bring down your arm, one, two, *three!*' It was quite extraordinary how Mrs Robinson dropped her arm and that as soon as she did so, it shot up again as if of its own accord!

'Are your subjects able to speak under hypnosis?' asked Katie Harbottle.

'Oh yes,' said Dr Porterfield and, turning to Mrs Robinson, told her to open her eyes. 'Now perhaps you will tell us if you received any visitors at home earlier today?'

An innocent enough question to be sure – but what a Pandora's Box was opened when Mrs

149

Robinson replied that her friend Mrs Thatcher had come round for morning coffee. 'Oh, yes,' said Dr Porterfield. 'And what did you talk about?'

Mrs Robinson replied: 'We had a most exciting conversation about Walsh, the new window cleaner who has taken over from Chamberlain who moved to Alwoodley last month. Walsh is a most personable young man and does his work far better than his predecessor.'

'He makes the windows shine brighter?' prompted the hypnotist.

'Never mind the bloody windows,' she said impatiently. 'It's his prick that Mrs Thatcher and I were concerned about.'

'His *what*?' spluttered Dr Porterfield, who was as shocked as anyone in the hall.

'His prick,' she repeated. 'After all, Chamberlain was hardly up to completing his round any more, what with trying to satisfy up to a dozen ladies who wanted to be fucked during one working day. But I think Walsh will be able to cope. He came round yesterday afternoon and after he'd done his work he came into the drawing room –'

'Stop her, Dr Porterfield, tell her to stop talking!' said Campbell Armstrong urgently, pulling Dr Porterfield's coat-tails to attract his attention. But the unfortunate hypnotist's foot slipped as he turned back again to instruct Mrs Robinson to keep quiet – though by now the cat was well and truly out of the bag – and he crashed over Reverend Armstrong's chair sending them both sprawling onto the floor. Although the curate was only slightly dazed by the impact, our poor speaker hit his head on the floor with a resounding crack and was as soundly out for the count as if a pugilist had felled him with an uppercut.

Barbara Dartland, who had undergone a first aid training course, frantically applied a cold compress to Dr Porterfield's head to revive him but, like the vast majority of the audience, I was far more interested in the revelations of Mrs Robinson!

She was well on her way telling us what she had told Mrs Thatcher what Walsh the window cleaner had been up to after she had rewarded him with a glass of beer for cleaning her windows. 'He said to me: "Mrs Robinson, I've always considered you to be a beautiful woman and you have one of the shapeliest figures in the village." As I listened to his shameless flattery, sitting snugly beside him on the sofa, he slipped his right hand into my blouse, under my chemise and began gently squeezing my breast. I raised my hand as if to stop him but my nipple already had swollen up to the size and hardness of a little red pebble. Yes, I know that I should really have stopped him right there but between you and me, my dear Margaret, I liked the look of this muscular young man! He then wormed his hand between my thighs and as we french kissed, he worked them into the leg of my knickers and touched the moistening lips of my pussey. My juices began to flow freely as my thighs tightened like a vice over his hand as I shuddered to a little spend as his fingers penetrated me.

'Then the naughty fellow began kissing my neck and throat and I suggested that we retire upstairs to a bedroom. He helped me undress down to my drawers and I lay back on the bed as he kissed my titties and my belly before rolling me over and kissing and licking me all the way back to my shoulders. My poor pussey was now sopping wet as he peeled off my knickers, kissing each inch of exposed flesh and he ran his hand lightly down the crack of my bum before rolling me back. He plunged his tongue inside my ear and then played the tip around my titties before his mouth travelled down to lightly bite the insides of my thighs. Then he drove me wild by licking and lapping at my dripping cunney and I was already on my way to paradise even before he found my clitty. He brought me off in style before I told him I wanted his prick inside me.

'Then he pulled off his shirt and undid his belt and let his trousers fall to the ground. Teasingly he told me to take off his pants so I carefully pulled them down over his hard, stiff cock. It wasn't that huge but his shaft looked well proportioned enough for a good fuck so, pulling back the foreskin, I rolled my tongue over his purple knob and sucked it right into my mouth. It tasted wonderful! This fully released my passion and I gobbled his cock until I felt it throb with desire. I released him so that he could climb between my legs and place his rigid rod inside my pussey. It stretched me nicely and I pulled my knees as far apart as possible to allow him to give me his full length. He fucked me beautifully with firm, pumping strokes, not too quickly, giving me the full benefit of his sinewy prick before shooting a huge jet of jism into my cunt as I squirmed my way to a tremendous spend.

'We clung to each other whilst he recovered but his cock was still semi-stiff when it slid out of my cunney. He raised himself up to his knees and the cheeky rogue placed his prick near my face. I reached out to hold the glistening shaft which was still wet from my juices and I decided to work him up to another full hard-on. I teased the knob by running the tip of my tongue all around the ridges of his helmet and then gave the underside a few quick licks and that did the trick, stiffening up his tool right back to its former firmness. I took his whole knob into my mouth and then eased in the rest of his stalwart staff. I bobbed my head up and down on his cock – three short, licking sucks followed by one long, fierce sucking was enough to send him off. The lusty lad was so excited by all this that in no time at all I felt his succulent cock shoving hard against the back of my throat and his hot, salty spunk was released and I felt it flooding down my throat. Walsh has got quite enormous balls, by the way, but by swallowing convulsively I drank every last drop of his copious emission, milking his tool of every last drop of the liquid of love.

'I managed to stiffen up his cock for one more fuck but then he had to leave as he was already late for Mrs Humphries and she wanted some special servicing too!' concluded Mrs Robinson. God knows what else she might have said but fortunately Barbara had by now revived Dr Porterfield and he quickly snapped the lady out of her trance. The audience had been stunned into silence, though one or two youths at the back had sniggered occasionally during her telling of this lascivious tale.

153

'There you are, I told you it was all hocus pocus,' said Mrs Robinson with satisfaction. 'I'd better be going now as I forgot to pay Mr Walsh the window cleaner yesterday and I'm expecting him back at the house.'

This brought forth howls of laughter but, quite undaunted, Mrs Robinson made her way to the exit. Reverend Armstrong stepped forth and, after explaining to Dr Porterfield what had occurred, called for silence: 'Ladies and gentlemen, I trust that what we heard this afternoon will never be revealed. Indeed, I am going to swear every person here to total secrecy. I will brook no exceptions, and Dr Porterfield agrees with me that, ethically, Mrs Robinson's words should be treated in the confidence she would have expected during a medical examination or, if she were of the Catholic faith, in the confessional. Would everyone please raise their rights hands and repeat after me an oath that we will never speak of what we heard just now. If there is anyone who has the slightest doubt about the justice of this, then I would remind him or her that Walsh is unmarried whilst Mrs Robinson's husband is a military man who is often away from home. Poor Mrs Humphries, as we all know, is a young widow. So only he that is without sin should cast the first stone.'

(Let me state here that I only mention the incident now in written form fourteen years after the event because Walsh married Mrs Humphries in 1904 and the couple promptly emigrated to New Zealand. Mrs Robinson and her husband, alas, perished along with Frank's father on the ill-fated maiden voyage of the *Titanic*).

We all went back to Barbara's house afterwards

for tea and, to everyone's relief, her parents were out for the afternoon. Reverend Armstrong said that he had some matters to attend to and would join us later.

Barbara insisted on opening a bottle of champagne from a case that an old French friend of her family had recently sent over to them, and the sparkling bubbly wine certainly loosened our tongues It seemed to make Barbara and Katie forget that I was present for the presence of a young lad did not inhibit them in the slightest in discussing matters of the utmost privacy and intimacy in front of me. For example, after discussing Mrs Robinson's hypnotic confessions, Katie said: 'You know, it was interesting that a member of the working class such as Walsh the window cleaner had the finesse needed to make a good fuck great After all, many men from the very cream of Society do not understand the subtle nuances of fucking, especially those who are well hung and who know it. Oh yes, they know that we can be excited by seeing a nude man with a flaccid cock, if his knob hangs over his balls.

'But simply just sticking your big shaft into a wet pussey isn't enough – after all, *anybody* can do that if he has the equipment for it. No, once a man gets a hard-on, I like a little foreplay like having him hover over me and rubbing his erect prick up and down over my breasts and belly and then finally on my clitty whilst he tells me how beautiful my breasts are or how juicy my pussey is and how much he loves my body. That will start me off and then I like him to begin inserting his shaft in my cunt, just a little at a time. First his helmet goes in and then when he pulls it out the feeling of the ridge rubbing against my pussey lips is simply divine. Fred Nolan is very good at foreplay, by the way. Once he starts fucking in this style he puts his hard shaft in just a little further each time and the tension builds up deliciously. I find this much more exciting than just having every inch of a cock inserted immediately. Mind, even after a good fuck, I am often still usually highly charged and it is really super if my lover licks my cunney or manipulates my clitty with his hand after he has spent because that will make me come or give me a second orgasm if I've spent already.

'What is really dreadful is if he just rolls over once he's finished and doesn't even kiss or hold you afterwards. And I hate it when a man says "Did you come?" If I have, he'll know it and if not, well, we can always try again. But when he asks me I have the feeling that what he's really trying to do is asking me to rate his love-making abilities, which is unnecessary. Simultaneous spending is over-rated anyway, in my humble opinion'

'You are really knowledgeable about *l'art de faire l'amour*, Katie,' sighed Barbara. 'As I said before earlier today, I do so admire your adventurous spirit. Here am I who have yet to experience the joy of feeling a prick up my cunt. Mind, I must confess that I am not totally without experience. For instance, I did have a very strange evening with a girl named Lizzie Hollywood the other week which led to my cunney playing host to other fingers than my own and, come to think of it, something else besides a strange hand!

156

'But let me first tell you about Lizzie. She is a pretty girl of about our age who I met for the first time at an exhibition of English Post-Impressionist art at the Manor Hall Gallery in Leeds The wealthy textile magnate, Sir Louis Segal, donated some works from his collection and I met Lizzie at a reception given by Sir Louis for supporters of the gallery (my Mama has been a patron for many years) We got to talking and she told me she was an art student. As I was on my own – I was staying the night with my old friend Angela Bickler and I had the keys to her house – I accepted Lizzie's invitation to dine with her at the Queens Hotel. We drank a bottle of wine with our splendid meal and what with the aperitifs we had consumed at Sir Louis's party, I was feeling more than slightly woozy by the time we had finished our desserts. "Come upstairs and lie down on my bed for a bit before you leave. Give me your friend Angela's address and I will ask the reception desk to send word to her and inform her that she should not wait up for you," suggested Lizzie and, taking my hand, led me to the elevator. It seemed like a good idea at the time. I certainly had imbibed not wisely but too well for I collapsed on the bed and in an instant was deep in the arms of Morpheus.

'I woke up a couple of hours later and for a few moments I was totally disorientated and wondered dizzily where on earth I was! Then I suddenly remembered as I looked at my wrist-watch, for the bedside light was still burning and I saw that it would soon be midnight. I shivered as I felt a cool breeze blowing through the half open window. I raised myself up to shut it and it was only then when I looked in the long wall mirror that I suddenly realised that I was stark naked! I looked wildly around for my clothes when Lizzie came in from the bathroom. She was only wearing a cream silk nightrobe through which I could see the dark protuberances of her nipples as she walked towards me.

' "Ah, you've woken up at last!" she smiled. "Do you feel better now?"

' "Yes, thank you, I feel fine and dandy after that rest. I am so ashamed though, falling asleep after dinner but I'm afraid the bottle of Château Mouton-Rothschild went straight to my head," I stammered in reply.

'She came and sat by me and stroked my hair. "It doesn't matter at all, it really doesn't. I hope you don't mind but the night air is so warm and you looked so uncomfortable that I undressed you whilst you were sleeping. I've hung your clothes up in my cupboard and before you worry your pretty little head about it, I've also let Angela Bickler know that you're staying the night here and that you'll contact her first thing in the morning."

'She then slipped off her robe and lay down next to me. "You don't mind if I join you, Babs, as I'm feeling rather tired too," she murmured, snuggling up close to me. Lizzie was really a very attractive girl with long blonde hair that she let down to fall over her shoulders, whilst her light complexion and slender figure contrasted so well with my own rather dark looks. She moistened her rich red lips with her tongue, showing her sparkling white teeth. Her legs were next to mine and I must admit that our figures complemented each other perfectly, even our pussies blended so well, mine brown-haired and curly, hers silky and blonde.

' "You still look tired," Lizzie said softly. "Why don't you put your head on my shoulders and close your eyes?" I readily complied, feeling totally relaxed and though Lizzie was soon stroking my nides and fondling my breasts in a most intimate fashion, I made only the slightest token attempt to stop her. "What are you doing, Lizzie? That's very naughty, you know," I admonished her drowsily.

' "Just relax my love and let me pay court to your beautiful breasts – aren't they large? They are so much bigger than mine," she cooed and I offered no resistance as she continued to caress my bosoms, cradling them in her hands. I closed my eyes as I felt Lizzie's lips close upon my right nipple and swirled it in her mouth, sending chills of desire running up and down my spine. She moved her hands up and down my body now in smooth, gentle titillating strokes and to my own surprise I found myself growing more and more aroused with each caress. As her knowing fingers inched towards my pussey I felt my thighs stiffen and my hips involuntarily thrust forward in tantalising anticipation of what was to come.

'She slid her long fingers into my dampening muff, moving them deliciously inside as the heel of her hand rubbed my clitty which rose up to greet it until it was as hard as a tiny walnut. "Ah, I've found your secret spot, have I not?" she whispered as she drew firm little circles around my clitty until my entire body was squirming with pleasure. Without ever taking her fingers from my clitty, she brought across her other hand and dipped a long

159

forefinger in my squelchy hole. The sensation was so electrifying that I sat bolt upright and moaned: "Oh Lizzie, that's wonderful!"

' "It's wonderful for me too, darling. Finger fucking your cunney makes me so wet," she breathed into my ear. "Feel my pussey, it's positively dripping waiting for your touch." Without protest I let her take my hand and place it between her cool, firm thighs. I trailed my fingers through her silky blonde cunney hair and we covered each other's mouths with burning kisses as we finger fucked each other's cunnies. Lizzie then moved her head down and nuzzled her red lips around my curly brown bush. "Darling, what a perfectly delicious crack you have! M'mmm, and what a stimulating, heady perfume it possesses!"

'Without further words she started to tongue my crack, moving all along my wet slit, exploring, tasting, teasing – and then suddenly she stopped! I gasped out my disappointment but Lizzie said sweetly: "Don't worry, sweetheart. I have a surprise for you." She reached out into the drawer of the bedside table and pulled out a strange black rubber dildo.

'Obviously, my surprise must have shown on my face for Lizzie said: "Barbara, have you never seen a ladies' comforter before?" "Oh yes," I said, still looking curiously at this strangely shaped instrument, "but never one like this."

' "Ah, this will be your first experience with a double-header – I promise that you will find it most exciting. One part of this dildo has been modelled upon the prick of the famous Shakespearean actor Mr Michael Beattie and the

160

other is fashioned from a plaster cast of the gallant prick of none other than Lieutenant Colonel Alan Brooke of the Hussars, perhaps the most famous cocksman in England."

'Without further ado she took out a small jar of pomade and poured some of the sticky oil over the dildo which she then pressed gently against my cunney lips as she continued to nibble around my pussey with her mouth. This made me so wet that she was able to work the dildo head (I believe it was the slightly less thick end which had been manufactured to the measurements of Colonel Brooke) into my cunt until it filled me completely.

'Lizzie then pulled herself up until she was sitting upon my thighs. Our eyes locked as she finger fucked herself with one hand whilst she vibrated this rubber prick inside my cunt with the other. When her cunney was nice and juicy enough she then raised herself up and slowly worked the other part of our rubber playmate into her cunney. She reached forward and pulled me to her until we were pressed tightly together, breast to breast and cunt to cunt with the dildo pleasuring us both at the same time as we jerked our hips to and fro along its long double-headed shaft. I wrapped my legs tightly around her back and she wrapped hers around mine as, rocking back and forth, we achieved a delicious rhythm that sent pulses of pleasure to every nerve centre in my body.

'As our excitement grew, our motions became even more frenzied and Lizzie pressed me flat onto the bed and stretched her body out across mine, the dildo still clamped between our suctioning pussies. I grabbed her waist and pulled her towards me, allowing the rubber cock of Colonel Brooke to slide even further inside my sopping cunt. This was the closest I have ever been to a genuine fuck and I loved every glorious second of it.

'Suddenly my body convulsed and my head thrashed back and forth against the pillow. "Oh my God! Lizzie, don't stop now whatever you do! Lordy, that feels so great!" Of course Lizzie did not stop, and kept fucking my cunney as well as her own as she rocked to and fro. As soon as she felt me spend she felt the stirrings of her own approaching orgasm and we climbed the peaks almost together, shuddering and heaving as our cunnies poured out generous libations of love juice upon the sheets which were already stained by our perspiration and previous spendings.

'We lay there, drained and exhausted, pressed together still and joined at the crotch by the dildo which we took out carefully, first from my cunt and then from Lizzie's and she deposited it back on the table. We took a short nap but this time I was the first to wake and whilst she slept I caressed her as slowly and lovingly as she had earlier made love to me. I licked and nibbled at her small but proudly jutting breasts and her nipples rose to greet my mouth. I ran my palm down her belly and into her soaking blonde muff which woke her up and she smiled happily, closing her legs gently upon my hand.

'I ran my fingers through her silky triangle and my forefinger slipped easily into her sticky pussey which made her purr with pleasure. I had never gone down on another girl before (though several girls had done this to me at boarding school) but my curiousity and pervasive lust to which should be added to the desire to please Lizzie too were enough to overcome any slight resistance I might have felt towards the idea. So I slid down between her slender long legs and clasped my hands around Lizzie's boyish, rounded bum cheeks. I separated them as she arched her back to bring her tangy cunney up towards my mouth. I licked and lapped around those savoury cunt lips, moist from both our juices and then sucked her clitty into my mouth. This made Lizzie thresh around under me and with each of her writhings I felt my own pussey spend a little. I managed to straddle her leg so that I was able to feel her knee against my clitty. We made love again and each time Lizzie moved passionately her legs pressed more heavily against my cunt. As my excitement rose even higher I sucked up her cunney juices with renewed vigour. Finally, her whimpers and groans gave way to one long full-throated scream and we came together for a second time in a total, blinding release. We lay there together in bed before falling asleep for the night in each other's arms.'

I was worried that my prick might literally burst out of my trousers for I had been inadvertently been playing pocket billiards throughout the recounting of this outrageous history. I wiggled about uncomfortably but my shaft remained as stiff as iron when Katie declared: 'You'll be ready soon enough to have Campbell or whoever you so desire poke you. Do insist that he stays the whole night with you, though, when you finally do decide to take the plunge. I adore it when my lover makes love to me in the morning after a good night's fucking. For example, quite recently I was fucked by Mr Harry Barr, the gossip columnist of *The Pink 'Un*, a sporting paper which wanted an interview with my Papa about his stable of racehorses. Mr Barr was a competent enough lover though nothing amazingly special as far as technique goes. But on the morning after we made love, I opened my eyes and found him licking out my cunney. Now I vaguely recall something pleasant about a dream I was having but I didn't connect it with what was actually taking place. I was dreaming that I was out on Scarborough beach when I saw a piece of wood carved in the shape of a huge black prick lying in the sand. I got up and took off my bathing costume and eased the piece of wood inside my cunt.

'Then I woke up and found Harry Barr deep inside me and he told me, as he pumped his prick in and out of my juicy wetness, that he had been playing with my pussey for at least ten minutes beforehand, being careful not to wake me up. This was most considerate of him in the circumstances as his cock must have been straining at the leash. We then enjoyed a truly superb fuck, much better than the night before, and I suppose it was the bridge between fantasy and reality that made the experience so memorable for us both.'

As she finished her recollection, Katie looked across to me and with a saucy grin, said: 'This has hardly been suitable conversation for young Rupert to hear – mind, from the look of that bulge between his legs, I don't think it has done him any permanent damage.'

Barbara blushed but Katie's blood was up from the recounting of the stirring adventures – almost as much as mine! 'Come here, you naughty boy and let me see what you have hidden away in your trousers,' she called. 'Is that a catapult you have hidden in your pocket or were you simply stimulated by hearing the private confessions of two young ladies? Come sir, don't be shy.'

I walked towards them awkwardly, trying to conceal my bulging prick. But as soon as I was in reach, Katie swiftly unhooked my belt and ripping open my fly buttons, brought out my naked stiff cock into the sunlight. 'Isn't he well developed for a lad of his age?' remarked Barbara. I looked gratefully at her for I was used to only Frank receiving such compliments about the size of his shaft!

'Oh yes, indeed! I think that a good boy like Rupert – with an enormous prick that looks desperate for relief – needs to be attended to immediately,' said Katie, pulling down my trousers and underpants as she knelt in front of me. She took my cock in her warm, soft hands which instantly caused it to twitch delightedly whilst Barbara joined her and cupped my balls with one hand whilst gently rubbing her fingers down the length of my staff.

'With respect, dear Barbara, I saw it first,' said Katie as she opened her mouth and took my uncapped helmet between her rich red lips. The feeling was simple unbelievable as her darting tongue moved to and fro along the shaft. As she palated my prick I felt my balls swell under the caress of Barbara's hands and I thrust my shaft frenziedly in and out of Katie's mouth, knowing that I could hold back my spend for only a very short while. Barbara must also have guessed my urgency for she took my balls into her mouth and sucked them which caused a fierce rush of sperm to be sent shooting through the channel to the "eye" on the top of my pulsating knob. I exploded inside Katie's sweet mouth, flooding her throat with a deluge of sticky spunk which she greedily swallowed though she could not cope with my copious spend. My spunk gushed out between her lips and ran down her chin and finally fell upon Barbara's nose as she continued to suck my balls.

When Katie had finally milked my prick of its last drops of jism I stood there in a daze with my prick limp. Then Katie pulled Barbara aside and whispered something in her ear that I could not quite catch. Katie then turned back to me and said: 'We would like to see your cock stand up stiff again, Rupert. Can you oblige us?'

'Not yet, I'm afraid,' I said sadly looking down at my flaccid shaft.

'Well, I have the answer. Take off the rest of your clothes please,' she commanded and so I did just that, carefully putting them in a neat pile by my chair.

Katie grinned and said: 'Good – now we are going to play a little game. We're going to imagine that we are back at your school – St Lionel's, if I am not mistaken – and you have been summoned to the Headmaster's study for bad behaviour Now sir, will you stiffen your prick!'

'I'm terribly sorry but I'm unable to just for the moment,' I mumbled.

'Very well,' said Katie crisply. 'Bend down, you

naughty boy, and touch your toes.' Again, I did as I was told, feeling rather nervous as Katie opened my legs slightly so that the girls could see my hairy ballsack hanging down. Then Barbara passed her hand lightly across my bare bottom cheeks and they began to wallop my arse with their palms, taking turns to smack me. It hurt a bit after a time but strangely enough did not feel as unpleasant as perhaps it should have done.

Smack, smack, SMACK! 'There, you naughty boy! How dare you visit us with a dangling tool!' Smack, smack, SMACK! 'Such an impudent fellow, isn't he? Take that, that and that!' I craned my head backwards and saw that whilst one girl was tanning my hide the other was busily undressing and by the time my arse was really stinging from their slaps, both girls were quite nude.

I looked down at my prick and saw that as if by magic it now stood up in a rampant state of erection, standing majestically high with the tip of my knob touching my navel. 'He's ready now,' cried Katie. 'Well, here's your chance, Barbara. I would let yourself be fucked by young Rupert, if I were you, so that when you and Campbell finally jump into bed you'll know exactly what to expect.'

'Do you think so?' said Barbara anxiously, as she thought for a moment before making up her mind. 'Yes, you're quite right, of course. Rupert, may I take it that you have no objections?'

My father had always drummed it in to my head that one should always help a lady in distress – not that I needed any encouragement as the lovely girl stretched herself out on the luxuriantly thick carpet. She really was an exceptional beauty with extremely large breasts topped by well-proportioned ruby nipples. Her mound was a veritable delight with a profusion of exquisite dark brown hair covering her furrow and the pouting lips of her cunney looked hugely inviting.

I knelt before this sensual goddess, spreading her legs wide as she grasped my rigid rod to feed it to her hungry pussey She guided my knob between her cunney lips and slowly, thrillingly, I inched my staff inside her willing wet cunt as it sucked in my throbbing cock I fucked her as slowly as possible, taking my time as her cunney muscles clutched sweetly at the sides of my shaft while I hovered above her, supporting myself on my arms. Then deeper and deeper, but still with deliberate speed, I thrust back and forth inside her. She began to moan and shudder and I paused. 'Am I hurting you?' I asked for this was after all Barbara's initiation into the grandest game, though her hymen must have been broken even before her tribadic double-ended dildo encounter with Lizzie with which we had just been regaled. I moved inexorably on, my hands holding her firmly just below her swaying breasts and I quickened my pumping at her request as I felt the walls of her love channel widen. She gyrated like a girl possessed and my cock was drawn in to the limit as I corked her cunt, my balls banging against her bottom as I plunged my prick in and out of her dark cavern.

The familiar tingle in my balls announced that the first surge of spunk was beginning its journey up to my rock-hard shaft. 'Can I spunk inside you?' I panted. Instinctively she opened her legs even wider, plumbing her hidden depths and as I drove in and out in the final passionate frenzy, her pussey exploded. She was wracked by great shudders that rippled through her body so that each time, however impossible it seemed to be, her cunney opened a little wider. As every current jolted through her she willed herself on, shouting. 'Yes! Yes! Shoot your spunk!' and she rose to meet me as I plunged yet again into her. The first unstoppable surge of sperm coursed its way up my cock. Time and time again I rammed into her, filling her cunt to overflowing with my jets of jism. Gush upon gush flowed into her from my spurting knob. My balls knocked unmercifully against her, throbbing with the mighty power of their emptying ejaculations.

A tide of relief washed over us as my pace slowed. Everything that was in me was now inside her cunt. The last irregular spasms of my come shook me and Barbara gave one last convulsive heave and then lay very still, her arms and legs splayed out, her breasts quivering still with the energy she had expended.

My lusty young cock was now truly spent and I pulled out my shrunken shaft and rolled off her. 'Well done, Rupert,' cried Katie, who had been following our coupling closely. 'I was most impressed that such a youthful prick could perform so well.'

'Well done indeed,' echoed Barbara. 'I came twice before you spunked. But I fear I have left little for you to enjoy, Katie. Poor Rupert will never manage another cockstand this afternoon.'

'Never mind, my sweet love; *carpe diem, guam*

minimum credula postero [*Seize the present day, trusting the morrow as little as you can – Editor*] and with respect to Rupert whose prick I would certainly enjoy having in my cunney or up my bum, I am well served for cock just now. If you recall, Mr Nolan the cinematographer has placed his Yankee pole at my disposal this evening and he really does know how to satisfy a girl.'

We decided to dress ourselves which was just as well because we had only just finished when the Reverend Armstrong arrived, to be followed shortly afterwards by Wallace in our best carriage Katie accepted my offer of a ride back to her home as she wanted to leave Barbara and Campbell alone to enjoy themselves in privacy! I was feeling satisfied with the way I had spent the afternoon but on the way back Katie suddenly said to me: 'Rupert, would you think it amiss if I gave you a word of advice?'

'Not at all, Katie but I do hope that I have done nothing to offend you,' I replied in genuine concern, somewhat puzzled by the serious tone of her words.

She shook her head. 'Oh no, my dear boy, far from it. I would just like to say this to you. Fucking is the finest sport that a young man can engage in However, if you ever reach the stage where one fuck is like another, when afterwards you cannot picture who it was you fucked and the particular taste of the girl concerned, then you should give your cock a rest and simply take yourself in hand – in every sense of the phrase if need be – until you are able to resume, refreshed and reinvigorated to enjoy the wonderful world of pussey and the ever-altering feel of one cunney from another.'

I pondered over her wise words. Over the years I have thanked the blessed providence for the fact that every pussey that I have ever encountered has been new and different in some way. Still, I have never forgotten Katie's counselling and there have indeed been periods – of as long as three or four weeks on occasion – when I have refrained from dipping my wick, even though the opportunity has been there for the taking.

At this early stage in my career as a cocksman, however, I simply filed Katie's warning in the banks of memory. I returned back to Albion Towers in the highest of spirits and naturally was eager to tell Frank about all my experiences.

'You should have come with me to Farnham, old chap, as I am sure that at worst, Katie Harbottle would have sucked you off even if she didn't want to fuck.'

'Not to worry,' said Frank cheerfully. 'I really did have a slight headache this afternoon and besides I had a jolly good time earlier on with Fred and Campbell whilst you were with Katie and Barbara.'

'Did you now,' I said, settling down in my chair as we idled away the time before dinner in the billiards room, undisturbed by any other members of the household.

'Yes,' he said smugly. 'I do not know whether it is the keen Yorkshire air that makes people so randy in this part of the world but I give you my word that I am not exaggerating a jot about what happened after luncheon. Fred, Campbell and I decided to trudge up to the ruins of Knaresborough Castle. Living so near, you must have been there many times, but Campbell told Fred

Nolan how the site of the castle commands prospects of great beauty and extent. Indeed, "Knaresborough From The Castle Hill" is a favourite subject with many artists.

'Campbell was telling us about a secret passage leading from the castle yard to the moat when we came across one of these artists, an extremely pretty lady in her mid twenties, sitting in front of an easel and looking earnestly at the scene in front of her. She was wearing a close-fitting costume in the modern style which showed off her slim body and lovely big breasts which jutted out like two melons. I don't mind telling you that my cock began to stiffen just at the sight of these two beauties which were only half hidden by a low-cut top.

'Well, what do ya know,' gasped Mr Nolan when we approached her. "It's Miss Patricia Miller or I'm a Dutchman. Hey, Patsy, how'ya doing, honey?"

'The girl looked up and, Christ, Rupert, she really was a beauty. Her mop of red hair set off the most beautiful face which lit up when she saw us. "My God, it's Fred Nolan," she cried out in a most pleasing Yankee drawl, "fancy seeing you here." They embraced each other heartily and Fred explained that Miss Miller was a distinguished actress in her home town of Boston and had played in many of the top theatres throughout the United States. "Are you working over here, Patsy?" he asked and she shook her head. "I'm over here purely for a vacation, Fred. The London impressarios have been badgering me and I was tempted by a generous offer from Konrad Kochanski to appear in *As You Like It* at

172

Drury Lane in London But I've turned him down along with all the others! I need to recharge my batteries and paint and sketch a little. I'm staying with Lord Hugh Hoffner at Hampsthwaite Where are you residing, Fred? You really must come along to see me there, especially if you bring along your camera. His Lordship is fascinated by the idea of moving pictures "

'Mr Nolan explained that he was staying at Albion Towers with your family, Rupert, and then after he introduced Reverend Armstrong and myself, Miss Miller showed us some of the pictures she had painted during her holiday I looked over Mr Nolan's shoulder as he leafed through her portfolio but to my delighted surprise there were no landscapes of Knaresborough Castle or the surrounds – instead there were twenty or thirty sketches and most were precisely drawn studies of those parts of the human body that we rarely see on canvas! There were titties and arses, cunts and pricks galore, Rupert My favourite was perhaps the one of a girl with her skirts thrown up and her naked bottom thrust out towards the beholder in such a fashion that, between the spread legs, one could see her furry auburn bush and her cunney lips that were already parted as if in eager anticipation of thrusting entry '

'How fascinating! Isn't it the very deuce of a coincidence that only last week Diana Wigmore, another female artist who loves fucking, was good enough to rid me of my troublesome virginity. I'll tell you something, Frank old boy, even if I pass all the University examinations when we leave St Lionel's, blow Oxford and

Cambridge, I'm off to art school in London, Paris or Rome.'

My pal chuckled and continued: 'And I think I'll join you, although my brother Roger assures me that there is plenty of fucking available to undergraduates in both those august establishments. Anyhow, as I was telling you, Mr Nolan was also much taken by this drawing and demanded to know who the lady in question might be. "Oh no, I cannot tell you," said Miss Miller roguishly. "It would be wrong to divulge the name of my sitter, for all these drawings were done for private exhibition only I mean, supposing I was to circulate a picture of your prick. I doubt whether you would want it bandied about amongst gatherings of strangers or passed from hand to hand even amongst those of your acquaintances Don't you agree, Reverend Armstrong?"

'Campbell took her point and commented: "I agree that your lips should remain sealed, Miss Miller, and that we must think of your sketch only as The Unknown Cunt. However, the love-channel in question does appear to be a most welcoming furrow and one can hardly blame any gentleman for being curious to find out the name of its owner." He pulled out another drawing that showed a pretty, buxom looking young woman with a happy smile upon her lips about to kiss the uncapped knob of a well-sized erect prick that she was lovingly cradling in her hands

' "Ah ha," said Campbell. "Now here is a sensitive sketch from life that I find most pleasing, with its suggestions both of vulnerability and of a half-ashamed boldness."

' "It does not offend you, Reverend?" twinkled the artist.

"Certainly not, my dear young lady," he quipped, "for it shows that the female in question has learned her catechism well. Does she not show that she knows what is the chief end of man? But I think you have based this picture upon an illustration from Mr Angus Gradegate's *Fucking For Fun* which must also be available in your country "

' "Well spotted," said Miss Miller with unconcealed admiration. "Only a very few people have ever made the connection."

Campbell replied modestly: "Well, I do have an unfair advantage here, as the girl who posed for the illustration in Mr Gradegate's valuable tome was my cousin Louise Lombert from Dumbarton and the member she is holding is that of her friend, Mr John Gibson of Edinburgh, a gentleman whose penis is reckoned to be perhaps the largest in all of Scotland."

' "Really now," said Miss Miller. "Is Mr Gibson still residing in Edinburgh? I plan to spend a few days there early next week and would appreciate an introduction." She turned to Mr Nolan and added: "You'll hardly credit it, Fred, but I've not had a good fuck since I came to England."

' "How terrible," said Mr Nolan as he took hold of the willing girl. "Let's put that right here and now! After all, we're old friends and I'm sure my companions will excuse me if I asked them to continue their stroll without me "

'Campbell whipped out a notebook and said that he would walk on to a park bench a quarter of a mile or so up the road. I would have joined him but the fiery-haired American girl said: "Don't leave us, young man. You may learn something to your advantage."

'Mr Nolan looked a little dubious but then his face cleared and he said to me: "Oh yes, I quite forgot, Patsy prefers an audience whilst fucking which I suppose comes from performing so much on the stage. Come on, let's go behind the clump of trees over there. After all, you're welcome to watch, Frank, but we don't want to admit the general public – especially as they would be able to see for free!"

'I followed the couple down the hill to the place Mr Nolan suggested and once we found an even piece of ground, I helped spread out the rug Miss Miller had brought with her and we laid it on the grass. Mr Nolan quickly stripped off and lay down on his back, his prick waving upwards like a huge, veiny truncheon. Miss Miller laughed gaily as she stepped out of her dress and slipped off her chemise. She wore no knickers (it was because the day was so warm, she later confided) and she paraded her naked charms which gave me a stiffstander in no time. What a ravishing sight she was, Rupert, and I almost spent there and then as her firm, thrusting breasts swung gracefully as she pirouetted lightly on the balls of her feet, letting me see her delectable figure. Straightaway I recognised her pussey from the picture that had so attracted us. "The Unknown Cunt", as Campbell had called it, was none other than a clever self-portrait for there in all its glory was the pouting little crack inside the curly auburn-haired triangle which nestled between her creamy white thighs.

'But I said nothing as she swooped down and washed Mr Nolan's knob with her tongue. She then wrapped her rich lips around the straining shaft and sucked lustily for a little before climbing up on him with her knees on either side of his torso She pulled open her pink cunney lips and I saw her take hold of his cock and guide it inside her. Like Mr Nolan, Patsy Miller was an expert equestrian and this was shown as she rode his prick with great assurance, twisting her hips and bouncing merrily away, leaning forward so that he could take her cherry nipples in his mouth.

'Her face was now flushed with excitement and she turned to me and gasped: "Come on, let me see what you have to offer." I unbuttoned my trousers and presented my cock to her. She took it in her hands and peeled back my foreskin as she massaged my shaft. "Hey, big boy, what a whopper, that looks like a prick big enough for a man twice your age. And such a fine smooth-skinned shaft, as hard and stiff as anything, yet like velvet to the touch."

'She continued to bounce up and down Mr Nolan's prick as she leaned forward to lick and tongue my purple knob. Then, with a practised hand, she cupped my balls in the palm of her hand and gently pulled me towards her so that she could feed all of my shaft inside her mouth. Perhaps it was the lewd sight of Patsy sucking my cock which brought Mr Nolan off so quickly. "Are you ready for it, Patsy?" he panted as she rocked backwards and forwards on his prick in rhythm with the grand sucking to which she was treating my delighted member I felt such delicious stabs of desire as she sucked my cock, teasing my helmet against the roof of her mouth with her tongue that I, too, soon felt the surge of a powerful spend coursing through my throbbing staff. We both spunked simultaneously and Mr Nolan filled her cunt with his copious emission of sticky white jism whilst I drenched her mouth with my spurtings of creamy sperm.

'"Thanks, boys, that was a nice brisk fuck. I really enjoyed that and I must tell you, Fred, that young Frank here has a lovely salty tang to his jism. M'mm, nothing tastes as clean and fresh as frothy spunk straight from the cock. My God, his prick is still stiff even after spunking! Oh well, let's not waste any time." She lay down on the sheet, and pulled me on top of her. I entered her easily, for her cunney was well greased from Fred's jism. I slid my full length deep into her and began to fuck her as she threw her legs around my waist. She arched upwards at every stroke, her bum cheeks coming off the sheet as she gyrated faster and faster. She wailed with ecstasy as I grabbed her breasts and brought my head down to suck those lovely red nipples. I felt her cunney contract around my cock as I thrust madly into her exquisite wetness and all too soon the sperm came bubbling up from my balls. Luckily, she reached port first, shivering and trembling as with one last push I started to spend, spurting my hot love juice inside her willing cunt. She gurgled with joy as my frothy white cream hurtled into her and she milked my prick superbly. Then Mr Nolan showed us his expertise at bum fucking and, as requested, I tossed myself off and squirted my sperm over her titties whilst her bottom hole was being flooded by Mr Nolan.

'So you see, Rupert, I didn't miss out too much by not joining you this afternoon at Farnham for I was absolutely shagged out and needed a rest!'

'You certainly did not,' I agreed and I asked him where Mr Nolan might be found. Frank informed me that our guest was still engaged in developing his film so I decided to go to my bedroom and take a bath as I was feeling hot and bothered after all that exercise at Farnham.

In my room, I took off my jacket when I suddenly remembered that our form had been set some holiday work by our English master Mr Bresslaw, the task being to write a poem of not less than twelve lines, a task which I had not yet completed. 'I wonder whether Frank has remembered either,' I muttered to myself as I took out the exercise book from my bedside drawer in which I had scribbled the verse to Diana which I have reproduced earlier in this narrative. Perhaps it was because we had been studying *Romeo and Juliet* and I had been much moved by the plight of the star-crossed lovers that I decided to try and pen some lines on the joyousness of love-making. I took off my jacket and sat down on my bed, willing the muse to assist me. The first few lines came quickly:

> *Tell me where are there such blisses*
> *When lips are joined in heavenly kisses*
> *When lovers both convulsive start*
> *The passion only love imparts*

Then, just as I was racking my brains thinking of how to continue, there was a demure knock on my door. 'Come in,' I called and Sally, our sensual servant, came in.

'What do you want, Sally, my room seems to have already been cleaned,' I said.

'I know, Master Rupert, it's been ready for you since noon,' said the blonde temptress. 'But Mr Goldhill told me to refill all the water jugs in the bedrooms – I'm sorry if I interrupted anything important.'

She set down the tray she was carrying with the jug on it and said: 'Are you writing another poem?'

I was shocked – how the devil did she know? As if reading my mind, she said: 'I read the verses you wrote to Miss Diana in that notebook. Well, don't be cross. You shouldn't have left it around if you didn't want anyone to see it. I'm good at rhyming, perhaps I can help you with your poem.'

Before I could reply, she was sitting besides me. To be honest, I did not believe for a moment that Sally would be able to complete my work. But I was wrong, dear reader, for Sally was blessed with an aptitude for versifying that put me to shame. It would bring a blush to all those of a reactionary disposition who insist that the labouring classes are incapable of anything but the most basic speech, thoughts and deeds. For Sally helped me greatly as I put together the following ode:

> Mutual keeping to one tether,
> Sweet it is to join together
> Throbbing, heaving,
> Never grieving;
> Thrusting, bursting,
> Sighing, dying!
> Decrepid age may beckon, teasing,
> Shrivelled up bodies we'll not abide,
> Vigorous youth, oh, that is pleasing,

It is worth the world beside.
Craving, wanting,
Sobbing, panting,
Throbbing, heaving,
Never grieving,
Thrusting, bursting,
Sighing, dying!

'Sally, you have hidden talents.' I laughed but she shrugged off what I now realise was an unintentionally patronising comment.

'Oh, we are quite capable downstairs of other things besides cleaning and cooking, you know. Mr Goldhill, for example, is a serious student of the art of ancient Greece and on his summer vacation last year went down to London to see the Elgin Marbles.' [*A group of fifth century BC Greek sculptures from the Athens Parthenon brought to England by the Earl of Elgin and now in the British Museum – Editor*]

'You surprise me, Sally, I suppose you'll tell me next that Wallace the coachman is a learned authority on the art of the Dutch masters.'

'No, Master Rupert,' she grinned. 'He doesn't even know much about Dutch caps. All that interests him is cricket, football, ale and fucking – which reminds me, as I've helped you with your homework, how about a farewell fuck before you go back to school?'

My eyes lit up. 'Now you're talking, Sally. Blow poetry and the Elgin Marbles.'

'Let me blow you instead!' she cried as she knelt before me and unbuttoned my trousers and peeled down my pants to allow my thickening bare cockshaft to emerge. My tool sprang out eagerly from its squashed state, stiffening up quickly as she cupped my balls in one hand. Coyly playing with my truncheon with the other, sliding her fingers up and down the hot, sturdy shaft, first played with my prick, then gobbled almost the whole length of my shaft inside her mouth. Her tongue played lightly at the swollen uncapped helmet of my prick as she gently but insistently squeezed my throbbing balls. Her mouth sucked hungrily up and down my rigid rod, sliding her lips up and down my rock-hard shaft, gulping noisily as my knob smoothed its way across the roof of her mouth and down towards the back of her throat. I managed to unbutton her blouse and took her proud young breasts in my hands, flicking her titties between my fingers as I thrust my cock in and out of her mouth until very soon I pumped a stream of creamy spunk between her lips which she swallowed with the same sweet urgency with which we began this encounter.

Gad, is there anything more thrilling than having a pretty girl suck your cock? It adds that indefinable extra dimension to a good fuck best expressed perhaps by my old friend, Sir Loring Sayers, who commented in *The Cremorne* recently: 'Sucking a man's cock is the deepest, most sensitive way in which a woman can acknowledge her lover's masculinity.'

I am sure this was so with Sally, who now had me in thrall. 'Now it's your turn to taste me,' she said, quickly stripping off the rest of her clothes. She lay back on my bed and the sight of her exquisitely fashioned quim with the two pink cunney lips peeping delicately through the mass of blonde hair of her pussey simply carried me away. With a hoarse cry I leaped up to join her and parted her thighs even wider. In an instant I was licking and lapping her around her dripping treasure-trove. My tongue slipped deep inside her and I could feel her clitty swell as I probed even further. There was a refreshing tang of our mixed love juices as with a soft moan of pleasure she wrapped her thighs around my neck, forcing her splendid silky bush into my face.

I nipped at her clitty with the top of my tongue until she reached a delighted peak. 'I want you inside me,' she moaned, releasing my head from between her legs. I let her flop back on the bed, threshing and writhing in her own secret world of pleasure. When she had regained her composure she told me to lie on my back and she knelt over my prick which was still semi-erect. She brushed her perky titties over my knob, and this had the desired effect of making my shaft stand up to attention straightaway. She grasped my slippery shaft and rubbed it up and down until it was more than ready. Then she squatted over my twitching knob and guided it between her squishy cunney lips. My cock slid all the way up her sopping slit as I reached up to squeeze her creamy breasts.

Sally began to ride me with long steady movements of her supple thighs. I began to move with her and played with her luscious red-stalked titties whilst she rode me faster and faster. This was no slow, lingering fuck. We were both so urgent in our needs that with every thrust downwards upon my prick, I rose upwards to meet her with equal vigour. Great gasps shuddered through our bodies and the tingling in my cock became stronger and stronger and I felt that first gush of spunk forcing its way up from my bollocks. My prick twitched and I jetted my first wodges of cream as her cunney quivered all round my shaft and she began to spend with me. The muscular contractions of her cunt increased my pleasure even more and I shot a tremendous flow of sperm into her gorgeous love box as she fell forwards into my arms, shaking and yelping in delight as her pussey milked my pulsing prick of every drop of spunk.

We lay entwined, exhausted, sucking in great gulps of air. Neither of us could speak but she smiled up at me and puckered up her lips in a little kiss. Still inside her, I felt her cunney relax and I took out my now deflated cock. I looked sadly down at it but Sally said: 'Your tadger has worked very hard. I give him nine and a half marks out of ten which is half a mark more than I have ever awarded.'

'How about Mr Goldhill?' I asked.

'Oh, Stanley usually scores seven or eight but I've yet to give out a ten. Perhaps we'll see if you can hit the jackpot during the Christmas vacation,' she teased.

Now the flush that had suffused our bodies began to subside and we pulled on our clothes. I took my bath and changed and knocked on Frank's door. 'Frank, are you ready for dinner?' I called out. He came to the door, looking very spruce. 'That was well-timed,' he said. 'I've just said goodbye to Polly who came up to my room for a last fuck before I go home. I say, Rupert, this has been the jolliest vacation we've ever spent together, hasn't it?'

'We've certainly spent a lot, old chap.' I commented and we burst out laughing as we made our way downstairs to the dining room.

CHAPTER FIVE

Back To School

I HAVE ALWAYS LOOKED WITH PITY ON THE
man who says that 'his schooldays were the
happiest days of his life'. It is an undeniable fact
that, when older men meet, they tend to hanker
for the joys of youth, remembering the roistering
of their salad days when they would besport
themselves with wine, women and song. Yet
whilst I enjoy ruminating over the fun of times
gone by, it is not in my nature to sigh wistfully
over past pleasures. I far prefer to look forward to
the opportunities afforded by the future.

However, let me stress that I count myself
extremely fortunate that my formative years were
spent at St Lionel's Academy for the Sons of
Gentlefolk, an educational establishment run on
more liberal principles than the usual public
school of its class. Great men have been scholars
there and many sportsmen of renown have
graced its playing fields. The majesty of the
ancient grey buildings, set just south of the
Ashdown Forest near the village of Maresfield,
makes its pupils appear in their imagination to
see themselves as heirs to a great tradition. Many,
I regret to admit, were tempted to hold an

186

unwarranted aloof sense of social superiority but Frank Folkestone and myself were amongst those who simply had a genuine love and pride for our old school.

In twos and threes we strolled along the tree-lined path leading to the Great Hall, exchanging greetings and comparing holiday notes with classmates we had not seen for several weeks. 'Should we tell them what we did on our holidays?' said Frank with a cheery grin as we entered Hall. 'They will all be so envious that I bet no-one will believe we now know the joys of fucking!'

I was about to reply when the deep, commanding voice of our headmaster Dr Keel-eigh boomed out: 'Folkestone! Mountjoy! I would like to see you in my study at once.' Frank paled and muttered: 'Hells bells! How could the old bugger have heard me?'

'He couldn't have done, don't worry,' I reassured him but nevertheless I was still more than a mite worried as we followed the headmaster through to his large oak-panelled study. As the Bard of Avon has it, conscience makes cowards of us all!

In fact, of course, Dr Keeleigh had not heard a single word of Frank's lewd remark. We entered his study and the headmaster must have been reading my mind for he put an avuncular hand on my arm and said: 'Sit down, boys, sit down. Now I don't want to burden either of you this term as it is important that you work and play as hard as you can. The Fifth Form this year is of an exceptionally high calibre and knowing your fathers as I do, if either of you don't finish well up

187

the examination lists at the end of each term, I know you'll be for the high jump.'

We smiled weakly as the headmaster added: 'But I've every confidence in you chaps and feel that your shoulders are strong enough to carry a further burden. I want your help in a matter not only important for the school but also for our country.'

These dramatic words had us bolt upright in our chairs. What could Dr Keeleigh mean? He saw he had captured our rapt attention and continued: 'Tomorrow, gentlemen, a very special new pupil starts at St Lionel's. Now we are not talking about the usual case of an eleven-year-old boy who would begin his life here in the First Form. Firstly, this new chap is sixteen years old and will start his schooling in your year. Secondly, this new chap is an Indian. His name is Prince Salman and he is the eldest son of the Rajah of Lockshenstan, a land of vital strategic importance on the North West Frontier. The Prince's father is an important ally in our fight against the Afghan irregulars and those agents of other European powers who would like nothing better than to see our position on the Indian sub-continent destabilised.

'I will let you boys into a confidence. Our government has persuaded the Rajah to let Salman be educated in the Mother Country. Previously he was educated privated by British tutors in the Rajah's palace so he speaks English perfectly. We have been honoured that on the advice of the Viceroy of India himself, the Rajah has chosen to send his son to St Lionel's. I would not be surprised if the Rajah knows of your father, Mountjoy. You lived in Delhi for some years as a young boy, if I remember rightly.

'What I want you boys to do for me is to take Prince Salman under your wing He has been to England several times and so he will not find life here totally strange. Show him the ropes and keep him out of trouble This should not pose too many problems because he is a studious boy and I am sure he will fit in well '

'We'll be happy to help out, sir,' I said. 'May I ask a question though? What do we call him: Your Highness, Prince Salman or what?'

The headmaster beamed and said: 'An excellent question, Mountjoy. I think the best solution is that he should be known as "Prince" to staff and boys alike. He will be at the school just before luncheon tomorrow and I will call you up here as soon as he arrives. Any further questions?'

'No, sir!' we chorused and Dr Keeleigh waved us away. 'Good lads, I will rely on you. I've already informed the teaching staff about all this but you must feel free to speak to me in confidence about any problem that might arise.'

After tea, our form was ordered into a classroom to hear 'an important address' by the school chaplain, the Reverend Percy Clarke, the contents of which was known to us even before he marched into the room. Looking back, I think it probable that the Reverend Percy was himself a closet arse-bandit [*a common Edwardian term for a homosexual – Editor*] for he liked nothing better than to question boys about whether they ever had wet dreams, whether they ever fantasised about naked women, whether they had ever experienced erections and whether they ever played with themselves. Of course, everyone denied everything (though in practice the true answer to any of his queries would have been in the affirmative for almost every boy!). But after a dare, one fifth former confessed to all of these 'sins' and was promptly ordered to dip his cock into cold water first thing in the morning and last thing at night!

So we knew what to expect when he cleared his throat and began droning on about the evils of 'the solitary vice'. 'Beware of this insidious disease which is the work of the devil,' he trumpeted. 'It cheats semen getting its full chance of making up the strong, manly chap you would otherwise be. Do not be tempted to throw away the seed that has been handed down to you as a sacred trust instead of keeping it and ripening it for bringing a son to you when you are fully matured.

'My advice to you all is this. Whenever you feel the impure urge coming on, say a prayer such as "Oh God, give me strength to resist the evil afflicting my body." I also recommend cold baths and long walks to help save yourself from this terrible scourge.'

'A final warning to you all – many of our finest doctors have written that, as surely as night follows day, self-abuse will lead to weak eye-sight, poor hearing and even insanity in later life. [*Unbelievable as this sounds to modern readers, Reverend Clarke was hardly exaggerating. It was only until after the Great War that medical opinion stopped preaching that masturbation was immoral because it wasted valuable sperm needed to make healthy babies! – Editor.*] So take heed and make a promise to yourselves that you will resist the forces of darkness.'

He burbled on for a few more minutes and Harry Price-Bailey, an athletic fellow and a good friend of both Frank and myself, grunted: 'I suppose that will keep us from pulling our puds for at least five minutes!'

For several years after I left St Lionel's I was especially cross with Dr Keeleigh for letting this clerical lunatic fill the minds of ignorant boys with such nonsense and I don't care who says anything to the contrary, I'm damned sure that a five-knuckle shuffle never harmed anyone I rest my case on no other grounds that if Reverend Clarke's view was correct, there'd be a bloody big demand for glasses and hearing-trumpets, that's for sure!

Any notice that might have been taken of the chaplain's words had gone by the evening, for that night, after lights out in the dormitory, Frank and I told our form-mates all about the excitements of our holiday. As we expounded in graphic detail about the several ways we had fucked Diana, Cecily, Sally and Polly, the lot of us soon sported gigantic hard-ons including Frank and myself! Within a minute, all the boys brought out their pricks and tossed themselves off, Frank and myself included. The experience was hardly unpleasant but since I had tasted the joys of a genuine fuck, I found that taking oneself in hand is fine as far as it goes but is only the first step on the road to sexual fulfilment.

I woke with the dawn the next morning and decided to go for an early morning run round Blodgett's Field, where football and cricket fixtures were played against other schools. Running before breakfast was a practice encouraged by Dr

Keeleigh but not to excess for it was banned during the winter months I rummaged through my locker and put on my athletic vest and shorts and went down the stairs as quietly as possible as I did not wish to wake up others who were still asleep. As I made my way out towards the front door I heard two of the servant girls who came in daily from the nearby village talking I recognised the dulcet tones of Melanie, perhaps the prettiest and certainly the girl who was most often drooled over by the older boys It was rumoured that she had gone for a walk with Claridge of the Modern Sixth Senior who had boasted that she had let him slide his hand inside her blouse But most of us, perhaps from envy, did not believe him!

I strained my ears and heard Melanie say: 'Yes, Dolly, so there we were, just the two of us in the changing room Well, I didn't know at first that Geoffrey had gone in to take a shower, I thought the place was empty.'

'My, my, so it's Geoffrey now, is it,' said Dolly, her companion, with a laugh 'It's plain Mister Ormondroyd to the likes of me and the rest of the girls!' My heart missed a beat – they were talking about my history master, a young man who had recently joined the school after leaving University. He had obtained his post at St Lionel's because Dr Keeleigh was always keen to keep a balance in the staff between youth and experience.

'Oh, go on with you,' said Melanie. 'Do you want to hear what happened or not? Yes? Well, I went in and heard Geoffrey singing in the shower I decided to stay around, especially when I saw his clothes lying in a heap on the floor. I peeped into the shower room and I saw him standing with his back to me under the shower, turning himself slowly round under the water jets, massaging the soap into his muscular body. What a fine figure of a man he is, Dolly, such a broad chest and such pinchable firm bum cheeks! When he turned round to the front I could take a long hard look at his big cock and it was so exciting when he soaped his shaft and it bounced up in his hand into the stiffest white truncheon you could ever wish to see! I don't mind telling you that my pussey started to dampen and I put down my mop and slipped my hand inside my blouse to rub my titties, which were already tingling unbearably as Geoffrey played with his prick, not knowing that an eager pair of eyes was watching his every move!

'So what did you do about it?' prompted Dolly, laughing lewdly as she sat down on the stairs to hear the end of the anecdote

'What do you think!' retorted Melanie, sitting down beside her. 'I went back to the changing room and bolted the door. Then I took off my blouse and skirt and stood there with just my knickers on waiting for Geoffrey to come out. I didn't have to wait long and he was even more ready for action than I was, being stark naked except for a towel with which he was wiping his face. His cock looked heavy and juicy, swinging between his thighs so he couldn't have brought himself off in the shower, I thought to myself, which would help things along.

' "My God, Melanie, how did you get in here?" he gasped, hastily draping the towel round his waist.

"I wondered if I might have some private instruction in indoor games." I said boldly, stepping towards him and pushing my body up against his I could feel his prick rising as I reached down and pulled down the towel, letting his swollen tool jump up to stand high against his tummy. I put my hands on his shoulders and pushed them downwards. He made no resistance as we sank to the floor and I thrust my titties in his face. He sucked them up marvellously as I clasped his massive cock and began to wank him. He then worked his hands inside my knickers and rubbed my pussey with the flat of his hand before he pulled down my knickers. Then he did something that's never happened to me before he leaned down and pushed my knickers over my ankles and then screwed them up in his hand and began rubbing the bundle against my soaking pussey! He made a sheath for his finger with the wet knickers and frigged my cunney with it. He wiggled his finger to the hilt until my knicks were saturated with my love juice. Then he eased them off his finger and frigged me with his bare fingers.

'So I wriggled myself around to bring my face up to his throbbing prick. I popped my lips over the crown of his cock and curled my tongue around his helmet, licking away whilst I cupped his tight ballsack. But I wanted him to fuck me so I only tongued the tip of his knob before lying down on my back. "Push that big dick in my cunt," I said and he didn't need asking twice! He slipped that fat bulb in my cunney. I came straightaway and could feel the juice running out of me, clinging to my pussey hairs as his cock crashed through my love channel. He kept ramming his well-greased tool until we were both screaming in delight until he filled me with his sticky spunk. We lay together and his shaft stayed hard inside me as I felt his sperm trickle out of my cunt and down over my thighs. I would have liked to have continued but it was neither the time nor the place. I had to finish my work and Geoffrey was the duty master at breakfast so we both went into the shower to refresh ourselves and got dressed again as quickly as we could '

'Are you going to see Mr Ormondroyd, oh, sorry, I mean Geoffrey, again?'

'I should say so! We've arranged to meet in his study tomorrow night at ten o'clock, I can't wait, Dolly! It's been three months since I've had a good fuck!'

I waited for the two girls to walk away before continuing my descent. Melanie's story had given me a huge stiffstander but I took Reverend Clark's advice and went for a brisk early-morning job instead of finishing myself off with a five-knuckle shuffle. It wasn't the chaplain and his dire warnings of perdition that stopped me relieving my feelings in the time-honoured fashion, but rather a gut feeling that somehow, somewhere, I was going to be involved in fucking. Since I was a small boy, my father had always told me to trust my instincts. I did so now, despite the total lack of credible evidence that might point to such a happy state of affairs. As it happens, such trust was not to be misplaced – though I would never have guessed in a million years just how such serendipity between fantasy and reality would be achieved!

I did, however, have to wait until the next day

for my dream to be realised. It all started when, as he had promised, Dr Keeleigh called Frank and myself to his study just before luncheon to meet Prince Salman – or, as the headmaster added, Salman Prince as he would be known at St Lionel's.

I liked the look of Salman from the moment we met – he was a tall, powerfully built chap with a firm handshake. 'Good to meet you, Mountjoy, and you too Folkestone,' he called cheerily. 'I hope I won't be a burden and I'm really grateful if you'll show me the ropes.'

At this point there was a tap on the door and, of all people, Melanie came in. 'You wanted to see me, sir,' she said and Dr Keeleigh asked her to show Salman where the laundry was situated, to explain how the household facilities of the school were run, and to take him back to the Fourth Form Common Room afterwards.

After they left Dr Keeleigh sat down in his superb red leather chair (donated a few years back by the Old Lionelsians on his fiftieth birthday) and said: 'There is just one further matter about which I want to speak to you. There may be, amongst some of the more vulgar of your form-mates or indeed other boys, a feeling of prejudice against our Indian Prince on the grounds of the colour of his skin. Any such foolishness is abhorrent in my eyes and in fact amongst the very highest in the land. "Mislike me not for my complexion" says the Moor in *The Merchant Of Venice* and it is an unfortunate fact that there will be those who may wish to make sneering remarks about Prince behind his back. If this happens, I want you to remind the offender that no less a person than His Majesty The King himself on a visit to India twenty five years ago berated some officials of the East India Company who spoke disparagingly about the natives. He told them that because man has a dark skin there is no reason why he should be treated like a brute.'

'Very good sir, but suppose someone says something out of place directly to the Prince himself?' ventured Frank.

A rare twinkled appeared in Dr Keeleigh's eyes. 'Ah, I don't think that will happen more than once,' he chuckled. 'I don't intend to broadcast the fact that Salman has taken lessons in fisticuffs from Harry Willoughby, the professional middle-weight boxing champion. He showed himself to be a willing pupil! I would rather wish you boys kept this information to yourselves and let anyone who tries to rag our new friend about his colour to find out for himself!'

After the last lesson of the day we took Salman to the study which he would share with Frank and myself. Coincidentally, we needed a third chap as our former studymate Nick Clee had left St Lionel's at the end of the summer term to join his parents in East Africa [*Rupert must surely be referring here to Major Colonel Sir Nicholas Clee VC, DSO, the High Commissioner of Kenya and Uganda from 1917 to 1929 – Editor*]

'I suppose this room must be a bit spartan after your father's palace,' said Frank as he busied himself with putting on the kettle for tea. 'And I bet you had something a darned sight tastier than bread and butter and a slice of cake for tea.'

'Yes, I was spoiled rotten,' agreed Salman. 'But

as it says in your Bible: "Better a dinner of herbs where love is, than a stalled ox and hatred therein." ' We looked at him in awe. 'Proverbs, Chapter 15, verse 17.' he added kindly.

'I thought you worshipped those funny statues with lots of arms and sacred cows and all that sort of thing.' I said.

'No, no, my dear Rupert, my family are Moslems and you are talking of Hinduism. I don't know too much about their religion except that the cow is regarded as a symbol of Mother Earth which is why the animal is sacred and many of my Hindu friends are vegetarians,' he explained 'Our holy book is the Koran though we do accept much of Jewish and Christian teaching.'

'Yes, we studied Mohammed and his teachings last term What I remember best is that men are allowed more than one wife, aren't they?' said Frank.

'If you're a glutton for punishment,' returned Salman with a smile. 'I think that like my father I shall settle for just one but keep a harem of concubines for pleasure.'

I licked my lips. 'When were you allowed to . . um –'

'Have my first woman?' said Salman, finishing the question for me. 'I had my first when I was thirteen. But that was quite unofficial and my father would have been furious, especially as the girl concerned was one of his favourites.' He paused and then, with a furrowed brow, he added in his perfect though slightly sing-song accented English: 'But since we're talking about this important subject, let me tell you that whilst I've been in England I have suffered from a grevious shortage of available bed-worthy females.

'But Miss Melanie, now, the girl who showed me round the school facilities before lunch, I would very much enjoy fucking her. My worry is that this might be against the rules of the school.'

Frank laughed out loudly. 'I don't see why, no-one's ever said anything against it. I would have thought a bigger worry was to persuade Melanie to come across.'

'Oh, that's no problem,' he said confidently.

'How do you know?' I demanded.

'Well, I've already asked her and she's coming here at half past eight this evening so we'll have an hour to enjoy ourselves before we have to go to bed.'

We stared at him in goggle-eyed astonishment. 'You asked her, just like that, if she wanted to be fucked and she immediately made an arrangement to see you tonight? My God, you're a fast worker. Perhaps your being a high-born foreign prince impressed her?'

But Salman shook his head. 'No, I don't really think so. I believe it is far more likely that she was impressed by my giving her half of this little piece of paper,' he commented, rummaging in his wallet to being out a carefully cut portion of a fifty pound note!

'Phew, I'll wager that Melanie hasn't seen too many of these,' I whistled. 'No, and I wonder if she's seen many of these either,' said Frank, giving his prick a suggestive circular rub with the palm of his hand.

'You don't think she is a virgin?' asked Salman anxiously.

'No, absolutely not,' I assured him firmly. I suddenly remembered that Melanie might have made an appointment with Salman this evening but that she had also made an assignation with Mr Ormondroyd for ten o'clock. 'She's no virgin, Salman,' I repeated and I told the boys what I had overheard on the stairs early this morning.

'Good,' said Salman with relief. 'I don't want any indignant fathers round here demanding that I marry their daughters and all that sort of nonsense. I shall enjoy myself tonight.'

We looked jealously at him as Frank poured the tea. 'Dash it, there's something else I'd better tell you,' he said.

'You've brought a girl from your dad's harem as well,' I sighed.

'No, no, old chap, it's about Melanie. I suggested that she bring two friends along tonight.'

'You jammy bugger!' grunted Frank enviously. 'Are you going to have three girls tonight?'

'I hope so,' he replied cheerfully. 'But my dear chaps, the other two ladies are primarily for your enjoyment '

'For us?' I exclaimed.

'Most certainly,' said Salman courteously. 'I do hope I haven't offended you but I thought we would have a little party to celebrate my arrival at St Lionel's and who better to ask than my two new friends. Of course, if you prefer not to indulge yourselves, do let me know.'

'Oh we wouldn't dream of letting you down, would we, Rupert?' said Frank. 'Salman, old boy, we'd love to take part – I can see that we three are going to get along very well indeed!'

It was difficult to keep our minds on our homework but we did our best until the dinner bell rang out. We bolted through our meal and were back in our study by eight o'clock. I must say that Salman was very cool about the whole affair, but Frank and I could hardly keep still as we were so excited at the thought of a big sex party. In the end Salman turned to us and said: 'I say, you fellows, why not sit down and relax. The girls won't be here for another half an hour. Use the time like me to relax your mind and body. You'll be in much better shape if you can try a spot of meditation.'

We followed his advice but in my mind's eyes I could picture Melanie's large white breasts with the pink rosebud titties and I let myself drool about how I would run my hands over those gorgeous globes and then let them rove across her belly to that curly growth of cunney hair which curled in rich, dark locks in a triangle between her legs, tapering to a tantalising thinness where her pouting pussey lips would be waiting for my sturdy shaft.

Naturally, these lewd thoughts made my prick swell up as I sat in my armchair so I propelled the chair round with my bottom so that it faced away from the others. My cock was now pushing up uncomfortably in my lap so I unbuttoned my trousers to accommodate my stiffstander which stood proudly to attention as I capped and uncapped the bulging red knob in my hand.

I was so engrossed in this reverie that I did not notice Salman standing by me. 'I don't think Melanie and her friends will be disappointed by that rampant weapon,' he said admiringly.

'You should see Frank's, it's massive compared to mine,' I warned him.

'Bigger than this?' he asked and he took out his bulging brown tool out of his trousers. There was something different about his prick which at first I could not make out. But then when he began pulling his hand up and down his throbbing shaft I realised what was so strange about it – there was no foreskin to pull back from his bare knob!

My curiosity must have showed on my face for Salman enquired: 'Is something wrong?'

'No, no, it's just that I have never seen a prick like yours before,' I said hastily

Frank came across to look and Salman said, 'Oh yes, of course, neither of you can be circumcised. Did you not know that, like the Jews, followers of the Prophet have our foreskins removed when we are small?' [*Circumcision did not become fashionable in Britain until the 1930s when it was widely practiced amongst the upper classes. Since the 1960s it has lost much of its popularity in Europe although the operation is still very much favoured in America. It remains, of course, a fundamental observance even amongst secular Jews and Muslims – Editor.*]

Frank showed Salman his giant whopper and, to my chagrin, my old pal's penis again took the top honours! But then there was a knock on the door and we hastily crammed our pricks away. As it transpired, we need not have been too concerned for it was none other than Melanie, who had arrived a little early along with two girls who I had never seen before They turned out to be friends of hers from Lord Nutley's big country house which was only a mile or so away. 'These are my friends Lucy and Tricia,' said Melanie brightly, pointing to two very attractive young girls of about eighteen. Lucy was a full-figured female whose pert, pretty face was encircled by a mob of blonde curls whilst Tricia was of a dark complexion, more slender of figure but with well proportioned breasts which thrust proudly against her tight-fitting blouse. We introduced ourselves and Salman asked: 'May I offer you ladies a drink?'

'Thank you, that would be very nice,' said Melanie and I watched in amazement as the hospitable Indian produced a bottle of brandy from his locker.

'I'm sorry there's no champagne,' he apologised, 'but we don't yet have an ice-box in our study. Rupert, remind me to ask Dr Keeleigh tomorrow if I can have one sent in.'

He poured generous measures for all of us though he abstained (his religion forbidding the consumption of alcohol). We polished off the bottle between us without his help! This loosened any inhibitions and we were soon paired off, each boy sitting in an armchair with a girl on his knee. Frank had made a beeline for Tricia from the very beginning of these proceedings and Melanie was cuddling up closely to Salman, which left me with my arms around Lucy, a fate I happily succumbed to as, though I would not have spurned any of these fine women, Lucy would have been my prick's first choice!

'This new electric light is much too bright,' complained Melanie with a pretended petulance. 'Who'll be a good boy and turn it off?' Frank

203

nobly volunteered and I called out quietly:

'And while you're there, turn the key in the lock, old chap.'

There was still enough light coming in from the corridor for us to see what we were about – and as soon as Frank settled down in the armchair all three couples began to snog passionately I was too busy engaging in a burning kiss with Lucy to see what the others were doing but I could see that Melanie was already half-naked, her discarded blouse by Salman's feet. When I removed Lucy's top I discovered to my delight that she was not wearing anything underneath it. So I cupped her lovely bare breasts in my hands as our tongues frantically searched each other's mouths until I thought my poor straining cock would burst! But then this delicious girl slipped from my arms and, standing in front of me, she kicked off her shoes and undid her skirt, letting it fall to the ground. She peeled off her brief white panties and in no time at all stood there fully nude, obviously enjoying to the full the way I was goggling at her beauty. She caressed her own heavy breasts with their dark raised nipples and stood directly in front of me so that her curly blonde bush was staring me full in the face. I kissed the snowy plain of her belly and then ran my lips lower, through the strands of her silky thatch. My hands circled round her glorious buttocks as I buried my head between her thighs and drew her against me. My tongue crept down her slit which was nice and moist. More by luck than judgement (for remember, dear reader, just how inexperienced I was at this age) I found her clitty almost at once and Lucy gasped as I found her magic button and started to roll my tongue around the erectile piece of flesh.

'Aaaah, that's lovely, you've made me spend already,' she moaned quietly. 'But now let me see what you have between your legs to offer me, as you're much younger than my boyfriend.' She expertly unbuttoned my flies and my naked penis sprung out to pay its respects. She wanked my cock with an amused look on her face and her wet, pink tongue flicked out to lick her lips. 'You're better endowed than I expected,' she admitted as she rubbed her hands round my pulsating prick. Then she bent down on her knees and encircled the tip of my helmet with her lips which made me groan with delight.

'Be quiet, you two, we don't want to be disturbed by any visitors,' hissed Frank so I gritted my teeth and leaned back in my chair as Lucy started to suck my knob lustily, licking and lapping as her soft fingers tickled my balls. She moved her lips and tongue up and down, each time taking more of my tool into her throat. This excited my prick so much that all I could do was to hiss out the first words of warning as I shot my hot spunky jism into the back of her throat. I withdrew my still swollen cock from her mouth and she took hold of it in her hand again as she jumped onto my lap. We peered across in the dim light and I could see that Melanie and Salman had wasted no time – she had leaned over the arm of their chair and Salman was fucking her doggie-style, whipping his thick brown prick into the glistening moist crack of her cunt from behind and slapping her bum cheeks lightly with every thrust forwards as he jerked his hips to and fro.

'Oh, what joy! Oh, what bliss!' cried Salman as he happily pushed his prick in and out of Melanie's squelchy slit. He held her round the waist until he was completely embedded and then shifted his hand round to fondle her superbly uptilted breasts, rubbing the pink titties until they were as erect as his cock which was nestling in her juicy cunt. His entire body quivered as he withdrew almost fully before pushing home, sheathing his cock so fully at each stroke that his balls banged against her rounded little bum cheeks. Melanie turned her head and waggled her backside. 'Harder! Fuck me harder!' she whispered fiercely. 'I'm coming, oh, I'm coming, oh, oh, OH' and she let out a screech of ecstacy as she shuddered to her climax. As she spurted her love juices Salman sent spouts of spunk flooding into her cunney, while he gave her lovely bum cheeks a final smack. He stayed still, however, with his cock still enclosed in her sopping crack.

'My, your prick's still nice and stiff. Can you carry on?' said Melanie hopefully.

'Certainly I can,' said Salman and he began gently to pull his gleaming shaft out from between her bum cheeks. His cock was still rock hard and he started to fuck Melanie more slowly this time. As Lucy rubbed up my own stiff staff, we turned our attention to Frank and Tricia. They were kissing rapturously and Frank had taken off all of her clothes, giving us an excellent view of Tricia's exquisite young breasts which were lusciously rounded, as white as alabaster and capped with superbly fashioned hard tawny nipples which were surrounded by large circled aureoles. 'Kiss my titties, Frank, they adore being made love to,' panted the adorable girl and Frank wasted no further time. He licked and nipped those lovely rubbery raspberries, running his hands along her thighs. The trembling girl turned sideways so that Frank could insert his hands between her legs and explore her pussey, which was thatched with a delicate covering of jet black hair. She moved across and over him so that her pussey was above his face as she lowered her head to kiss his throbbing tool. Her soft hands caressed his heavy balls as with a sensual slowness she slicked her tongue up and down the length of his thick shaft, taking her time to reach the red mushroomed helmet which was twitching frantically as she finally coated it with the tip of her pink tongue. Then she suddenly engulfed his shining knob, sliding down his foreskin and gobbling greedily on her fleshy lollipop.

Frank's tongue was now pressed against her pussey and he licked at her dripping crack, moving around the outer lips and gently slipping his tongue inside the rolled lips until the juices flowed into his open mouth.

My own cock was now quivering with unrequited lust but (as she told me later) though she would have loved me to fuck her again, Lucy kindly decided to offer my tool to Tricia who loved threesomes but rarely had the opportunity to indulge herself.

Lucy murmured: 'Why don't you fuck Tricia's bottom, Rupert? I know she'd really enjoy that very much.' I hesitated for a moment but the sweet girl pulled me up by my cock and brought me round to the armchair where Tricia was sucking Frank's cock whilst he licked out her cunney. She had one leg over the chair and the other over Frank and the firm, curvaceous cheeks of her bum were spread out deliciously, giving me an excellent view of her wrinkled brown rear dimple. Lucy released my cock to bring forward the chair from my desk which I knelt upon to enable me to lean over Tricia and wedge my cock between her glorious buttocks. Then the thoughtful girl pulled me back and washed my knob with saliva before taking hold of my shaft and aiming my knob at Tricia's winking little rosette which beckoned me so alluringly. She eased my glowing crown between those gorgeous bottom cheeks which I fairly ached to split with my iron hard cock. Her work soon achieved the desired effect. My shaft enveloped itself beautifully between the rolling buttocks until it was fully ensconced in her warm, tight bum and I leaned over Tricia's gleaming body to play with her luscious breasts.

I worked in and out of her arse very slowly at first but then, as Tricia artfully waggled her bottom provocatively, at a faster pace, pushing my entire body backwards and forwards, making Tricia's divinely proportioned bum cheeks slap loudly against my belly. I screwed up my eyes in sheer bliss but opened them again with a gasp as I felt Lucy's hands pressing against my thighs. The lewd sight of Tricia's cunney and bottom being pleasured at the same time had fired Lucy so intensely that she now knelt behind me and thrust her head between my legs. She took my ballsack into her mouth, moving her head in time with my thrusts.

Salman and Melanie now joined us and I turned round to see the young prince position himself on his back so that his head was directly underneath Lucy's cunt. She raised herself to accommodate him and then with a squeal of joy lowered her enticing golden cunney onto his lips and he noisily nuzzled into her golden honeypot, flicking his tongue into the soft folds of her juicy pussey. Melanie was now down on her knees beside them and straddling his body, holding open her pink cunney lips as she sat firmly upon his stiff penis, sitting with her luscious buttocks towards him while she rode up and down his delighted pole. Salman grasped her bottom cheeks with both hands and squeezed them rhythmically as she pushed up and down, contracting her powerful pussey muscles with every downwards movement, to their joint delight. At the same time she reached between his legs and took his balls in her hand and began to jiggle them, scraping the hairy sack with the fingernails until Salman was crooning with delight

This was my first multiple fuck and I must confess that it was most stimulating to see all those fine cocks and cunnies in action. All three of us boys came closely together, Frank jetting his spunk into Tricia's mouth whilst I spurted my sperm into her bottom and Salman sent up a stream of jism into Melanie's cunt. The girls, too, all achieved copious climaxes, especially Lucy whose love juices poured into Salman's mouth as he swallowed her tangy spendings.

There was just time for one more fucking chain.

This time Melanie sucked me off whilst Frank fucked her as he lapped at Lucy's titties whilst Salman was diddling her pussey at the same time as he plunged his prick into Tricia's sopping cunt, with Tricia completing the circle by finger-fucking Melanie's bum. We would have liked to have changed positions for yet a further joust but it was approaching the time when Melanie had arranged to meet Mr Ormondroyd. So Salman passed the second half of the fifty pound note to Melanie with our grateful thanks as the girls began to dress.

'Thank you very much,' panted Melanie as she buttoned up her skirt, 'we must do this again next week. And this time, you don't have to bring your wallet. It's been a pleasure to fuck with such vigorous young gentlemen, hasn't it, girls?'

'I should say so,' echoed Tricia. 'It would be grand to spend the night together, wouldn't it?' Lucy agreed and said she was free any night next week and that we could use her cousin Amanda's house as her parents would be away. 'You'll have to find another boy for her, of course, but I'm sure that can be easily arranged.'

'No problems there,' said Frank cheerily and we kissed the girls good-night. We were in the dormitory spot on time at ten o'clock but perhaps I was over-fatigued by all the fucking for I simply could not get to sleep. So I quietly got out of bed and slipped on my dressing gown to fetch a book from our study. Like many other boys, I also had a torch which I used to read in the dark.

I kept the study in darkness as I searched the bookshelves for it was strictly against the rules to leave the dormitory after lights out. I found the book I was looking for, a ripping adventure story by Tom Shackleton, my favourite author, when I was startled by the opening of the door. I spun round with a gasp to see the figure of Melanie framed in the door.

'Gosh, you gave me a fright!' I said. She apologised and explained that she was missing a earring and hoped that one of us might have discovered it on the floor. 'I'm afraid not,' I said quietly. 'I wouldn't mind helping you to look for it now but I'm not supposed to be here so I can't put on the light.'

'Never mind, it wasn't a very expensive one and perhaps you'll find it in the morning. But what are you doing here anyway?'

I explained how I could not sleep and Melanie said: 'Well, Mr Ormondroyd won't be coming round looking for you, that's for sure. I've left him fast asleep in his bed!'

'Is he good between the sheets?' I asked.

'Oh yes, I've no complaints but don't worry, you silly boy, I was more than satisfied with the way that you and your friends performed – especially the lad with that monster cock, what's his name, Frank Folkestone! Still, Geoffrey – that's Mr Ormondroyd – knows how to use his tackle. We wasted no time and as soon as I got to his room I sat on the bed, fondling his stiff cock through his trousers which he unbuttoned for me to let his tadger shoot out like a coil. He sat down beside me and worked his hand down to my muff which was already damp with all the spendings from you. He moved his fingers between the edges of my crack as we kissed and I wrapped my legs around his hand as I lowered my head to suck his cock.

' "Let's continue this in bed,' he said and so we undressed and snuggled up together. As we embraced I felt his hard tool press against my tummy and then he rolled me over on to my back and pressed his helmet through my pussey lips. I was really enjoying myself as with a deep groan he thrust his strong shaft straight in and his balls slapped against my bum. I lifted my bottom up to get as much of him inside me as possible. I wrapped my legs round his back and clawed his shoulders with my fingernails as he started to pump his rod in and out of my squishy pussey. It took only a few strokes before I was twisting away like crazy. His cock seemed to swell inside my cunney and I spent first, soaking his shaft with my juices. Then I felt his whole frame shiver and he flooded my cunt with a spurt of hot spunk so huge that I could imagine it splashing against the rear walls of my love box. There was so much jism that my thighs were lathered as he pulled out his cock and rubbed it in my sticky cunney hair.

'He rolled off me, heaving and panting with exhaustion and said: "What a succulent little cunney you have there, Melanie It sucked in my cock so sweetly that I'm spoiled now for any other." '

'You should think yourself honoured! He never compliments anyone in class, and I don't think he has much of a sense of humour,' I said with a gloomy laugh.

'Oh I don't know about that,' said Melanie, who somehow now found herself in my arms in one of the armchairs we had used for our escapade earlier in the evening. 'I said to him that

I had to really stretch my legs to accommodate thick pricks like his and do you know what he said? "Don't complain, Melanie – have you heard the rhyme about the girl who was worried about that? No? Well it goes like this:

> There was a young lady from Harrow,
> Who complained that her crack was too narrow,
> For times without number,
> She'd use a cucumber,
> But could never accomplish a marrow."

'And it was just after he'd finished reciting this poem when something quite extraordinary happened ..'

[TO BE CONTINUED]

VOLUME II

Introduction

FROM THE MIDDLE OF THE NINETEENTH century to approximately one hundred years later sexuality was a taboo subject in Britain.

Whilst the upper classes paid only lip service to the strict and often unpleasantly hypocritical morality urged upon the populace by the then powerful Church and all other organs of the Established order, the world of our great grandparents was one in which an astonishingly high number of people lived in ignorance, their natural feelings numbed and inhibited as Society successfully established stringent control over this area of their lives.

Working class adolescents learned what little they knew from their peers at school or at work, though as Dr Steve Humphries commented pithily in his fascinating book *A Secret World Of Sex: The British Experience 1900-1950*: 'Young people, from whatever background, generally taught each other about the facts of life – though there were strenuous efforts by adults to control their knowledge and keep them in ignorance ... moral reformers constantly complained that poor children knew too much for their own good.

217

Better-off parents usually exerted greater control over their children's sexual knowledge and development. If a boy or – even more worrying – a girl from a well-to-do background indulged in this kind of sexual experimentation, the parents would usually intervene very rapidly to put an end to it.'

However, in wealthy houses, boys were often not actively discouraged from enjoying their first sexual lessons from female servants, though of course any untoward consequences usually resulted in the girl being thrown out of the door to fend for herself. Often their own families were no less harsh, rejecting their 'wicked' daughters who ended up in either the local workhouse or one of the bleak, spartan homes run by such organisations as the Salvation Army. No doubt, several girls preferred to swell the throngs of 'unfortunates' who crowded the streets of London and other major cities.

Yet is has always been the self-imposed duty of the upper and middle classes to protect the lower orders from their own base instincts. But human nature cannot be denied and recent republication of late Victorian underground erotic novellas such as *The Intimate Memoir of Dame Jenny Everleigh* show that under the all-enveloping public respectability of the age, there was another world peopled by high-spirited consenting adults who revelled in sexual enjoyments.

By the turn of the century, basic adult literacy had almost been fully achieved and amongst the most popular entertainments for young Edwardian men was the 'horn' book, of which

Rupert Mountjoy's salacious autobiography is a typical example. Not only did such books provide sexual stimulation, but they preached a gospel that sexual activity was to be enjoyed, and in addition they provided valuable instruction in sexual techniques and thus offered a platform of resistance to the suffocating guilt-ridden climate in which they originally appeared.

Professor Warwick Jackson gives a thumbnail sketch of Rupert Mountjoy's interesting life in his introduction to the first book of these memoirs: *An Edwardian Dandy 1: Youthful Scandals*, which was published earlier this year. Suffice it to say here that our author enjoyed a typically sybaritic lifestyle of a wealthy young gentleman around the turn of the century, and his many tales of intimate intrigue, clandestine affairs and all the many thrills of lust were further enhanced for himself and his contemporary readers by the spice of prohibition.

These diaries were first published (illicitly, of course, as the explicit, uncensored writing is bawdy even by modern liberal standards) just before the outbreak of World War One, in 1913. Rupert certainly took part in a wide variety of sexual adventures about which he writes with a liveliness which distinguishes his work from certain pale imitators and shows how much he enjoyed his many erotic escapades as he and his friends, male and female, discarded the constraining yoke of the manners and mores of the Edwardian Establishment.

As Rupert Mountjoy himself wrote in 1909 to Heather O'Fluffert, one of the trio of writers who

219

composed the multi-volume *The Intimate Memoir Of Dame Jenny Everleigh* (now also available in a series of paperbacks from Warner Books): 'All animals copulate but only man is capable of extending a physical need into an act of love. This ability sets mankind apart from the lower species, although it is surely a most unfortunate fact that far too few of us recognise and develop this unique talent with which we have all been blessed.

'So many people are being hindered by the lack of open exploration of sexual matters and are cursed by the innate, often hypocritical, prudery in Society that the merest discussion of a morality based upon more reasonable precepts is forbidden. At least there are some of us who strive to formulate a set of ethical principles for the twentieth century that will be based upon a saner understanding of our own natural desires.'

Happily, the original manuscript of Rupert Mountjoy's memoirs was recently discovered and this has afforded us the opportunity to relive his amorous adventures that show to the modern reader a very different side to the starched picture of life in Great Britain some one hundred years ago.

Kevin Plymouth
Ipswich
August,1992

Green grow the rushes O,
Green grow the rushes O:
The sweetest hours that e'er I spent,
Were spent among the lasses O!

ROBERT BURNS
(1759-1796)

CHAPTER ONE

A Freshman's Tale

'HERE'S A LITTLE TRICK WHICH WILL amuse the ladies at your party tonight,' said Barry Jacobs, a fellow undergraduate I met during my second week of the Varsity when we were both chosen to play football for the college team on the strength that we had both captained our school elevens at soccer. He was a clever chap and though our life paths took very different directions after leaving Oxford, Barry and I have remained close personal chums. 'Do you have a pencil and paper to hand?

'Listen carefully now, Rupert – take your age and double it; then add five. Right? Now, think of any number between one and ninety-nine; and now take away the number of days in a year. Finally, add one hundred and fifteen and divide by one hundred. Now see where the decimal point comes. Your age will be to the left of it and the number between one and ninety-nine that you chose will be to the right of it! Isn't that amazing?'*

---

*Alas, this party trick does not seem to work! – Editor.

But dear readers, I feel that I am in too much haste in beginning these recollections of my splendid years spent 'twixt the dreaming spires of the internationally famous University of Oxford, in the heart of England's green and pleasant land. For those of you who have yet to read of my early exploits in the grand *l'arte de faire l'amour* I had best swiftly sketch the bare details of my life so far. [*Rupert Mountjoy's first amorous adventures were republished for the first time in uncensored, explicit form in* An Edwardian Dandy 1: Youthful Scandals – *Editor*].

Although my family seat is in Yorkshire, I attended boarding school down in Sussex at St Lionel's Academy For the Sons Of Gentlefolk. I was initiated into the joys of sensuality, however, by Diana Wigmore, the beautiful daughter of a neighbour and my friend Frank Folkestone (who also crossed the Rubicon during that never-to-be-forgotten summer holiday) and I enjoyed further liaisons at school with Prince Salman of Lockshenstan. Salman, the son of a fabulously wealthy maharajah, liked nothing better than to fuck himself into a stupor at any and every opportunity and the girls of the nearby village queued up to receive his spunky libations and twenty pound notes which he generously distributed to his female companions.

Nevertheless, all play and no work is a recipe for disaster as Dr Keeleigh, our dear old headmaster used to say, and Salman took his wise words to heart. My Indian pal was a diligent scholar and I was sorry that he did not accept the place offered him at University College, Oxford but preferred to continue his scientific studies at Trinity College, Cambridge. However, we did keep in touch from time to time as will be recorded in this narrative.

My other inseparable schoolfellow was Frank Folkestone and to our mutual delight we were both accepted by Balliol College to study law. Our rooms were on the same landing in college which pleased us both and, as will be noted, this arrangement proved to be extremely convenient for, how shall I best put it, our often joint extra mural activities.

Hopefully this will set the scene for you, dear reader. Let us now return to a pleasant day in early October, 1899. I was walking down St Cross Road with Barry Jacobs after we had taken part in an hour's training for the football match against Brasenose College to be played on the following Saturday. It had been a dry, warm summer and the weather had yet to turn cold and walking slowly away from the playing fields I felt at peace with the world. In the quiet lane I thought I could hear some conkers falling and I noticed that the ash-keys were turning gold along with a few adjacent leaves – but all other leaves on the ash-tree boughs were still green. Barry had also been affected by the beauty of our surroundings and he exclaimed: 'We're really lucky chaps to be at Oxford, aren't we Rupert? How did the poet put it:

Towery city and branchy between towers;
Cuckoo-echoing, bell swarmed, lark-charmed, rook-
*   racked, river rounded;*
The dapple-eared lily below thee; . . .

'Very well said – especially coming from a mathematics scholar!' I joked, 'but frankly I'm thinking of a more down-to-earth matter. I've been invited to a reception this evening given by Doctor Nicholas Blayers at Jesus College. He's a cousin of the headmaster at my old school and probably the most radically minded senior tutor in the entire University. He believes in mixed colleges with boys and girls studying together. Now you know how resistant most Oxonians were to the idea of women being admitted at all and how today their colleges are strictly out of bounds to us.

'Well, because he believes (and quite rightly in my opinion) that undergraduates of both sexes should mix freely without undue hindrance, at his own expense Doctor Blayers is throwing a party for a group of first year female students from Somerville College and a similar number of male freshmen. Now I happen to know that several of these girls have come to Oxford from Trippett's Academy For The Daughters Of Gentlefolk down in the West Country. This is a school run by Dame Agatha Humphrey, the famous champion of higher education for women and frankly, I'm more than a little apprehensive about meeting sophisticated young ladies from there. You attended a day school in London and I doubt whether you can appreciate what a sheltered life one has to live even at a progressive English boarding school like St Lionel's.'

Barry looked at me in some astonishment. 'What on earth have you to be scared about? What a marvellous chance you have to meet some girls – gosh, Rupert, I wish I had been given an invitation to such a spiffing party. I just can't imagine any problem or are you just very shy?'

'Yes, I suppose I am,' I admitted, for with the exception of my initiation into the joys of fucking by Diana and her friend Cecily, along with some uninhibited horseplay with some housemaids at St Lionel's with Frank and Salman, I had little to no experience of social intercourse with the female sex. 'I'm worried that I will find myself quite tongue-tied. How do I continue a conversation with a girl after enquiring about the state of the weather? To be honest, I'm uncertain about what to say next!'

'Now this can often be a thorny problem for boys,' admitted Barry as we trudged along. 'It has to be said that girls are not usually interested in current affairs (except those of an intimate nature!), sport or other masculine pursuits, and we are hardly enraptured by feminine chit-chat. Also, they have been told by their mamas that they must not be too forward in the initiation of conversation with young men and should only speak when spoken to – so this makes the situation even more difficult.

'My solution is to try your luck with subjects such as the weather, gardening, food, the latest plays or the current exhibition at the Royal Academy. This usually works although, of course, I cannot give you a cast-iron guarantee of success. However, just before I came up to Oxford my uncle, Sir Lewis Osborne, invited me to a splendid dinner-party to celebrate the eighteenth birthday of my cousin Philippa. I was sitting next to an extremely attractive girl named Adrienne and I tried my best to impress her with some smart, sophisticated conversation. In vain I went through all the subjects I have just mentioned but I couldn't raise the slightest glimmer of interest. I even tried talking about the magnificent dishes being served which were all strictly kosher [*prepared to Jewish dietary laws – Editor*] but she barely concealed her boredom and was even beginning to yawn.

'At this stage I was frankly ready to throw in the towel but just then a footman approached and handed me a note on a silver salver. "A message from your cousin Philippa, sir," he whispered into my ear. I opened it surreptitiously under the tablecloth and with difficulty deciphered Philippa's scrawl. She had written: *Try Votes For Women,* so I pocketed the scrap of paper and tackled Adrienne again. "What do you think of Mrs Pankhurst and the suffragettes?" I asked and *voila!* instantly into her lovely brown eyes leapt a bright gleam of genuine interest.

'Philippa had noticed how I was struggling and her kind message certainly did the trick for me. Adrienne was an ardent supporter of the emancipation of women and as I have never understood why women should be treated as second class citizens I could honestly put my hand on my heart and tell her that I agreed with every word she said. I told her of my father's letter on the subject which had been published a few weeks back in *The Daily Chronicle*. He had argued that women's suffrage would come once the present social, educational and economic changes now taking place had worked themselves through the system. The choice is not between going on and standing still, it is between advancing and retreating, he had written in his forceful conclusion.

' "Oh, so it was your Papa who wrote that letter," said Adrienne, now flashing a luscious smile at me. "How silly of me not to have realised that Leonard Jacobs was your Papa. I know of his reputation as a generous philanthropist and I am glad to hear that he holds progressive social views."

' "Like his son," I added with a twinkle in my eye and she squeezed my hand as she said: "I'm very glad to hear it." Well, from an unpromising start the evening could hardly have gone better. After dinner we sat and chatted and she even accepted a lift home in my hansom, sending her parents' carriage back, telling the coachman that she had made other arrangements. I escorted her to her front door and she invited me in for a night-cap.'

He paused and I said: 'Well go on, old boy, don't stop there. This sounds like a story with a jolly interesting ending!'

Barry laughed and said: 'Well, it does get a little spicy, Rupert, and I wouldn't want to offend your aesthetic sensibilities. Are you sure you want me to continue?'

'You'd better watch out for your own aesthetic sensibilities if you don't carry on!' I retorted, and so with a grin he continued the tale.

'Well, it was well past midnight when we arrived at her parents' house in Allendale Avenue. Everyone had retired and she told the footman who had waited up for her that he too could now go to bed. She poured out large cognacs which we sipped as we sat together on the sofa. "You know, Barry, it's funny that I did not realise that Leonard Jacobs was your father," she said thoughtfully, "but then we don't always know everything about our parents, do we? Why, only last week I discovered that my own Papa has a collection of sketches by poor Aubrey Beardsley. He has kept them under lock and key in the library but by chance I picked them up the other day. Would you like to see them?" [*Aubrey Beardsley (1872-1898) was a brilliant young illustrator best known for his distinctively stylised work and also for his explicitly rude drawings which scandalised London Society one hundred years ago – Editor*].

' "I certainly would, Adrienne," I said, and she brought over a folder from a bureau in the corner of the room. I opened it and the first picture was of two plump nuns lying naked on a bed working dildoes into their open cunnies. They were being watched by two monks peeping round the door who had thrown up their cassocks and pulled out their pricks, each tossing off the other as they looked upon the lascivious women playing with themselves. The next drawing really made my cock swell up. It showed a beautiful dark-haired girl seated on the lap of her lover. Both were nude and between her thighs you could see that her pussey was engorged with his swollen cockshaft. She had one hand round his neck and in the other she was cupping his hairy ballsack.

'It became quite obvious that Adrienne's blood had also been fired by sight of these erotic drawings. She pressed her thighs together and made no objection when my arm stole round her shoulders and she cuddled into my body as we looked at another illustration of this same couple, only this time the girl was kneeling between his legs, her bottom well stuck out and the furrow in between shown in loving detail. She was shown opening her lips in order to take the shiny knob of the young fellow's stiff lovestick inside her mouth. The next sketch showed her flat on her back with her legs wide open. Her handsome lover was balancing on his forearms above her and this time her cunney was engorged with the thick prick of her lover who had inserted his staff in to the very roots of his pubic hair.

'I could no longer contain my feelings and I burst out: "My God! Wouldn't I give anything to be in his place." I bit my lip as soon as I had uttered this heartfelt but uncouth plea. Surely she would recoil away in disgust! But to my surprise and absolute joy, Adrienne placed her hand directly on my straining cock. She unbuttoned my trousers and brought out my throbbing tool which she stroked gently with her hand, saying with a mischievous chuckle: "Yes, Barry, your pego confirms the truth of your last remark."

'Well, you don't look a gift horse in the mouth! I covered her lips with my own and instantly we were exchanging the most passionate, burning kiss. Our tongues fluttered in each other's mouths as I raised her dress and petticoats and she arched her back upwards to allow me to pull down her knickers as she tugged down my trousers and drawers to the floor. She continued to rub my cock in her hand as I played with her moistening pussey

231

which was daintily fringed with light brown hair and her cunney lips opened immediately when I inserted my finger between them. We continued to pet and I frigged her juicy cunt with two and then three fingers, faster and faster as I knew that the warm touch of her soft hand would very soon bring me off.

'I could now simply no longer control the tidal flow of jism which was boiling up in my balls. Adrienne sensed that I was about to spend, for with her other hand she quickly pulled down an antimacassar from the top of the sofa and placed the linen cloth on my thighs as she slicked her hand up and down my rigid rod. I began to pant and she felt my cock contract before I squirted my spout of spunk all over her hand. She came too, drenching my fingers with her love juices, but we used her knickers and the antimacassar to wipe up the traces of our escapade before I left shortly afterwards.'

'So you didn't get further than that?' I said, and the disappointment must have shown in my voice for Barry turned round and replied: 'Well, surely you don't think she'd let me fuck her, do you?'

'Why not? You'd be surprised how many girls are just as keen as you on fucking. Don't you listen to anyone who says they don't enjoy it as much as us.'

Barry looked at me and frowned. 'Are you telling me you've already had a woman, young Mountjoy? You lucky so-and-so. I've come pretty close on several occasions and we once employed a Welsh chambermaid named Gladys who sucked me off but I've never actually gone all the way.

Damn it, here am I telling you how to talk to girls and all the time you're way ahead of me!'

'I've just been very lucky,' I replied modestly and I swiftly recounted how I had surrendered my virginity to Diana Wigmore and of my subsequent successes with my pal Frank Folkestone, who Barry had already met at a Liberal Club reception for college freshmen. 'Look, Barry, I know how frustrated you must feel, never having been able to complete the journey, so to speak. Look, I've a splendid idea. Come with me to Doctor Blayers' party tonight. You'll be more than welcome, I'm sure, especially as Frank won't be able to come as he is suffering from a rotten head cold – and you'll make up the numbers.'

At first he demurred. 'That's very kind of you, Rupert, but I just can't barge into a party without being asked. I'm as shy as you when it comes to gate-crashing!'

'Look, if it will make you feel any better I'll ask Jackson to run over with a note to Doctor Blayers asking if you can come in Frank's place.'

He looked gratefully at me. 'Thanks, old boy, I'd much rather go with a proper invite.'

As soon as we arrived back at College I scribbled a quick letter and told the College messenger boy to wait for the reply. Then I strode across to Frank Folkestone's room to see if the poor chap was feeling any better. I didn't knock on the door in case he had fallen asleep and I opened the door very slowly and carefully so as not to disturb him. But though he had earlier told me that he was going to spend the rest of the afternoon trying to sleep off his cold, his bed was

233

empty, though the eiderdown had been thrown back and the bedclothes were ruffled. I was about to leave when suddenly I heard a low moan coming from behind the closed door of his bathroom. Oh dear, I hope Frank isn't feeling really ill, I thought as I marched across the room and flung open the bathroom door with a theatrical flourish.

I needn't have concerned myself! For there was Frank, sitting in the large bath of warm water – not moaning with pain but with passion for with him in the water was Nancy, our young maidservant, who was lathering his erect penis which stood up out of the water like the periscope of a submarine. They were so engrossed in their sexual play that they did not realise that I was there. Nancy got up on her knees and her succulent large breasts jiggled invitingly, which made my balls tingle and my prick stir in my pants. She now rinsed Frank's enormous erection with water and said: 'Now it looks really nice and clean, doesn't it? Let me see if it tastes as good as it looks.'

His eyes closed in ecstacy, Frank leaned back and arched his back up slightly as this time Nancy washed his shiny round knob with her slithering tongue as Frank cupped her big breasts in his hands. Well, the sight of this gorgeous creature holding Frank's shaft whilst she sucked his cock drove me wild and my fingers began to tear wildly at my trouser buttons so that I could release my own stiffstander, which was threatening to burst through the thin material of my flannels. My hand flew to my trusty tool and I wanked away frantically as Nancy now pulled out the plug. As the water level fell, I could see Frank snake out his right arm and plunge his fingers directly into her slippery pussey.

Nancy looked up at me through her half-open eyes which widened to their full extent as she gave a tiny scream. 'Oh, Frank, Frank, someone's come in!'

Frank woke up from his delightful reverie in alarm but as soon as he saw that the uninvited guest who had caught him *in flagrante delicto* was none other than his old chum from St Lionel's his face creased into a grin. 'Not to worry, Nancy, why, it's only Rupert Mountjoy. He and I are best pals and we do everything together. All for one and one for all and all that nonsense.'

She considered this for a moment and said: 'You do, do you? Well, in that case Rupert, why don't you stop rubbing your own cock and let me do it for you once Frank has fucked me with his tremendous tadger?' Here we go again, I thought, for readers of my earlier diaries will note how often I have had to grind my teeth whilst a girl hymns a paean of praise to Frank's gigantic member!

However, I proceeded to shed my clothes whilst Nancy and Frank climbed out of the bath and dried themselves with the huge bathtowels Frank's Mama, Lady Folkestone, had packed for him in his valise when he left home for the Varsity. Nancy and Frank now exchanged a series of slurping kisses and his hands massaged her breasts as her hips swayed in hypnotic rhythm. I cupped my hand over her hairy pussey, rubbing the exposed, erect clitty with my middle finger. But she pushed my hand aside to press in Frank's bulbous bell-end between her cunney lips. She

235

drew about two inches of his thick, meaty shaft inside her cunt and this was enough to drive her insane with desire. Arching her back, she raised herself on tiptoes, forcing more of his prick inside her as she grasped my own iron-hard rod in her right hand.

'I want more of this cock in me – all the way,' she groaned as his fat shaft slid out of her slippery pussey and flopped against her belly. Still holding my cock tightly in her fist, she turned her back to Frank and leaned over the bath, offering her chubby little bottom to him. He parted the peach-like bum cheeks and she turned round and said: 'Frank, don't go up my arse, there's a good boy. I'd be frightened that you'd rend me in two with that mighty tool of yours.'

'Have no fear – I'll only ream out your cunney,' assured Frank as he shoved his truncheon in the inviting cleft between her buttocks and entered her cunt from behind. Nancy pushed her hips back as he plunged his prick all the way into her sopping slit. I watched her hips rotate in a sensuous circular motion as she enjoyed this grand doggie-style fucking. I saw Frank's cock slew in and out of her hot, juicy cunt and Nancy's hand shot up and down my own boner which triggered off my orgasm and my cock unleashed a fountain of sticky white jism that arced across the bath and splashed against the wall. The lewd girl came at the same time as Frank, who sent a gush of warm spunk deep into her cunney, and she came with a full-throated scream of pleasure as her love juices flowed down her thighs.

'How about letting me fuck you now?' I asked

236

Nancy as, although my cock had lost some of its stiffness, my still enlarged shaft was still swinging heavily between my legs.

'I'd love to, Mister Rupert, but honestly I don't have the time. I'm late as it is and I've still got to clean up the bathroom,' she replied with what appeared to be genuine regret in her voice.

Naturally, after we dressed ourselves we helped Nancy finish her work and I saw Frank slip a sovereign in her hand as she left the room. 'She didn't ask for anything,' he explained as the door closed behind her, 'but yesterday Nancy told me about how she is saving up for a new dress this Christmas and I thought I would help her out.'

'Very generous, I'm sure,' I commented, 'but actually I thought you were down with a bad cold and wouldn't be going to Doctor Blayers' party tonight.'

'I am suffering from a chill though I feel much better after that fuck with Nancy. But I don't think I'll risk going out in the night air, Rupert, if you don't mind. You don't need me to hold your hand there, do you? No, I'll stay in this evening and think of you enjoying yourselves with all those pretty girls.'

'Thank you, Frank, and certainly I don't need you to hold my hand – or anything else for that matter! But I'll certainly be thinking of you wrapped up in bed all on your own.'

Frank flashed a wicked smile. 'Wrapped up, yes but not alone for too long, old boy, for after she's finished her chores, Nancy's promised to tuck me up for the night!'

I rolled my eyes upwards – there had been no

stopping Frank Folkestone ever since Diana and Cecily had first allowed him to cram his cock into their cunnies. 'Bye then, I'll see you tomorrow,' I said as I waved my farewell, thinking that at least Frank's absence might well provide an opportunity for Barry Jacobs to begin his rites of passage.

The messenger returned just as I was about to take a shower to wash away the perspiration from what had just taken place in Frank's bathroom. As expected, Doctor Blayers was disappointed that Frank could not come to his gathering and wished him a speedy recovery, but was delighted that I had procured a substitute at the last minute as he believed in keeping even the numbers of young men and women at his *soirées*. I decided to take down this note to Barry as it would put him at ease, knowing that he would be genuinely welcomed at the reception.

So slipping on a dressing gown, I popped downstairs to his room, and would you believe it, who should be with him when I opened the door which had been left slightly ajar but the voluptuous Nancy. They were entwined together naked on the bed, kissing mouth to mouth as Barry's hand was squeezing her full breasts and she pulled her hand up and down his twitching staff.

'Ahem, we meet again, Nancy,' I said and the shameless minx looked up and grinned saucily, saying: 'Oh fuck, I thought I hadn't closed the door properly. Be a love, Mister Rupert, and shut it firmly behind you.'

I couldn't help laughing as I obeyed her request and I said: 'Do carry on, don't mind me.'

'Fine,' she said, her fist wrapped round Barry's

prick as she moved her hand up and down in regular stroking motions. 'Is that nice, Barry? I'll rub your cock a little harder if you like.'

'Yes please, Nancy, rub a little harder and put your other hand on my balls, move your fingers further back, still further, ahhh, that's wonderful, truly wonderful.' She obliged him and rubbed his shaft at a faster pace until with a hoarse cry he spent, and great globs of frothy, creamy spunk shot out from the top of his purple helmet.

'You're a busy young lady,' I observed as Nancy twisted her body off the bed and bent down to slip on her knickers.

'Yes, there are always a great number of first year students who appreciate my personal services,' she agreed, pulling on her chemise.

'How did you know that I wouldn't have appreciated being asked if I wanted to try out these services?' I wondered.

'Oh, you're on tomorrow's list,' she replied blithely. 'I was going to leave Mister Barry till then but when I came in to empty his wastepaper basket he looked so forlorn I thought I'd see if I could cheer him up a bit, poor boy.'

Barry gave a nervous laugh and added: 'Nancy came in just at the right time to boost my confidence for tonight's affair.'

My eyebrows rose as I exclaimed: 'And I thought that I was the shy fellow. Now I can't even use the gambit of that weird mathematical puzzle you showed me earlier today to open a conversation!'

But before Barry could utter a choice riposte, Nancy sat on the bed and, taking Barry's cock in her hand, said with a puzzled look on her face.

'Do you know, I've only just realised what it is that made Barry's prick look so different to any other tool I've ever handled. What's happened to your foreskin, love – did you have to have it surgically removed? I hope you never caught some kind of nasty disease.'

'No, no, not at all. I've been circumcised, Nancy, and I must say I'm rather surprised that you've never seen a circumcised cock before. Let me explain – circumcision is the biblical covenant God made with Abraham and his descendents, and all Jewish boys have their foreskins removed eight days after birth *[or as soon as the infant is deemed medically fit – Editor]* by a religious official known as a *mohel*. Muslims too chop off the prepuce for the same religious reason. But quite a few Christian chaps at my school were also circumcised in infancy because a growing number of doctors believe the practice to be hygenic.'

'Yes, there were a few Roundheads in the sixth form at St Lionel's,' I agreed, 'but one poor chap had to undergo the operation when he was fifteen because his foreskin was too tight. It must be a jolly painful operation.'

'For him, maybe,' chuckled Barry, 'but as I was only eight days old when the cut was made, I remember absolutely nothing about it.'

Nancy eyed his circumcised shaft which was beginning to swell up again in her palm. 'Well, you learn something every day. I've never seen one of these shafts before and I must admit that it is not displeasing to the eye. I would imagine that it must feel nice to fuck or to be sucked or tossed off without any additional covering over your cock.

'What an awesome and responsible job for the *mohel*,' she added before licking her lips and jamming them over Barry's rubicund mushroom knob and sucking him up to a rock-hard stiffstander.

'It doesn't command any salary as he's expected to donate his fees to charity,' gasped Barry as Nancy's hand cupped his hairy ballsack whilst she continued to lick and lap his pulsating penis which had risen up majestically under her skilful sucking, 'but as any *mohel* will tell you, the wages are poor but the tips are great!'

I smiled my appreciation at this witticism but Nancy was far too involved in palating his prick to have heard his jest. She somehow managed to take almost all of his rampant rod between her lips and bobbed her head up and down so that Barry fucked her mouth without even having to move a muscle! It took less than a minute for Barry's prick to begin to twitch uncontrollably and Nancy's mouth was soon filled with frothy white foam as she swallowed all the jism from his throbbing tool, gulping down every last milky drop of spunk as his shaft shrank back into submission.

'I'm always the best man but never the groom,' I complained as my own prick was now bulging up high against my belly. Nancy flicked open my robe and seeing my raging stiffstander she grinned: 'I'll come round one day soon and we'll see what we can do for Mr John Thomas then.'

There was no time for any further conversation so I went back upstairs to my room and dressed, consoled somewhat by Nancy's promise. By the time Barry and I were ready to go the evening air was rather chill, although a soft light still shone through the windows as we made the short journey across Broad Street to Doctor Blayers' rooms in Jesus College. But when we reached the gates a college servant informed us that the good doctor had booked a hall for his reception at a nearby tavern. At the same time two girls who had also been invited to the party arrived and we escorted them down to a small turning just off Cornmarket Street where the party was taking place. We introduced ourselves as we walked to the new venue and, as always happens in a foursome, we paired off almost immediately. I squired Beth Randall, a charming tall, blonde girl whilst Barry chatted to Esme Dyotte, an equally attractive young lady whose mop of slightly disordered brown hair and dashing hazel eyes spelled out a promise, I thought to myself, of possible further delight later in the evening if my friend played his cards correctly.

Doctor Nicholas Blayers himself welcomed us at the door. He was a jolly, fine-looking man of about forty, edging towards plumpness, sallow complexioned and wearing gold-framed spectacles and a jolly smile. 'Good evening, good evening, how nice to see you!' he beamed as we came in. He had met Beth and Esme before when, at the headmistress' invitation, he had travelled down earlier in the year to lecture to the sixth form at Trippett's Academy. I introduced myself and Barry to him and as the girls turned away temporarily to converse with former schoolfriends who had also won places at Somerville College, Doctor Blayers told us: 'I do hope that you all have an enjoyable evening tonight. You would be surprised at the battles we have had to allow women even to study at the University let alone mix together. Why, many of my own colleagues say to me that the presence of women destroys the atmosphere of Oxford. Only yesterday a certain professor was moaning to me that soon the women will turn round and say: "If we win degrees it is illogical to withold from us the privileges of the High Table." [The elevated table in the college dining halls at which the principal professors, etc sit – Editor]. To which my reply, of course, is that it would be so much more pleasant to dine in the company of ladies – and this does shock such old dodderers as the gentleman who spoke in such a way to me.

'I believe in the rules of nature and I would like to see young people grow up untrammelled by the burdens of sexual shame. Any tendency of celebration or joy regarding these matters is frowned upon by Society, yet the most elemental expression is itself the act of sexual congress upon which the very preservation of our species is dependent! It is for this reason that Nature made this union extremely pleasurable. We did not ask it; it is the gift of a beneficent Creator and it is thus quite absurd that we are ashamed of our natural inclinations. Do you not agree with me?'

We murmured our assent as we took glasses of iced champagne from a tray proferred to us by a passing waiter and our host continued to ride his hobbyhorse: 'Let me stress that there must be *some* strict regulations by Society – for otherwise we would revert to the laws of the jungle. But in my opinion if two consenting young people wish to follow their natural inclinations, then I say jolly good luck to them – especially if they are responsible enough to take proper care not to bring unwanted children into this overcrowded world.

'Enjoy yourselves tonight,' he added as he turned away to welcome some other guests.

'Gosh, what on earth was that all about?' asked Beth, who only heard the latter part of Doctor Blayers' miniature lecture.

'I believe that he wishes to propound a new morality,' I said, sipping a glass of champagne, to which she gravely nodded and said sweetly: 'Is that so? Personally, I thought he was just expounding upon the joys of fucking.'

I almost choked on my drink as she gave me a saucy smile and murmured throatily: 'Do you like fucking, Rupert? I love it! There is nothing better in the whole wide world I am sure and you don't have to answer the question really because my cousin has already supplied me with your answer!'

'Your cousin? Who is that?'

'Why Diana Wigmore, of course! Yes, she wrote to me about you as soon as she knew that we would both be going up to Oxford together this year. Don't blush, Rupert, she only said nice things about you and your sturdy instrument, which since her tuition you now know how to play to good effect! As soon as you told me your name I thought to myself, it must be fate that has brought us together so quickly.'

Whilst I digested this not unwelcome information, Beth asked: 'Tell me about Barry Jacobs – has he any experience in the art of love-making or like most boys of your years is he still *virgo intacto*?'

'Barry is still untested,' I admitted candidly,

opposite effect and frankly it excited me to think that they might be watching as I took the initiative and unbuttoned Beth's blouse and slid my hand over her rounded bosoms. Now perhaps our exhibition had encouraged them because when she brought my stiff shaft out into the open I heard a gasp behind me and I surmised that Barry and Esme had begun their own new play. I probed the inside of Beth's mouth with my tongue and slid down the straps of her chemise over her shoulders to expose her proud, jutting breasts. She closed her fingers around my palpitating pillar and began to toss me off with regular stroking motions which sent tiny shivers of pleasure all over my body.

Behind us I could hear that Barry and Esme were already one step ahead as I could distinctly hear the wet, squishy sounds of Esme's pussey being finger-fucked, and her moans of delight stimulated Beth who pulled her dress and petticoat up to her waist, exposing her frilly French knickers. She arched her back to assist me in removing them and she spread her legs as I let my palm smooth its way into her silky pubic thatch. My fingers easily found her moist crack and I slowly stroked the entire length of her slit before dipping my finger into her wet cunney, which sent her wild, and she twisted and turned as I moved first one and then two fingers in and out of her dripping cunt.

I turned my head to watch Barry performing the same service for Esme and then Beth pulled down my trousers and drawers and in a flash her head was between my legs as, shaking a lock of blonde hair from her face, she took my shiny uncapped helmet into her mouth. She sucked slowly, tickling and working round the little 'eye' on top of the bulbous dome. Her magic tongue encircled my helmet, savouring its spongy texture and her teeth scraped the tender flesh so deliciously as she drew me in between those luscious lips. She lowered her head to take in more of my shaft and ran her tongue along the side of my throbbing tool which again sent almost unbearable waves of sheer ecstacy coursing through my entire frame. Every time she sensed I was on the verge of spending she would ease her wicked tonguing, thus prolonging our mutual enjoyment which was reaching new, unscaled heights of desire.

'You'll come too quickly if I don't stop for a while' Beth whispered as she reached round and unfastened the hook of her dress, leaving me to unbutton the garment. She slid gracefully out of it and I drank in the awesome beauty of her glorious naked body. Her bare breasts rose and fell with her heavy breathing and until my dying hour I will never forget the sight of the firm swell of those proud young beauties, perhaps the most perfect I have ever viewed. They were firm and globular, each looking slightly away from each other and tapering into lovely curves until they came to the rich, crimson points of her taut nipples.

I kissed and sucked these pretty, erect titties and she took my stiffstander in her fist for a second time but now she lay back and held my pulsating prick against her warm, white belly. I moved to insert my knob between Beth's inviting cunney lips but instead she pulled my cock forwards into the cleft between those divinely rounded breasts and rubbed my cock between the exquisitely formed globes whilst she cupped my ballsack in one hand and frigged her own pussey with the other. It was impossible to hold back and I spurted my spunk all over her bosoms. She let go of my shaft to rub the hot, sticky cream all over her titties until I had emptied my balls and my staff began to flag, settling down in a semi-erect state, between her breasts.

In our frenzy we had taken no notice of what was happening behind us, but now as we were in a more composed state, we looked back to see what stage of the game Barry and Esme had reached. It was immediately apparent that they were not far behind us as both had shed their clothes and Esme was kissing Barry's thick prick which was quivering in anticipation. Her tongue encircled his knob, savouring a blob of pre-spend juice which had already formed there as she drew him in between her generous red lips, sucking lustily. Barry instinctively pushed upwards as her warm hands played with his heavy, hanging balls and her pliant tongue washed over the purple mushroom of his helmet.

'A-h-r-e, A-h-r-e!' he growled softly as Esme took her lips away from his prick and lay back, her legs wide apart to give us all a full view of her curly moss of cunney hair and the pouting pussey lips and delicious red love chink. She took his cock in her hand to press the glowing head between the soft moist cunney lips and I thought to myself, here you go, old boy, your cock is about to enter a cunt for the first time and experience those grand thrills which only a good fuck can induce.

But then disaster struck! Poor Barry's prick,

which before was as hard as an iron bar, appeared to bend as he frantically rubbed his knob against Esme's juicy cunney lips. Indeed, the harder he rubbed his rod against her sopping slit, the softer it became until it lay as limp as could be in her pussey hair. Beads of perspiration were now evident on his forehead as he cried out in frustration: 'What the hell is happening to my cock? I've waited years for this and now it's letting me down!'

'Calm down, it isn't unusual for a lad about to fuck for the first time to be so nervous that his prick won't stand up,' Beth assured him. 'Look, watch Rupert fuck me and I'll wager you'll be ready to play a tune on your organ in no time at all.'

Barry was not to be consoled as in vain he frantically attempted to frig his recalcitrant cock up to its former erection. 'It won't go up, it just won't go up. Oh Esme, I am so sorry – what you must think of me!' he groaned as he slid his hand up and down his dangling dick.

'You silly boy, you must try not to think about it, and I guarantee that Mother Nature will take its course,' said Esme soothingly. 'And before you say anything more, you have no need to fret about my feelings as I always enjoy watching a good fuck. It makes me very horny too and we'll enjoy ourselves that much more afterwards.'

I don't know whether Barry was entirely convinced but naturally I was more than ready to help out my friend by fucking the beautiful Beth, who said: 'Move up you two lovebirds, Rupert and I will join you on the bed and you will both have a grandstand view of his cock entering my cunt.'

We embraced as we rolled together on the bed next to the other pair and as we writhed about in each other's arms my prick began to leap and dance about between her thighs, seeking an entrance in the silky mass of blonde pussey hair which formed a perfect veil over her pouting pussey. I wanted to fuck the sweet girl then and there but I knew that I had to instruct Barry in how to approach a cunt with subtlety. So I disengaged my mouth from Beth's burning kiss and rose up on my knees between her parted legs. My hands roved around her gorgeous breasts and I fingered the engorged, rubbery nipples that stood out like little red soldiers. I heard her gasp with joy as I buried my face in the golden fleece of her pubic bush, inhaling the delicate aroma of her cunt. I grasped her bum cheeks as I flicked my tongue around her crack and she whimpered as her pussey opened like a budding flower and I slipped the tip of my tongue inside her love lips to probe against her stiffening clitty. I licked and lapped as her cunney gushed love juice and her body rocked with unslaked desire.

'Fuck me, Rupert, fuck me,' she moaned and so I scrambled up to kneel between her marble white legs as she reached out and clasped her hand round my swollen shaft.

'I hope you're watching very carefully, Barry,' I said as Beth guided my cock into her dripping love channel. Ah, to hold her creamy buttocks was sheer delight and to suck her erect rosy titties was heaven itself as I slid my cock in and out of her warm, clinging cunney.

Our movements became more heated as I

thrust forward, sending my prick deep inside her. How I enjoyed this magnificent fuck, sliding my willing cock in and out of her wet and juicy pussey. Beth yelped as she felt my knob touch the innermost walls of her cunt and she wrapped her legs around my waist to hold me firmly inside her as I continued to pound away, my prick driving in and out of the tender folds of her cunney from which her juices were flowing liberally. Then she started to buck to and fro with her bum cheeks lifting themselves off the sheets and I pumped into her back and forth as her body gyrated wildly. I felt her body tremble as she closed her legs around me like a vice.

'Yes . . . yes . . . I'm coming . . . yes, yes, Oooh! Oooh! Ah!' Beth yelled as she shuddered her way to a delicious spend. When she had calmed down I set up another rhythm, fucking her with short, sharp jabs and she spent again as I warned her that my own spend was near. She massaged the underside of my ballsack and this brought on my final surge as I emptied myself into her, flooding her cunney with tremendous spurts of hot, sticky spunk and she screamed with delight as the gush of my juices sent shock after shock of erotic energy coursing through our veins.

I heaved myself off Beth and we turned ourselves to our right to see that, as we had expected, the sensual spectacle of our fucking had achieved the desired effect and that Barry's battering ram was impatiently pushing its way through Esme's curly forest of cunney hair. However, his inexperience showed as he was unable to find his way through the hirsute veil to her cunt, so I said to him: 'Wait a second, Barry, let me help you.' I inserted my hand between their bellies and told Barry to lift himself up for a moment. Then I took hold of Barry's rock-hard cock and directed the fiery knob towards Esme's pouting pussey lips. 'Now slide your prick forward and you will see that the key will fit into the lock,' I ordered as I took my hand away, and with his first thrust he was within the lips, with the second he was half way home and with the third his entire pulsating shaft was firmly ensconced inside her wet, willing honeypot.

Barry's body trembled with excitement and his tight little arse cheeks quivered. As Beth and I noted with satisfaction, Barry had a natural understanding of what was required of him and he refrained from rushing in and out of Esme's juicy cunney in a mad frenzy but instead forced himself to push in and out as slowly as he could. This was most pleasing to Esme who responded with upward heaves to his downward thrusts. Her bottom rolled violently as she clawed Barry's back and he grasped her shoulders and started to ride her like a cowboy with a bucking bronco. Her legs slid down, her heels drumming against the mattress as she arched her back, working her love channel back and forth against the hot, velvety hardness of Barry's thick, glistening tool.

With a hoarse cry of rapture he sheathed his shaft so fully within her that his balls nestled against the top of her thighs. This so affected Esme that she rotated her hips wildly, lifting her lovely bottom to obtain the maximum contact with his cock. He groaned as Esme's fingernails raked across his back and she panted: 'Oh lovely, that's really lovely, Barry, ah, it's so delicious! Make me come now, you big cocked boy! Shoot your spunk into me!' She threw back her head in abandon and a primordial sound came from deep within her as her climax spilled out and she swam in her sea of voluptuous delight just as Barry shuddered convulsively as he squirted his tribute of frothy white jism into her yearning cunney, on and on until the last faint dribblings oozed out and he sank down upon her in a blissful swoon of unalloyed happiness.

My own cock was now standing as straight and erect as before and Beth could see that I was game for another bout, but the unselfish girl turned to her friend and invited her to make use of my pulsating prick. 'Thank you, my sweet,' said Esme, smiling lasciviously at me. 'My cunt is a little sore from Barry's big cock but I would love to suck this fine-looking cock, if its owner has no objection.'

'None at all, please help yourself,' I said as I wriggled my way towards her until she could pull my aching shaft towards her rich red lips. She squirmed towards me to leave Barry lying on his own as she took my knob inside her mouth and washed it all over with her tongue, making me shudder all over. She quickened the movements of her tongue, lashing away at my rigid rod as her right hand snaked down and frigged busily away at her still juicy cunt. Esme's mouth was like a cavern of fire which warmed yet did not burn as she licked and lapped away, stroking her tongue up and down the sensitive underside which made me almost faint away with the pleasure of it all.

Then she cupped her hands around my balls, gently rubbing them as she slowly took every inch of my prick into her mouth. She squeezed her free hand around the base of my cock, sucking me harder and harder until I felt the tingling sensation which heralded the nearness of my spend. I shouted that I was going to spunk very soon and the randy girl let my twitching tadger slide out of her mouth.

For a moment I thought this was simply because she did not want to swallow my sperm and would simply finish me off with her hand. But I was wrong for she cried: 'Pump into my cunt!' So I slid myself down her trembling body, ramming my prick into her soaking pussey which was still wet from Barry's and her own juices, but she waggled her bum so artfully that her cunney muscles gripped my cock wonderfully as I drew my chopper out and then darted it in again to engorge this marvellous cunney, which held my thick prick like a soft, moist hand. To be absolutely truthful, as I must in these memoirs, Esme was an even better fuck than Beth for she was expert in the use of her vaginal muscles to contract and relax her cunney, and she somehow managed to tighten her passage so when I slowly drew out my gleaming shaft until only the tip of the purple dome remained embedded inside her, it caused so great a suction that it sent electric shocks of delight fizzling through me. I worked away for as long as I could hold back and she spent twice until the sensitive contractions of her clever little love channel milked my cock of a torrent of hot, sticky cream that lubricated her innermost passages.

The sight of this sensual show had so stimulated Beth that when I recovered my composure I turned my head to see her lying on her back with her legs apart, her hands provocatively rubbing her blonde muff. 'Go on, Barry Jacobs, what are you waiting for?' cried Esme, pushing him towards the other girl. Their bodies met and Barry slid his hand over her dripping pussey, then he spread open her cunney lips and she purred happily as he rhythmically finger-fucked her.

'Have you ever eaten pussey?' Esme demanded and Barry looked up and shook his head.

'Watch closely and I'll show you how to do it,' I said and I doved down into Beth's blonde bush, rubbing my face against her silky golden hair. Barry withdrew his fingers as I worked my tongue along that delicate crack. My mouth was now put to good use as it slid up and down the warm slit and I savoured the tangy taste of drops of love juice which pattered down from her cunney. I heard Beth gasp with pleasure as I probed her love lips and thrust my tongue deep into her cunt, finding her erect clitty and sucking it into my mouth as she moaned with pleasure and brought herself off by rubbing her cunt against my mouth. Almost of their own volition her legs splayed wider as she sought to open herself still more to me. I slurped lustily, swallowing her salty libation that was flowing freely from her pussey and Beth's hands held my head as her legs, now folded across my shoulders, twitched convulsively with joy as the waves of pleasure from her spend engulfed her.

'Somebody fuck me please,' she called out and

my head jerked up from between her thighs as Barry's circumcised cock passed inches away from my face on its way to the slippery entrance which was waiting to welcome it. I could see my friend's whole being was shaking with excitement as the swollen helmet of his rock-hard rod teased Beth's pussey lips before he edged his shaft deep inside her juice-wet love furrow. His hands roved around her jutting breasts, arousing the rosy nipples until they stuck out proudly, as he began to fuck her at first slowly but then increasing the speed of his strokes until his prick was hammering like a piston, his balls beating a tattoo against her backside. Barry showed that he was an ardent cocksman but all too soon he felt himself approach the ultimate pleasure stroke.

'I'm coming! I'm coming! I can't stop!' he shrieked as his body exploded into a climactic release and he shot his hot, creamy froth into Beth's delicious cunt as she writhed beneath him, lifting her shapely bum cheeks to obtain the maximum contact with his raging cock.

We were not yet sated, dear reader. As I lay flat on my back, my love truncheon standing as high and straight as a flagpole, Esme struggled up and stood over me, her legs apart like a female Colossus. Her teeth flashed in a lustful smile, her hazel eyes twinkled merrily and then, holding her cunney lips open with her hands, she slowly lowered herself onto me. As she went down on me, my greased shaft slid straight into her at the first attempt and our pubic bones ground together. She paused, like a rider testing a new mount, clamping her cunney muscles around my penis as I flexed myself, heaving myself upwards and delighting in the silky clinginess of her cunt which fitted my cock like a hand-made glove.

Esme pumped her tight little bottom up and down, digging her fingernails into my flesh, and each voluptuous shove was accompanied by wails of ecstacy. I pulled her body forward so as I could rub her red titties between my fingers and then I moved my head up to take one of the stiff little strawberries between my lips. She panted away as she bounced up and down on my pulsing prick so violently that I was forced to hold her bum cheeks to keep her in position, helping her in her ride by pushing her up and letting her drop down hard upon my cock. The supreme moment arrived and her cunney clung to my cock even harder as she pulled me in as firmly as she could, squeezing her legs against mine as if fearing that I would leave her. She sighed and squirmed, the lips of her cunt tightly clipping my shaft as we spent profusely together, my jets of sperm spurting up her pussey as her own love juices cascaded down her thighs. Her buttocks quivered in my hands as we drained each other dry until Esme slowed her movements down and came finally to rest. We lay entwined in euphoric peace and she exclaimed in a tone of rapture: 'Oh, that was a truly magnificent fuck, Rupert. I must award your cock full marks for his performance. You know, Beth, it has to be said that boys are adept and considerate lovers. We have chosen our bedmates well tonight.'

'Let me say that the feeling is mutual,' Barry said, his voice cracking with emotion. 'I will never forget either of you helping me so patiently to lose my cherry. I count myself most fortunate in making love for the first time with two such understanding girls.'

Beth acknowledged the compliment and said: 'Perhaps we should all drink a toast to Dame Agatha Humphrey of St Trippett's Academy for The Daughters of Gentlefolk. Unlike the vast majority of schools, we were given guidance on sexual matters.'

'Yes, I can remember telling Dame Agatha without any embarrassment of my first sensual stirrings,' Esme chipped in brightly. 'I had been waking up in the night and finding myself shivering with excitement, with my nightdress damp from a thin fluid which had trickled down my thighs from my then lightly haired pussey. Now I knew from other girls who I had seen giggling over the pages of that rude magazine *The Oyster* that boys entering puberty have nocturnal emissions but I never knew that girls could have wet dreams.

'Golly, I was so worried and confused but in the end I plucked up courage and asked Dame Agatha about what was happening to my body and she told me how entirely normal these nightly emissions were and how my body was preparing itself for sexual congress.'

'Not that we were totally innocent about sex by the time we had the first hairs growing around our pussies,' said Beth brightly.

'Did you play games in the dormitories like we used to do?' I asked her.

'Of course, although we made ourselves follow to the letter some strict regulations about such

259

matters,' she rejoined, passing a glass of wine to me. 'Perhaps the most charming rule concerned the bathrooms in the evenings as we prepared ourselves for bed. Naturally, shut up as we were with little chance of contact with the opposite sex, passions and crushes freely abounded. Many a swift hip-to-hip rub was exchanged as a signal that greater intimacies might be enjoyed in the near future. But to counter the shame and embarrassment of rejection we all accepted the convention that if the girl you fancied was bending over a washbasin having her before lights-out wash, it was totally permissible to approach her from behind and to touch and stroke her – mark you, without a word being uttered. If she did not check these advances it was permissible to reach under her nightie and clasp the swelling cheeks of her bum. Then, so long as she continued to show no objection, one might rub one's pussey against her bottom and then reach round and play with her hairy bush, though more than a little diddling was frowned upon as it might upset other would-be suitors. A caress of one's cunney held the promise of fun and games between the sheets later that night.'

'But wasn't it rather difficult for anyone to repel such an advance?' enquired Barry.

'Not really, for one could easily reach back with one's hand and remove the persistent hand. There are many subtle ways by which one can quietly yet firmly refuse unwelcome attentions and I think that Esme will agree that women are far more skilled than men in expressing themselves in this unspoken language.'

Esme nodded her head in agreement. 'It was also so nice to be able to use this very delicate way of accepting a loving, exploratory caress. My goodness, when I think back how many times whilst splashing water over my face I sensed a warm presence behind me and felt the soft touch of an unknown hand running up and down my back and sliding under my nightie to squeeze my bottom. It was such fun to close your eyes, cradling your head on your arms against the cold rim of the wash-basin, nestling against the unseen girl whose hands would reach round and cup your breasts in her palms, rubbing up the titties until they rose up to greet her.

'Yes, and how stimulating it could be to feel a quiver of delight run through the body of the girl you were stroking, to look in the mirror and see her blush as she shyly raised her bum to show that she welcomed your attention. Then would come the magic moment when you raised the nightdress over the hips and the white orbs of her bottom were exposed to be cupped, caressed or even lightly slapped. And ah, the delight if afterwards she welcomed the insertion of your finger into the dampness of her cunney, wriggling so sweetly as you prised open the yielding love lips.

'Beth and I often used this stratagem before starting to play games in bed, though perhaps we should not mention such sport to you,' added Esme with a saucy look.

'Oh, please go on, Esme, don't be a tease,' begged Barry. 'Rupert and I would really love to hear all about what you got up to together, wouldn't we, old chap?'

261

Before I could answer (in the affirmative, of course!), Beth interrupted and said: 'All right, we'll tell you all but you must confess your early experiences to us afterwards.'

This was a fair enough exchange so we agreed and settled down to listen to Esme, but she had little to say except that 'actions spoke louder than words' and so she and Beth would demonstrate what they often did, cuddled together in bed at St Trippett's, and this proved to be so exciting that Barry and I never got round to fulfilling our side of the bargain!

Barry and I settled down to watch as the two girls entwined their arms lasciviously around each other. I looked again at Beth and how magnificent her breasts looked, rounded like two snowy white balloons topped with two cute, rosy nipples. She squeezed her legs tightly together and her right hand went down to snake its path through the golden silk of her blonde mound. She started to rub it gently with the palm of her hand and to move her backside slowly, lazily dipping her fingertip into her itching cunney. Esme now knelt beside her, stroking and fondling Beth's nipples as she removed the blonde girl's hand and replaced it with her own, inserting two fingers into her sticky pussey, jerking them in and out, whilst her thumb brushed over the erect clitty which protruded between Beth's cunney lips.

This was but the *hors d'oeuvre* to the main course of a girls-only fuck because she rolled herself on top of Beth, taking care that her hand did not lose contact with the juicy love nest which was becoming more moist by the minute. Her apt fingers toyed with Beth's erect clitty as Esme breathed: 'What a gorgeous wet cunt you have, darling. Can you feel my fingers dipping in and out of your honeypot? Does that feel good – or would you prefer a big fat cock like Rupert's piercing you through and through?'

Beth moaned an inaudible reply as Esme now kissed the damp yellow pussey hair around the cunney lips and her pretty pointed tongue licked lewdly along Beth's crack. She soon found her clitty, fully swollen as she sucked the little button, letting the very tip of her long tongue go around it in tiny circles. Barry and I craned our heads forward to watch her teeth nibble all along the glorious love slit, her pink tongue teasing Beth's tasty pussey with rasping licks.

'Oh! Oh!' Beth gasped, her eyes closed in heavenly bliss and she took hold of Esme's tousled head in her hands. 'Oh, you tongue me so divinely, darling.' Her soft limbs quivered as Esme pressed her face even harder against Beth's cunney lips so that her tongue could delve even deeper and she lapped around the innermost walls of the orifice. Beth writhed around in frenzied momentum as Esme's tongue, now glued to her cunney lips, worked sensuously inside the hole to be rewarded by a sustained flow of pungent love juice which she swallowed as Beth worked herself off with wild, rising cries of joy.

Now it was Beth's turn to be the gentleman and she rolled off the bed and padded across to the table on which stood the tray of refreshments we had ordered. She brought back an empty bottle of champagne with her and then she took out a small jar of cold cream from her handbag. Barry and I looked on curiously as she turned Esme gently on to her side. Beth's ideas for pleasuring the other girl soon became apparent as she rubbed the cream in and around Esme's wrinkled little bum hole, and the auburn-haired beauty wriggled deliciously, her smooth white globes jiggling as Beth lubricated her rear dimple. Then Beth took the champagne bottle and with great care slid the neck, which was as thick as my prick, into Esme's behind. The girl gave a cry of alarm but then her pretty face relaxed, the hazel eyes wide and appealing as Beth now began work in earnest. With one hand she manipulated Esme's sensitive cunney lips and clitty and with the other she moved the neck of the bottle back and forth gently in and out of Esme's anus.

'Aaaah! Aaaah! Aaaah!' she cried out as Beth continued this inexorable masturbation. 'Oh Beth, you are a naughty girl to fuck my cunney and bum at the same time. All I need is a thick cock in my mouth and I will be filled to the brim. Where are you, Barry, I need you!'

This was all he had to hear – for like me, Barry's prick was now standing high against his belly and he shuffled forward, his prick in his hand, and to his delight Esme grabbed hold of it and her mouth opened greedily over his knob as she took it between her lips, slurping lustily on the shaft, sending him into paroxyms of delight. I could no longer stand idly by and I crawled round behind Beth and parted her peach bottom cheeks and inserted two or three inches of my bursting prick into her damp cunt from behind. She turned her head so that our lips could meet and she drew my tongue into her mouth as she cleverly wriggled her bum so that I could embed my entire eight and a half inches of cock inside her. With a passionate jolt of our loins my shaft was fully inserted and she cried out in glee as I started to fuck her and our hips began to work away in unison. How tightly her dripping cunt enclasped my cock and we gloried with each tremendous thrust as her juices dripped upon my balls as they slapped against her arse.

She threw back her head in ecstasy, tossing her blonde mane over her shoulders as she urged me to drive even deeper and with her firm bottom cheeks cupped in my broad palms, she writhed savagely whilst my sinewy shaft rammed its passage in and out of her soaking slit. I could feel the throbbing of Beth's excited pussey increase to boiling point as she screamed out her climax so loudly that I feared we might disturb other guests in the hotel. Her shuddering cries soon led to my twitching cock ejaculating great gushes of jism inside her cunney just as her orgasm was dying down, giving the sensual lady the pleasure of a second spend which arose from the sensation of my spunk hurtling into her love channel. Now Barry could contain himself no longer and he thrust his hips forward and his sperm spurted into Esme's waiting throat. She tried hard to swallow all of the creamy emission but he shot such a torrent between her lips that some of the fluid dripped down her chin and onto her breasts.

This led to Beth increasing the speed of her finger-fucking of Esme's pussey and together with continued insertion of the champagne bottle up her bum soon brought off the sweet girl to a magnificent orgasm.

This last 'whoresome foursome', as my first lovely partner-in-fucking Diana Wigmore was wont to call such jousts, completely exhausted us and we all fell fast asleep under the warm eiderdown Beth and I pulled across the bed. Our tangled limbs rested in comfort until the grey dawn of morning woke me from my slumber. The others still lay deep in the arms of Morpheus when as quietly as possible, I slid out of bed and padded to the bathroom to make my ablutions.

Ah, what sweet recollections this memoir brings back to me, of how Beth, Esme and Barry lay naked on crushed and rumpled sheets whilst I watched the weak autumn sunlight caress the dreaming spires as the town woke up to another day. I looked out at the early risers walking down the street and I idly wondered how many of them had enjoyed as good a fucking (if at all) as Barry and I.

An attractive dark-haired girl in jodhpurs strode towards the Bodleian Library *[one of the most famous libraries in the world with an unrivalled collection of rare books and manuscripts – Editor]* and two or three male passers-by turned their heads to stare after her. I pondered as to what private thoughts were passing through her mind and those of her unknown secret admirers. What ideas were spinning around those people, hiding behind bland, expressionless faces, what lovers, real and imaginary were being wooed in their minds, what triumphs and failures were being lived and relived in their daydreams? Take this girl who turned heads on this October morning, for instance; what were the thoughts of the young butcher's boy who was so entranced by the fetching swell of the girl's buttocks tightly encased in the riding breeches which clung so lovingly to her figure, that he pulled his bicycle over to the kerb so he could gaze at the girl's delicious backside for a few moments more? Perhaps he was thinking of how he would like to see her peel off her clinging jodhpurs and expose her naked charms or maybe how she might caress his erect cock or even be persuaded to take his knob in her mouth?

It is this gap between reality and fantasy, between what is and what might be or might have been which has for me been an endless source of fascination. Will the fucking of a particular girl turn out to be an anticlimax? Will the reality be but a pale imitation of the untrammelled adventures of the mind? Fantasy should not be discouraged for it represents perhaps the only time when one can be certain of taking the lead role in delicious daydreams in which one can become famous for whatever one wishes. All grievances can be righted, all one's actions will be applauded and, of course, a variety of the most gorgeous women in the entire world will be conquered almost without effort! Curmudgeonly critics may carp at fantasising as a fruitless exercise – but surely the only harm in pursuing this occupation is when one finds it difficult to leave cloud-cuckoo land for the harsher world of reality upon which we have so little chance to influence the way events great and small unfold around us.

The rays of the sun roused me from this reverie and I turned back to see that my companions were still asleep. But Beth lay on her back, her nude charms half uncovered by the bed-clothes which sent my prick rearing up to a fine hard stiffness. I gently climbed between her open legs and kissed her blonde furry pussey. Then I spread the pouting cunney lips with one hand and taking hold of my cock with the other, I lowered my uncapped helmet until it touched her pouting cunney lips. I managed to insinuate my knob inside her cunt without waking her. She made a few uneasy movements as I slowly withdrew my blue-veined pole but Beth slept on as this time I engulfed my staff fully into her love channel, overcome as she was by the fatigues of fucking the previous night. I would have liked to continue this delicate fuck but alas, *tempus fugit*, and I had to leave shortly to attend a lecture in political philosophy. So I was forced to begin heaving and bucking in earnest and this woke the pretty girl, who fondly kissed me, and we engaged in a wonderful contest, each striving to be first in climbing the mountain to the highest peak of pleasure. My thrusts forward were met with her impetuous heaves upwards and as my shaft slid to the hairs inside her honeypot my balls knocked against Beth's thighs and the delicious wriggles of her splendid bottom soon roused me to an erotic fury.

Our frenzied fucking woke Barry and Esme and

they immediately copied our example. It was so arousing to see Esme's beautiful cleft in its hairy auburn grotto with the large white shaft of Barry's weapon appearing and disappearing through the luxuriant curly thatch of pussey hair as he drove his cock in and out of the open, rosy chink. Our frantic heaves and shoves were received and returned by our lusty partners with a gradually increasing intensity until we all four spent near enough simultaneously, swimming in a sea of lubricity as we melted away in a glorious excess of sensual rapture.

We lay there for a while longer but then it was time to wash and dress and we ate a hearty breakfast. Barry paid the bill and we made arrangements to meet the girls again in a few days' time. 'Will you get into trouble for staying out all night?' I asked, much concerned that this escapade would have no serious consequences for the two lovely ladies.

'No, Mr Holland the porter is very obliging and a half sovereign will buy his silence,' said Esme with a giggle as we exchanged fond kisses of farewell. 'How do you boys plan to get back into your rooms?' Barry explained that we hoped to enter our college through a secret back entrance our maidservant Nancy had shown us (we didn't venture any further information about the other services Nancy provided for her scholars!) and we waved goodbye as we walked through town.

By taking the seldom-used side stairs that Nancy had pointed out, we managed to sneak into our college unnoticed and I hastily changed and ran down the stairs to the lecture hall just in time to take my place before our senior lecturer, Professor Simon 'Beaver' Webb, entered the room. He was a large, indeed somewhat corpulent gentleman with twinkling blue eyes and a luxuriant red beard which doubtless accounted for his admittedly vulgar nickname. An ardent supporter of the suffragettes, his radical views were hardly hidden in his dissertation on the so-called 'wild women' who were determined to change the country's social structure.

But frankly, I was so tired after all the exertions of the previous night that my eyes fluttered shut more than once whilst the Professor gave us his views on why women should be allowed to vote. However, he became quite steamed up at the end of his lecture and I woke up with a start as he thundered: 'We must allow for the fact that there is no reason to suppose that in any respect women will show themselves superior in sagacity. Blunders will undoubtedly result occasionally from the new freedom when it finally arrives – and I say "when" and not "if" advisedly for the river of social progress can only be stemmed, it can never be rolled back. And if the new movement has no other effect than to rouse women to rebellion against the madness of producing large families, it would confer a priceless blessing on themselves and upon humanity!'

A burst of applause came from a small group of girls from Girton College, Cambridge who had been specially invited with other students from London and Edinburgh to attend a special three day seminar presided over by Professor Webb on

'The Emancipation Of Women'. Not all the undergraduates agreed with the Professor's sentiments however, and a few ill-mannered boors had the temerity to hiss as Professor Webb gathered up his papers.

At first I thought the Professor was going to ignore the jeers but he changed his mind as he reached the door and he suddenly whirled round and accosted Lord Blaxonberry who had led the dissenters. 'So you and your friends do not approve of votes for women,' he snapped angrily. 'Perhaps you do not approve of votes for men either.'

'Not particularly,' the wealthy young landowner coolly replied. 'I would have to agree with you that the prevailing democratic tendency is the prevailing fashionable theory. The idea of government by the absolute majority has superseded the thought that government should be conducted for the benefit of all by the enlightened and capable – the genuine aristocracy in the strict sense of the word – who have been born and bred to such a task.

'In my view, Professor, the only benefit of granting women the franchise might be to show the innate fallacies inherent in the pernicious democratic doctrine and weaken the belief in the wisdom of purely popular government.'

'Stuff and nonsense!' called out a very pretty girl from just a few seats away from me. 'I would rather be governed by a council of working men who know at first hand the needs of the great majority of our citizens than a gathering of chinless drones who know nothing except how to idle away their days whilst the rest of their fellow countrymen engage in back-breaking toil.'

'Hear, hear! Well said!' I cried out loudly, and this interjection brought me a friendly smile from the speaker and a disdainful look of utter contempt from Lord Blaxonberry.

Professor Webb stroked his luxuriant red beard and said: 'Carry on, sir. What would you add to this discussion?'

I thought carefully before rising to reply. 'I would just wish to add this thought, sir,' I said, trying as hard as possible to prevent my knees from shaking, as public speaking has always filled me with dread and was one of the major reasons why I recently refused the kind offer of Mr Lloyd George to stand as the Liberal parliamentary candidate in the safe seat of West Gloucestershire during the recent General Election. 'There is no sadder sight in the world than that of a wasted life, yet how wantonly Society condemns to waste the lives of thousands upon thousands of bright, intelligent young women all over Britain whose powers are worn down and diminished by long courses of boring trivialities and mental stagnation.'

Though I stand in danger of being labelled a braggart, I can truthfully record that my words were cheered to the echo, not least by the attractive girl whose own speech had sparked off my contribution. Professor Webb brought the discussion to a close and enjoined us to read a variety of books on female emancipation – both for and against – and told us to write essays upon the subject that he wanted handed in to him in three weeks' time.

As we left the lecture hall, I smiled back at the

girl whose cause I had supported and she made her way round to my desk and introduced herself. 'My name is Gillian Headleigh from Girton College, Cambridge and I'm the secretary of the college branch of the Cambridge Society for Women's Rights,' she said, holding out her hand. 'Thank you very much for supporting me against Lord Blaxonberry and his little coterie of silly young reactionary idiots.'

'I'm Rupert Mountjoy and I'm studying here at Balliol,' I said, shaking her proferred hand. 'The authorities here are usually so stuffy about male and female undergraduates mixing together that I'm surprised you managed to obtain a pass to listen to Professor Webb's lecture.'

She laughed and though we were talking of serious matters I could not help but be diverted by her mop of bright curls that set off her tiny, slightly *retroussé* nose and large cornflower-blue eyes which sparkled with promise. Her slim, lithe body was delightfully shown off by a close-fitting grey costume in the modern style, which accentuated the swell of her small but gorgeously rounded breasts that jutted proudly forward like two soft peaches ripe for my mouth . . .

'Doctor Blayers arranged it for a group of us to come over to Oxford and attend a number of lectures as part of our PPE [*Politics, Philosophy and Economics – Editor*] course. There are many excellent scholars at Cambridge but it is generally agreed that Professor Webb [*a distant relative of the well-known social reformers and educationalists Beatrice and Sidney Webb who helped found the London School of Economics in 1895 – Editor*] is the most important figure in the drive towards social progress.'

'What a coincidence,' I exclaimed. 'I was at a party given by Doctor Blayers last night.'

'Yes, I was there too and I saw you talking to a pretty blonde girl,' she said with a little smile which showed two delicious dimples on either side of her lovely red lips.

'Would you like to take morning coffee with me?' I asked hurriedly, for I had no desire to let the conversation drift down this particular avenue! Gillian agreed and fortunately I had no further lectures until mid-afternoon so after coffee I was able to walk down with her to her lodgings in Pusey Street, just off the Woodstock Road. We chatted in animated fashion and by the time we reached the house in which Gillian and three other girls were staying for the week, almost to my surprise, I noticed that we were holding hands.

'I have some reading to catch up on,' she said, 'but you're welcome to join me if you are free.' I accepted this invitation with alacrity for the sun had come out and the weather was warm enough to sit outside, which I thought would be especially pleasant as the other girls were studying elsewhere and so we had the house to ourselves. I pulled out a rug and two deckchairs from the garden shed but Gillian sat herself down on the rug and of course I followed suit.

At first we both attempted to read but when I put my book down and took the trembling girl in my arms she did not push me away but giggled delightfully and brought her face up to be kissed. Our mouths met and in an instant her tongue was filling my mouth, probing, lapping and caressing, which made my prick swell up to its full height. My fingers found their way to the buttons of her blouse and I undid enough of them to allow me to slip my hand inside and squeeze the succulent spheres of her breasts, feeling the hardening nipples push against my palm. My excited prick was now threatening to burst its way out from the confines of my trousers but she slid her hands down to the bulge in my lap and quickly unbuttoned my flies as I wrenched off my belt. She drew out my swollen chopper and held it tightly in her hand as it stood up stiffly, twitching slightly as she worked her hand slowly up and down the throbbing shaft.

Our mouths were still glued together as I slipped my hand under her skirt but immediately she pulled my arm down and muttered throatily: 'You naughty boy, Rupert! I haven't quite finished my monthly so we can't consummate our friendship this morning. But I do fancy sucking your delicious-looking cock.'

We rolled about on the rug as I helped Gillian pull down my trousers and drawers and then she sat on my legs, her hands clasping my stiffstander as she bent her head down to kiss the rubicund bare knob. I closed my eyes and groaned with delight as she washed her tongue all around my helmet, nibbling at it with her teeth before gently easing my pulsating prick into her mouth, sucking furiously as instinctively I put up my hands to cup her breasts which swung invitingly before me. Then she placed a hand on my ballsack which sent wave upon wave of exquisite pleasure crashing through my body. I thrust my cock forward and pressed the crown further inside the warm wetness of her mouth.

She was happy to engulf my shaft, sheathing it between her lips and licking and lapping my prick with gay abandon. No man's penis could resist such a cleverly wicked stimulation and I whispered hoarsely that I would be unable to hold back my spend for much longer. I always let this be known for there are girls, admittedly few in number, who enjoy sucking cocks but do not wish to swallow the spunk. I still find this difficult to understand for it can do them no harm whatsoever, but naturally their wishes must always be respected. But as Gillian said later when I mentioned this to her, she adored the taste of sperm and now she nodded as she squeezed my balls through their hairy wrinkled skin and with an immense shudder I expelled my creamy jism which hurtled into her mouth and which she swallowed with evident enjoyment. She sucked my cock with great skill, coaxing out every last drop of jism from my prick until I had been milked dry and she lifted her head with a sigh, smacking her lips in satisfaction.

'Rupert, your spunk has a gratifying tang. Perhaps we could meet at this time tomorrow when I shall be fully ready for you and you may fuck me for as long as you can keep your cock stiff!'

'I look forward to it,' I declared, smiling my approval as we lay motionless, recovering our senses as the autumn breeze cooled our heated bodies. She gave my prick a final friendly rub before I stood up and put my clothes back on. 'Wild horses would not keep me away from you.'

After supper I went to Frank's room where he, Barry and another friend, Leonard Letchmore [*a nephew of the infamous Sir Jonathan Letchmore, a founding member of the fast South Hampstead set which revolved around Count Gewirtz, Sir Ronnie Dunn and Lord Tagholm. He was one of the most infamous rakes of the 1890s of whom it was said that large blue eyes like his might be found in many a stately nursery – Editor*] were gossiping about the events of the previous night. 'I'm sorry in a way that I didn't take up my invitation to Doctor Blayers' party after all,' said Frank. 'Still, I did fuck Nancy and I'm pleased for Barry that he finally got his end away, as the vulgar colloquialism has it.'

'It was good of you, Frank, and I will never forget your kindness – nor that of Rupert, Beth and Esme,' said Barry with some emotion. 'Oh, Rupert, I almost forgot to tell you, the girls sent round a note insisting that they make dinner for us when we see them again. They have suggested next Tuesday which is fine with me. Is it convenient for you? Good, I'll write back tomorrow morning. God, aren't they two smashing girls. I'm so lucky to have met them.'

'Don't get too carried away,' advised Leonard as he poured out glasses of port for us. 'First love can often be idyllic and you were well served. But there are plenty more fish in the sea to be landed, old chap, and as my uncle Sir Jonathan always says, keep playing the sport until you find the special girl with whom you want to stay with for the rest of your life.'

'What, and never fuck any other girl again?' said Frank ironically.

'Supposedly not, though in my uncle's case that practice has certainly never been put into effect! Mind, he's a rogue of the first order though jolly useful as far as I was concerned. I'll wager that few chaps received such a sixteenth birthday present as I was given by Uncle Jonathan.'

'This sounds interesting – tell us more,' I said, settling down in an armchair.

'Well, my birthday is in July and I had just come down from Eton. Actually, my birthday was on the very day I came home and to be honest I was rather miffed to discover that every single one of my relatives and friends, with the sole exception of Uncle Jonathan, had remembered the day and sent me cards and presents. I was especially mortified as he had been perhaps the closest of my many uncles and aunts. But then later that evening I received a hand-delivered letter marked "Strictly Private" and which was delivered to me in great secrecy by our butler, Conway, when my parents were elsewhere in the house, as Uncle Jonathan had previously instructed him. It read:

Dear Leonard,

I haven't forgotten your birthday although it might have so appeared to you. Now you know my flat in Albemarle Street off Piccadilly? We met there in Spring before we went to the theatre with Aunt Anita and your cousins. Be there sharp at three o'clock tomorrow afternoon and you'll have your present. But whatever you do, don't tell your parents about this or it will spoil the surprise.

Your affectionate uncle,

Jonathan Letchmore

'What was I to make of this note? Naturally, I obeyed his instruction and told my parents the next day that I fancied a brisk constitutional in Green Park. We live in Belgravia so I hailed a cab to take me to Uncle Jonathan's *pied à terre*, which he kept partly as a spare apartment for visitors from abroad as Aunt Anita hails from the United States and partly (as I thought in my naivety) for certain business purposes. As we circumnavigated the hazards of Hyde Park Corner, I racked my brains wondering as to what birthday present Uncle Jonathan had in mind and why it could not be delivered like all the others.

'Despite the usual heavy traffic I arrived there just before the appointed hour and the porter recognised me as he swung open the front door. "Good afternoon, sir, your uncle told me to expect you. He'll be with you later but you're to go right on up and wait for him, if you don't mind." So I took the lift up to the fourth floor and saw to my surprise that the door of Uncle Jonathan's apartment was slightly ajar. This is becoming curiouser by the minute, I said to myself as I pushed it open. There seemed to be no-one else there and one look sufficed to tell me that there had been no burglary. I stood by the sideboard in the lounge and was about to pour myself a sherry when the door from the bedroom opened. Had the flat been visited by robbers after all? I gripped

279

the decanter in my hand, ready to wield it as a weapon.'

He paused dramatically and Frank asked excitedly. 'Go on, Len, who on earth was it? A sneak thief who had managed to climb in from the fire escape?'

'A jolly good guess, Frank, but no, nothing like that – the unexpected visitor had been invited by Uncle Jonathan and she immediately apologised for startling me.'

'It was a woman, then – a friend of your uncle no doubt, who the porter had let in before you,' suggested Barry Jacobs.

Leonard beamed and continued: 'You're getting closer to the mark now. Yes, the porter had let her up to the flat on my uncle's specific instruction. She told me that her name was Fiona but I hardly heard her sweet voice as I gazed upon the pert mass of dark curly hair which had popped round the door. Then a tiny hand brushed the hair away and I could see the most exquisitely beautiful girl framed in the doorway, as pretty as a picture with a face that was somehow disembodied as she smiled, showing pearly white teeth which sparkled in the sunlight that poured through the windows. She came in and shut the door behind her and when I saw her figure, dressed in a loose cotton white dress that was as good as transparent in the bright rays of the sun, I noticed that she was barefoot – and in the back of my mind I somehow thought that I had somewhere before seen this heavenly apparition. "Hello Leonard, we've never been introduced but I know who you are – and we're not total strangers as you saw me when your uncle took you to the theatre last April," she said, taking my hand in hers. "Ah, were you about to pour yourself a sherry? I think I'll join you if I may."

'Of course! This sweet girl was on the stage of the Alhambra and to her delight I remembered her name and the song she sang so delightfully in the musical show *Berkeley Close*. "You're Fiona Forster and you sang *Love In The Park*," I said with a great effort of memory and she clapped her hands in glee. "Oh Leonard, how clever of you to remember the song. Did you enjoy the show? It's just finished its run after almost ten months at the Alhambra."

' "Very much so, and I remember how well you sang and how pretty you looked on stage," I said, blushing to the roots of my hair. She squealed happily at this compliment. "Oh I can see for sure that you are your uncle's nephew. What a nice compliment and I'm so pleased you could come round to the flat this afternoon.

' "I know why you're here as well. You've come to collect your birthday present," she added roguishly. I looked at her in astonishment and in all innocence asked: "How on earth did you know that?"

' "Goodness me, you silly boy, don't you know? *I'm* your birthday present!" she said happily and in one quick movement she raised her dress over her head and for the very first time in my life I looked in awe at the sensuous beauty of the naked body of a pretty girl. I could hardly believe my eyes as she smoothed her hands over the creamy spheres of her firm breasts. I was rooted to the spot as she pirouetted gaily about the furniture, flaunting her tight rounded bum cheeks and the curly mass of hair which sprouted in a thick triangle at the base of her flat, white belly.

Then she stood still in front of me and held out her hand. "Come on, Leonard, don't be shy. Come into the bedroom and take off your clothes." I still could not believe what was happening – as if in a dream I followed Fiona into the bedroom and she sat me down on a chair and bent down to unlace my shoes. My heart was pounding, I could feel the perspiration on my forehead but I slowly regained control though surprisingly, even though this delicious nude beauty was peeling off my socks, my prick remained obstinately limp and the thought crossed through my mind that I wouldn't be able to get it up, even though this problem had never occurred during our circle jerks at school or when I had read the copy of *The Temptations Of Cremorne* in the Geography master's study!

' "Didn't naughty Uncle Jonathan even give you a hint of what your present was going to be?" she cooed as she helped me unbutton my shirt. I shook my head and she giggled as she loosened my trousers. In a trice I was naked save for my undershorts. She made me stand up and on her knees slowly pulled down my pants. Perhaps not surprisingly I now felt curiously vulnerable for I was so overcome by a mixture of lust for this gorgeous girl and concern that she might laugh at my fumbling efforts to fuck her that my prick dangled uselessly between my legs.

But Fiona was wise beyond her years and she whispered: "Don't be nervous, Leonard, it's always a little difficult beginning the race but you'll run well enough once you reach the starting line." Slowly at first, she gently stroked my cock and peeled back the foreskin to expose the domed mushroom of my bell-end. This instantly produced the desired effect and as my truncheon stiffened she allowed her fingers to trace a path around and underneath my balls which made my whole body tingle with gratification. After a while she closed her fist around the burgeoning shaft, sliding her fingers along its length until my prick stood up proudly at full erection. "There, that's a lovely thick tool for such a young boy. It looks good enough to eat," she said admiringly and I trembled with joy as, still on her knees, she opened her lips and her pink tongue shot out to lick my shaft from base to tip. I clung to her tousled head as she now kissed my rampant chopper, letting the tip of her tongue flick out to tease my bare knob. Then she opened her mouth wide and encircled my cock with her lips before jamming the throbbing tool inside its heavenly wetness. Her head bobbed down and like a serpent her tongue slid round and round my rod, rolling it cunningly across the swollen knob, and I could feel the playful bite of her pearly teeth as she nipped the sensitive skin of the underside.

'My prick swelled to bursting point and very quickly I spurted a creamy emission into her luscious mouth. She eagerly swallowed every drop of spunk and perhaps because I had spent so quickly my prick was still ramrod stiff as I slowly withdrew it from her lips. The dear girl planted a series of butterfly kisses on my glistening helmet and heaved herself to her feet. "Now for your next lesson," she murmured as she gripped my prick in her hand and led me to the bed. She threw herself down upon it and drew me upon her. I looked down at her exquisite nude body, her slender long legs, her uptilted pointed breasts with the flat belly below which her curly haired pussey glinted in the warm sunshine. I may have lacked any previous experience but Nature told me to take her in my arms and with my mouth on hers I lovingly caressed Fiona's smooth thighs and then raised my hands to rub my fingers against her raised raspberry nipples. But my kind mistress was not yet finished teaching me the refinements of *l'arte de faire l'amour*. "Eat my pussey, Leonard, don't be shy. I adore having my cunney licked out," she panted, pushing my shoulders down with her hands. Again, I had read about this practice in *The Oyster [a spectacularly rude underground magazine – Editor]* but had never had the chance even to attempt it before. In fact, the nearest I had ever come along this path was to French kiss Joanna the parlourmaid and squeeze her breasts through her clothes whilst she rubbed my cock against my flannels.

Yet by now I had lost much of my nervousness and I prised her legs apart and buried my face between her unresisting thighs. I sniffed her delicate feminine aroma and let my tongue lap freely around the moist curly hair around her cunney lips. She pressed my head forward with her hands and lifted her bottom off the bed, forcing my nose against her cunney. I moved my head slightly upwards and as my hands slipped under her quivering body to clasp her bum cheeks, I slipped my tongue through the pink love lips and licked between the inner grooves of her cunt which was now starting to gush love juice. I tasted her fragrant sweetness, rousing her to new peaks of delight, and I sucked deeply on the pouting cleft that rubbed up and down on my mouth as I tongued her erect, rubbery clitty. Her hands now ran wildly through my hair, pressing on my temples as if to direct this onslaught. She exploded as I continued licking and lapping, swallowing her salty fluids as her hips and bottom moved in synchronised rhythm with my mouth. My face rubbed against her curly bush as she screamed again with delight and, heaving violently, Fiona managed to achieve a second spend before pushing my face away from her juicy crack.

' "Fuck me, Leonard! Oh, you must fuck me now!" she gasped as she drew me up until my face was level with hers. Then, throwing her arms around my neck, she drew my lips to hers as she thrust her wicked tongue into my mouth with all the wild abandon of love, shoving her backside upwards to meet my charge. But I was so excited at the thought that I was about to fuck my first girl that I could not find the entrance to her cunney! I jabbed my hips backwards and forwards, moaning with frustration as I failed to sink my shaft into the eagerly moistened channel that awaited it. Fiona opened her legs wider to make it easier for me. She placed her hand around my raging cock and directed it towards the waiting gap. I sighed as I felt the first thrilling sensation as it eased between the puffy outer lips of her cunt. This was all the help I required and like an iron bolt my prick battered through the cunney flesh, separating the folds of sticky skin and fucking deeper and deeper as my throbbing tool plunged into her, stretching the resilient love channel to its utmost. She spread her legs and bent her knees so that her heels rested upon the small of my back. I pressed home slowly and I marvelled at the wonderful sensations produced on my swollen staff by her tight little cunney. I began to find a rhythm and fucked her with long, simple strokes, glorying in the electric tingle that spread up and down my spine as I slowly withdrew my glistening pole before plunging it right back in.

'If I may say so without seeming smug, we both enjoyed my first fuck, for Fiona was an excellent teacher, slowing me down and then urging me to quicken the pace as her juices lubricated her cunney walls, making my shaft squelch merrily in and out of her honeypot. She twined her legs about my waist and asked me to put my hands under her hips as I pushed forward and buried the entire length of my cock in her hungry snatch. As I did so she began to rub her clitty hard against my rigid rod and her soft moans turned to a rising scream as she urged me on. "A-h-r-e! You dear boy, push on! Come now, Leonard, empty your balls!" she cried out and I began to pump wildly, feeling my ballsack smack against her bottom as together we scaled the heights of ecstacy. I crashed huge shoots of love cream into her sopping cunney and this brought down her flow of pussey juice, which flooded her luscious nest, and our fluids oozed down in a trickle across her thighs.

'We lay panting as I slowly withdrew my glistening cock which was still almost as stiff as before it first entered her glorious quim. When we had recovered our senses she began to fondle my cock and her hand moved rhythmically up and down my stiffening shaft between her long fingers. As my prick hardened I felt myself being pushed upon my back and Fiona said: "There are other ways to enjoy fucking, Leonard. I particularly like being on top because it allows my clitty to be rubbed by the tip of the cock but some men, rather foolishly to my way of thinking, find it demeaning in some way to be beneath a female during love-making. Mind, these are the rough kind of fellows I would never let get in between my legs. Still, that's another story. Let me show you what I mean about the girl-on-top position."

'She climbed up on top of me, bending forward to kiss my lips as I cupped those voluptuous breasts in my hands, feeling the hard little titties against my palms. Her oily cunney lips were just touching the very tip of my helmet, which made my staff tremble with anticipation. When she moved her hips so that her cunney lips slid over my knob, I thrilled in the clinging wetness as she lowered herself gently until almost all of my throbbing length was inside her. "There, isn't that nice?" she asked, and I gasped back how perfectly splendid it was as she raised herself up and then suddenly plumped herself down hard, impaling herself on my cock which revelled in its surround of warm, wet cunney flesh.

'How she squealed as she moved her body up and down, using her thighs to ride me, bobbing herself up and down so that her breasts jounced up and down as I met her downward thrusts with jerks of my hips upwards. I panted heavily with this exertion as Fiona heaved herself up and down on my twitching tool, taking every last inch of me deep into her hairy pit, and the continuous nipping and contractions of her clever pussey soon brought me to a rip-roaring spend. At first I tried to hold back but I could not deny the boiling spunk that was racing up from my balls and I sent a tremendous jet of jism up into her cunt as she rocked up and down, faster and faster until with a delighted yell she writhed in convulsions of joy as her orgasm enveloped her body and she shivered all over, almost swooning away as her cunney disgorged a rivulet of love fluids all over my matted pubic thatch.

' "Well, what do you think, Lenny, was that as good as before?" she gasped as she rolled off me to lay panting in my arms. "Just as good if not even better," I replied truthfully. "I read somewhere that this method is known as the lazy man's fuck and I can see why. You have to do most of the work."

'But before she could answer we were startled by a fruity chuckle from our right. "Well now, you look as if you've been working well enough already, nephew," commented the gentleman whose portly frame filled the doorway. It was none other than Uncle Jonathan himself! "I'm glad to see that my birthday present has been opened," he continued, smacking his lips with evident gusto.

' "He's a chip off the old block and fully deserved his treat," said Fiona. "Oh, do come in, Jonathan, if you are staying and shut the door. I want to fuck Leonard again so you'll have to share if you want to join us."

' "I will with pleasure," said my randy uncle who tore off his clothes with an amazing rapidity and in a trice was on the bed with us, his veiny cock heavy as it lay semi-erect over his thigh. "After all, there's nothing like keeping it in the family." I motioned as if to leave but Fiona caught my arm. "No, no, don't go – let's see if I can stiffen you up to ride your cock again, and while we're at it your uncle can fuck my bum if he can't get in my cunt," she suggested.

' "Sounds like a good idea," agreed Uncle Jonathan, reaching out for a pot of cold cream whilst Fiona knelt down and popped my cock into her mouth. Could I rise to the occasion one more time? Her darting tongue moved along my rod and as she licked my knob my shaft began to grow and swell up as hard and as stiff as ever. She gave my cock one last long lick and said: "Oooh, what stamina – I envy the lucky girl who'll be fucked by you now you've got the hang of it."

'In no time at all she was back between my legs, her cunney lips slipping over my knob in an instant, and she bounced up and down, repeating the pleasure as Uncle Jonathan tried to insert his thick member in her cunt alongside mine, but this was impossible to achieve. So my uncle clamped his hands on her arse and parted her rounded bum cheeks and then he dipped a hand into the cold cream and liberally anointed her rear dimple. Fiona stuck out her bottom as he wet his sizeable knob with yet another dollop of cold cream. Then he pushed his thick shaft between her buttocks and soon his vigorous shoves gained an entrance as Fiona wiggled her bum lasciviously in front of him, enjoying the feel of his domed knob which was well burrowed inside her backside. Clamping her firmly, Uncle Jonathan pushed forward until his entire shaft was sheathed inside her back passage. For a brief moment we rested with our two cocks throbbing against the other with only the thin divisional membrane of the anal canal separating them.

Then I started to jerk my body up and down, my cock sluicing through her engorged quim whilst Fiona wriggled her *derrière* in time with each sliding motion of Uncle Jonathan's lusty organ. I found this threesome fucking so exciting that I came very soon after, injecting soul-stirring spurts of spunk, and this led to Uncle Jonathan pumping his prick in and out of Fiona's bum at a fast rate of knots until he ejaculated a hot gush of juice into her bottom. He gallantly withdrew his prick slowly until with an audible plop! the avuncular tool emerged and he sank back, mopping his brow. "Phew, that was fun," he grunted. "Now who would like a drink?"

I spent the rest of the afternoon and evening with Jonathan and Fiona, my kindly uncle telephoning my parents to say that he was taking me out to supper as a birthday treat, which was in fact the case, although I dare say Uncle Jonathan could be justly accused of being economical with the truth!'

Frank slowly expelled a great breath of air. 'Damn it, I wish I had an uncle like yours, you lucky blighter.'

'Yes, he's a real good sport, and on my seventeenth birthday he took me to a Victor Pudendum contest at the Jim Jam Club [*a notorious meeting place in Great Windmill Street where the very highest in the land took part in discreet affairs and wild orgies – Editor*]. I must be going now as I have to prepare some notes for a tutorial,' said Leonard, rising to his feet, 'but all of you please remember, if any of you ever find yourselves short of a good fuck in London, just call me. I'm now an associate member of the Jim Jam and for just ten bob [*fifty pence – Editor*] Solly the doorman can always be relied on to provide a couple of pretty young dollymops.'

'I'd better leave too as I also have work to prepare for tomorrow,' I said, though thinking more of my assignments with Beth, Esme and Gillian than the boring pages of my books on political economy. 'See you at breakfast, chaps,' I added as I strolled back to my room with a smile on my face, as it suddenly struck me how funny it would be for one of my uncles, the Rector of West Finchley, to be offered an evening at the Jim Jam Club. However, the old boy was no fool and whilst passing the port after dinner one evening whilst a guest at our house, he made it clear that before marriage he had himself enjoyed what he described as 'The Fleshpots Of The Metropolis', and that he considered it right and proper for

291

any young man to enjoy some happy years of freedom. 'Mind, I cannot countenance over-familiar dalliances with young, attractive members of the opposite, ah, gender.' I listened in respectful silence, stifling my amusement when he proceeded to lean over and in a conspiratorial whisper murmured in my ear: 'But if you do find yourself tempted by the sins of the flesh, my advice is to go for a girl with large titties. For as we often said in officers' mess when I served with the Hussars: like titties, like clitty.'

Of course, by that time Uncle Arthur had downed the best part of a full decanter of '96 Old and Crusted so to be fair, it was the port rather than the clergyman giving me that sound advice!

I shook myself free of this pleasant reverie as I opened the door to my quarters. For a moment I thought I had entered the wrong room for Nancy the maid was lying on my bed, dressed only in a flimsy nightdress and lying on her tummy. Alongside her, completely naked, was a most attractive tall girl, finely formed with blonde hair falling down in ringlets onto her shoulders. She had smaller breasts than the generously endowed Nancy but possessed firm, chubby buttocks which quivered as she lifted her head and said: 'Nancy, is this the young gentleman you were talking about before supper?'

'Yes, this is Rupert Mountjoy,' said Nancy, waving her hand lazily at me. 'Rupert, I want you to meet my friend Rosa Crouthampe, who works at Brasenose College but comes over to visit me as often as she can. Rosa is my very best friend, aren't you, dearest? Isn't she pretty,

Rupert? Look at the rolling swell of her bum cheeks. Now turn over, Rosa, and let Rupert see the tight yellow curls around your cunney and the dear little love lips peeking through them. Wouldn't you like to plonk your big cock between them, Rupert, you randy devil? Oh dear, you must forgive my naughty language but we've had a few drinks to celebrate my birthday, and anyhow, I'm sure you'd want to fuck Rosa because you and Barry and Frank are the randiest boys out of all the first year students.'

'You're very probably right,' I agreed as I shut the door behind me.

'But you shouldn't speak to Rupert in such a familiar way and I think you owe him an apology,' said Rosa, and despite my protestations that I was not in the least offended by Nancy's remark, Rosa insisted that Nancy should be punished for her indiscreet observations. Nancy herself did not seem to want to challenge her friend on this point and offered no resistance when Rosa turned her over on her belly and, throwing up her chemise, exposed Nancy's perfectly rounded little bum cheeks to my lascivious gaze. She then rose to her knees and began to smack the two beautiful white hemispheres of Nancy's backside, saying: 'This will teach you to be so forward, you bad girl.' She slapped lightly and it was plain that both girls were enjoying this little scene. Rosa's lithe naked body glistened as her hand rose and fell, her round, nut-brown nipples rising and falling quickly with each sharp stroke, her cheeks slightly flushed with her exertions and her blue eyes sparkling with excitement as she chastised her naughty friend.

'Oh! Oh! Oh! No more, Rosa, ouch, it hurts, it hurts, Ouch! Please stop!' begged Nancy as she winced and wriggled under the rapid succession of slaps.

'Quiet now, Nancy! Stop making such a fuss,' snapped Rosa fiercely. 'You have been a very bad girl and all bad girls get smacked. Besides, Rupert and I love the way your bum cheeks jiggle as I smack them. Now we want to see your lovely botty colour up. See how nicely your buttocks are blushing! They should always be bright pink, shouldn't they, Rupert?'

This lewd scene had made my cock swell up unbearably and as I watched this stimulating scene Nancy called out to me: 'Come on then, show us your stiffstander.' The thought flashed through my mind of what would occur if we were caught (for there were no locks on the doors) but as the maxim of the great Count Gewirtz of Galicia has it: *ven der putz shtayt, ligt seichel oif'n fenster [when the prick stands up, common sense flies out the window – Editor]* and I shucked off my clothes in record time. I jumped onto the bed and huddled up next to Rosa who, without missing one beat of her rhythm as she continued her inexorable spanking of Nancy's now tingling backside, clamped her wide, red lips around my rampant cock.

Mercifully for the other girl, this excited Rosa so much that after bobbing her head back and forth to suck in as much of my shaft as she could, she ceased her slapping of Nancy's poor bum and instead she jammed her hands around my pulsating prick which already had a blob of milky jism formed on the tip of my knob. She jammed down the foreskin and lashed her tongue round my pole which was now thudding away like a steamhammer. I worked my hips backwards and forwards as her pliant tongue washed over my bared helmet, thoroughly enjoying this delicious sucking-off.

Meanwhile Nancy had raised herself on her hands and knees and had lowered her pretty head between Rosa's legs, splaying open her buttocks to make room for her lips to kiss between the ripe, white globes, worrying her tongue around her corn-coloured pussey hair which I imagined was already dampening with love juice, teasing the tip around the pouting pussey lips before slipping in and out of her juicy quim.

Fired by this tribadic activity I pulled my prick away from Rosa's mouth and positioned myself behind Nancy, whose rounded bottom cheeks were moving in rhythm as she suctioned Rosa's blonde-haired pussey between her lips. Nancy took hold of my sinewy shaft with her right hand and directed its purple-domed head to the glorious vale between her buttocks and to the tight-looking wrinkled hole that lay between them. After further wetting my tool with spittle, I attacked this fortress with vigour, but as my member forced its way past the sphincter muscle she wailed: 'Ah, stop! Stop! You'll rend me if you don't withdraw!' Fortunately I keep a small jar of pomade [a perfumed ointment for the hair – Editor] on the bedside table so I swiftly greased my cock and again set my knob at the little brown bum-hole. The pomade worked like a charm for this time when I pushed forward Nancy wriggled her arse until I was firmly ensconced inside her bum.

For a brief moment I rested and then slowly began to pull in and out whilst I threw my arms around her waist and frigged her pussey. Nancy responded to this double stimulation by squirming under the surging strokes of my prick. Her legs began to shake and I knew that her spend was approaching. She gripped hold of Rosa's thighs as she lapped furiously at the girl's soaking slit. Nancy's juices flowed freely and she worked her bum to bring me off, and I flooded her arse with a copious discharge of sperm which both warmed and lubricated her superb bottom. As I spunked into her I continued to work my prick back and forth so that it remained as hard as rock as, with a 'pop', I uncorked my tool from her bum-hole. We screamed loudly in the frenzy of emission as Rosa also spent over Nancy's lapping tongue and we collapsed in a heap on my bed.

When we had recovered Nancy thanked me for taking the trouble to use the pomade and not simply pushing forward and ignoring her plea to withdraw. 'I sometimes think that there are some men who enjoy hurting their partners – or at best they are uncaring,' she complained. 'Most girls enjoy a good fuck up the bum but only when the cock has been well oiled beforehand with butter or some other substance.' Since this day I have heeded her words and have always kept a jar of cold cream handy for this purpose. But now we were fired up again and we engaged in some splendid three way kisses, pressing our lips together and waggling our tongues around in a most sensuous manner. If we had had any inhibitions they were now cast aside, so I had not the slightest intention of ducking the challenge when Nancy placed her hand on top of my head and drew it down towards Rosa's hairy mound, saying: 'Rosa loves having her pussey kissed. I've brought her off, Rupert, now let's see if you can do so.'

I drew my body up until my tongue was level with her titties and began by nibbling at her nipples, licking and sucking on their rubbery hardness until they were sticking out like two tiny stalks. Then I let my tongue travel slowly down the velvety white skin of her tummy, pausing briefly to encircle her belly-button before sliding down into the curly smooth hair of her mound. Like a snake I slid myself down between her legs as I parted her soft, lightly scented pubic bush with my fingertips to reveal her swollen clitoris, and as I worked my lips into the long gash of her cleft I breathed in the delicious aroma from her clean, appealing cunney, a fragrance which has always greatly excited me. By slipping a hand under her bum, I pressed her even more closely to me as I placed my lips directly over her clitty and sucked it into my mouth, where the tip of my tongue began to explore it from all directions. I could feel it growing even larger as her heels drummed against the sheets and her legs twitched up and down along the sides of my body.

Rosa became hugely agitated when I found the tiny button under the fold at the base of her clitty and began twirling my tongue around it. The faster I vibrated my tongue, the more she twisted and turned and I was forced to move both of my hands to her shoulders to keep her cunney pressed against my face. She now started to gyrate her pelvis as I increased the stimulation and she planted her feet firmly on my back as if she desired to mould our two bodies into one mass of quivering flesh.

'Oooh! Aaah! Stick your cock in me now!' panted Rosa, and this was an opportunity my bursting prick was happy to take. So I heaved myself up and fixed my lips on one of her horned-up nipples, and the strawberry stalk grew long and hard as I sucked it between my teeth. At the same time her cunney responded to the urgings of the three fingers I had buried inside the clinging sheath and I frigged her slippery clitty with my thumb. The more I frigged her, the quicker she jerked her hips and she grabbed my cock and began pumping my shaft, sliding her hand up and down in such insane excitement that she spent then and there and I felt the sticky moistness of her honey cascade over my hand. This set me off and I spunked a profuse libation of hot, creamy jism that drenched her hand. She directed my spurting shaft up to her belly and smeared my cream all over her white tummy.

'Now who's been a naughty girl,' stormed Nancy. 'See how you've wasted poor Rupert's semen. Get up and bend over the chair in the corner.' To my surprise, Rosa meekly did as she was told and when she had placed herself over the chair, Nancy gave me one of my slippers and told me to chastise the wayward girl.

'No, I can't do that, Rosa would not want to be spanked,' I laughed nervously as I took a long look at the plump, well-shaped cheeks of Rosa's behind.

'Oh, but Nancy's right,' Rosa called out, turning her head to look at me. 'I have been a bad girl and deserve to have my bum smacked.'

Well, there is no accounting for tastes, and although in my time I have spanked a good number of female bottoms I have never been a fervent devotee of *le vice anglais*. Perhaps this is because at St Lionel's Academy, corporal punishment was unknown and we suffered none of the sadistic beatings inflicted upon pupils at most other English public schools. But be that as it may, whilst I draw the line at really whipping one's partner's backside, if the girl really likes to be stimulated in such fashion, so be it, and I cannot deny that I achieve some mild satisfaction from distributing the occasional few passionate slaps on the swells of feminine rears.

So I jumped out of bed and went across to where Rosa lay inert over the chair, provocatively wiggling her arse as I approached. I passed my hand caressingly over the cool, soft skin of the swelling cheeks of her buttocks. I brought the sole of my slipper down upon these pretty posteriors but my first few strokes hardly changed the colour of the flesh and Rosa turned her head round and said: 'You may hit harder than that, Rupert. Honestly, I can hardly feel anything.'

'Are you certain that this is what you want?' I asked, 'Because if it is, my girl, I'll give it to you!' She nodded and so this time I lifted my arm high and brought down the slipper with a thwack which must have made her bottom tingle. I struck her again in similar smart fashion and her bum cheeks soon assumed a glowing, rosy hue as I administered a good, sound spanking. This pleased both girls for Nancy went down on her knees and sucked up my cock between her lips, palating my prick so sensuously that my shaft swelled up to bursting point in her mouth. After a dozen strokes I threw away the slipper and led Rosa back to the bed where, as I surmised she would find her backside too painful to lie upon, I pushed her face downwards, her legs apart but on the floor and her forearms on the bed. She knew what was about to happen so she stuck out her backside for me to part the two tingling cheeks and I plunged my trusty cock into her warm, juicy slit from behind, my balls fairly cracking against her bottom.

'Keep going, that's the ticket!' she laughed merrily, and her backside responded to every shove as I pounded her pussey, driving home until, excited to such raging peaks, the contractions of her deliciously tight cunney lips sucked the spunk from my prick. The sweet friction of her pussey lips against the sensitive skin of my knob sent the sperm pumping through my shaft into her waiting love box as I thrust my twitching tool to and fro with all my youthful vigour.

Nancy threw herself down to lie beside us on her back, her hands busy parting her pussey lips

300

as she frigged herself excitedly, somehow managing to turn her head across to lick Rosa's goregous titties. My own climax was nearing and our surging cries of joy echoed around the room as the three of us began the journey down the road to ecstacy. Then I started to tremble and began shaking like a leaf from head to toe, until a huge wave of delight flooded through my body and I sent thick wads of creamy spunk crashing into Rosa's sopping cunney and she too screamed with delight as she shivered through a powerful orgasm just as the hot, frothy jism drenched her womb.

Well, of course I would have liked nothing better than to have continued to fuck both girls throughout the remainder of the evening. But I had an important essay to prepare for Professor Webb and reluctantly ordered the girls to leave my room and go back downstairs. They were most disappointed and even my insistence on giving each of the girls a pound note as a farewell present did not mollify them.

'I bet you've already found some posh tart from one of the women's colleges. These girls are supposed to arrive here all sweet and innocent but it doesn't take them long to snap up any young boy who has had some experience and knows how to fuck like a gentleman,' sighed Nancy. 'Rupert, don't forget now, any time you want your cock sucked, please let me know.'

I smiled my goodbyes and with difficulty turned my mind to such stimulating legal matters as the rights of landlords and tenants and the ramifications of the judgement in the case of The Attorney General versus The Borough of Fulham in the High Court fifteen years ago. It was devilishly hard to concentrate upon such affairs. When I banished Nancy and Rosa from my mind, Beth and Esme stepped up smartly to take their place and when I finally forced them out of my brain, a picture of the beautiful Gillian Headleigh formed itself every time I tried to focus my eyes on the page. My heart began to pound as I remembered her words: *'meet me at this time tomorrow and you may fuck me for as long as you can keep your cock stiff!'* The old, familiar tingling began to make itself felt in my groin. My hand wandered down to smooth itself over my shaft, but I had no need of the five-fingered widow after tonight's fun and games, and anyhow I needed to keep up my strength for Gillian tomorrow morning. So I cleared my mind of everything except the need to prepare for Professor Webb's tutorial and doggedly read six more pages from my textbook, scribbling some notes and memorising some important points before slamming the book shut, and after a refreshing warm bath I settled down in bed, as happy as a sandboy.

As is still my custom, I picked up a newspaper to read for a few minutes before turning off the light and in the *Oxford Mail* my attention was captured by a report of the speech made at the Empire Club by Dr Whibley of Merton College attacking 'the monstrous encroachment of women upon the University' and how a mixed University – 'the dream of the farcemonger' – will lose its unique distinction. 'The University will be destroyed because once more the patent truth has been ignored that men are men and women women.'

For how long will such reactionary views be propounded in this new twentieth century, I thought to myself as I chucked the newspaper on the floor in disgust, because no force on earth can turn back the clock once a sizeable proportion of the population (for better or worse) refuse to accept the old established order. By and large, women will never again be content with a subservient role in society despite the rantings of Dr Whibley and his ilk, and will rightly demand the same privileges and duties as men.

As far as I was concerned, it was a most pleasant discovery to find out that inside the ivy-covered college walls, away from the prying gaze of the outside world, the opportunity arose for many girls to shed a cloak of modesty which could be safely stripped away. My first days in Oxford, alone and apprehensive as to whether I would be happy spending three years here, were miserable indeed – but after meeting these jolly girls who revelled in their new-found freedom, there was now no doubt in my mind that the student life had much to commend itself to a red-blooded young man who enjoyed the taste of forbidden fruit!

CHAPTER TWO

Extramural Studies

MY HEART SANK WHEN DURING BREAKFAST the
following morning a college servant presented me with a letter which had been
hand-delivered by a young lady just half an hour
beforehand. 'Damn and blast!' I muttered as I
gave myself the mental odds of a pound to a
penny that the envelope contained a note from
Gillian cancelling our mid-day tryst.

At first glance my pessimism seemed to have
been well-founded for indeed the letter was from
this pretty girl and as I had forecast, she could not
meet me as planned. But as I read on my face
broke into a smile for this was no mere cold
cancellation but a hot-blooded *billet-doux* which I
still have in my possession and so can reproduce
it in full:

> *Dearest Rupert,*
> *First, the bad news; I cannot meet you as planned*
> *this morning because I have to attend a lecture*
> *which has been brought forward from four o'clock*
> *this afternoon.*

But this leaves me free from one o'clock and at the risk of sounding over-forward I would like to suggest that we meet for a late luncheon at Carlo's Restaurant which is in Woodstock Road just before the junction with Little Clarendon Street. If the weather is good we could take a bus or train to Woodstock and see Blenheim Palace [A richly furnished palace with many art treasures designed by Sir John Vanbrugh for the Duke of Marlborough and mostly paid for by Parliament in recognition of the Duke's victory over the French at the Battle of Blenheim in the War of the Spanish Succession – Editor].

On the other hand, if it's raining, we could go back to my house as, like yesterday, my room-mates will be away until at least six o'clock. Somehow, even if the sun is shining brightly, I think I can speculate what you would prefer to do and oh, Rupert, to be honest, I wouldn't be too disappointed if we went to Blenheim Palace on another day!

For if I were forced to make a choice between viewing the marvellous Blenheim gardens laid out by Capability Brown [a noted eighteenth-century landscape gardener – Editor] *and sucking your cock, I would always plump for the latter. I do love sucking a fat juicy prick, caressing the red mushroomed crown with my lips and then washing it with my tongue. It is so thrilling when the shaft trembles in my mouth and so exciting when the frothy cream shoots out of the tiny hole and I can spread the sticky jism all around the knob with my tongue. I love swallowing mouthfuls of tangy spunk too and cannot think of anything that tastes so fine and clean.*

Enough now, for writing this frank confession is making my pussey damp and soon it will be crying out for relief which I can only partially satisfy by frigging myself. Only a proud, throbbing stiffstander like yours will be able to quench my voracious sensual desires . . .

If you aren't free this afternoon, leave a note at my house. Otherwise, I'll be at Carlo's restaurant at around twenty past one this afternoon and look forward to seeing you there.

Love,

Gillian

Well, dear reader, I doubt whether you would have to ponder for more than a second about a choice between walking round Blenheim Palace or fucking Gillian Headleigh! The only problem facing me now was how to collect my thoughts for Professor Simon Webb's tutorial which would begin in ten minutes' time. Somehow I managed to concentrate upon my work and after what seemed an eternity the hands of the clock finally came together at noon. I gathered my books up in a rush and was about to fly out the room when the Professor beckoned me. 'Mr Mountjoy, a quick word if you have a moment,' he said and though I could hardly wait to get back to my room to change I could hardly refuse to listen to a senior lecturer.

'I am inviting a few undergraduates over for an after dinner soirée in my quarters tomorrow night and I wonder whether you would care to join us at about half past eight?' This was an honour indeed and I accepted his invitation with sincere pleasure, especially as he had not, as I had feared, engaged in further discussion upon our work, which was just as well because already I had little time to spruce myself up before my appointment with the lovely Gillian at Carlo's Restaurant.

In fact I arrived at Carlo's in good time and was welcomed effusively by the eponymous owner, Signor Carlo Justini, who has of course since found fame and fortune as the proprietor of the Trattoria d'Argento in Piccadilly which is patronised by the *crème de la crème* of London Society. 'Come this way, sir. Miss 'Eadleigh has booked a table in a private room upstairs. Perhaps you would like a glass of wine whilst you wait for her?' he suggested, but before I could even answer him Gillian had entered the restaurant and I greeted her. In front of Carlo we exchanged a formal handshake, though once he had brought us a bottle of chilled white wine and taken our order, I leaned over the table and kissed her firmly on the lips.

'Thank you for your lovely letter,' I said as I resumed my seat, 'but you win no prizes for guessing what I prefer to do after luncheon.'

'You mean then that I shall have to wait for another occasion to walk round Blenheim Palace,' she said, returning my smile. 'Well, I think I can live with this disappointment so long as you can provide me with an equally pleasurable entertainment this afternoon.'

'Gillian, I promise you that will prove to be no problem,' I assured her as our eyes met in a knowing glance and, when I felt her foot rub sinuously against my ankle, I knew that this sensuous girl was feeling just as randy as me! But there was no huge hurry for we had until six o'clock to ourselves and we first enjoyed a delicious luncheon, the highlight of which was grilled chicken with a *panzanella* bread salad of plum tomatoes and parsley. We both ate sparingly for we knew that fucking on a full stomach is not a practice to be recommended. As we sipped our *grappa*, the little minx must have slipped off her shoes for I felt her silk-clad foot move up between my legs under the cover of the sparkling white linen tablecloth. Gillian giggled as Signor Justini bustled in with a fresh pot of coffee and she stroked the stiff length of my shaft with her toes.

'Have you ever fucked in a restaurant, Rupert?' she whispered throatily as her toes continued to stroke my stiffstander.

'No, but I'm more than willing to try out the experience,' I replied.

Gillian leaned forward and as she was wearing a jacket with a low neckline, I was given a clear view of her firm, ripe breasts. 'Well, it's very nice to repair to a couch immediately after leaving the table, but as there is a nice, comfortable bed waiting round the corner, perhaps it would be as well to wait until another time. I do have a fondness for such sport you see, because it was in a private dining-room such as this at the Café Clive that I became a woman.

'Yes, Rupert,' she continued. 'I was first fucked by Sir Andrew Stuck, perhaps the randiest rogue in all London.'

'I hope he did not take advantage of you,' I

commented, for even then I knew that an extra bottle of champagne often led to a remorseful morning.

'Oh no, I was more than willing to surrender my virginity to him. I was like the Lady of Kent in the limerick:

There was a young Lady of Kent,
Who said that she knew what it meant
When men asked her to dine
And also to wine,
She knew what it meant – but she went!'

I was keenly interested to hear more but Signor Justini knocked on the door and presented us with the bill. As I busied myself writing out a cheque, Gillian muttered: 'I'll tell you more about it when we get home, although you must fuck me first.'

'Your wish is my command,' I replied quietly as Signor Justini and his staff ushered us out into the street. It was less than five minutes' walk to Gillian's rooms and, as she had promised in her letter, none of the other girls in the house were present. We ran straight up to the bedroom and in an inkling we had shucked off our clothes and embraced each other's naked body as we rolled around on the soft mattress.

'My darling boy! Tell me how you are going to fuck me,' she cried.

I thought for a moment and said: 'How am I going to fuck you, Gillian? Well, first I am going to roll you over on your back and then I shall mount you as I decide which way we shall first take our pleasure. To begin with, perhaps I shall simply lie

309

on your belly and slowly insert my long, thick cock into your inviting little wet snatch. Then I'll push forward until my shaft is fully inside your velvety sheath before I pull it out and then tease the lips of your pussey with my knob. Then I'll crash my cock back inside your cunney and pump away, increasing the tempo gradually until I'm pistoning such hard, deep thrusts that my balls crack against your thighs. Then we'll come together, my throbbing tool spewing out a sea of sperm whilst your pussey creams itself with the sweet love juices from your hairy honeypot.'

'What a magnificent fuck that sounds! But let me first salute your proud prick.' She dived down to brush my iron-hard member with her cheek as she licked my heavy, hanging balls with her wet tongue. I writhed in delicious agony as she transferred her attentions to my cock, licking the shaft from base to tip in long, langorous strokes. She moved round to make herself comfortable as she played with my prick, pressing it to each of her smallish but beautifully rounded breasts, squeezing it between them and then softly biting and tickling my purple knob with the end of her wicked little tongue. Then suddenly she thrust her mouth down and took my entire eight inches into her mouth and her salacious sucking almost brought me off there and then.

It was far too early to shoot my load so I placed my hands gently under her shoulders and heaved her back onto the bed until she was lying down and she whispered: 'Suck on my titties, please, Rupert, this really makes me feel very randy.' She spoke the truth for she started to squirm as soon as my lips touched her stalky nip. As I sucked it into my mouth I ran my hands all over her body, lingering on her inner thighs whilst I took one and then the other rubbery red tittie between my lips, licking and lapping at the succulent flesh as Gillian's hand now circled and slid up and down my raging staff. Then it was her turn to pull my body upwards as she parted her long, slim legs and as I entered her I paused to savour the sensation as my mushroom helmet squelched its way inside her damp, soft-walled tunnel. She raised her legs high as our loins locked together, our hips bucking wildly as we thrashed around and I pounded in and out, my hands clasping the firm white globes of her backside as the spunk boiled up in my balls and thrust upwards through my pulsating penis.

Alas, I simply could not wait for Gillian to climax and with a mighty groan I flooded her cunt with a torrent of warm sperm as jets of jism poured out of my prick so abundantly that her thighs were well lubricated. I withdrew my tingling truncheon, rubbing it amorously against the sticky lips of her pussey.

'Oh dear, I am so sorry,' I apologised as I rolled over to cuddle her in my arms, 'but I just could not hold back any longer.'

'There is absolutely no need to apologise, you sweet boy. You fucked me delightfully and I don't have to spend every time, you know,' she said generously.

'But surely it *does* matter,' I persisted. 'If you don't manage to climax then I must be doing something wrong.'

Gillian sat up and put a finger against my mouth. 'Let me give you some good advice, Rupert. You really must not become obsessed with timing your spend or you will be in danger of forgetting everything else! Although I grant you that some men do have a problem about spending too quickly, I assure you there is very little to be gained in holding back or forcing forward merely to achieve a simultaneous spend.

'Of course it can be great fun to climax together but this is but one joy of love-making which need never interfere with any other pleasures. Why, I've often found that spending at different times allows the partner who comes first to concentrate on exciting the other which can be very, very nice for them both.'

Maybe I still looked doubtful for she added: 'Rupert, if you don't believe me, I'll gladly lend you my copy of that marvellous textbook *Fucking For Beginners* by Nigel Andrews and you'll read for yourself that what I am telling you is plain, simple fact.'

Of course as I matured I soon realised the complete truth of Gillian's words though at the time they were spoken I did believe that she was perhaps slightly gilding the lily for my benefit. Anyway, I nodded my head in agreement and quickly changed the subject. 'What about telling me instead the story of how you were fucked by Sir Andrew Stuck?' I demanded as I threw my arm around her shoulders.

She giggled and said: 'Oh yes, I mentioned something about my first poking by young randy Andy at the restaurant, didn't I? It was quite an

312

adventure really as naturally I was still at Trippett's Academy. I had come home for the Easter holidays and I decided to visit my friend Estelle Kenton, who happens to be Andrew's cousin. I'd never met Andrew although like most girls of our class living in London I had heard of his reputation as a ladies' man. As luck would have it, Andrew had also decided to visit Estelle that fateful afternoon and when I was introduced to him I could see why so many young women (as rumour had it) offered themselves for his delectation. There's no getting away from the fact that he's a handsome chap with a friendly face and a witty turn of speech.

'Andrew is one of those chaps who is so blessed with the gift of the gab that if fate had placed him in a different strata of society he would have made an excellent career as a salesman in one of these new huge emporiums in the West End.

'To cut short a long story, before he left us, Andrew asked me to dine with him the following evening. Normally I would have had to ask permission from my parents but they were spending a few days away in the country with some friends so I was free to accept Andrew's invitation without any hindrance. He called for me punctually at eight o'clock in his new motor vehicle and as Grahame, his chauffeur, drove through Oxford Street Andrew told me that he had booked a table at the Café Clive in Museum Street, Bloomsbury. Now I had read about this establishment in the illustrated papers and knew it to be a favourite haunt of the smart 'fast' set, and this already added an extra spice to the evening.

'When we arrived there was already quite a gathering at the restaurant as Lord George Lucas had booked a table to celebrate his birthday. Along with a clutch of other young men his party consisted of chorus girls from the musical comedy at the Alhambra Theatre which was due to open in three days' time. This merry throng dominated the atmosphere but I found it all terribly exciting, especially when the handsome Lord George himself came up to our table. "Hello, Andrew, you lucky so-and-so. How in heaven's name did you manage to persuade this gorgeous young lady to dine with you tonight?

' "I don't think I've had the pleasure," he added as he turned to me, his sensuous grey eyes locked into mine, and I smiled demurely, trying hard to act the part of a shy, blushing maiden.

' "Yes you have, George, but not with that pretty girl," called out one of his friends from his table. "At least, not yet!"

'Andrew was not overpleased by Lord George's intervention especially when the young peer invited us to join his party, and he murmured his thanks after I had politely declined and Lord George returned to his guests, where his jolly friend Mr Stockman was regaling the company with a risqué story about how he had recently encountered a pretty young woman who turned out to be a witch whilst driving his carriage along a country lane. He knew she was a witch for when she put her hand on the front of his trousers he turned into a lay-by!

'We enjoyed a splendid meal and then Andrew suggested that we took our coffee and liqueurs in one of the small private rooms upstairs. Monsieur Clive himself ushered us into the room which was richly decorated with fine furnishings. I noticed immediately that what appeared to be suspiciously like a bed frame and mattress stood in a corner, covered in cream linen sheets along with two big matching pillows plumped up against the wall. I said nothing but sat across the table from Andrew who poured out two steaming cups of black coffee as he asked me whether I would care to join him in a glass of cognac or some other liqueur from the clutch of bottles on the small sideboard. I accepted his offer of coffee and chose a kummel [a Central European aniseed and cumin liqueur favoured by Queen Victoria – Editor] to accompany it.

'We held hands as we talked and Andrew must have slipped off a shoe for I felt his foot insinuate itself between my ankles and I was so aroused as his toes moved higher and higher that my silk knickers were soon damp even before his foot had reached my thighs!

'I shall spare us both further blushes except to admit that I was no match for Andrew Stuck's polished technique of seduction. In my defence I shall simply say that few girls could resist the charms of this handsome, wealthy young baronet and very shortly afterwards he moved round to sit next to me and we exchanged a passionate kiss. As his tongue probed inside my mouth I felt his hand fondling my breasts. "What divine bosoms, Gillian. I am sure your titties will be as beautiful to the eye as they are to the touch."

315

'After this sweet compliment Andrew unbuttoned my dress and gently eased off the front of my chemise so that my naked breasts lay in his hands. We kissed again and he squeezed my nipples so wonderfully that they became hard and pointed. He rubbed them between his fingers and as he stroked them he put his head down and began to kiss and suck my erect little red soldiers.

'Soon I was lying naked and trembling on the bed watching him undress and admiring his wiry, athletic body – and no doubt like so many girls before and after this experience, I gasped with wonderment when he pulled down his drawers to reveal his astonishingly thick prick which sprang upwards from the mass of black hair at the base of his belly. Although technically I was still a virgin (though I had often used the ladies' comforter I had purchased by mail-order from Madame Nettleton's – you must have seen their advertisements in *Society News* with their famous guarantee that "all purchases are sent in discreet plain parcels" – and had previously frigged and sucked a certain number of cocks) I knew that Andrew would want to fuck me, but I was worried that I could never accommodate that enormous shaft inside my little cunney.

'Andrew took me in his arms as he knelt down and laid down beside me. His French cologne smelled beautifully and I revelled in the sensation of his abundant chest hair tickling my so sensitive nipples. Our bodies pressed even closer together and he put his hands around my bum cheeks which pushed his huge cock against my soft tummy. At first I didn't hold it as I had no desire to appear a wanton but I could not resist letting my hand wander across the enormous shaft when his right hand slithered around from my bottom and the palm of his hand rubbed itself against my pussey, which was by now moistening like a dew-drenched flower in eager anticipation of what was to come.

'But before we proceeded any further down the path of passion, Sir Andrew Stuck showed himself to be a true aristocrat. "I would love to fuck you, dearest Gillian," he whispered quietly, "but you are only seventeen years old and may well be a virgin. I do not want you to regret this evening so even now if you decide to hold back, I will respect your wishes."

These kind and caring words made my heart warm even more towards this considerate young man and looking steadily into his sensual dark eyes I said softly: "Andrew, I very much want you to fuck me. Yes, I am a virgin in that no cock has ever actually entered my love-tunnel, but I lost my hymen some time back thanks to all the frigging and the joys of Madame Nettleton's famous dildoes!"

'With a smile he nodded his head but still asked again: "So you are absolutely certain that you want to be fucked, Gillian?"

' "Yes, oh yes, very, very much – and right now!" I answered with some vehemence and I grasped his meaty tool, making a fist around the pulsating shaft with my fingers and I gently masturbated this tremendous love-truncheon as his fingertips slid their way into my juicy cunney. He now raised himself over me and plunged his

317

head down to wash his tongue for a second time over my titties and I arched my back upwards as he licked so thoroughly that when I passed a hand over my tittie it felt as hard as an unripe red berry. For a split second our hot eyes locked together as I took his bursting cock in both hands and placed the purple domed helmet against the pouting cunney lips which were more than ready to receive it. He carefully inserted an inch or so of his tremendous tadger as he moved forward to lay on top of me. I spread my legs as wide as possible and wrapped my legs around his waist as our lips collided and meshed together.

I had been concerned that I would be unable to accommodate Andrew's monster chopper but I discovered that by wriggling my bottom to and fro I could embed even more of this thick bell-end inside my cunt. As if by magic, further and further inches of pulsing prick disappeared into my creamy cunney as my pussey lips engulfed more and more of his great boner until, with a convulsive jerk of his loins, his cock was fully inserted to the very root and I cried out with glee as our bodies moved up and down in unison. What a glorious first fuck this turned out to be! How tightly my saturated slit held on to Andrew's throbbing tool! We gloried in each other's thrusts as my love juices dripped against his balls as they slapped against my bum. I implored him to drive deeper by twirling my tongue in his mouth and my buttocks rotated almost savagely in his broad palms as his lusty, gleaming joystick drove furiously into my soft depths.

' "Fill me with your spunky cream!" I urged Andrew, who for answer plunged his face between my breasts, sucking furiously at my right nipple whilst the friction in my cunney reached new heights. His wonderful prick slicked in and out of my wet crack at an even faster rate, making us both breathless with excitement. I was finding out what the glorious pleasures of a good fucking could be as my fingers now dug into the flesh of his back and my bucking torso wildly sought more and more of his magnificent prick as our pubic hairs crashed together. All the time I squirmed lasciviously and I began to shudder uncontrollably as I felt my inner depths exploding into the most delicious waves of ecstacy which bathed me in a marvellous glowing release which flowed across every fibre of my body. Each spasm racked through me and I bit poor Andrew's shoulder, which made him pump even harder. Very soon I screamed with joy as he shot powerful spurts of spunk inside my receptive cunt, his rigid prick jetting its jism into my innermost cavities with such vigour that dribblings of our mingled love juices dribbled down my thighs.

'Slowly he pulled out his gleaming penis which was still hard and when I lovingly squeezed the shaft it throbbed with latent energy. I lowered my pouting lips and flicked my pink tongue across the massive dome, juicing his shaft with my saliva as I forced the ripe plum between my lips. He trembled as I moved one hand to massage the insides of his thighs and let the other cradle his heavy, hairy ballsack. Andrew moaned as I sucked on my splendid sweetmeat, until my mouth was full and I began to move my head forwards and backwards, slurping noisily on this monster rod which tasted so tasty with that unique masculine tang. His hands clutched at my hair as I closed my lips around it as tightly as possible and worked on his knob with my tongue, easing forward gradually to take in a little more of the shaft. I circled the base with my fingers and worked my hand up and down the shaft, sucking Andrew's delicious cock until the tip almost touched the back of my throat and I cupped his balls, feeling them harden until the frothy white sperm rushed up his shaft and my mouth was filled with gorgeous gushes of sticky foam as his prick bucked wildly while I held it lightly between my teeth. I gulped down his copious emission, gratefully swallowing every last milky drop of spunk.

Not till his delicious prick had fully shrunk back to its normal flaccidity did I withdraw my lips and then we returned to the table to partake of some more coffee which was bubbling away on a tiny gas burner and Andrew and I toasted each other before we returned to the makeshift bed where he finger-fucked me to another delicious orgasm. We finished this lewd encounter with a final *soixante-neuf* before making our way downstairs where members of Lord George Lucas's party were also set to leave.

' "Hey there, Andrew," shouted out the good-looking young son of Viscount Sevenoaks. "We're going to continue celebrating my birthday at Matthew Cosgrave's house in Grosvenor Street

320

– why don't you and your lovely companion join us there?" Andrew looked at me and murmured: "It's up to you, Gillian, I don't mind whether we join them or go straight back home. In all fairness, though, I must warn you that Charlie's parties have been known to, shall we say, get a little out of hand if what they tell me at the Jim Jam Club is to be believed."

' "Well, unless you are too tired, why don't we find out for ourselves?" I suggested. "We can leave at any time so long as your chauffeur is capable of getting us home."

' "Oh, there's no worry on that score, Grahame never drinks and drives," replied Andrew and so we agreed to join Lord George's gathering which was to mean, dear Rupert, that although I had only just an hour before enjoyed my very first fuck, I was now to be introduced to the wild bachannalian revels of the fastest set in London.'

At this stage she paused and giggled: 'I'll wager this lewd story has given you a big stiffie, you naughty boy.' She reached down to feel my throbbing prick which as she had correctly surmised was now at bursting point and I kissed her warm, soft lips and played with her hard titties which instantly aroused the sensuous girl.

'We need some exercise, Rupert, all this lying in bed is fine as far as it goes but we must put other muscles to use besides those in your cock and my cunney,' she said as she jumped out of bed. 'Come on, darling, you can fuck me in the Irish style, that'll be good exercise for us both.'

I looked at her with a puzzled expression until she added: 'Some people call this method "the wheelbarrow position". Does that mean anything to you?'

'Yes, I've read about this way of fucking in *The Intimate Memoir Of Dame Jenny Everleigh* but I've never actually tried it out. Still, *experientia docet*, so if you're willing, by all means, let's see for ourselves what it's like.'

Gillian turned away from me and dropped to her hands and knees on the floor. I picked up her legs and supported much of her weight by holding her spread thighs so her arms could be fully extended and her lithe body was in a slanting position with her bottom on the same level as my cock. As soon as we were comfortable I pushed my knob forward between her bum cheeks – the only question now, as the snooker player might ask, was whether to go for the pink or the brown! I decided to slide my cock into her cunney and slipped in my length quite easily. It took a little while to achieve a satisfactory rhythm as she matched my movements with her own and I managed to 'steer' her into a position where my shaft slid very nicely in and out of her clinging sheath. I plunged in hard and in time the boiling spunk rose and, with a woosh, it surged out of my pulsating prick in a spend that seemed to last and last as I loosed a stream of sticky spunk into her dark, squelchy love-box. I withdrew and creamy drops of sperm dribbled down her thighs as I gently eased her body down onto the floor. She scrambled to her feet and kissed me, saying: 'Well, for a novice, you managed very nicely, though I must admit that I would only like to fuck this way very occasionally as it isn't the most comfortable position – it makes all the blood run into one's head.'

I was hardly surprised that Gillian was not too keen on this position for I was not that enamoured with it either – perhaps I'm old-fashioned but there's a minimum of physical contact involved and a lack of the emotional intimacy which I believe adds that little extra something to a good fucking. Mind, I'd rather take exercise in this fashion than run a mile before breakfast or in summer swim a similar distance along the River Windrush like my old pal Colonel Goldstone of the West Oxfordshire Rifles! And may I pass on a tip, dear reader, should you or your partner wish to try 'the wheelbarrow position' for yourselves? If the woman supports herself on a bed or chair, the man can place his arm round her middle and fondle her titties or pussey and she can turn her head and look at him, both of which allow a closer contact between the two of you. I find this variation preferable but as they say in that haven of devotion to the pleasures of the flesh, the Cock and Crop Club in Manhattan, 'diff'rnt strokes for diff'rnt folks'!

We climbed back into bed and Gillian lay her head on my shoulder and toyed with my still damp shaft which was in a state of half limber resting on my thigh. She said: 'I suppose you would like me to continue this tale of debauchery, wouldn't you?'

'Yes, please go on, your words are so much more interesting than anything I've heard in my lectures!'

She laughed and gave my balls a playful

squeeze. 'Very well then – where was I now? Oh yes, we followed Lord George Lucas's party back to Matthew Cosgrave's house and there must have been about a dozen or so of us in the lounge toasting the birthday boy with a jeroboam *[a huge bottle holding as much as four normal bottles – Editor]* of Mr Cosgrave's best champagne. We were all certainly a little worse for wear when one of the girls (who were all very friendly but remember, they were all from the chorus line at the Alhambra and, like most theatrical people, had few inhibitions) beckoned me to a corner where her friends had gathered.

' "We're going to give Lord George a very special birthday present," she giggled. "Do come and join the fun." She signalled to Matthew Cosgrave who called for silence and announced: "George, my dear old fellow, in honour of your birthday, we would like to present you with a little something that you'll never forget."

' "How kind of you all," murmured the dashing young peer who allowed himself to be led to a superbly made Chesterfield *[a large, tightly stuffed sofa upholstered in leather, named after the nineteenth-century Earl of Chesterfield – Editor]* in the centre of the room as Carrie, the girl who had told me about the plan, explained what she and the others – Pippa, Lucy and Suzanne – had in mind. I don't mind telling you that I was a little shocked but as I said just before, we were all quite tiddley from the champagne which was flowing like water.

'Anyhow, Lord George sat on the Chesterfield and as quick as a flash he had the four girls piled on top of him. Pippa and Lucy held down his

324

legs whilst Carrie and Suzanne pinioned his arms, though to be truthful I can't say that our birthday boy struggled overmuch against the overpowering odds! "Gillian, I need your help," cried out Carrie, who was a real stunning girl of no more than twenty at the most blessed with an exquisitely rounded figure and an extremely pretty face with deep blue eyes set off by long dark lashes, a full mouth and a brilliant set of pearly teeth. I hurried across and took her place, holding down Lord George's left arm against the soft leather upholstery.

' "Are you going to feed him some birthday cake, girls?" laughed Roland Phillips, one of the other gay young blades who along with my escort Sir Andrew Stuck and the other men, was watching this little game unfold from the comfort of an armchair. "In good time he might be given something to eat," replied Carrie, unpinning her long tresses of light, gold-tinted auburn hair, "but first I want to find out how hungry he is." And to my astonishment she pulled open the flap of Lord George's trousers and proceeded to unbutton his flies!

' "I say, steady on, Carrie, old girl," he protested but I noticed that he did not struggle overmuch when the lovely girl tugged down his trousers and Pippa and Lucy (two lissome blonde beauties) had only to hold his legs steady whilst in one dextrous movement Carrie removed the offending garment. Along with the other girls I looked with great interest at the wisps of black pubic hair which were showing over the waistband of his drawers which had been slightly

325

pulled down in the Mêlée and I could see his erect boner practically tearing through the fine mono-grammed silk material of his aristocratic under-pants! Carrie yanked these off with a whoop of joy. His rigid rod sprang up to attention and Pippa grabbed it in her fist and pumped her hand up and down with a squeal of delight.

' "Hold on there, you'll make him spend if you're not careful," warned Carrie who was now on her feet and busy unhooking her dress. "Oh, I'm terribly sorry," said Pippa, removing her hand immediately. "George, you be a good boy and wait for Carrie, do you hear?" Carrie shucked off her clothes very quickly and she flaunted her gorgeous naked body in front of us. She smoothed her hands across her magnificent swelling breasts which were round and firm and topped with large, stubby nipples. The pure whiteness of her belly was accentuated by a bushy mound of curly auburn hair through which I could just perceive the outline of her crack. Her luscious charms appealed to the other men too and I could see Roland and Andrew's trouser fronts bulge as they gawped in awe at this delicious nude apparition. But it was poor Lord George who was given the most tantalising view as Carrie began to writhe sensuously in front of him. She knelt down and let her bare breasts dangle in front of his face and then straddled him so that the tip of his straining shaft just touched her soft pussey hair. She leaned down and gave a swift series of butterfly kisses upon his blue-veined length and by now the perspiration was pouring down his forehead as he frantically tried to free himself from his captors. However, he was no match for four strapping girls and soon he was almost weeping with frustration.

' "I think he's hungry enough for you now, Carrie," smiled Suzanne and our prisoner spluttered: "Hungry enough? I'm bloody starving!"

' "Come on Carrie, it is his birthday," shouted Andrew and the gorgeous girl nodded as she climbed over George, rolling all over him and rubbing her superb titties in his face before taking hold of his enormous erection in her hand. Then she lifted herself up and sticking her bum up in the air she sat down hard on his stiffstander which slid all the way into her slit as her buttocks bounced against his thighs. She purred contentedly as she screwed herself from side to side on his bursting cock and then she began to ride her mount like a jockey on a thoroughbred. I could see his rigid rod flash in and out of her juicy cunney and then George arched his back and jetted a copious gush of spunk as she enjoyed her own climax, uninhibitedly screaming out her delight.

'She nimbly swung her legs round and jumped off her exhausted lover and Pippa piped up: "Who's next to give George a birthday present?" Andrew heaved himself up from his chair and looking at Lord George's limp prick he suggested that some girl might like to bring back this exhausted tool to life. Well, Rupert, my blood was up from watching Carrie in action and so I must admit to you that I volunteered for the job. Carrie took my place, although we hardly needed to keep hold of our victim who appeared a little *hors de*

327

combat after his vigorous fuck, even though Carrie had done much of the work.

'I began by running my tongue along his hairy ballsack and then slowly I licked the soft length which was still wet from Carrie's spendings. This soon had the desired effect and his prick gradually swelled up until I found it difficult to accommodate its throbbing thickness between my lips. So I went back to his scrotum and kissed his sweet nuts whilst I gently rubbed his strong, sinewy shaft with my hand. I took my time and his cock and balls received a prolonged salivating which made him groan in ecstacy. When I had sucked up his sabre-curved cock to its fullest erection, I reached behind him and inserted a moistened fingertip into his bottom hole. With my other hand I cupped his tightening ballsack and set up a rhythmic motion, bobbing my head up and down in time with my finger. As I now know, there is not a man in the whole wide world who can resist a good gobble and I only had to squeeze his balls two or three times before he rolled his hips and sent thick wads of creamy, hot spunk down my throat. To the applause of the other guests, I eagerly swallowed his spend which tasted slightly sweeter than Andrew's sperm.'

'Did you then let him fuck your dear little cunt?' I asked breathlessly, reaching down to stroke her damp pussey.

'Certainly not,' she retorted sharply, 'don't forget it was only an hour or two earlier that evening I had first had any prick penetrate my pussey. If I was to be fucked again, it would only be by Andrew Stuck, the man who had so carefully and considerately taken my unwanted virginity.'

I apologised profusely for my hasty remark which Gillian gracefully accepted in the nicest way possible – by opening her legs and letting me rub her dampening slit whilst she took hold of my burgeoning boner and the next thing I knew I was looking down at her and my sturdy prick was being guided between Gillian's welcoming pussey lips. She whimpered and closed her legs around my waist to hold me tight as she began that rapid rippling contraction of her cunney muscles which so excited me. This was to be no slow, lingering fuck for we were both urgent in our needs and as I thrust into her again and again she rose to meet me with equal vigour. Great gasps swept through our bodies and she cried out: 'Rupert, Rupert, I'm spending, you big cocked boy! I'm spending, shoot your spunk inside me!'.

It was an easy command to obey for already I could feel the first spurt of milky cream forcing its way along my pulsing prick. This was shortly followed by another as I discharged a powerful stream of sperm and Gillian's own juices flowed liberally in response. She seized tight hold of me and we fucked away quite uncontrollably, writhing and twisting on the bed until we were both totally drained. As we lay there entwined in each other's arms, panting and sucking in great gulps of air, we were so overcome that neither of us could speak for a while as we shared our post-fuck fatigue.

Gillian was the first to recover her senses and she said: 'What a simply marvellous bout of love-making. I came at least three times, Rupert, you have such a clever cock.'

'Thank you very much,' I said modestly, though like all men I was delighted to be complimented upon my performance. 'But any credit must be equally shared with your divine cunney and I suppose the wonderfully lewd account of your rite of passage also helped stir my imagination.'

She smiled and continued: 'Oh, I am pleased you enjoyed it. Don't think too badly of me because I sucked Lord George Lucas's cock after Sir Andrew Stuck had fucked me.'

'Good grief, of course not, Gillian, why, so long as you had no objection I must confess here and now that if a lovely girl came into the room and asked me to fuck her, I would have no compunction about obliging her.'

'Really, Rupert? You are not just saying that to make me feel less guilty after telling you how free I was with my favours that night?'

'No, honestly, darling, I'm doing nothing of the kind,' I assured her in all truthfulness, though I wondered why she wanted to lead the conversation in this very personal direction. 'Why on earth shouldn't a girl let herself go once in a while just in the same way a man can without being labelled as anything but a chip off the old block.'

'Why indeed, Rupert, but there is such an overwhelming prejudice against women enjoying themselves in bed that even though I surmised you were not so blockheadedly chauvinistic about

330

this matter, I wanted to make sure before imparting any information about a party being held at the aptly named Oxford Playhouse on Saturday night. I've been invited and told I may bring a friend but I didn't want to mention anything to you until I was sure that you wouldn't be stuffy about it.'

'Who's throwing the party? Is it town or gown?' I asked, more than a mite puzzled by this little speech.

She smiled and replied: 'Neither really, my love, it's for the cast of *A Nice Little Stroll Does You Good* which has been running at the theatre for the last two weeks before it transfers to Birmingham and then on to the Holborn Empire in London. The show is one of Mrs Susan Moser's lush musical comedies and the impressario, Mr Louis Segal, is so pleased with the reviews it's attracted in the provincial papers so far that he is putting on this party for the cast and some friends. You might know that he often tries out his productions in out of town theatres before spending a lot of money putting on a show in the West End.

'But you see, I've been invited because one of Sir Andrew Stuck's hobbies is to invest in theatrical productions, and he is one of the major backers of *A Nice Little Stroll Does You Good*, and all four of the girls who were at Lord George Lucas's birthday party are in the chorus and naturally they will also be at the party. But if their presence or Andrew being there would bother you, then I'm quite happy to go on my own.'

'For heaven's sake, that won't be necessary,

you silly goose. We are both free agents and can live our lives as we alone wish to live them.'

She puckered up her lips and planted a kiss on my cheek. As she snuggled up to me I felt her relax, but moments later we were disturbed by a soft knocking on the door.

'Who is it?' asked Gillian with an unconcerned yawn.

'It's Chrissie,' came the whispered reply. 'May I come in, please?'

I looked questioningly at Gillian's naked body. 'Hadn't we better make ourselves decent?'

'There is no need, Chrissie is a very close friend and to be frank I've discovered her in a similar position more than once so it hardly matters one way or the other if she now sees me in a state of undress in bed with my lover.'

'Come in, Chrissie,' she called out and the door opened to reveal a tall, dark-haired girl dressed in a short tennis dress. Her willowy figure was capped by an attractively pert face with bright brown eyes which matched her long tresses of soft hair falling down in ringlets to her shoulders. 'Chrissie, meet Rupert Mountjoy; Rupert, this is Miss Chrissie Nayland-Hunt, one of the three girls who shares this house with me.'

I heaved myself to a more upright position, but our visitor said with a twinkle in her eye: 'A pleasure to meet you, Rupert. Please don't get up, it looks as if you have had a tiring afternoon.'

'He has performed splendidly, Chrissie, and it is truly a serendipitous coincidence that you have joined us at this time. We were just discussing some intimate matters and I don't think it's more than five minutes ago that Rupert declared that so long as I have no objection – and I have none as far as you are concerned – he would happily oblige any pretty girl who desired the thrill of his stiff cock in her cunney.'

'Is this true, Rupert?' enquired this scrumptious lass as she came in and sat on the bed. 'Let me see for myself what exactly you have to offer.' And before I could say or do anything more she pulled the covers off my side of the bed and exposed my dormant but still swollen shaft which was in a state of half limber.

She took hold of my prick and commented: 'Gillian, you must have really extracted great pleasure from this fine instrument.'

'I have indeed, Chrissie, along with a copious amount of hot, frothy, masculine seed,' agreed my pretty bedmate. 'Would you care to take your pleasure with Rupert? He is a true gentleman and though his cock must be somewhat fatigued after our strenuous exertions, I am sure that with a little assistance this fine organ will be capable of rising to the occasion.'

Perhaps I should have been angered by Gillian's cool suggestion to her friend which took no account of *my* feelings about whether or not I wanted to fuck Chrissie, though to be fair I had been hoist by my own petard through my rash remark about happily obliging any girl etc, etc, the words of which Gillian had glibly repeated to the newcomer. Anyhow, Chrissie looked simply ravishing in her skimpy white tennis dress which set off her long dark tresses and large brown eyes and only a confirmed homosexualist would have failed to have been aroused by her sensuous pulchritude.

So I raised no objection when Chrissie leaned forward and proceeded to take my penis in her smooth, soft hands, resting her forearms on my belly and thighs. As Gillian had forecast, it needed little further encouragement for it immediately began to swell to its fullest extent under her warm touch. She cupped my ballsack in one hand and lightly ran the fingers of the other along the bright blue veins of my distended love truncheon.

'Master John Thomas looks to be well on the road to recovery, but to make sure I'd best give him the kiss of life,' she murmured and I gave a huge grin of approval as she leaned forward and took my throbbing tool between her ruby lips, teasing my knob against the roof of her mouth. Ripples of ecstacy flowed out from my delighted stiffstander as her darting tongue moved to and fro along the thick shaft and I closed my eyes and lay back, totally engulfed in the exquisite sensations which were now washing all over my body.

Frankly, I sometimes wonder whether being sucked off isn't even more pleasurable than actually fucking though I suppose it depends upon one's mood and the skills of one's partner. Certainly Chrissie was a fellatrix *par excellence* and as she licked the tip of my cock I felt my balls begin to tighten and fill with jism. Chrissie sensed this and for a moment took her sweet lips away. Then with a wicked smile she returned to the fray, stroking her tongue along the underside of my cock, making it ache with excitement as I jerked my body upwards and thrust frenziedly into her oral orifice. She squeezed her hand around the base of my prick, sucking it even harder and this exquisite sensation sent me to paradise. But I could contain myself for only a short while longer and I let out a short, sharp cry of despair as my lusty young prick pulsed in her mouth and I jetted spurt after spurt of creamy white semen full into her adorable mouth. She managed to suck in and swallow every last drop of my libation, licking all round my knob to take up the final sticky dribbles of jism.

She raised her head and looking me squarely in the eye said mischievously: 'Well, that was a truly delicious *hors d'oeuvre*, Rupert, but now how about the main course? I'm glad to see that your cock's still quite hard, can you keep it up whilst I undress?'

'I'll help to keep his organ on song,' said Gillian brightly, taking hold of my moist length and rubbing it gaily between her hands. This had the desired effect of keeping my shaft stiff as Chrissie slipped out of her clothes. For a girl with such a slim, almost boyish figure, Chrissie had a surprisingly full bosom with rounded, firmly shaped breasts tipped with pert raspberry nipples surrounded by large red aureolae. I watched closely as she ran her hands along the smooth skin of her flat, unwrinkled belly and into a luxuriant fleece of dark, almost black hair which extended between her thighs and completely covered her pussey. She leaped into bed beside me and straightaway took a pillow and placed it under her bottom as she spread her legs to wait for the arrival of my twitching tool which under Gillian's continuing rhythmic ministrations was now standing proudly upright in all its glory, the purple helmet uncapped and glowing as she worked my shaft up and down in her hands.

'Chrissie, are you ready to receive His Majesty, King Cock?' she gaily enquired.

The darling girl replied: 'Yes, dear, please put Rupert's tool in my cunt, I have a great fancy for it just now. I want to feel his knob nudge between my pussey lips and drive straight through into my cunney.'

Gillian moved a hand across to delve into Chrissie's thick growth of pubic hair. Her clever fingers spread her friend's pussey lips and exposed the pink chink where my pulsating prick was now yearning to enter. With Gillian's hand still firmly clasped on my tadger, I rolled over on top of the trembling girl and she opened the lips of Chrissie's cunt and placed the tip of my helmet between them. 'Push on, Rupert,' she hissed in my ear. 'Chrissie has a marvellously tight little cunney and she wants to feel every inch of your big cock inside her!'

I needed no further urging and planting my lips on hers, I plunged forward, embedding my knob and just an inch or so of my shaft inside her delicious, velvet-walled cunt. Quickly, we established a fine rhythm with Chrissie pushing her hips upward to meet every push forward of my prick into her already sopping cunney. We enjoyed an excellent fuck (though is there such a thing as a bad one!) with her rapid jerking spurring me to further fast plunges into this delectable cunt which held my member in its warm, silky embrace. Her juices lubricated her little love-channel so that my cock slid in and out of her pussey with consummate ease though it was tight enough for me to feel my foreskin being drawn backwards and forwards with every lascivious shove. I fucked away with surprising energy considering how Gillian had emptied my balls before Chrissie had sucked me off just before. But the throbbing contractions of her cunney muscles spurred me on and we shared a truly memorable experience.

'Ah, you lovely boy, ram home that fat joystick!' she urged me as her eyes sparkled and she writhed in delicious agitations as within us the pent-up waves of ecstatic bliss rose to tidal proportions. A few more rapid, impetuous thrusts together with one last straining of her body to mine and her fingers clawed up and down my back as she reached the highest pinnacle of pleasure. Very shortly afterwards I joined her and I spouted a stream of milky seed inside Chrissie's cunney which mingled deliciously with her own copious rivulets of nectar that overflowed down onto her thighs. I pounded my spurting shaft until I was spent and I collapsed on top of her soft body, and the two of us were almost fainting with fatigue after this torrid fuck.

Both Chrissie and I had been so highly involved with each other's bodies that neither of us had noticed Gillian slip out of bed whilst we had been fucking ourselves into a stupor. But the kind girl had busied herself whilst my love trunk was battering its way into Chrissie's cunt and she had set up a table upon which she had placed a selection of fruits and a jug of lemonade from the ice-box. The clever girl knew full well that a prolonged bout of fucking uses a great deal of energy and that even our strong, youthful bodies required refreshment to regain our strength. We were so warm from our fun and games that we stayed quite naked as we enjoyed our informal tea, during which I asked Chrissie what she was studying at Oxford.

'I'm reading for a degree in the history of art,' she explained as she sat up in bed munching an apple, 'and as I enjoy painting, for my own amusement, I am also studying watercolour techniques in an informal weekly class under the tuition of Professor Tim Titchfield of All Souls, who offers his kind guidance to any budding artists among the first year students.'

Now I had dabbled a little in painting since my first encounter with art which had led directly to my crossing the Rubicon with the divine Diana Wigmore [see An Edwardian Dandy 1: Youthful Scandals – Editor] that in turn had given me the unexpected but highly delightful chance to lose my unwanted virginity. Sadly, my efforts with the brush and palette were so far undistinguished, though I was told by Diana that I would do far better once I had been taught to harness my technical skills to create my own personal style.

So I asked Chrissie if any student could avail himself of Professor Titchfield's classes. 'Most certainly,' she replied. 'Why, would you like to come along? We meet on Thursday evenings at eight o'clock in the small lecture hall just next to the Playhouse Theatre.'

'I'll be there,' I promised and, turning to Gillian, I said: 'Talking of the Playhouse, will Chrissie be invited to this party on Saturday night? I'm sure you could wangle her onto the guest list.'

'Of course, but unless I'm much mistaken, she'll be wining and dining with her new special boyfriend who's coming all the way over from Cambridge for the weekend just to be with her.'

Chrissie blushed and said: 'Now you know full well, Gillian, that Salman is just a boyfriend, and there is nothing special about him – except of course that he is a very charming young man—'

'– who has pots and pots of money and a very, very big cock!' finished Gillian with a giggle.

'Wash your mouth out, you bad girl!' scolded Chrissie although she was not really offended by the jest. 'Salman's cock is certainly sizeable but it is not the very biggest I have ever entertained in my pussey. That honour would go to "Donkey Dick" Dinchley, the gardener's boy at my Uncle Rodney's country house in Buckinghamshire whose erect tool measured almost twelve and a half inches, though he was by no means the most satisfying fuck. I mean, we both had that good-looking chap Harry Barr at your birthday party in May and he was superb in bed even though his member was if anything smaller than the average cock. Don't you agree that this obsession with the size of their penises makes many men almost neurotic? And it's all so unnecessary because as an American girl in my college says, it isn't the size of the ship that counts, it's the motion of the ocean!'

'Yes, although I suppose it is a similar problem

that we women have in never being quite satisfied with our weight!' said Gillian thoughtfully, but before she could continue airing her views on this admittedly interesting subject, I suddenly woke up to the fact that Chrissie's boyfriend could be none other than my old school chum Salman Marrari, the eldest son of the Maharajah of Lockshenstan who had, as I noted at the very beginning of these memoirs, spurned a place at University College, Oxford to take up a place at Trinity College, Cambridge as he wanted to continue his scientific studies with some noted group of physicists who were based there. He was also a great cocksman and very popular with the servant girls at St Lionel's amongst whom he distributed a generous number of twenty pound notes for favours great and small!

So I asked her excitedly: 'Are you talking about Salman Marrari who went up to Cambridge from St Lionel's? He shared a study with me at school and it would be marvellous to see him if he is coming to Oxford this weekend. Is this the chap who you are seeing, Chrissie?'

'Yes indeed, what a lovely coincidence,' she said, clapping her hands together. 'Oh, Rupert, you must join us for dinner on Friday night.'

'That's very kind but surely you two prefer to dine *à deux*.'

'No, really, you must come along – I won't tell Salman so it will be a lovely surprise for him to see his old school chum again,' she insisted.

It was time for us to take our leave but Chrissie assured me that she would send round a note about where I should meet her and Salman on

Friday night. After kissing the two girls goodbye I walked back briskly to my college, making a mental note as I looked at my watch that I would need to employ a social secretary if invitations were to keep flowing so freely into my diary. When I reached my rooms I jotted down my immediate engagements – this evening I had planned to see Beth Randall after dinner and take her for a walk and perhaps visit one of the quaint old Oxford inns frequented (though much frowned upon) by students of the University. Tomorrow I had to attend two lectures and write a long essay which had to be given in the next morning, but time would be at a premium as I had already accepted Professor Webb's invitation to his soirée. I had some reading to do as well but the weekend was already filling up for on Friday I was to dine with Salman and Chrissie, whilst on Saturday night I would squire Gillian to the party at the Oxford Playhouse. I gnawed my lip in a gesture of irritation as I suddenly remembered that on Saturday afternoon I was due to play soccer for Balliol against Merton College and I really should fit in at least a couple of hours of training before the match. Of course, I could always cut a lecture or two, but at his specific request, I had promised my godfather, Major Fulham, that I would never allow this to happen during my first year and since my earliest years I have always maintained that a promise is a promise – and especially when you have just been handed a cheque for fifty pounds 'to be spent on enjoying yourself, my boy; your father can look after the college fees and your account at Blackwell's bookshop'!

This left Sunday as the only day free to work and though my family have never been strict observers of the Sabbath, I knew full well that if the Saturday party turned out to be the kind of affair I hopefully expected, I would be in no fit state to study the day afterwards! Still, these were pleasant problems to solve and I resolved to lighten my load by postponing my tryst with Beth until the following week and instead making a start on my essay after dinner, even though Frank and Barry would do their best to inveigle me into playing a few rubbers of bridge. I would be very tempted as I much enjoyed the game, but however hard it would be, their blandishments would have to be resisted, I said to myself as I made my way downstairs to spend half an hour reading the newspapers in the library before going into the dining hall.

In the library I picked up a copy of *The Times* and coincidentally one of the first reports to catch my eye was a review of *A Nice Little Stroll Does You Good*. Under the heading 'A Jolly Evening Well Spent' the critic had written: 'As several friends in the profession have told me about the rousing reception *A Nice Little Stroll Does You Good* has been given in the provincial theatres before opening in two weeks' time in London, I ventured out to Oxford to see Mr Louis Segal's latest musical comedy for myself, and am pleased to report that this latest offering is about as good and as clever as any play in this genre. The songs are jolly and the story, though of the sort we have seen more often than not, is at least well paced and, though relying on mishaps and misunderstandings for its dramatic effects, all ends happily with the hero and heroine reaping their rewards and the villains getting their just deserts. It is conceived as a downright, rollicking, noisy comedy and the humour and praiseworthy characterisations evinced by the principals, Mr Michael Bailey, Mr Frederick Shackleton and Miss Deborah Paxford undoubtedly caught the imagination of the audience. They are abetted by one of the prettiest chorus lines, whose shapely forms are clothed perhaps in too scanty a fashion for the older generation, but all can act and sing as well as they can dance. From first to last, all on stage appear to revel in the fun and the company complied with repeated requests for encores without displaying any symptom of weariness.'

Then and there I decided to check with Gillian as to whether she already possessed tickets for Saturday night, because after such a review the playgoers of Oxford and the surrounding villages would flock to see the show. I scribbled a note and found a young college servant who for sixpence was willing to deliver the message that evening and (so long as Gillian was at home) wait and bring back her reply.

The gong sounded as I gave the lad my note and made him repeat the address I had just given him (for the matter was important and I did not want my note to go astray) and Frank Folkestone ambled up and accompanied me into the dining-hall. 'Hello there, old boy, I haven't seen much of you since Len Letchmore regaled us with his lewd tale about his uncle and the chorus girl.

'Talking of chorus girls,' he added, 'how about

coming along with me to see the show at the Playhouse one night? I've spoken to a few chaps who have already seen it and they all say that it's great fun with some cracking chorus girls. Do you know that Malcolm Ross, the fellow from Winchester who rowed for Oxford in the Boat Race this year – well, he went backstage with a bunch of flowers and a note for one of the girls and she accepted his invitation to dine at Carlo's Restaurant after the performance the following evening.'

'You think she sang for her supper?' I said with a grin.

'I don't honestly know, but the newspapers say the chorus line is well worth watching especially as some of the costumes are rather naughty,' said Frank with undisguised relish. 'So how about it, old boy?'

Trying hard not to sound conceited, I explained to Frank (and to Barry Jacobs who had just joined us) that I already had an invitation to meet the cast on Saturday night at a private party after the show, but that if I could smuggle my pals in, I'd let them know as soon as possible. 'Gosh, you're a fast worker, Rupert,' said Frank admiringly. 'Talk about being quick off the mark. If this gathering is anything like the theatrical revels I've read about in the *Jenny Everleigh* books, it's just as well you're playing football before and not after the party!'

'Yes, especially as I'm playing with you in the team on Saturday afternoon and Esme Dyotte is coming to watch the game. I want to be on the winning side, Rupert, so be a good chap and keep your mind off your cock and on the match until we've beaten Merton by at least six goals!'

344

Frank shook his head in warning. 'You'll be lucky if you manage to scrape a draw, Barry. Merton plan to field four Corinthians [*a famous English amateur football club in the early years of the century whose members were mostly drawn from the top public schools and that often played matches against leading professional sides – Editor*] in their line-up.'

'Gosh, we'll have a real fight on our hands,' said Barry gloomily. 'It jolly well serves me right for wanting to show off in front of Esme.'

'Cheer up, old lad – at least you aren't playing in goal so she won't have to see you bending down every ten minutes to pick the ball out of the net,' said Frank, though perhaps not surprisingly these words of comfort elicited only a glare from Barry.

'I think I'll take up golf instead,' he muttered. 'At least I can only let myself down on the course. Still, I'm sure that win or lose Esme will keep to our arrangement on Sunday. She can't see me after the match because she's going with your friend Beth Randall to see *The Taming Of The Shrew* at the New Theatre on Saturday night along with some other girls. But I'm planning to take her out to Standlake for luncheon on Sunday.'

'I didn't know there were any public houses serving meals on Sunday round there, though it's a pretty part of the county,' I commented.

'You're right, Rupert, there aren't any but Mr and Mrs Greenacre, some old friends of my parents, live there and yesterday Mr Greenacre called and asked me to join them for lunch on Sunday. He said that I should bring a friend if I would like to, so I've asked Esme.'

'And has she accepted?' asked Frank.

'I'm waiting for her reply as I only left a message at her rooms this morning. I wrote to her after what happened at Doctor Blayers' party, and I do hope that she will come to Standlake with me. To be frank, I'm a bit worried as I went over the top a bit when I wrote to her.'

'Oh, don't worry at all about that,' I said with all the assurance of an eighteen-year-old man of the world. 'I don't think you can over-flatter a woman. Remember what Ovid said: *Quae dant, quaeque negant, gaudent tamen esse roatae.*'

'Whether they give or refuse, women are pleased to have been asked,' translated Frank and Barry's face brightened.

'You think so?' he said as we stood up to greet the dons who marched their way through to the High Table. 'I wrote her a little poem,' he added as we resumed our seats. 'Would you like to hear it?'

'Why not?' said Frank and as Nancy (of all people!) plonked brimming plates of oxtail soup in front of us Barry fumbled in his pocket and brought out a piece of paper and began to read his Ode to Esme:

'I care not what other men may say,
The maid that suits my mind,
Is the girl who meets me on the way
And while she is free, she is kind.
With her beauties never could I be cloyed
Such pleasures I find by her side;
I don't love her less because she's enjoyèd
By many another beside.

346

She opens her thighs without fear or dread,
And points to her dear little crack,
Its lips are so red, and all overspread
With hair of the glossiest black.
Reclined on her breasts or clasped in her arms,
With her my best moments I spend,
And revel the more in her sweet melting charms,
Because they are shared with a friend.'

'A splendid effort, old chum,' I said, although I wondered how Esme would take to Barry's emphasis on the fact that Beth and I had also romped with her during that wild night at The Cat and Pigeons hotel.

Frank also congratulated the poet and Nancy whispered a 'well done' in Barry's ear as she waited for us to finish our soup.

The fish course was a rather undistinguished piece of grilled cod but when this had been cleared away Nancy brought a fine roast joint of beef to the table and placed it before me to carve for the eight of us who were sitting at our table.

My father had taught me to carve at an early age so I had no worries as I rose, knife and fork in hand, to make the first incision into the mouthwatering piece of beef in front of me. But as I looked up the table to the students furthest away from me and asked whether they preferred their meat rare or well-done, I was startled by what appeared to be a small hand grabbing my ankle underneath the table. I cast a glance down but could see nothing as the overhanging white tablecloth concealed all. Saying nothing except to enquire as to how the other diners wished to have their beef prepared, I manfully carried on carving as the mysterious but determined hand started to stroke first my ankle and then the upper part of my calf.

I wondered whether it was Nancy playing a practical joke and looked around for her, but she was nowhere to be seen and another maid brought bowls of roast potatoes and green vegetables to our table. Now I enjoy a good joke as much as the next man but there was a time and place for this admittedly agreeable massage. However, right now I wanted to tuck in to my dinner so I simply ignored the wandering fingers which by now had reached my knees. What should I do? I had no wish to call over a steward for certainly poor Nancy would face instant dismissal without a reference. So I just sat down and savoured the first delicious mouthful as Nancy's hand moved speedily along my thigh and reached into my lap. There it thankfully rested for a moment as Humphrey Price, the broad-shouldered captain of our football team, called across from an adjoining table: 'Rupert, I hope you will be able to score goals on Saturday afternoon with the same facility as the way you carved that hunk of beef.'

'I'll do my best, Humphrey,' I responded as burrowing beneath my napkin, Nancy's hand felt for and grasped my cock. Now in normal circumstances, such behaviour would have caused Mr Priapus to swell up in greeting but even when she undid my fly buttons, my prick stayed quiescent – but when she slid her hand inside my drawers and started to caress my naked shaft it now began to stir perceptibly with a swelling excitement, especially when she pulled back my foreskin and washed the exposed smooth-skinned knob with long, lingering licks of her tongue as she coaxed my shaft up into life by sliding her hand up and down its expanding length.

Nevertheless, I was determined not to allow this strange turn of events get out of hand, but the mundane task of passing the salt to Frank Folkestone almost shattered my mask of calm as Nancy's hand had now won the battle and my prick stood high, erect and throbbing. Her firm fingers now pulled it towards her soft lips which kissed my knob lightly before opening wide to admit my twitching tool inside the deliciously wet cavern of her mouth. I took my glass and swallowed down a draught of wine as, drawing a deep breath and making a supreme effort to relax, I impaled a piece of beef on my fork. At the same time, inch by inch, Nancy was fucking my cock with her mouth, bobbing her head backwards and forwards as I chewed on the equally tender food on my plate. For a short while I managed to continue eating without showing any outward signs of agitation but soon I became aware of the first rising spasm of sperm starting its journey up from my balls and along my distended staff. I tried to hold back but the insistent pressure from Nancy's lashing tongue was too much and with an involuntary jerk of my hips, I sent a stream of hot spunk crashing into her mouth. This sudden movement caused me to choke on a barely chewed wedge of cabbage as the wicked girl gobbled furiously on my spurting prick.

Barry Jacobs shifted his chair to move closer to me and slapped me on the back. 'Are you all right, Rupert?' he asked anxiously. 'Has something gone down the wrong way?'

'Not exactly,' I spluttered, drawing in fresh gulps of air whilst Nancy hungrily continued to suck and swallow the last drains of spunk from my now thankfully deflating shaft. 'I'll be all right once everything has gone down.' I could have sworn that I heard Nancy giggle at this and I looked around sharply but fortunately no-one else had heard her. As we finished our main course I deliberately dropped a spoon on to the floor and bent down ostensibly to pick it up but in reality to catch a glimpse of the tousled mop of hair still nestling between my thighs. Nancy looked up at me and winked as she gave my flaccid cock a final lick before pulling her head away, which allowed me to hastily button up my gaping flies.

The plates were now cleared away and Frank said: 'There's apple and blackberry tart to follow, gentlemen, the perfect finish to an old-fashioned English dinner, don't you think?'

As I nodded my agreement, however, I noticed with a smile that another diner at our table, a jolly, gregarious Scot from Stirlingshire named Michael Beattie who had this evening donned his traditional Scottish dress, was sitting bolt upright in his chair with a startled expression on his face. One didn't need to be the winner of a scholarship to guess that Nancy had lifted his kilt and in her own inimitable way was cementing the Act of

Union! Wicked though it was, I just could not restrain myself from leaning forward and asking Michael (who was a great theatregoer and a leading light in the Oxford University Dramatic Society [OUDS]) whether he planned to see the show at the Playhouse this week. 'There are supposed to be some sparkling songs which could be considered for the Christmas revue.

'And you could always use some new jokes, couldn't you? I mean, we all know the good old stories from the music hall like the girl asking you what's worn under the kilt and your answer being, nothing's worn, Miss Jones, everything is in perfect working order,' I added mischievously.

He seemed unable to reply but instead threw me a glassy smile and I surmised that Nancy had now taken his claymore out of its scabbard and was, so to speak, busy Tossing the Caber. It would have been cruel to carry on teasing poor Michael but so not to arouse suspicion, I steered the conversation along a tangent to the Dramatic Society's current presentation of *The Taming Of The Shrew*, of which Michael was the stage manager. 'But we mustn't neglect the OUDS offering at the New Theatre,' I said, turning to the other side of the table. 'Everyone who has seen the play has praised the production to the skies, not least the performance of Lily Brayton in the title role. I would imagine that our amateur players must have been in awe at treading the boards with such a distinguished Shakespearean actress. *[Professional actresses playing female roles in OUDS productions was a well-established tradition until the nineteen-twenties, when there were enough female undergraduates available for selection by the Dramatic Society. Miss Lily Brayton, who Rupert mentions here, was indeed an accomplished actress who had played Katharine in a West End production the previous year – Editor].*

'You went to see the play last night, Roger,' I said to the Honourable Roger Tagholm, the younger son of Viscount Bloomsbury and a polite young man who was sitting across from Michael Beattie, whose face was now screwed up in a contortion which suggested he was suffering from indigestion though I speculated that Nancy was about to draw a large dram of Highland Cream from Michael's Caledonian cock. 'Tell us frankly whether you enjoyed it. Michael and his friends would want your honest opinion on the matter.'

'I enjoyed it very much and that's a fact,' said Roger warmly. 'Lily Brayton plays her part as Katharine so well that I could believe she is a real shrew off the stage as well as on it, though I'm sure that is not really the case at all. She brought out the best in Fred Newman who I think hit on the right method of playing his difficult role. Petruchio is after all a gentleman who pretends to be a ruffian and Fred realised this, blustering through his lines as a noisy bully yet showing that he is only acting the part, yet not so clearly that Katharine will see through the pretence. I also thought the quieter scenes between Bianca and Vincentio were very well played by Gwendolen Bunbury and Arthur Cuthbertson, who made a very handsome couple indeed.'

This generous critique was interrupted by a

long drawn-out sigh of release from Michael Beattie whose balls had obviously been relieved of a copious discharge of *uisge beatha* via Nancy's unseen palating of his prick under the table. 'I'm so pleased you enjoyed the play,' he said, his voice croaking with emotion which the others may have believed was brought on by Roger's praise but which I guessed was caused by Nancy nipping his sticky knob with her teeth as she licked up the remains of his spend, 'and I'm especially glad that you thought Gwendolen and Arthur played their love scenes so convincingly, as they had a little problem last night and I had a hand in solving it.'

But when we pressed him to say more he declined and we rose to take our coffee outside the dining-hall. Nevertheless, after Frank, Barry and myself had settled down with Michael in a quiet corner of the large, high-ceilinged common-room, we asked him again to enlarge upon his curious remark. At first he declined but then his face crinkled into a broad grin and he said: 'Look, if you will all promise me faithfully that none of you will spread this story to anyone else, I'll tell you what actually happened backstage last night between Gwen and Arthur because looking back, it was really rather funny – though I didn't find it all that amusing at the time!'

'Of course, we promise that we won't tell a soul,' we chorused and it is only now, some years after the events here described took place and after I have received the written permission to record the facts of the matter from both Arthur and Gwendolen (now Lady Royce-Mainwaring), that I am setting down Michael's secret story for a far wider audience than when it was first recounted to me.

'All right then,' said Michael, as we took up Barry's usual generous offer to buy a bottle of port for the table. 'I'll start at the beginning. Perhaps you won't be surprised to learn that since women have been allowed to join OUDS there has been a marked increase in the number of fellows willing not just to tread the boards but to take on such work as set construction, scene-shifting, prompting and all the many other jobs necessary to mount a successful production. After all, you might not be paid for your time but there's usually a good chance of meeting any number of pretty girls during the rehearsals, and afterwards, when we invariably go out for a drink, there's usually time to try and form a closer relationship. And working backstage, especially when you're putting on a historical play, there are often several quick changes of costume to be made, and I've never found it a bother to help scantily dressed girls to change into their clothes.

'Now it was clear to all of us involved in putting on *The Taming Of The Shrew* that Arthur and Gwendolen were clearly enjoying their love scenes on stage – so much so in fact that during the dress rehearsal, after a farewell kiss lasted more than a minute, the director, Sidney Smyth, had to shout out: "Hey, that's enough, you two, this is Shakespeare not a Victor Pudendum show at the Jim Jam Club!"

'This admonition worked only as far as the first night and since then their on-stage kisses have been becoming longer and longer and a few days ago Sidney Smyth threatened to throw a bucket of water over them if they embraced for longer than ten seconds! Well, last night he deputed me to ensure that Gwendolen and Arthur behaved themselves. Now there is a thirty-five minute break between when the pair leave the stage to when they have to make their next entrance so I thought I would keep a close eye on them during this interval.

'I made my way to Gwendolen's dressing room, which was at the far end of a small, badly lit corridor. There was a light shining through the door which was only slightly ajar and I could hear the soft murmur of voices as I approached. As I had guessed, Gwen was talking to Arthur, but I was shocked and faced with a difficult dilemma when I heard her whisper throatily: "Suck my titties, darling, you know how that excites me!" Should I or should I not make my presence known and break up their spooning? I peered in through the gap left by the half-shut door. Gwendolen looked simply stunning – if you've never met her, let me tell you that she is a most attractive girl, well-built with long curly strawberry-blonde hair and a curvey figure. She had taken off the dress she was wearing in Act One and was lying in Arthur's arms on a pile of clothes heaped on the floor wearing only a silk camisole which had ridden up to reveal her frilly white knickers. She had let the shoulder straps fall down and Arthur had cupped her large creamy white breasts in his hands. He had taken off his shirt and vest but had kept on his tights which bulged so much between his legs I thought that the material would soon give way! Gwendolen stroked this enormous bulge as she repeated her request for Arthur to suck her titties. She made herself comfortable on his lap, put her arm around his neck and pulled his face to her naked nipples.

' "Oooh! Oooh! How lovely," she moaned as he nibbled gently away, tweaking one erect red tittie between the fingers of his left hand as he twisted his tongue around the other, and Gwendolen moaned with delight, holding him in a vicelike grip as with his right hand he lifted her camisole even higher to rub his palm against her pussey. She arched her back upwards to allow him to pull down her knickers and I don't mind telling you that this sight made my own cock swell up so much that I was forced to unbutton my flies and let my stiff shaft spring out of my trousers. My hand flew to my rigid rod but somehow I managed to resist the temptation to toss myself off. Instead, I squeezed my bursting prick as I watched Arthur's fingers burying themselves in Gwendolen's furry mound, which made her shake in a series of spasms before she gasped: "Arthur, let me do something for you." He pulled away for a moment and attempted to take off his tights. He pushed them over the protuberance made by his swollen prick and let them down together with his underpants down to his ankles.

'Gwendolen reached out and grasped his tumescent tool, sliding her hand up and down the thick veiny shaft and they frigged each other frenziedly as they exchanged a long, deep French kiss. I could no longer contain myself and indulged in a rapid five knuckle shuffle. Gwendolen lay back and spread her legs and the sight of Arthur's fingers sliding in and out of her hairy crack brought me to the boil very quickly and turning aside I ejaculated a stream of creamy jism all over the wall behind me. In double quick time I mopped it up with a handkerchief as best as I could. Then as I dried my knob I looked back again at the frenetic couple in the room in front of me who by now were about to progress to an actual fuck. Gwendolen was now on her back with her head resting on a plump cushion and Arthur was on his knees between her legs. He grabbed a second cushion and slid it under her backside and then he nudged her knees further apart as he took his thick prick in his hand and carefully inserted the uncapped bulbous helmet into her cunney. I swear I could hear the squelchy sound of his shaft parting her love lips and entering her cunt as she clasped her legs around his waist and he fucked her in a slow yet steady rhythm, his hands cupping her breasts as he pumped in and out of her juicy love channel.

' "Go on big boy, fuck my pussey with that big fat dick. Ram your cock into my crack you dear lad!" she cried out as she drummed her feet against the small of his back to force every inch of his pulsating tool inside her. Arthur was now panting from his exertions as he pounded away, his body rocking backwards and forwards between her spread fleshy thighs. Gwendolen was obviously spending as she raked his back with her fingernails as she thrilled to the sweet sensations of her spend, but as he trembled on the brink of his climax she gasped: "Best not come inside me tonight, Arthur, it's not a good time of the month." "Oh, damnation!" he grunted, clearly disappointed but gallantly and wisely, he jerked his hips upward and withdrawing his gleaming, throbbing penis, proceeded to shoot a flood of milky white semen all over her belly. Gwendolen wriggled out from underneath him and wiped her pussey with the corner of one of the discarded old costumes upon which they had been lying. "Time for another quick one?" she asked and before he could answer she leaned forwards on her hands and knees and presented the full moons of her soft rounded buttocks to Arthur's (and my own!) delighted gaze. His cock was still meaty looking but it swelled up again to a full erection after he slicked his hand up and down his wet shaft. Then when his prick was ready again for action he pulled open her rounded bottom-cheeks and, after wetting his knob with spittle, inserted the tip of his chopper inside the wrinkled brown rosette of her rear-dimple. She writhed with the pleasure and the shock afforded by this new sensation and Arthur had his work cut out to keep his cock in place.

Her plump bum slapped nicely against the back of Arthur's thighs as he pounded away and reaching behind her she caressed his heavy ballsack as she rocked to and fro in time with Arthur's piston thrusts. My own cock had swollen up again but before I could even think of frigging myself for a second time, Arthur's torso suddenly went rigid and he spurted spasm after spasm of spunk into Gwendolen's arse-hole.

'But now came the disaster that nearly led to the abandonment of last night's performance of the play! For as Arthur emptied his balls he cried out not in ecstacy but in agony: "Ow! Ow! Ow! My back! My back!" as he fell forward on top of her, his prick still embedded in Gwendolen's back passage as they collapsed in an untidy heap. Poor Arthur was in obvious pain, his back muscles having seized up so badly that he was unable to move his body by even an inch. "Arthur, what's the matter? – please get off me!" cried Gwendolen in vain. They were joined together by Arthur's prick but she managed to wriggle free from this tender trap, leaving Arthur moaning in agony on the carpet of old costumes.

' "For God's sake get help, Gwen, I'm in terrible pain," moaned Arthur and hearing his plea I decided to make my presence known. I quickly walked back a few yards and then walked briskly towards the room, knocked on the door and threw it wide open. I feasted my eyes on Gwendolen's delicious naked charms for she was so agitated she made no attempt to cover her titties or her silky pubic muff of light brown curls.

' "Oh Michael, thank goodness you're here," she said with undisguised relief. I pretended to look shocked as I replied: "Good God, what's been going on here, Gwendolen? Did Arthur attack you?"

'Despite the desperate situation, she smiled briefly before replying: "Not in the way your question suggests; we were, er, um, doing some

359

indoor exercise when suddenly Arthur keeled over and now he can't move!"

' "You'd better change, Gwendolen, your next scene opens in just over ten minutes' time," I said crisply, picking up Arthur's tights from the floor. "I'll go next door to Arthur's room and slip these on, pronto. Luckily we're near enough of the same build so I'll be able to change into his shirt and doublet as well. I'll take your boots as well, Arthur, if you don't mind. You know the first rule of all thespians – no matter what, the show must go on."

'Gwendolen clapped her hands together and looked admiringly at me. "Oh, Michael, I didn't realise what a masterful chap you are – but do you know Arthur's part?"

' "I've heard you rehearse often enough and we studied the play at school, but if I lose my place, young Sheena Walshaw is an excellent prompter and she'll help me out. Luckily the action takes place when the set won't be lit too brightly so hopefully the substitution won't be too glaring even for those people in the front stalls."

'I promised Arthur that I would send someone to help him as soon as possible and then went next door and changed into his costume. I grabbed Gwendolen's hand and pulled her along the corridor and upstairs to the side of the stage, where Sidney Smyth glared at her and whispered: "I was just about ready to send out a search party." Then when he saw me dressed as Vincentio his eyes bulged but he only had time to gurgle an imprecation before Gwendolen and I sailed onto the stage. The Gods were with me and I managed to get through my lines without once having to take recourse of a prompt. In the wings, the rest of the cast gathered to find out what was happening, and as Gwendolen and I finished our scene to a storm of applause we were almost mobbed when the curtain came down at the end of the Act. I hastily explained what had befallen the stricken Arthur, tactfully omitting the prurient details of his unfortunate accident. Sidney went in front of the curtains and asked if there were a doctor in the house and fortunately Dr Fulham of the John Radcliffe Infirmary was in the audience and he kindly offered his services to us. During the interval, we managed to get Arthur up on his feet but I continued to play the role for the rest of the evening and Sidney made a further announcement to the audience explaining that the actor playing Vincentio had been taken ill and that I would act as understudy for the remainder of the play.

'Gwendolen was very grateful. Not only had I saved the day as far as the play was concerned but also that I had not breathed a word about how Arthur came to strain his back so badly! By the time we went back to our dressing rooms, Arthur had been helped back to his college and Gwendolen turned to me and suggested that I brought my clothes into her room so that we could change together. When I returned with my clothes she said: "I do so admire the way you solved our problem, Michael. But do you know, all this stress has given me all kinds of aches and pains. Would you care to massage my back for me?"

' "Certainly I would," I replied, "although I had better tell you that I have never tried to massage anybody before."

' "Oh, I'm sure that a clever chap like you will have no difficulties," she replied and before my very eyes she slipped out of her costume and gave me full view again of her delectable naked body. She lay face downwards on the small sofa and I licked my lips when Gwendolen wriggled her luscious bum cheeks. I moved over and put my hand on her shoulder. "Start from the top and work down," she suggested and nothing loath, I gently rubbed the smooth, warm skin of her neck with my fingertips.

' "M'mmm, you have a wonderful touch, Mr Beattie," she purred in a soft voice, "are you sure you have never before given any girl a massage?" For reply, I began kissing her, starting at the nape of her neck and then my kisses followed my hands which were soon clutching her glowing, rounded buttocks. As I frantically tore at the buttons of my doublet I rained rapid kisses down her backbone and over her bum cheeks down the backs of her thighs which made her body quiver all over.

'When I had managed to shuck off my tights, she turned round to lie on her back and her beautiful body lay sprawled before me, her legs flung invitingly apart and the white globes of her breasts acting as magnets to my hands which roved freely across them to feel the elongated red nipples. I kissed her pretty ankles and began travelling ever upwards. Gwendolen trembled with lustful anticipation when my hot lips reached the curly hair of her cunney and she moaned with desire when I sucked the pouting love lips into my mouth. She grabbed my hair and pulled me even closer as my tongue inserted itself into the damp crevice of her cunt. My tongue soon found her stiffening clitty and she gasped: "Yes, Michael, finish me off as quickly as you can!" So I gave her clitty my full attention, nibbling the hard flesh as her body jerked from side to side as I tongued her cunney and played with her titties until she threw back her head and in a paroxysm of erotic fervour cried out: "I'm coming, Michael, I'm going to come! Push your tongue in further! That's the way!" With a huge shudder she gained her release, mewing happily as her love juices dribbled over my lips and I swallowed as much of her pungent nectar as the flow ran over my face.

'When she had recovered she sat up and took my bursting prick in her hands. I tried to move on top of her, but she gently pushed me back and rising to her knees she said: "No, Michael, I don't want to go further now. Apart from anything else, it would hardly be fair to Arthur if I let you fuck me. But I tell you what, I'll relieve your feelings in a way which I think you'll like!"

'She slid her hand up and down my straining shaft as she lasciviously ran her tongue round her upper lip before stooping her head and kissing my uncapped helmet which sent a current of delicious sweetness flowing throughout my body. She played with my prick for some moments, slipping the crown in and out of her mouth whilst her tongue glided slowly up and down my pulsing pecker. She bobbed her head up and down so that I could fuck her mouth in a most delightful manner. Indeed, she sucked me off so beautifully that all too soon I could feel the rush of sperm hurtling up from my balls and with a cry I pumped out a stream of hot spunk between her rich, red lips. Gwendolen enjoyed this and she sucked up and swallowed every drop of my vital essence, milking my cock until it wilted under the frenetic urgency that it had encountered.

'There was no time for further petting even if we had wanted to continue as the theatre staff wanted to close up for the night. We dressed ourselves and made our way out and joined up with the other players at The Cat and Pigeons for a nightcap – but as you can all appreciate, I didn't stay too long for I was exhausted both physically and mentally by all that had happened earlier!'

Now Michael Beattie had told his stirring story so clearly that Frank, Barry and myself had listened with such rapt attention that none of us had noticed that several other fellows had quietly ended their conversations and had gathered round to listen to him. So at the conclusion of his colourful narrative, we were startled by the sound of a number of chaps who suddenly burst into a spontaneous round of applause. Poor Michael was dreadfully embarrassed and appealed to all those who had listened in to his tale to swear that they would not repeat his yarn to anyone else. Everyone readily agreed that to spread the story would be a caddish act – 'though in return I think Mike Beattie must tell us all the details when he finally fucks Gwendolen!' called out a fruity voice

364

from behind me.

Michael raised his hands in surrender and said: 'We'll cross that bridge when we come to it – though I wouldn't be surprised if Gwendolen and I never actually go any further. Our snogging was spur-of-the-moment stuff and tonight when I'm playing Vincentio, as although Arthur's making a swift recovery he won't be able to resume his role until Friday's performance, I don't expect Gwendolen and I will do anything more than kiss each other on the stage.'

Frank called over the waiter and asked whether anyone would care to help him finish a second bottle of port. 'Not for me, thank you. I've really enjoyed listening to Michael's saga, but I must retire to my room as I've an essay to finish for tomorrow,' I said, rising to my feet.

'Oh come on, my friend, all work and no play makes Jack a dull boy, you know,' protested Barry. 'I was looking forward to a few rubbers of bridge this evening.'

'Get thee behind me, Satan,' I warned him with a smile. 'You know how much I enjoy a game of bridge, but please don't tempt me any further. I've a hellish day tomorrow though I'm quite looking forward to Professor Webb's party in the evening.'

'Have you also been invited to old Beaver's get-together?' drawled Frank. 'He asked me to come too but I didn't want to mention it before in case you hadn't been favoured with an offer to attend, what does he call it, his *conversazione*. It could be fun and I've been told that he owns the best cellar in the whole University.

'Jolly good, Frank, I'm sure we'll have a fine time. Knock on my door at eight o'clock tomorrow night and we'll go to the bunfight together.' And before anything else could draw my attention, I waved a goodbye to my friends and made my way up to my room, resolving to burn the midnight oil until I had finished my essay.

CHAPTER THREE

A Test Of Endurance

IT WAS NEARLY TWO O'CLOCK IN the morning when with a sigh of relief I put down my pen and shuffled together the papers upon which I had written my essay which was about the tiresome political situation in Ireland. As I yawned and stretched my arms I thought to myself that this might not be the most elegant essay I had ever composed but though on the short side it was competent enough and would have to suffice. Indeed, I had been sorely tempted simply to write that there were no solutions to the Irish problem except build a border fence like the Great Wall of China between Ulster and the rest of the country though it would be hard to decide on which side lay the barbarians, but aphorisms of this kind would not please my tutor, Professor Cuthbert Cumberland, who was a man of acerbic wit and well-known to be merciless to students who sent in below standard work for his perusal.

He was also somewhat of a snob, a characteristic I abhor, although I still smile at the story about his involvement in a planned visit to the

University by the Crown Prince of Japan. An official from the Japanese Embassy visited Professor Cumberland to make the necessary arrangements and the Professor, who was a stickler for protocol, asked how the young man should be addressed. 'At home we refer to him as the Son of God,' said the diplomat, to which Professor Cumberland is supposed to have rejoined: 'That will present no problem. We are used to entertaining the sons of distinguished men at Oxford.' He had a perverse sense of humour too as shown by this probably apocryphal anecdote. It is said that a colleague rushed up to him one morning with the news that a member of the philosophy department had committed suicide. Professor Cumberland is said to have raised his hand and said: 'Please, don't tell me who. Allow me to guess!'

But I would just have to hope that my essay pleased the Professor for I was so sleepy that I could not have written another sentence. I fell asleep as soon as my head touched the pillow and would have missed breakfast and perhaps my first lecture if Nancy had not have woken me up in time. It was not part of her duties to rouse undergraduates from their slumber but the jolly girl wanted to apologise for slipping under the table and sucking me off during dinner the previous night. She had knocked on my door but when I had failed to reply she quietly entered as she had correctly guessed that I was still in bed.

I must say that I preferred Nancy's way of waking me up to that of any alarm clock! I felt my shoulder being shaken and as I came to my senses

I felt soft fingers snake their way around my stiff cock (since the age of thirteen I have always woken up with a boner) and I heard Nancy whisper: 'Wake up, Master Rupert, it's getting on for eight o'clock.' My head cleared quickly as her words seeped through and I slowly came to my senses, though for a few seconds I was puzzled by the fact that my tool was throbbing with pleasure even though I was not frigging myself. Then I quickly realised that Nancy was playing with my prick, rubbing her hand up and down the hot shaft, capping and uncapping my helmet as she said: 'Would you like me to finish you off, Master Rupert, or shall I run you a bath instead?'

'Time enough for both I think, Nancy, if you don't mind,' I said, now fully aware of what was going on. She grinned and increased the pace of motion, her hand flashing up and down my swollen shaft as I lay back and enjoyed the very pleasant sensation of being woken up by what is vulgarly known as 'a hand job'. Nancy's sensual rubbing soon brought the inevitable result and I spunked copiously, the sticky froth shooting out from my knob all over her hand and over my curly pubic hair.

This sight so excited her that she whispered: 'Oh dear, now we can't let all that luscious spunk go to waste,' and she bent down and sucked up as much of my emission as possible, licking my cock clean until my prick began to lose some of its stiffness. 'I do love sucking your cock, your sperm has just the salty tang that I like to swallow. Just the thought of taking your pole in my mouth makes me ever so randy,' she added, massaging

'I'd love to fuck you, Nancy, but it will have to be at another time as I'm already late for breakfast. Please run my bath now whilst I shave, there's a good girl,' I said, heaving myself out of bed.

She sighed and said: 'Well, how about this evening before dinner?'

I shook my head and said regretfully: 'Nancy, this must sound awfully conceited, but I'm afraid that I don't have the time. I'm only going to have half an hour or so to change before dinner and then I'm going to a reception at Professor Webb's house. Believe me, it's not that I don't want to fuck you but I'm not really free till after dinner tomorrow evening at the earliest and then only briefly because I'm going out again to an art class.'

'I can't meet you till Friday then because I'm going out myself tomorrow night,' she complained crossly. 'My friend Rosa and I have been given tickets to see *The Taming Of The Shrew* at the New Theatre.'

'Really? I do hope you enjoy it – who was the kind gentleman who provided your tickets?'

This question put her back into a good humour for she giggled and replied: 'Mike Beattie, of course. Why do you think I gobbled his cock under the table last night? Actually, I came in this morning to apologise if what I did during dinner upset you.'

'No, of course it didn't,' I hastened to assure her, 'although I must say I was very worried in case you were discovered.'

'It wouldn't have mattered too much, I would have just said that I was cleaning up some spilt

370

food,' she said coolly, 'and I'm sure that none of you would have given me away! I had only planned to suck off Michael but I'm particularly fond of your prick, Rupert, and I couldn't resist it.'

'Thank you, Nancy, I'm always very pleased to hear a girl say nice things about my prick because at school we were all a little jealous of Frank Folkestone's gigantic tool.'

Her remark at hearing this confession well illustrates why, as I have just written when recounting the anecdote about Professor Cumberland's snobbery, I detest this particular vice. More often that not, I was to discover that several college servants like Nancy possessed far more common sense than many of the fellows of the college including those who sat at the High Table. She laughed openly at this confession and exclaimed: 'For heaven's sake, don't disappoint me now, Master Rupert. Surely you're not one of those silly boys who measure themselves against what they see in the changing rooms and worry that their own pricks seem smaller than those dangling around them.'

I coloured slightly at her well chosen words which you may well recall, dear reader, gave further credence to Chrissie Nayland-Hunt's rebuke to Gillian Headleigh when the latter made an appreciative remark about the size of Salman Marrari's member.

Nancy continued: 'My last boyfriend, Billy Bucknall, who still works down the road in Blackwell's bookshop, had such a tremendous tadger that at school his form-mates used to whistle and cheer whenever they saw him take a shower. And of course he enjoyed basking in their approval and admiration, but this proud self-confidence soon vanished when he first had the opportunity to spoon seriously with the maid-of-all-work back in his parents' house.

'At first all was well and she allowed him to caress her breasts through her blouse and she rubbed her hand against the huge bulge in his lap – but when she unbuttoned his trousers and took out his prick she was so startled that she began to giggle. Now you can imagine what effect this had on a shy boy who had never even gone further than a furtive kiss before. His cock shrivelled down in double quick time and he couldn't coax it back up again for love or money. Still, I helped him to forget about his problem by explaining to him that a girl's cunney expands or contracts to take in whatever size cock is being placed inside it.'

'You must have had great fun giving Mr Bucknall a practical lesson,' I said drily.

'Yes, I taught Billy all he knows about fucking,' said Nancy with justifiable pride in her voice. 'We went out together for almost a year but neither of us want to settle down yet so we have agreed to go our separate ways for now, although you never know how things might turn out, do you?'

I gave Nancy a kiss as I stripped off and as I marched into the bathroom I called out: 'Nancy, thank you once again for waking me up this morning. Look, there's half a crown *[a coin worth 12½p which disappeared when Britain changed to decimal currency in 1971 – Editor]* on my bedside

372

table. Please take it and buy yourself and Rosa a nice box of chocolates for the theatre tomorrow night.'

'That's not necessary, Master Rupert, really it isn't,' she protested as she followed me inside the bathroom and turned on the bath-taps while I rummaged around in the cupboard for my razor and shaving cream.

'I know it's not *necessary* but I'd like to show my gratitude to you, so please accept my gift as a sincere token of appreciation not as a fee for a service,' I said grandly and this pompous little speech made us both smile. Anyhow, Nancy finally accepted my little present and I just managed to get downstairs before the kitchen closed. After breakfast I left my essay in Professor Cumberland's pigeon-hole and spent the rest of the day hard at work. Nevertheless, I made sure to post two notes, one to the gorgeous Chrissie telling her that I would attend her art class the next night when she could give me further details about when and where we would meet my old pal Salman Marrari, and the other to the equally lovely Beth Randall, apologising for not having contacted her before but that I hoped she would be free to see me one day next week.

My crowded social calendar would certainly keep me busy, I thought, as I changed for dinner and Professor Webb's evening party. Still, we work to live, not live to work as our wealthy village squire and family friend Mr Buckingham was fond of saying when he called round in the morning to pick up my father for a day's fishing. Mind, my mother, who holds radical views upon what she calls the shockingly unfair distribution of wealth in our society, once asked the squire with some irritability how he would know this to be true as he had never done a day's work in his life!

'It's becoming quite difficult to fit everything in – as the maidservant said to the chauffeur!' I said to Frank Folkestone as we met as arranged after dinner.

'Don't complain,' advised Frank as we walked briskly out of the college gates. 'Despite the many opportunities to enjoy oneself here, there are very many first year students who are still lonely and homesick.'

'Very true, I have no right at all to grumble,' I sighed. 'And you seem to be getting on nicely, Frank. I can't believe that you really miss our life at St Lionel's.'

'Good God, I should say not, although I must admit that occasionally I do miss the friendship you and I shared with Prince Salman. We had some great times together, didn't we?'

This reminded me to tell Frank the good news about Salman coming to Oxford for the weekend. 'I'm sure you could join us for dinner tomorrow night,' I said but Frank shook his head.

'Damn, I've already arranged to dine with the Matthew Arnold Society, but try and bring him over for coffee on Saturday morning,' he said, a sensible suggestion with which I was happy to comply, though I speculated that Salman had planned to spend the morning in bed with the delectable Chrissie!

Professor Simon Webb's party turned out to be a fine affair – frankly, I had expected to mix in a small, exclusive gathering but there must have been at least fifty young people present. Frank and I were delighted to see that like Doctor Blayers, the good Professor believed in letting young people of both sexes engage in social intercourse and as I scanned the room looking to see if I knew any of the other guests besides Frank, I wondered whether Gillian Headleigh might be present.

'Are you looking for someone?' said a sweet feminine voice and I turned round and saw a truly ravishing girl standing beside me. She was a most beautiful creature, rather above medium height with shining bright brown hair, a fresh complexion and a pretty face which was set off by a merry smile that played upon her rich, red lips. Furthermore, this exquisite young lady was wearing a low cut crimson dress which revealed a goodly amount of her firmly-rounded breasts.

'Yes, I was looking to see whether Gillian Headleigh or her chum Chrissie Nayland-Hunt were here. Would you happen to know these girls by any chance?'

She looked at me closely and then with a lilting laugh in her voice she said with a fine theatrical flourish. 'I am acquainted with both of them and your question leads me to believe that your name is Rupert Mountjoy from Balliol College. Am I right or wrong, my dear sir?'

With a chuckle I raised my hands in surrender. 'The prisoner pleads guilty as charged. But we have not been introduced, so I can't imagine how on earth you come to know my name.'

'Elementary, my dear Watson,' she replied,

wagging a finger at me. 'Indeed so elementary that we hardly need employ the services of Sherlock Holmes or Sexton Blake. I am sharing lodgings with Gillian in Pusey Street whilst we are in Oxford and she has told me all about you, you naughty fellow.'

'Goodness me, I hope you don't believe everything that you are told.'

'It depends upon who is doing the telling and as you would-be lawyers might say, *cui bono? [who benefits? – Editor]*. As far as Gillian is concerned, I am sure that I can believe every word she has said about you, especially about your abilities to please members of the female sex.'

I blushed at the thought of what Gillian had told this gorgeous girl about our escapades. 'Of course you can, I didn't mean to even hint that Gillian would ever deliberately utter an untruth.'

'Of course you didn't,' she agreed. 'But alas, neither she nor Chrissie are here to defend themselves even if you did. They've gone to see the Dramatic Society's production of *The Taming Of The Shrew* at the New Theatre this evening.'

Well, dear reader, this led me on to mention my friend Michael Beattie's involvement in the play, though naturally I did not breathe a word about the truth of just how he came to take over the part except to say that Arthur Cuthbertson had suddenly taken ill during a performance and that at very short notice, Michael had bravely stepped into the breach.

'Anyhow, whilst I am sorry that Gillian and Chrissie aren't here, I'm delighted that their absence has brought us together, Miss, ah, now

376

you have the advantage of me as you know my name but I don't know yours!'

'I'm Marianne Dawson and I'm pleased to meet you, Rupert, and please don't worry, Gillian said only the nicest things about you!'

This chance meeting was indeed fortuitous for me. Marianne and I chatted animatedly especially when I discovered that we shared an interest in photography. I told her of how Frederick Nolan, the American cinematographer, had come to my family's home [see An Edwardian Dandy 1: Youthful Scandals *for a full account of Rupert's involvement in making one of the earliest 'blue' films made in Britain – Editor*] and I was saying how popular moving pictures had become with the general public, when Professor Webb himself joined in the conversation.

'Moving pictures, young Mountjoy?' he snorted. 'Can't abide them, to be frank with you – all that jerky flickering gives me a headache after a time but I suppose they'll form an interesting library of material for future historians to complement the newspapers and official records. I grant you that now people are flocking to see cinematograph shows but these only have novelty value and won't pose any threat against the music halls and the theatre.'

Marianne took issue immediately with this view. 'I can't agree with you, sir. The film offers a new entertainment to an international audience. A film-maker such as Frederick Nolan makes his film and can have copies shown all over the world. All Frenchmen, Spaniards, Italians or what have you need do is to insert title slides in their own language where needed. I grant you that the actors cannot be heard but against this, the action is more realistic, being able to switch at will from inside to outdoors and from the past to the present and if necessary even to the future. Of course, whilst the film remains without the power of speech, the theatre remains unchallenged but I would wager that sooner rather than later, some clever inventor will marry sound and colour to film and there will be machines available that we can buy so that we can view these films in the comfort of our own homes.'

'Oh, I think you are now entering the realms of fantasy, my dear,' said the Professor doubtfully although I strongly backed up Marianne's prophecy. *[In the fullness of time, an ironic coincidence would see Rupert in New York on the evening of October 6th, 1927, squiring a pretty actress to the premiere of 'The Jazz Singer', the very first film in which the cast were heard to talk – Editor]*

'Well, one matter upon which we can surely all agree is that the moving picture will never replace the art of painting, although like the majority of my friends, I was most disappointed at this summer's Royal Academy Exhibition,' I declared roundly.

Professor Webb beamed and said: 'I am pleased to hear you say so, young Mountjoy. I looked in vain for evidence of new genius coming to the fore but was castigated for my criticism by my young brother who sits on the Hanging Committee. He had the cheek to call me an old fogey! Well, he could hardly level the same charge at you and your chums!'

'I was not able to see this year's Exhibition as I spent the summer with my family in America,' confessed Marianne, 'but I don't think we should judge the newer artists too hastily. The language of art varies – what may have been expressive yesterday may be regarded as merely commonplace today. But from what I've seen at previous exhibitions, I would say that the danger comes in that once an artist is admitted into the Academy, he often becomes too contented with himself to care to do anything that he had not done before.'

'There we are most certainly in agreement,' said the Professor, running a hand through his bushy red beard. 'I've been collecting landscapes by Stanley Brendah *[a British landscape artist whose Hertfordshire scenes became extremely popular and fetched high prices around the turn of the century – Editor]* for the last ten years and I would have to agree with you that since he was given the *imprimateur* of an Academician, his work has suffered. The bold, dashing style seems to have become muted, as if he were afraid of experimentation in case his admirers might turn away, just as I must turn away from this interesting debate, dear Miss Marianne, for I must circulate amongst my guests and make some introductions where necessary. Many young people are terribly shy and stand around all by themselves, lonely in the thronging crowd, and I consider it my bounden duty as host to help them break into a friendly circle.'

As Professor Webb plunged through the crowd, I said to Marianne: 'What a decent old stick! It's very thoughtful of him to make sure that his more reticent guests enjoy themselves. Mind, I never knew he was a connoisseur of landscape pictures.'

'Ah, there's probably quite a lot you don't know about our host,' said Marianne brightly. 'He specialises in other artistic fields too.'

'Really? In poetry perhaps, or in sculpture?'

'Neither, Rupert, and I doubt if you would ever guess the answer. You see, the Professor's chosen speciality is in sucking pussey.'

I looked at her blankly for I could hardly believe my ears. 'Yes, it's true, I do assure you,' she said, trying hard to suppress a giggle. 'How do you think he came to have a nickname such as "Beaver"?'

'Well, blow me down, I would never have suspected it,' I said, taking a large gulp from my glass of the excellent fruit punch. 'My, this also has quite a bite to it.'

We looked at each other and spontaneously collapsed into roars of laughter at this unintentional witticism. Frank strolled over to see what all the fun was about but we could hardly repeat the story and he retired muttering that we must have been pouring the punch down our throats too quickly for our own good. 'I say, Marianne, you're not having me on about "Beaver" Webb, are you?' I asked when we finally recovered our composure.

'No, of course not, Rupert,' she replied indignantly. 'Why, I myself had the pleasure of being brought off by his brilliant oral skills earlier this evening. I came here an hour before the party was due to begin because I had heard of his reputation as a cunnilinguist from my cousin Lucinda, who studied under Simon Webb last year. I was attracted to the idea of having my pussey pleasured in this fashion by an expert for the art is alas not practised as widely in this country as it is on the Continent and in America.

'As I had arrived so early, I was shown into a small sitting-room to wait until the Professor had finished dressing though it was not long before he came bursting in, saying that he was sorry not to have received me before but he had not expected such an early arrival. He opened a bottle of fizz whilst I told him that I knew I was early but that I shared his interest in art and wondered if he would be interested in an early Stanley Brendah picture I had uncovered, as my cousin Lucinda had told me of his interest in this artist. It was an unusual painting for it was a nude study and I had always thought of Brendah as a landscape specialist. Simon's face lit up and he explained: "Ah, well you see, Stanley was quite a ladies' man in his early days and every time, how shall I say, he sowed some wild oats, he made figure studies of the girls concerned."

' "How fascinating! So his lovers have been immortalised on canvas! I would have loved to have been one of his models but I don't think I have quite the figure for it."

' "Stuff and nonsense, my dear Miss Dawson, I am sure that any artist worth his salt would be honoured to have you pose for him," he replied. I looked at him with a wide-eyed innocence and said: "Do you really think so, Professor?"

' "Oh come now, let's not be so formal, we're

not in the lecture hall now. My name is Simon," he said. "Very well, Simon, thank you, but then you must call me Marianne," I replied as I hitched my skirts up to my knees. I stretched out my legs and enquired: "Tell me truthfully, Simon, don't you think my calves are a little too plump for someone like Stanley Brendah to paint me?"

' "No, no, not at all, they are quite beautiful in my judgement," he said, swallowing hard as I crossed and uncrossed my legs. Then I stood up and moved forwards towards him. When I reached his chair I deliberately leaned forward so that my bosom almost spilled out of this low-cut dress. Now false modesty is as foolish and vulgar as overweaning pride, so I have no hesitation in telling you that like all men, Simon Webb was overwhelmed by the nearness of my soft, rounded breasts. He gulped again as I said seductively: "What I would really appreciate is for you to give me your opinion on perhaps my best attributes." He gaped in silence, his mouth hanging open in amazement as I fiddled with the hook behind my back to loosen the top of my gown and he stood up and helped me unbutton my dress so I was able to step out of it without creasing the material too badly. With a graceful movement I pulled off my chemise so that my bare breasts were exposed to his excited gaze and then I took his trembling hands and pressed them to my titties which made the nipples pop up like two little bullets.

'It was time for me to display the *pièce de résistance* so with a deliberately accentuated wriggle I pulled down my frilly lace knickers. As I stepped out of them I bent down and picked them up from the floor. I held my knickers in my hand as I stroked my sides sensuously before placing my knickers on the silky mound of hair between my legs and rubbing them against it. Now the merest touch of my fingers against my pussey is always enough to get me going, so throwing all modesty aside I tossed them to Simon as I teasingly purred: "Sniff them and tell me if you like the aroma of my pussey. Then if you wish to sample what you see on display, I would very much like you to suck my pussey. Otherwise I will assume that you want me to wrap the goods up again and place them back on the shelf!"

'He did not reply but wordlessly he rose and took me in his arms. Then he planted his mouth on mine and we exchanged a lingering kiss before I felt myself being gently laid back on the floor. Simon pulled down a cushion from a chair to act as a pillow for me as I lay back and relaxed, thrilling to the movement of his lips sliding down my body. He kissed each raised tittie in turn as his hands prised open my unresisting thighs. Then he buried his face between my legs and licked the dampness round my pussey lips as I lifted my bottom so that he could clasp my buttocks and pull them forward to him. My cunney opened out like a flower as he slipped his tongue through the pouting pink pussey lips and lapped with long, thrusting strokes between the inner grooves of my cunt, which by now was beginning to gush out love juice.

'Simon certainly deserved first class honours for his ability to bring a girl off with his mouth. To add to my pleasure he slipped two fingers into my slit which made me thrash around wildly until the electric sensations subsided. But what took me up to the highest realms of ecstatic pleasure was how he attacked my clitty, driving his tongue into the ring of my love channel and then as the tiny bean broke from its pod he gripped it in his strong fingers and tugged at it quite vigorously, which made me spend profusely as I writhed my hips dementedly. Then he lowered his mouth again and slurped noisily on my drenched pussey, his tongue driving fast round the juicy crack from which dribbled a flow of tangy love juice which he swallowed with evident relish.

'I would have liked nothing better to have repaid the compliment by sucking his prick but the first of the other guests would soon be arriving and I needed time to put my clothes back on. Simon also understood why I would not let him fuck me with his sizeable prick which he had let free from the confines of his trousers. I am sure you will agree, Rupert, that it would have been far too forward to let oneself be fucked after so brief an introduction.'

'Oh absolutely so,' I said gravely, nodding my head in agreement. 'I never fuck with any girl I have known for less than thirty minutes.'

Marianne's delicious dimples showed as she smiled broadly at my ironic comment and said: 'A very wise maxim to follow – and one should be most careful when recounting the pleasures of one's fucking, though I know I can trust you to keep the tale I have just told you under your hat. For as Molière rather cynically wrote: *le scandale du monde est ce qui fait l'offense, et ce n'est pas pêcher que pêcher en silence'* [It is a public scandal that gives offence and it is no sin to sin in secret – Editor].

'So poor Professor Webb must be feeling rather frustrated unless he has sought relief from the five-fingered widow,' I commented.

'Perhaps, though I think it more likely that he asked one of the girls in that group over by the window to toss him off.'

'That would be rather dangerous, wouldn't it?'

'Not really, for I am certain that he has probably fucked at least three of them. Amanda Wellsend, the tall blonde girl, told me only this evening that she rode a splendid St George on Simon's cock the other afternoon.'

Marianne looked down and lightly touched the bulge in my lap with her hand. 'I think that you might be more frustrated than Professor Webb,' she murmured. 'Do erotic anecdotes make you feel randy too? I must say that after telling you that lewd story, I'm also feeling pretty horny myself.'

My blood *was* on fire and I muttered: 'What a pity there are no private rooms to which we could repair.'

'But there are, my dear – wait here for just a moment and I'll arrange everything for us,' she replied, a lascivious smile forming across her lips as her hand dived down to give my swollen cock a friendly squeeze.

Marianne then made her way through the chattering crowd to where Professor Webb was holding court with his *amorata* Amanda Wellsend and her friends. I saw her whisper something in

385

his ear after which he passed something small from his waistcoat pocket to her which she clutched in her fist. When she returned to me she opened her hand to reveal a key. 'For one of the bedrooms upstairs?' I hazarded.

She gave a wolfish grin and said: 'Who's a clever boy, then?' and she took my hand and pulled me towards the staircase. I was hardly unwilling to accompany her but as we climbed the stairs I glanced back to see how Frank was fairing – and I was pleased to see that he had now joined Professor Webb's little group and was deep in discussion with a striking red-haired girl who was laughing at some witty remark Frank had just made if the rather smug expression on his face was a true guide to what was happening down there.

When we reached the landing Marianne pulled me across into the passage leading to the bedrooms and unlocked the door to our left. We went in and she closed the door behind us as I switched on the electric light. The room was richly furnished and I was delighted to see there was a large double bed for us – fucking on a narrow single mattress can be fine but I am sure you will agree, dear reader, that *un lit matrimonial* offers more room for both partners. Be that as it may, Marianne and I wasted no time in tearing off our clothes and in under a minute we were rolling around quite naked on the Professor's huge bed, our mouths glued together in a passionate kiss, our tongues lashing away inside the other's mouth, hugging and clutching each other in a frenzy of loving voluptuousness.

Finally, I was forced to break away from our embrace to draw breath – and raising myself on my elbow I looked down upon the soft, quivering body of this exquisite girl. She had unpinned her hair and her gorgeous face was now set off by soft waves of chestnut hair which cascaded down over her shoulders. Her firm, jutting breasts stood out proudly whilst her well-rounded shoulders tapered down into a surprisingly small waist. Yet her thighs were full and beautifully proportioned whilst between her long legs lay a furry fleece of brown hair which formed a delicious veil over her pouting pink cunney lips.

Marianne whispered: 'Let's start with a *soixante-neuf*. Why don't you lick my cunt whilst I suck your cock?' I have always maintained that this is the most ingenious yet easiest erotic position after the simple man-on-top-woman-underneath-on-her-back 'missionary' position, so called because our more bigoted evangelicals have always taught that this is the only permissible way to engage in intercourse.

I have always delighted in the magic of *soixante-neuf* and Marianne and I assumed the position which led to me repositioning myself so that my legs were up against the bedstead with my cock by Marianne's mouth whilst my own lips were just inches away from the succulent goal of her sweet pussey. I inhaled and savoured the piquant fragrance before burying my face between her legs in this aromatic nest of love. I kissed her creamy crack and my tongue began whipping back and forth, taking on a life of its own when I slipped the tip of my tongue between her cunney lips which opened in salute as it bored deep inside her juicy wet cunt. I felt for her clitty and ran my tongue up and down the sides, teasing it into a full erection as taking it now between my lips I tweaked its plump unsheathed base with the tip of my tongue, which sent tremors of lustful passion hurtling through her.

Meanwhile Marianne closed her lips around the bulbous uncapped knob of my raging stiffstander and it was my turn to shudder as her tongue flicked over my helmet, down the shaft and over my balls before reversing the route back to the mushroom dome. Her moist mouth worked its way over every inch of my rock-hard cock, her hand grasping the base as she pumped her head up and down, keeping her lips taut, kissing and sucking my pulsating prick as she ground her now sopping cunt against my face – our tempos matching in increasing speed, faster and faster as our twitches grew into tremors, the tremors into convulsions as first Marianne climaxed, moaning her joy as she flooded my mouth with her liquid spendings. Soft and yielding, the delicate cunney flesh was slippery against my tongue and I was engulfed in her spasms which sent waves of love juice coursing their way through her love channel and into my mouth and over my face.

Now I felt the first unmistakable rise of spunk rising up from my balls as Marianne continued to suck my throbbing tool, somehow managing to take almost all my shaft deep down into her throat. Her tongue slid juicily up and down until, with a low growl I cried out: 'Ahhh, here it comes!' and I shot an explosive stream of sticky white froth into her mouth which she gulped down as best she could though my emission was so strong that some of my spunk dribbled down her chin. I sat up and she leaned forward, tasting ourselves as we exchanged a long, lingering kiss.

Much like artichokes and olives, cunnilingus is an acquired taste but I would urge all young men who wish to pleasure their partners to try it. After all, is there a chap to be found anywhere in this world, regardless whether he prefers blondes, brunettes, or redheads in bed or indeed even if he is of the homosexualist persuasion, who does *not* love having his cock sucked? And if your bed-mate pleasures you, should you not play the game and return the compliment? Pussey-eating is an art in its infancy in this country which is, I am convinced, one of the reasons why English girls seem to fall so readily into the beds of the Latin races who practice cunnilingus almost as a matter of course.

Certainly, as far as Marianne was concerned, having her pussey pleasured by my mouth made her terribly randy. 'Rupert,' she said throatily, her voice crackling with desire, 'I want you to fuck me now, so slide your lovely cock in my cunt straightaway, if you please.'

Well, though putting myself in danger of sounding like an alehouse braggart, I should record here that my ability to keep a stiff prick at the ready has often been a source of joy and sometimes delighted surprise to my bed-mates, and at the age of eighteen, when the incident I am now describing took place, my prowess was at its peak and I could spend six or seven times a night without over-exerting myself in any great fashion.

So to return to the tale, despite spurting copiously into Marianne's mouth, my cock retained much of its tumescence and the soft touch of Marianne's fingers soon had my shaft standing stiffly to attention. She lay back on the bed, and I raised myself on top of her superb body and looked down upon the delicious curves of her breasts with their elongated erect nipples pointing outwards. My eyes then travelled downwards to her milky white thighs, which were as perfectly proportioned as any Grecian statue and spread wide to reveal every exquisite fold of her juicy cunt.

Slowly I eased myself down upon her, my cock sliding between her slicked cunney lips into the clinging moistness of her love channel, driving deeper and deeper until my prick was fully embedded inside her and our pubic hairs mashed together. Instantly, our bodies began to thrash back and forth in a fit of lustful passion. Clinging madly to each other, Marianne clamped her legs around my waist, squealing with delight as I pumped away and her hips writhed and twisted in time with my thrusts to maximise her pleasure. What a marvellous fuck this was! Her cunney had been so well-oiled by her previous spend that I was able to slide my cock in up to the hilt and her pussey absorbed every inch of my shaft, rippling over my length as her body exploded into a series of tiny spends. She tossed her head from side to side, biting her lower lip for she was worried that letting out her emotions in an ardent scream might be heard above the din of the partying guests downstairs. But when my own orgasm arrived and I flooded her cunney with a vibrant stream of hot, frothy spunk, she could not contain herself and whilst spout after spout of sticky sperm poured from my cock deep inside her velvety cavern, she let out an uninhibited howl of pure ecstacy as she shuddered to a magnificent climax.

Now despite my previous remark about being able to fuck all night at the peak of my youthful vigour, I was now gasping for breath, almost insensible from my efforts and I flopped down beside Marianne and my cock languished limply over my thigh. 'Oh my, I hope you have not over-exerted yourself,' said Marianne anxiously as she placed her head on my chest and listened with concern to the thumping beats of my heart. I ran my fingers through her hair and smiled contently, at peace with the world.

'Just give me some time to recover, my love, and I'll be as fit as a fiddle,' I said, closing my eyes for a well-deserved little nap, and so Marianne obediently snuggled down and moulded her soft curves into my body as we held each other tight for our short journey to the Land of Nod. She woke first and roused me by kissing me all over my body. By the time her head burrowed down to reach my burgeoning prick I was already awake and I grunted my appreciation as she washed my uncapped knob all over with her tongue. She pulled her head back and flipped herself round to lie on her belly, pulling a pillow underneath her so the rounded globes of her backside were pushed out cheekily as with a sensuous little wriggle she signalled her readiness to be bottom-fucked.

I needed no further invitation and immediately heaved myself up to kneel behind her. Carefully I pulled apart those delectable bum cheeks and angled her legs a little further apart to afford a better view of her puckered little nether orifice. Then I gently eased my knob between her buttocks and pushed into the tight little rosette. My cock was still moist from our previous spendings and I encountered little difficulty for her sphincter muscle soon relaxed and I slid my tadger in and out of the tight sheath, plunging my prick to and fro as Marianne reached back and spread her cheeks even further to widen the rim for me, jerking her arse in time to my rhythm as I wrapped one arm around her breasts, frigging each of her titties in turn and with my other hand I diddled her sopping pussey, rubbing her clitty, which afforded her the greatest of delight, doubling her pleasure now being fucked from both in front and behind.

Her bottom responded to every shove as I jerked my hips to and fro and my balls fairly bounced against her smooth bum as I cornholed her to the very limit. The unique, almost indescribable tingling one experiences in the cockshaft towards the end of a fuck soon heralded the approaching arrival of my spend. I moved my stout shaft faster and faster as Marianne worked her bum with a will until she brought me off and I injected her rear with a lavish libation of gushing jism which warmed and lubricated her delicious bottom. When I had finished emptying my balls I withdrew my cock from her well-lathered back passage with an audible plop and sank back to rest after this lascivious episode for a well-earned rest. We had been at it for only just over an hour and already I had fucked her three times and from the gleam in Marianne's eyes, I suspected that the night was still young as far as she was concerned!

Sure enough, in a short time our bodies were locked together as we mashed our mouths against each other's lips. With a fluttering tongue, she explored the inside of my mouth whilst I ran my hands over her proud thrusting breasts, letting my fingers delve into the crevice between the two white rounded beauties.

'Am I naughty to love fucking so much?' she sighed thoughtfully. 'Would you be shocked if I confessed to you that I like nothing better than a thick prick sliding in and out of my pussey?'

'Of course not, so long as you take care to guard against unwanted consequences and choose your lovers with care,' I murmured, brushing away a stray lock of hair from her face.

'Well, naturally I wouldn't have let you spunk inside me without a johnny [a condom – Editor] if I had not already taken precautions,' she said indignantly. 'And I would be very upset if the thought ever crossed your mind that I let any Tom, Dick or Harry fuck me.'

'It never crossed my mind and I assure you that I did not mean to imply any such dreadful imputation,' I said hastily. 'Furthermore I don't think you are wrong to love fucking – I also can't think of a nicer way to spend my time and after all, if the parsons are right to condemn intercourse except for the purpose of procreation, why did our Creator make love-making so pleasurable if he did not want us to enjoy it?'

To my astonishment my rhetorical question was answered! 'I could not agree more with you. Apes have been observed to finish their sexual union in six seconds, the male using some seven or eight thrusts of the phallus to complete the act. Would the puritanically inclined wish us to behave in such fashion? Is this a benchmark to which we should aspire?' said a fruity male voice by the door.

I sat up in shock at this interruption but Marianne appeared to be very little disturbed by the stranger's entrance. 'Don't fuss, Rupert,' she said soothingly. 'It's only our host who I am sure has come up here only to make sure that we are having a jolly time.'

By Gad, she was absolutely right regarding the identity of the intruder for this uninvited visitor was indeed none other than our host, Professor Webb. He stood at the foot of the bed and flourished what must have been a spare key of the door before putting it back in his pocket. He beamed at us and said: 'You're not too tired to accommodate a fresh cock, are you, Marianne?'

'So long as it's rock-hard and ready to do its duty,' she answered. And before I could venture to give my opinion on the matter, our host was unbuckling his trousers and sitting down on the bed to bend down and take off his shoes and socks. 'I do owe Simon a good fuck, you remember. I had no time even to suck his cock before the party began after he had creamed my cunney so superbly with his mouth.'

'Be my guest, Professor,' I said rather sourly and moved across the bed as our uninvited guest climbed into bed with us. Although the bed was large, we only just had enough room to allow him in with us. For he was naturally broad shouldered and over the years had developed a corpulent figure which tended to sag somewhat without the power of clothing to pull him into shape. But there was nothing amiss with his massive love truncheon which stood out from a mass of grey-flecked ginger hair at the base of his belly. He climbed rather awkwardly on top of Marianne and I must say that I was concerned that her tight little crack might make it difficult to take in such a mighty weapon.

But perhaps because she had just absorbed my own sizeable prick, even a shaft the girth of the Professor's presented no problems for her and I watched in awe as the gigantic crown of the Professor's cock slid between Marianne's pouting cunney lips. He took a deep breath and then let out a deep growl of satisfaction as inch by inch his thick tool disappeared inside her warm, juicy pit.

'There, do you like my thick prick slipping into your juicy cunt, m'dear?' he asked roguishly.

'Yes, I love it. Push it all in, you randy cocksman!' she gasped, but teasingly he pulled back and she wailed with dismay as with a passionate jolt of his loins the randy pedagogue plunged it in again, which made her roll her hips and clasp her legs around his waist whilst his large hairy ballsack banged against her bum.

They fucked away in joyful unison, with Marianne clutching his ample buttocks to draw him even closer inside her and they heaved merrily away as he screwed his shaft in and around her luscious crack.

'Oh what a perfect pussey! How it sucks and clasps my cock! A-h-r-e, I'm coming, I'm coming, I can't hold back!' he groaned and she panted:

'It's all right, don't worry – I'm almost there too. Shoot your spunk, you thick-pricked fucker!'

These lewd words sent them both passing the point of no return and the lewd pair gloried in the joys of an unforced simultaneous spend as they writhed around in ecstacy with Marianne's pussey awash with the Professor's jism as well as the love juices flowing freely from her own cunney. Then, when they had completed the course, he moved off her, flopping over to lie down on her side that was furthest from me.

Watching this erotic exhibition had so excited my flaccid cock that it had swollen back up again in a fine state of erect stiffness. I rolled over back to Marianne and began to kiss and cuddle her. The insatiable girl relished the idea of a further fuck and responded by embracing me whilst I played with her titties. I guided my hand between her legs and parting her cunney lips with my fingers, began to massage her wet pussey which made her purr with pleasure. Shortly her bottom began to jerk up and down to the rhythm of my frigging and she opened her legs wider to receive me as I clambered on top of her. We were both leaning on our sides as with a squelchy swishy sound my cock slid into her sopping love channel. Marianne rotated her hips, working her soft, wet flesh against my hot, hard shaft as I matched her rhythm, letting my length slide in and out of her clinging dampness until our surging cries of fulfilment echoed round the room as her cunt milked my prick which was thrusting faster and faster out of her sated body.

'Aaah! Aaah! One last push!' she screamed out and she bucked and twisted under me as her spend sent thrilling waves of electric delight crashing through every fibre of her being. She arched her hips and with a huge final shudder, sank happily into the bliss that follows the draining of love's reservoir.

When we had all regained our strength, the three of us spent the rest of the night engaged in further fucking and sucking. I think my favourite position was fucking Marianne's cock-hungry cunney whilst she lustily sucked on the Professor's prick, though we tried several variations on this and similar themes until the first rays of daylight heralded the dawn.

After bidding the others farewell (for neither Marianne nor the Professor needed to rise at an early hour), I walked back to college with some difficulty, taking only small, bandy-legged steps as my over-indulgence had left me saddle-sore. God knows how long Marianne will need to recover from her all-night orgy, I thought as I hauled myself up the stairs to my room. There's just time for forty winks before breakfast, I decided whilst taking off my coat and dinner jacket, and without further ado I threw myself down upon my bed. But I was so completely worn out from the violent erotic excesses in which I had participated, that, this time being without the kind assistance of Nancy, I fell into a deep sleep from which I did not awake until shortly after eleven o'clock.

Still, both my mind and body felt refreshed when I finally awoke, and after undertaking what my fellow undergraduates rather vulgarly know as a triple S [*a shower, shit and shave – Editor*], I was ready to face the day. Unfortunately, I had missed a seminar on the law of property, which meant that I had inadvertently broken the promise which those readers with good memories will recall I had made to my godfather about diligent attendance at lectures during my first year as a student. However, I did not feel too badly about this as the offence was not one committed deliberately and most fellows cut some work at some time or other without getting into any trouble. Mind, this did not hold good for one poor fellow who was summoned to the office of the famous Oxford don Dr Spooner, who when excited would often transpose the initial sounds of pairs of words, and was told by the angry don: 'You have hissed all my mystery lectures and are suspended from your studies. Leave college immediately by the next town drain.' [*W A Spooner (1844–1930) gave his name to such slip-ups of speech now known as Spoonerisms. One of his most notorious bloopers was standing up to toast Queen Victoria when she visited his college in 1889 and saying: 'Ladies and gentlemen, here's to the queer old dean.' – Editor*].

To make up for taking the morning to recover from the night before, I resolved to spend the rest of the day in the library. But as I was about to leave my room I noticed that a letter had been placed under the door. I did not recognise the writing which I deduced to be in a feminine hand but decided to take the envelope with me and read the letter in the common-room over a cup of coffee before I shut myself up in the library.

Who could be writing to me? I opened the envelope and found to my disappointment that the scribe was Chrissie Nayland-Hunt and that she was the bearer of sad tidings . . .

For the record, I reproduce her letter and the missive which accompanied it:

> Dear Rupert,
>
> I am sorry to tell you that Salman Marrari has been forced to postpone his visit to Oxford this weekend. I enclose his letter which is self-explanatory. Do let me have it back as he writes so well that I become greatly excited just reading it.
>
> Still, I hope we can still dine together on Friday night though I will quite understand if you prefer to cancel our arrangement.
>
> Love,
> Chrissie

Salman's letter read as follows:

> Darling Chrissie,
>
> It is with heartfelt apologies that I must write to say it will not be possible to come to Oxford on Friday. My uncle Pandit, who is one of the members of an important Indian governmental consultative council on native education, has arrived in Britain for a short visit and naturally he wishes to see me this coming weekend in London.

You will understand, I am sure, that this is an invitation which I cannot refuse. Perhaps you will let me know whether you will be free in two weeks' time and I can come over to see you and Rupert then. Perhaps you would ask Rupert to tell Frank Folkestone of my visit so we can have a reunion of our old gang from St Lionel's. I know you'll be back here in Cambridge by then but would you mind going back to Oxford as I would so like to see my old school chums again.

However, wherever we do meet is no great matter so long as we see each other very soon. Chrissie, it is you who I will miss most on Friday, for I had planned a weekend of l'amour which will now have to wait for at least a fortnight. Shall I tell you what I had in mind and what I still hope will happen when we finally do manage to see each other again?

Do you remember how we first made love this summer after watching the lawn-tennis championships at Wimbledon? We had just eaten strawberries and cream and were sitting in my carriage which had the blinds drawn when I leaned over and kissed you and then one thing led to another and the carriage rocked so violently that we startled the horses which began to neigh and chafe at the bit. Wasn't it lucky that they calmed down before old Johnstone the driver returned!

Ah, the memory makes my prick harden up as I recall that delightful afternoon! But enough of the past – let me look forward to the future and I'll tell you what I have in store once we are together. I shall place you naked on a cool white sheet on my bed and smear your quivering soft body all over with cream from a large bowl into which I will dip my bursting cock and then, taking hold of my shaft and using it like a paintbrush, plaster your sumptuous breasts and the crisp dark curls of your pussey hair with cream from my cock. Then I'll take a big banana, peel it and roll it over your titties until it is covered in cream and then slide it between your moist pussey lips deep inside your cunney, leaving only a little piece sticking out. Then I'd place my head between your legs and eat the sticky fruit, drawing it out slowly piece by piece as I taste the delicious mixed aroma of banana and cream laced with cunney juice!

Here Chrissie scribbled a note in the margin: 'I'd love to have my bubbies smothered in cream, perhaps with a cherry on each nipple – so long as I had the right man to eat them and lick it all off, of course!'

Now you know, dear Chrissie, that we promised never to keep any secrets from each other. So I will not hold back from recounting what occurred last Thursday afternoon when I went into town to buy you an 'unbirthday' present which I had planned to bring with me to Oxford this weekend. My original idea was to buy you a book but whilst browsing through the shelves at Heffer's, I bumped into Johnny Crawford, a fellow member of the University Polo Club, and when I told him that I was searching for a present for my girlfriend, he suggested that I go down the road and purchase something suitable in Madame Antoinette's French lingerie shop in Green Street instead. I protested that I had never been inside such a shop before but he dismissed my fears, saying with a strange smile upon his face: 'There is no need to feel apprehensive.

From my own experience, Salman, I can tell you that Madame Antoinette's girls give a splendid personal service to all their clients, both ladies and gentlemen alike.'

Well, it was worth a look, I thought, so I thanked Johnny and made my way to Madame Antoinette's, a small establishment tucked away in an alley set between two large emporiums. I felt slightly embarrassed at going into such a shop but nobody had seen me go into the alley so I screwed up my courage and opened the lace-curtained door. At first there appeared to be no-one inside the place as well, but in a few moments a young sales girl came through from the back of the shop.

'Bonjour, monsieur, can I help you?' she asked. I looked at her with interest. She was a slim brunette with long, curly hair and despite having probably worked in the shop all day, her flawless skin still had a fresh, vibrant glow. She was dressed in a dark skirt and a white open necked blouse which exposed enough cleavage to make my prick stir in my trousers, especially when she leaned forward to pick up her tape measure which had fallen to the floor. 'Madame Antoinette?' I asked nervously and she showed a set of dazzling white teeth when she smiled and replied: 'Mais non, monsieur, my name is Cherie, Madame Antoinette's niece, and I am helping her run her shop whilst I am staying in Cambridge to gain more practice in speaking English. Tell me, are you also learning English here, monsieur, ah, I don't think you mentioned your name?'

'Salman, Prince Salman Marrari at your service, mademoiselle. And no, I am studying science at the

University, because English happens to be my mother tongue, the language in which I think and the one in which I can best express myself to other people. But I am fluent enough in Hindi and Gujarati, which occasionally we speak back home to our servants or when we don't want the British to understand us!'

She chuckled at this and I added that I wanted to buy something for my girlfriend who I was seeing soon for a weekend reunion. 'I would like something elegant yet revealing for she has a lovely figure, much like yours,' I said boldly and Cherie put her hand on my arm and said: 'Then in that case I will model one or two garments for you.' She looked up at the clock and said: 'Good, it is near enough closing time,' and she drew a bolt across the door and hung the closed sign on it. I sat down whilst she went back into the back office which doubled as a showroom. In just a few minutes she emerged wearing a negligee of such fine silk that it was almost transparent. She was wearing nothing underneath the negligee and I could make out the rounded globes of her bottom as she executed a little pirouette in front of me and the dark buttons of her nipples pushed out provocatively from their light covering.

Cherie must have seen my cock shoot up when she smoothed her fingers over her firm breasts, for then she rubbed her nipples against the palms of her hands and said softly: 'Does your girlfriend have sensitive titties, Salman?' Unable to speak, I simply nodded and she continued: 'I wonder whether they are as sensitive as mine. Would you care to help me find out?'

The gorgeous girl giggled as she saw me blush but though I was still speechless, she nevertheless sat down on my lap and putting an arm around my neck, pulled my face to her breasts. I threw my arm around her waist and pulled up the frilly garment so that I could see her firm, jutting breasts which were topped with large, nut-brown nipples which I tweaked between my fingers. 'Suck my titties, Salman,' she moaned and I complied, rolling the erect, rubbery flesh between my teeth, nibbling gently on one nipple and then the other as Cherie squirmed in ecstacy. Now in my experience, playing with titties is a prelude to the main event but Cherie needed nothing more as, shaking all over, she spent with a happy little yelp of delight.

'Wait a moment and let me show you something else,' she panted as she returned to the dressing room. My poor prick, which was already threatening to burst out from my trousers, now throbbed uncontrollably as Cherie re-entered the shop naked except for a pair of lace crotchless knickers which made the ravishing girl look even more inviting, especially when she turned her back and bent over the counter, spreading her legs to reveal her glistening wet cunney framed by twin trails of white lace.

Now Chrissie, I have always been true to you, darling, in my fashion. Yes, I've always been true to you darling in my way – but I will have to confess that I found this erotic tableau simply too exciting to bear and I ripped open my trousers and grasping my cock in one hand and wrapping my other arm around her waist so that I could again play with her titties, I eased my knob between her bum cheeks and sank in to the hilt. Wisps of frilly lace tickled my shaft as I pumped in and out of her juicy cunt and what made the love-making even more thrilling was that I could see myself fucking this delicious girl in the long mirror on the wall in front of us. Watching our naked bodies heaving and shoving was so stimulating that I spent very quickly, shooting a torrent of sperm deep inside her longing pussey.

Straightening up, she turned and stood before me, rotating her hips in a tight rhythm. Obviously she had not yet spent a second time so I dropped to my knees and breathed in her musky aroma as I fingered her cunney and began to massage her clitty. 'Ah, c'est magnifique! Continuez, continuez!' she yelped as I licked and lapped around her pussey lips.

Now I placed my lips firmly over her clitty and sucked it into my mouth, with my hands now squeezing her bouncy buttocks and I found the magic button under the fold at the base of Cherie's clitty and twirled my tongue all around it. The faster I vibrated my tongue the more excited she became and she gyrated madly as my darting tongue licked and lapped up the delicious juices which were now running down in a veritable stream from the clinging grooves of her cunney. With each stroke she arched her body in ecstacy, pressing the erect clitty, which was protruding out quite two inches like a tiny cock, against the tip of my flickering tongue.

This oral stimulation soon served its purpose and I brought her off wonderfully. She flooded my face with her juices as she spent exquisitely in great, tumbling spasms.

I had an appointment with my tutor so regretfully I could not take up her kind invitation to go upstairs and fuck in the comfort of her bedroom for the rest of the evening. Now this tale might make you jealous but please note that I also declined the chance to visit Madame Antoinette's shop the next day before Cherie's aunt returned from her brief holiday. And not only have I bought you the negligee and knickers that Cherie modelled but two lovely muslin petticoats with flounces of broderie anglaise and baby ribbon edgings that I am certain you will love to wear – and I hasten to add that these were chosen solely by myself without any help from Cherie!

Despite this erotic encounter, I only have eyes for you, Chrissie, and am counting the hours until we meet again.
All my love,
Salman

I laid down the letter and called over a passing serving girl to refill my cup from the common-room coffeepot which was kept bubbling under a small spirit lamp from after breakfast until midnight.

The maid was a pretty wench who I had not seen before in the college. She could have been no more than eighteen years old, a strawberry-blonde girl who had been blessed with a pert prettiness with wide cornflower-blue eyes, a tiny nose and generously wide red lips through which showed pearly white teeth that sparkled in the bright autumnal light which poured through the large windows.

'Some more coffee, please,' I said, lifting up the

cup to her.

'Thank you, Mr Mountjoy,' she said sweetly.

How did this gorgeous girl know who I was? My fame must have travelled before me, I smiled to myself as I asked her how she knew my name, and the lovely creature coloured slightly as she replied: 'My name is Polly Castle – hasn't my cousin Nancy said anything about my starting work here? She arranged this position for me and Nancy was here a moment ago and pointed you out whilst you were reading your letter. She told me some nice stories about you, Mr Mountjoy.'

'I'm afraid she hasn't mentioned a word to me about her cousin starting work in the college, although I'm not surprised as she would hardly welcome such lovely competition for her favours. But Polly, I sincerely hope that you won't believe everything that Nancy might have told you about me.'

She stole a quick glance down to my groin where my prick, which had stiffened up whilst I was reading Salman's *billet-doux*, was bulging out like a miniature mountain from my lap. 'Well, Nancy did say that you had the sturdiest tool in Balliol,' she said quietly. 'Was this something that I shouldn't believe?'

I looked straight into her large, liquid blue eyes and said: 'I would be happy to let you discover the truth of her observation at any time of your choosing.'

Frankly, I never expected her to take up this lighthearted challenge but to my delighted surprise she immediately replied: 'There's no time like the present as far as I'm concerned. I had just finished my duties when you called me over to pour out some more coffee for you. Oh dear, I don't think there is any left in the pot – I'll have to boil up some more hot water.'

I rose from my chair and winked at her: 'Polly, do *not* put the kettle on! Take off your apron and instead find out if Nancy was telling the truth about my capabilities.'

She hesitated only for a moment and then she gave a cheeky grin. 'Well, why not? I know where your room is, Mr Mountjoy – I'll be there in five minutes.'

'You really don't have to address me as Mr Mountjoy, Polly. All my chums call me Rupert and I trust that we are going to be very close friends – do you agree with me?'

'Oh yes, I do hope so,' she said. 'Very well then – Rupert – I will come upstairs just as soon as I've cleared the rest of the tables.'

All thoughts of spending time in the library had now vanished from my mind and after gathering up my books I ran up the stairs back to my room. I took off my jacket, shoes and socks and was debating whether it would be too forward to take off my trousers when a knock on the door announced Polly's arrival. 'Come in,' I sang out and sure enough, it was the delectable little miss who stepped inside. 'Hello again, Polly, now do sit down on the bed and for a change let me see if I can serve you. Would you care for a glass of wine?'

'Not just now, thank you, but perhaps a little later,' she rejoined as she stood still for a moment and then suddenly, as if remembering why she was here, set to work unhooking her dress and loosening her clothes. I copied her example and in no time at all she stepped out of her garments, naked except for her brief white knickers, whilst I also stripped down to my undershorts with the stiff shaft of my boner standing up like a flagpole against my belly and the rounded red knob poked up over the waistband of my drawers. Polly's bare breasts were simply superb, two proud, firm creamy spheres each tipped with taut crimson titties. My hands were instinctively drawn to these delicious beauties and I reached out and gently squeezed the succulent globes whilst our faces moved slowly forward until our lips melded together into a passionate kiss.

Now the gentleness gave way to a frenzy as, locked together in a tight embrace, we staggered towards the bed and fell upon the mattress, still joined by our mouths. Polly wasted no time and immediately pulled down my drawers and grasped hold of my throbbing tool as she lifted her bum so that I could remove her knickers. I smoothed my hand over the flat expanse of her belly, dimpled as it was with a sweet little navel, like a perfect plain of snow which appeared the more dazzling from the curly locks of silky brown hair that formed a hirsute triangle around her pussey. She opened her legs slightly to allow me a view of the pink chink of her cunney before she climbed up on her knees and moved her hand up and down my blue-veined staff which was now pulsating furiously in expectation of the delights to come.

'What a splendid looking cock!' Polly said admiringly, now holding my engorged truncheon in both hands. 'I like a dick this size which isn't too small for me to feel or too big so that it's hard to take into my cunney. Now I must find out whether this nicely proportioned prick will taste as good as it looks.'

'Please feel free to do so,' I murmured as I lay back and enjoyed the sight of this sensuous girl licking her lips before kissing. my knob and thoroughly wetting it with her tongue. She gave my bared helmet a short series of licks before opening her mouth and engulfing it inside her. She closed her lips around it and worked in as much of my shaft as she could, sucking lustily all the while which made me almost faint with sheer delight. As she increased the tempo of her sucking and her teeth scraped the tender cockflesh, she cupped my balls in her hand and this sent me over the edge so that my rigid rod jerked convulsively against the roof of her mouth. In seconds I filled her mouth with a veritable jet of jism which spurted out from my prick and she swallowed the gush of milky love juice until the fountain of frothy seed eased to a mere trickle.

When she had finally drained my twitching tool of the last dribble of my vital essence, Polly looked up at me, my sated prick still between her lips, as she brushed back a lock of hair which had fallen over her face. She bobbed her head up and down for a few moments to keep my prick from sliding back into limpness and kept hold of it in her hand as she scrambled back to lie down again. Then she levered herself up on her arms and looked me full in the face.

'I'm pleased to tell you that your spunk is quite

delicious to swallow, Rupert,' she said happily as she snuggled down beside me, 'and so I award John Thomas ten out of ten on both his looks and the taste of his love liquid.'

'Are there any further tests you would like him to take?'

Polly considered this question with a merry smile thoughtfully before answering: 'Well of course, so far he has only passed the entrance examination. He has yet to attempt his finals which of course means seeing how stylishly he performs in my pussey.'

This was a challenge from which my prick had no intentions of shirking! I said nothing but pulled her closer to me and she responded at once to my embrace and playfully started to rub her soft body against mine. Her mouth was biting at my shoulder and the top of her head was level with my chin. Her nipples traced tiny circles against my chest as she ground herself against me. I gloried in the sensuous warmth which emanated from this divine creature and my cock, now back to its prime state of erectness, found its way unerringly between her legs and her pouting pussey lips were brushing the tip of my knob, frigging my cock up to bursting point.

'May I ride you?' she enquired and I nodded my assent. She wriggled herself between my legs and rising to her knees, she took hold of my iron-hard rod and placed it firmly to the mark. Then Polly pressed herself down and effortlessly her cunt encompassed the entire length of my swollen shaft. She moved sideways a little before settling herself down so that her bottom cheeks

411

sat comfortably upon my thighs. She twitched her shoulders and I watched with awe as her jutting breasts swung free and unencumbered above me. I reached up as she leaned forward, placing her breasts inside my cupped palms and I squeezed and fondled them as she began to bounce up and down upon my own proud stiffstander.

Her red titties rose like twin projectiles as I sucked them into my mouth and Polly leaned further forward, sticking out her tongue, thrusting it deep inside my mouth as I moved my chopper upwards in unison with the downward pistoning of her bum. She adjusted herself slightly so that I could now also feel her silky pussey hair and fleshy clit rubbing along the upper side of my cock, and she rocked backwards and forwards so that her furry mound pressed damply against my own pubic bush.

We matched thrust with counter-thrust until I suddenly had a fancy to fuck Polly doggie-style and gently wrenching my lips from hers I asked if she had any objection to being taken from behind.

'Not in the slightest,' she gasped and obediently turned herself over onto her elbows and knees and raised the delectable soft spheres of her bottom high in the air. Cradling her head on her arm she looked backwards at me with a cheerful smile through the tunnel of her parted thighs. Like her breasts, her bum was beautifully divided and I was tempted to cork my cock into the winking little eye of her rear dimple, but below the glistening damp hair of her pussey hung like an inviting tropical forest. I let my shaft ease its own passage between her bum cheeks which I clutched in my hands. I slid directly inside her and started to fuck her juicy cunney with great relish. I pushed in and pulled out at a steady pace and I looked down with pleasure to see the white shaft of my cock disappearing into the crevice between Polly's buttocks like a gleaming piston of a river steamer.

Deeper and deeper, but still with deliberate speed, I continued to fuck the quivering girl and she moaned and trembled whilst my cock scythed in and out of her squelchy cunt. I held Polly firmly just below her breasts as they swayed from side to side, the nipples touching the sheet as she lowered herself even further.

'Faster! Faster!' she panted and I raised the speed a notch, flashing my prick in and out of her juicy pussey at a quicker rate. But I wanted to make these marvellous moments last as long as possible for I was determined to savour every second of this magnificent joust. So I closed my eyes and tried to keep tight control over my balls which were already threatening to send a foaming gust of spunk hurtling out through my cock. After all, when would I be able to fuck Polly again? Already I would have to find time to service Gillian, Chrissie, Nancy and Beth on a regular basis let alone any other willing girl that came across my path. And I would not be surprised if Nancy ordered her cousin to stay away from my cock if I did not give Nancy enough attention.

However, try as I might, the divine sensations of reaming Polly's slippery love channel soon finished me off and I could not withstand the early familiar feeling of an approaching spend. My balls tightened as, swollen with their load, they slapped against Polly's bum as I pushed inside her pussey one more time.

Polly sensed that the end was near for she suddenly lay down and turned over onto her back, opening her legs to display her sopping cunney. Without pausing I immersed my prick inside her and the clever girl did not close her legs around me but opened her thighs even wider, which allowed me to move my shaft all around her love channel, plumbing any hidden depths which I had not previously touched with my straining knob. Her love juices now poured out from her, soaking the sheet as well as the back of her thighs as the first unstoppable surge of jism coursed its way through my cock and seethed out into her welcoming cunt. This set her off and she twisted in delicious agony as her body was wracked by great shudders which rippled out from her sated pussey as each jolt drove through every fibre of her body.

She rose to meet me as again and again I rammed my spurting cock home and my balls banged vigorously against her bum as now a tide of blissful relief ebbed through me. My pace slowed and the last irregular spasms shook my body as Polly gave one final convulsive heave and then lay very still, her legs and arms splayed out, only her breasts still trembling from the frenetic climax which we had experienced.

I slid my now shrivelled joystick out of her and moving down, replaced my cock with my face which I pressed against the wet warmth of her soaking pussey. I breathed in the aroma of our combined spendings and licked at her pussey hair that shone damply around her cunney lips. I licked the inside of her thighs before my head drooped and I rested it upon her pubic mound, thinking how a painter would rejoice in the chance to contrast the silky blackness of Polly's bush against the smooth unblemished whiteness of her belly and thighs.

Now what would be Polly's verdict on my love-making abilities? 'Did you enjoy yourself?' I asked, looking up from my pillow of cunney hair.

'A truly wonderful fuck, Rupert,' she replied lazily, 'and your cock has passed its test with first class honours.' And she then paid me the most tremendous compliment by adding: 'My cousin was right – you have a beautiful cock and what is even more important, you know how to use it.'

'Thank you very much, Polly,' I said with what I hope sounded like a dignified modesty, though inwardly I smirked because those readers blessed with good memories will remember that Gillian Headleigh had paid me a similar compliment after I had fucked her when she had finished telling me the story of the orgy at Lord George Lucas's birthday party. 'There can't be an undergraduate in the whole of Oxford – or Cambridge for that matter – who wouldn't be greatly flattered by such a kind speech, and what makes your words extra special for me is that I have a friend, Frank Folkestone, whose rooms are just across the way, incidentally, who has the most enormous plonker and occasionally, when we have been together with young ladies *au naturel*, I don't mind telling you that once or twice I've been miffed when one of the girls starts talking so admiringly about the huge size of Frank's bell-end.'

'The size of a cock never really matters though I know that all you boys think that an extra couple of inches would come in handy,' said Polly, echoing the words of Gillian and Chrissie after the aforementioned fuck. 'And I admit that the sight of nine inches of proud, rock-hard cockflesh can often excite me. But for me and most of the girls I know it's the look of the owner of the prick which is far more important. We want to see if a man is clean, well turned-out, jolly, generous – and we all have little special likes and dislikes when it comes to physical appearances. For instance, I like a neat, tight bum myself and my cousin Nancy certainly knows what she fancies in a man.'

'And what does she specially like?'

She gave a naughty little giggle. 'Well, come to think of it, there isn't much that Nancy *doesn't* fancy about a man,' she giggled naughtily, 'and in fact she has already warned me about your friend Frank's big cock. I haven't fucked as much as Nancy but one of my best lovers was the local policeman in the little village near Lord Brecklesbury's country house outside Witney, where I worked till Nancy found me a position here when I told her I wanted to live in town. His prick was thick enough but it only stood at less than five inches from base to tip, though he almost always managed to bring me off every time we made love.'

I record Polly's comments *in toto* for as a noted cocksman, I cannot overstress the importance of her observation which had been mirrored of course by Gillian and Chrissie as well as by my very first fuck, the delicious Diana Wigmore, who had always impressed upon me the importance of never worrying about the dimensions of my equipment or about the fact that at times my young prick might jump up to attention for no apparent reason or that it might obstinately refuse to swell up when required – say when the lovely girl you have been wooing finally consents to place her hand inside your trousers!

However, it was time for Polly and I to get dressed for she had further chores to get through whilst I knew that I would find myself in real trouble if I did not make my way post-haste to the library. I kissed the charming girl goodbye and we made an arrangement to see each other the next week when to her great joy I promised to take her to the first house of the music hall and on to a café for some supper.

For the second time that morning I gathered my books together and told myself that nothing would stop me from going to the library except a visit to the college from His Majesty, King Edward VII, Defender of the Faith, Emperor of India 'and all stations south of Birmingham,' I muttered to myself as I raced down the stairs, determined to put in at least an hour's work before luncheon.

But it was not to be! For who should I meet at the foot of the stairs but Beth Randall and Esme Dyotte, the two girls with whom Barry Jacobs and myself shared a splendid night's fucking courtesy of our host Mr Waterbrick of The Cat and Pigeons.

'Hello, stranger!' squealed Esme. 'We haven't

seen you for so long that Beth and I decided to see for ourselves that you were still in the land of the living.'

'Or to ensure that you had not been rusticated [temporarily expelled from the University for bad behaviour – Editor] which we thought more likely,' added Beth with a roguish grin.

Oh no, I groaned inwardly, as the wise words of Mustapha Pharte, the perhaps unfortunately named Oxford-based disciple of the Indian philosopher Tagore, whose teachings were beginning to influence very many young people at this time, rushed through my brain – 'Take care that an overindulgence of your favourite pastime (in my case, chasing pussey) does not overtax your strength'. Now it was not difficult to see from the glint in their eyes that both girls had not come to my rooms simply to pass the time of day, but I had spent almost all the previous night fucking Marianne and if that were not enough, pretty little Polly Castle had twice emptied my balls. Even if I agreed to comply with the wishes of these two lovely ladies, would I be physically able to do so?

'Well come on, Rupert, aren't you going to invite us to your room to show us your etchings?' said Esme impatiently.

There was nothing for it but to smile and wave the girls upstairs, I reasoned, for the girls would rightly consider it the height of rudeness to spurn the offer of a freely offered fuck.

'It will be my pleasure to entertain you both,' I said with as much enthusiasm as I could muster. 'Though I have no paintings to show you, perhaps I can offer you a glass of wine or some other refreshment.'

'Or maybe both?' enquired Esme wickedly, slipping her arm in mine as we walked back upstairs to my rooms.

'Don't be too impatient, Esme – we'll begin with a glass of wine,' said Beth, settling herself down on the small sofa whilst I hung up their coats and busied myself selecting a decent bottle of white wine from the icebox, which incidentally was one of the first purchases I made in Oxford and is still in full working order.

'I'm afraid that I don't keep any champagne here, Beth,' I apologised, 'but let's open this bottle of Vernaccia from Sardinia your cousin Diana Wigmore sent me after she returned from her Grand Tour this summer.'

'I'm sure it will be lovely,' said Beth. 'More and more people are coming to realise that many Italian vineyards produce wine of an excellent quality. We do not look at Italian wines as seriously as we should because the Italians regard wine as something to be drunk and enjoyed rather than talked and written about like the French, who have cleverly conjured up a mystique of unique quality about their wares, from fashion to liqueurs.

'But it's funny that you should bring up Diana's name, Rupert. I had a letter from her the other day and she asks me to send you her love. When she was in Italy this summer, you know, she took a course in painting with the famous Professor Arturo Volpe in Milan.'

'Did she really? Even I have heard of the great

419

Arturo Volpe. He is one of the top teachers in Europe and he must have thought very highly of Diana's work to allow her to join one of his classes.'

'Yes, I suppose so,' said Beth slowly, 'though I think Diana helped matters along by offering to pose nude for his students. She wrote to me what happened when she finished one session and all the students had filed out of the room, leaving herself together with Professor Volpe. Look, I have her letter with me – would you care to read it?'

She rummaged in her bag and passed me a couple of sheets of paper from it. Good grief! I had only just finished perusing Salman's sensual epistle to Chrissie, but I was curious to read how Diana had managed to wriggle herself into one of the best master classes in Europe, so I took the letter and sat down next to Beth and began to read. I skipped through the text until she came to the incident Beth had mentioned, and readers will note that Diana indeed had used all her wiles to secure a place with the great man.

So when the last student had left, I slipped off the pedestal and made my way across to Professor Volpe who was sitting at his desk. Luckily he speaks excellent English (for my Italian is disgracefully poor) and I asked him what time I would be required the next day, and whilst he was replying I pretended to see a coin on the floor and I bent down to pick it up. This gave him an excellent view of my bottom which was only inches away from his face. I looked up and saw that he was appreciative of the two soft globes and so when I straightened up I said that I had been mistaken. Then I affected to trip forwards and fell across him, taking good care that my breasts fell nicely into his hands.

At first he was embarrassed but I quickly made clear my intentions by taking his hands and pressing them to my naked nipples. He looked startled for a moment but then he responded and we were soon engaged in a long, lingering kiss. I felt for his cock but there seemed nothing stirring in his lap so I slid off him and stood directly in front of him. Then I opened my legs and I began to stroke my cunney through the blonde silky bush of my mound. I slipped a finger into the moistening crack and started to rub myself off.

Professor Volpe obviously enjoyed watching me masturbate as I caressed my breasts seductively with one hand, tweaking my titties lasciviously, whilst finger-fucking myself with the other. He unbuckled his trousers and pulled them down to reveal his now hard, stiffstanding shaft. I looked down at his prick which was of no great size but of quite a thick girth and decided to stop the show. Instead, I dropped to my knees to suck upon his knob and run my fingernails lightly up and down the veiny length. He groaned with delight when I switched to his ballsack which with one gulp I had in my mouth, and I massaged his thick staff up to its throbbing, twitching peak whilst I sucked his heavy balls.

Before long we found ourselves on the couch upon which I had been reclining for the students and I moved round, my lips still around his cock, so that my cunney was above his head, and as I lowered myself down he wiggled his tongue all around my dripping slit. By this time we were both moaning with genuine pleasure and I urged him to move round and get on top of me. When he was in position I took his shaft in my hands and guided him into my longing love-channel.

He fucked me very nicely for about a couple of minutes until he shot a great spurt of spunk into my honeypot. I didn't spend myself but this pleasant little fuck was very enjoyable and certainly did the trick as far as getting me into his classes was concerned. In fact, I would never have let anyone fuck me simply to further myself in some way. If Professor Volpe had asked me to suck his cock, I would have been delighted to comply with such or any other erotic request as I regarded it as an honour to be fucked by the great man.

I passed the letter back to Beth who looked at me curiously and said: 'Rupert, you look somewhat pale and tense. Are you feeling unwell?'

'Yes, I'm quite fit, thank you, but I do feel a little tired even though I overslept this morning and truthfully, I'm also getting very worried about all the work which I have to plough through and how I am going to fit it all in with my social arrangements.'

'Oh, you must never let business interfere with pleasure,' chirped up Esme. 'You're probably just feeling out of sorts because you woke up late. My granny always says if you lose an hour in the morning you'll spend the rest of the day looking for it.'

But Beth could see that I was really out of sorts

and after we had drunk our wine she whispered something to Esme who nodded her head and smiled at me, saying: 'I have a couple of small errands to perform, Rupert. Will you excuse me for an hour or so? But Beth will stay and she'll help you relax.'

What was all this about? Beth soon answered my unspoken question by taking me by the hand and guiding me onto the bed. 'No, I don't want you to fuck me,' she said. 'At least, not until I've managed to clear your mind and refresh your body by giving you an Oriental massage. I've always been a great believer in the principle of *mens sana in corpore sano [a healthy mind in a healthy body – Editor]* and I promise you that you'll feel so much better afterwards. I hope you'll let me try this out on you because you don't look your usual sparkling self.'

'I do need toning up in some way,' I admitted sheepishly, 'so I'd be more than grateful if you'd give me, a what did you call it?'

'An Oriental massage, Rupert. I was shown the secrets of the art by a friend who has spent several years in Hong Kong and if I say so myself, I picked up the technique extremely well.'

'I'm sure you have, Beth. So how do we start the ball rolling?'

'Lie down and let me help you undress,' she instructed as she sat down on the bed and unlaced my shoes. I unbuttoned my shirt and unbuckled my belt whilst she pulled off my shoes and socks. I arched my back to allow her to ease my trousers and drawers over my bottom and in a trice I was naked as nature intended. 'Now it's my

423

turn,' she said softly, stepping out of her shoes. Then she slipped off her blouse before unhooking her skirt and letting it fall to the floor. She sat on the bed and peeled off her stockings and lifted her chemise over her head to reveal her bouncy white breasts with their pert ripe nipples which almost appeared to be stiffening as she wriggled out of her knickers. She smoothed her hand across her fluffy blonde bush and I reached up to place my hands upon her breasts.

But she stepped back a pace and said: 'Not yet, Rupert, you're not yet in trim. First, I want you to turn over and lie on your tummy.' I sighed but obeyed her command and Beth jumped up on the bed. On her knees between my parted legs, she placed her hands on the back of my neck and began to massage me, not too fiercely but at a slow, sensual pace, starting at my neck and working her way down my back, over my buttocks and thighs until she came to my ankles. She surprised me with the strength of her fingers but I must say that my muscles relaxed under the firm pressure of my skilled masseuse.

She worked her way back up to my neck and then began to run her fingertips ever so lightly down my body. When her fingers reached the small of my back she slid her hands back and forth across my buttocks, then down the outsides of my legs to my feet and back up the insides until she came to my balls which she softly caressed from behind. Naturally, my cock rose up to greet Beth's hands even though she did not actually touch my shaft.

After a minute or so she told me to turn over

and I rolled over on to my back. 'Keep your arms down by your side,' she said as I moved my hands to cup her gorgeous breasts which dangled so invitingly when she leaned forward to repeat this fabulous massage. So I simply closed my eyes and enjoyed the feel of Beth's hands pressing and kneading my muscles and though my stiffstander was waving frantically at her she kept her hands away from the throbbing pole. But relief was soon at hand for once she had given me the soft butterfly touch of her fingertips, she lowered her mop of silky blonde hair and planted a smacking wet kiss on my lips. With difficulty I restrained myself and kept my arms resting on the eiderdown as she worked her tongue down my body, stopping briefly to circle my nipples before at last descending to my aching cock.

She licked all round my helmet and then sucked in as much of my straining shaft as she could manage, stroking my length with one hand and teasing my balls with the other. She opened her mouth and sucked in almost all my cock until it touched her throat. Up and down, up and down bobbed her head until I almost fainted away with pleasure. Once she had thoroughly anointed my pulsing prick, Beth climbed aboard for a ride. She leaned over so that her stalky red nipples brushed my chest and this time she raised no objection as I slid my hands under them and rubbed her titties against my palms. This was a short, sharp fuck but memorable for its intensity for her cunney muscles clung deliciously to my cock as it slid up and down inside her tight, wet sheath. All too soon, the spunk came rushing through my twitching tool and with a low growl, I sent a mighty burst of hot, seething jism upwards into her eager nook. Gush after gush spurted deep inside as Beth's climax followed almost immediately.

'There, do you feel better now?' she enquired with a smile as we lay in each other's arms.

'I should say so,' I said enthusiastically. 'Let's finish that bottle of wine and have another little fuck before luncheon.'

'What a splendid idea!' said a voice from the doorway and we looked over to see that Esme had returned. 'I'll just undress and then I'll fill our glasses,' she added as she took off her coat.

Esme was as good as her word and the three of us lay naked on the bed, drinking and laughing until Esme took hold of my semi-stiff love trunk and rubbed it between her palms until it stood up to attention, waving slightly as Beth and Esme knelt down in front of it and took turns to lick my shaft. Esme then gobbled my purple knob before taking about three inches of my cock into her mouth. As she sucked lustily on my delighted tadger, Beth kissed and licked my ballsack and then the girls swapped places and Beth lapped at my bared knob with the tip of her tongue, savouring the salty pre-cum which had already formed around the 'eye'. I thrust my slippery shaft upwards between her lips as she jammed my cock between them.

There was time for just one more turnabout as Esme took my pulsating pole inside her mouth and she slid her lips as far down my shaft as possible, feeling my wiry pubic hair tickle her nose. She sneezed and Beth left her exquisite palating of my hairy ballsack to say gaily: 'Esme dear, Lady Scadgers' Book of Etiquette expressly states that one should never sneeze with one's mouth full of cock.'

I thought that Esme would choke with laughter but she sucked away vigorously until the girls finished me off and she swallowed my spunk in great gulps, pulling me hard into her mouth as I delivered the contents of my balls in a fierce squirt of white frothy cream. They licked up the last drains of my spend together until my prick had been totally milked and my shaft began to shrink back to its normal size.

Beth and Esme would liked to have continued playing three-in-a-bed – who was the dolt who laid down the old law about the female being the weaker of the sexes? – but I was saved by the resonant sound of the dining-room gong and I invited the girls to quickly dress themselves and join me for luncheon.

By good fortune Mike Beattie and his friend and fellow-Scot Allan Campbell were taking luncheon in college that day and I took the opportunity of introducing the Caledonian duo to Beth and Esme. When the girls left us to wash their hands I hurriedly explained my predicament to the two Scottish lads. 'I may be wrong but in all probability Beth and Esme are expecting to be fucked this afternoon and frankly, I'm just not capable of performing any more till tonight at the earliest. Would you kindly offer your cocks to the girls if need be?'

'With pleasure, Rupert,' said Mike warmly.

'Shall we inform the ladies that our pricks are at their disposal or would you prefer to tell them yourself?'

'It's probably best to play it by ear,' I advised the eager lads who were only too willing to please the two insatiable girls if required. 'I think you'll know well enough if your services are required.'

'It's a pity I'm not wearing my kilt or they could see something to tickle their fancy without too much bother,' commented Allan, but as it turned out, the four of them got on splendidly and after polishing off two bottles of the college claret, we were all feeling very merry. Esme asked Allan what was his field of study and when he replied that he was taking a degree in English Literature, she made us all roar with laughter when she said she also enjoyed poetry and, when being told that Allan's home city was Dundee, recited the following limerick:

There was a young man of Dundee,
Who one night went out on the spree;
He wound up his clock
With the tip of his cock,
And buggered himself with the key.

'I hope I have not offended you,' she said, but Allan shook his head and replied:

'Of course not, Esme, would you like to hear another rhyme about my home town?

A pretty young girl from Dundee
Went down to the river to pee.
A man in a punt
Put his hand on her cunt,
By God! How I wish it was me.'

'It must be the influence of McGonagall [*William McGonagall (1830-1902) was a deluded Dundee-born writer of bathetic doggerel of poor scansion who imagined himself to be a divinely inspired poet – Editor*] which makes people laugh when they find a Dundonian who is studying poetry,' said Michael Beattie.

'Probably so,' said Esme, 'but tell me, from where do you hail, Michael?'

'From Perth, another city on the silvery Tay, as McGonagall might say.'

'Very good,' said Esme, finishing off her glass of the very passable college claret. 'Then I dedicate a verse to you – how about:

Mike Beattie who hails from Perth
Had the biggest balls e'er seen on earth.
They grew to such size
That one won a prize
And goodness knows what they were worth.'

Perhaps it was as well that a two shilling [*ten pence! – Editor*] bribe to Mrs Woodway, who supervised mid-week luncheons, afforded us the luxury of dining in a small private room off the main hall. When it was time to pass the port we were all rather flushed and certainly far merrier than when we sat down to begin our meal. This free and easy atmosphere afforded me the opportunity to ask Beth if she and Esme would agree to my leaving the party. 'Please don't be offended but if I don't get on with my work I really will have good cause to worry and not even your delightful Oriental rub down will be able to help me – not even if you massage Professor

429

Webb and my tutor!'

'It's quite all right, Rupert,' she said kindly. 'You run along – Esme and I will be well taken care of by these two strapping Scotsmen, won't we boys?'

Allan and Michael chorused their agreement and so I kissed the two girls goodbye and walked back slightly unsteadily to my quarters. But after a brief rest, dear reader, at the third time of trying I finally managed to find my way to the library where I spent the rest of the afternoon with my nose to the grindstone!

But no, I cannot conclude these memoirs with an economy of truth! I did take a ten minute break at four o'clock to see if the girls had stayed with Allan and Michael. I left my books and papers on the library desk and made my way up to Michael Beattie's rooms. I thought I could hear some familiar sounds but as I discovered as I tried slowly to turn the handle of his door, he had taken the sensible precaution of locking the happy group out of sight of prying eyes.

Now if he reads this manuscript, Mike Beattie will discover for the first time, that what went on that afternoon did not go unseen! For as I cursed Mike for being so careful, who should I meet on the landing but Nancy, who had also been drawn to the scene by the muffled cries and giggles that emanated from (as he is now entitled to be known, having joined the Scots Guards after graduation) Major Beattie's bedroom.

Carefully, she unlocked the door with her skeleton key and I pushed the door slightly ajar so that we could see inside – and what we saw was worth the effort we had made to view the lewd girls and boys!

Allan Campbell lay sprawled naked but *hors de combat* on the carpet, fast asleep, with his prick dangling over his left thigh as he lay dead to the world. But Mike Beattie was obviously made of sterner stuff for he was engaged in an interesting situation with Beth and Esme on the bed. Beth was on her back and Esme was lying on top of her so that the two girls' tummies and titties were pressed together with Esme's legs stretched out to encompass her friend's limbs. But behind her, Mike had climbed up and Nancy and I saw him guide his thick cock in the crevice between Esme's luscious buttocks.

'Is he fucking her up the bum or in her cunney?' whispered Nancy as the broad shouldered Scot eased his knob into one of Esme's orifices.

Mike unknowingly answered her question by groaning aloud: 'Esme, what a lovely juicy cunney you have, my prick is sliding into it like a knife through butter. And as he fucked her from behind, Esme sucked upon Beth's erect rosy titties as she pushed a thigh up against the blonde girl's pussey and began to rub it sensually against her silky fleece. Their gentle caresses rapidly acquired an urgency as the lusty Mr Beattie slewed his sturdy prick in and out of Esme's moist, yielding love channel and in turn she sucked furiously upon Beth's firm nipples, all the while massaging those divinely full high breasts.

'Oooh! I've come!' squawked Esme.

'You lucky girl – then may I have Mike's cock inside me to finish me off?' Beth responded.

'Certainly you may, and I'm sure Mike has no objection,' said Esme graciously and she wriggled off her friend to let the handsome young Scot mount Beth and place the tip of his glistening cock inside her.

'Aaaah! That's the ticket – slide all your fat prick inside me,' cried Beth as she raised her hips sharply to meet his initial thrust, forcing more of his shaft inside her, though it slid out as she fell back on the pillow. On stiffened arms, he teased her cunney by only inserting a couple of inches of his sizeable length but then with a growl he drove down and she took in the entire veiny staff as their pubic hairs entwined together. She wrapped her legs around his waist as Esme kindly slid a pillow under her hips to intensify the pressure of his cock against her pubes. Beth thrashed around, caught up in a wild ecstacy as she spent again and again before Mike's body went rigid and he trembled all over before releasing his flow of sticky white love cream.

Esme now re-entered the fray by pulling Mike off and rubbing his twitching tool between her hands until she was satisfied that it stood as high and firm as before he shot his load. Then rolling him upon his back, she straddled him and with a single downwards motion impaled herself upon his throbbing tool.

With long, lingering strokes she slid her hungry pussey up and down the towering pole and Mike used one hand to play with Esme's breasts and the other to continue to finger-fuck Beth's cunney as she lay with her legs wide open, crooning with glee as sparks of excitement from her big spend continued to excite her.

At this point Nancy and I closed the door quietly and the little minx squeezed my cock which, as may well be imagined, was bulging out from my trousers. 'Time for a quickie?' she suggested but I knew that I had to decline.

However, I did not give the real reason for my decision not to slip into an empty bedroom with her, but said in as regretful a tone as I could muster: 'Oh Nancy, I'd adore fucking you but we won't have enough time to make love as fully as you deserve. Come to my room later this evening and we'll be able to relax and make love without having to keep one eye on the clock.'

This satisfied the sweet girl though I knew that my cock needed a longer rest from all this frenetic activity. Still, after several years engagement in a similar routine, I can report that despite the warnings of certain jealous gentlemen, it is still in fine fettle and shows no sign of wear and tear!

ENVOI

HERE I CONCLUDE THIS ACCOUNT OF my first term at my old *alma mater*. But I will pen a frank, uncensored narrative of my further adventures with Chrissie, Beth and some new girls and boys who were to cross my path during my stay midst the dreaming spires of Oxford. Gad! How lucky I was to have enjoyed the company of such a merry and uninhibited crew during these formative years.

My thanks to them and finally of course to you, dear reader, who I sincerely hope has enjoyed reading my recollections of what some prudes might call a mis-spent youth. But I don't regret a single day of the time spent at the Varsity, especially (as was not always the case afterwards as will be seen in my next volume of intimate memoirs) as I dallied with impunity so many times in beds which were not my own without any unfortunate consequences.

Till then, *au revoir*.

TO BE CONTINUED

VOLUME III

Introduction

THE GLITTER OF RANK, WEALTH and fashion associated with the early years of the twentieth century were not confined to Great Britain. In Vienna, the glittering capital of the Austro-Hungarian Empire, the cavalry officers replete in their magnificent uniforms were waltzing the nights away and dining with their mistresses in discreet little supper-rooms; in America, the idiotic extravaganzas of the robber barons and their families made the headlines in the rapidly burgeoning popular press all over Europe and in Paris, the Left Bank seethed with many daring new artistic, social and philosophic ideas.

Yet without doubt it was the lives of the wealthy upper class English Edwardians, the heirs and custodians of an awe-inspiring Empire upon which the sun never set, that occupy centre stage during this so-called Golden Age when taxation was low, inflation unknown and masses of 'common' people were eager to be hired as domestic servants for absurdly small wages.

Of course, this colourful decade is too often viewed through nostalgic rose-tinted glasses. Living conditions for poor people were shocking, with at least one third of the population in the slums of London and other major cities, eking out a wretched existence below a decent level of subsistence. To quote the writer J.B. Priestley: 'They were overworked, underpaid and crowded into slum property that ought to have been pulled down years before . . . in London, the West End was already establishing "missions" in the East End, just as the Victorians had sent their missionaries to India, China, and darkest Africa.'

But for the idle, hedonistic rich, the years between the death of Queen Victoria and the Great War offered tremendous opportunities for enjoyment. These were aided by the rapid development of such luxuries as motor transport, the telephone and above all a monarch such as the extrovert Edward VII, who made little secret of his enjoyment of the pleasures of the flesh!

Rupert Mountjoy was a typical young man-about-town of these times with plenty of money and little inclination to work at anything except the diary which he began at the age of fifteen just before his initiation by the pretty daughter of a neighbour into the joys of sex. Since then, as he frankly admitted, his chief interest was in *l'art de faire l'amour*, which led to his pursuit (with no little success) of a never-ending number of the most ravishing and desirable girls in London.

And he had plenty of time to indulge himself, for though he was unquestionably possessed of a kindly, liberal disposition and attached much weight to the idea of *noblesse oblige*, he had little to occupy himself with in London except the pursuit of pleasure. For Rupert Mountjoy, this involved making love to a wide range of nubile females, from cheery young servants at home or in his friends' houses to the wild, fun-loving contemporaries of his own social class.

He was a member of the notorious Cremornites Club, a semi-secret fraternity of young rakes, and was a frequent visitor to the plush headquarters of the Club in Green Street, Mayfair, where King Edward VII is known to have brought his mistresses for discreet romps, often with such raffish companions as the Honourable Randolph Joynes, Sir Nicholas 'Mad Nick' Clee and Colonel Alan Brooke of the Household Cavalry.

As the distinguished social historian Dr Warwick Jackson drily noted in his foreword to the first book of Rupert's reminiscences, *The Intimate Memoirs Of An Edwardian Dandy Volume One: Youthful Scandals*, 'Rupert Mountjoy's lifestyle was hardly stressful! It consisted of huge luncheons after lazy morning recovering from the nights before, followed by unhurried afternoons spent leafing through the sporting magazines at the club, and the day was rounded off, perhaps, by a formal dinner party or by an evening at one of the popular West End theatres and afterwards, to complete matters, he and his cronies would visit one of the *maisons privées* to take their pick of the pretty girls available as bed-mates for the night.'

As his memoirs make clear, Rupert and his comrades left no stones unturned in their search for novel erotic entertainments. They threw themselves into London's night-life, shedding the shackles of convention as easily as they pulled off

439

the garters of the saucy chorus girls who joined in the revels which took place behind closed doors but which were chronicled by Rupert in these uncensored, uninhibited memoirs.

We are fortunate that his extraordinarily explicit account of his day-to-day and night-by-night erotic escapades has survived for they were not originally written for public consumption. But in 1913 Rupert found himself frighteningly short of funds, after a huge row with his father and an unwise speculation involving the purchase of three racehorses, and was forced to bow to parental pressure and decamp to Australia.

But before he left London for Sydney he wrote to the family solicitor, Sir David Godfrey, asking him to sell his scribblings for the best possible price. Sir David was an adroit negotiator who had built up a thriving practice hushing up potential scandals and sorting out the often tangled affairs of cuckolded country gentlemen and indiscreet titled ladies, including several from the King's own charmed circle of friends. He was also himself a man of varied sexual proclivities and so had no qualms about selling Rupert's diaries to Max Dalmaine, the editor of the Cremornites quarterly journal in which they were serialised until the autumn of 1917. Few copies of these magazines have survived – but in 1990 an almost complete set of The Cremorne Dining Society Journal from 1913 to 1918 was discovered in a locked wooden cabinet during the refurbishment of an old water mill on the River Windrush in Oxfordshire and it is from these rescued pamphlets that this and other books in the series are taken.

A particularly interesting point of social history in this book concerns Rupert's involvement with an exhibition in London of pictures by among others, his first lover, the young Yorkshire artist Diana Wigmore, and some far more famous and distinguished French impressionists such as Cézanne, Matisse and Gauguin.

I believe that he was not over exaggerating the furore caused by these paintings which the critics labelled as 'filthy and depraved', for at a famous exhibition in 1910 at the Grafton Galleries of modern foreign artists, Desmond MacCarthy recalled: 'Soon after ten the Press began to arrive. Now anything new in art is apt to provoke the same kind of indignation as immoral conduct and vice is detected in perfectly innocent pictures . . . anyhow, as I walked about the tittering newspaper critics busily taking notes I kept overhearing such remarks as "pure pornography", "admirably indecent" . . . and from the opening day the public flocked and the big rooms echoed with explosions of laughter and indignation . . .'

Similar explosions of gaiety and anger may well have been caused by the publication of Rupert's intimate diary; his robust vitality must have shocked even readers of The Cremorne Dining Society Journal. His lusty narrative, penned with an unselfconscious gusto, contains some of the frankest evocations and descriptions of a variety of sexual acts to be found in erotic writings of this era. Lovers of gallant literature will surely be delighted that Rupert's saucy narrative is once again available and this time to a far wider audience. Social historians too will also find much of interest, not least in Rupert and his contemporaries' fierce resistance to the suffocating, guilt-ridden and above all hypocritical moral climate of the time.

But above all, this novel is for the general broad-minded reader, as Louis Lombert commented in *His Mighty Engine* – a seminal study of turn of the century erotica: 'Copies of Rupert Mountjoy's memoirs have fortunately survived to delight and amuse, as well as providing us with an unusual and unconventional insight into the manners and *mores* of a vanished world.'

Alexander Raspis

Birmingham. January, 1993

'I am not over-fond of resisting temptation.'

William Beckford [1759-1844]: *Vathek*

CHAPTER ONE

A Menu To Savour

I WELL REMEMBER STANDING IN front of the fire in the drawing-room after breakfast on the morning of October 28 1905. Outside in Bedford Square the weather looked distinctly chilly and a brisk wind was winnowing the last big harvest of leaves from the trees. It was a good morning to stay indoors, I reflected, as a sudden squall briefly rattled the windows, though I would have to go out at about half past twelve, as I had accepted a luncheon invitation from a new acquaintance, Miss Nancy Carrington.

Of course, I could have always telephoned and pleaded that a trifling indisposition would prevent my presence at her table, but on the other hand, Miss Carrington only lived across the road and, even more important, she was a good-looking, young American lady from Boston whose wealthy family had rented a house for her in Bloomsbury to enable her to continue her studies in the nearby British Museum during the six months she planned to stay in London.

Nancy Carrington had called round last Thursday, which happened to be my twenty-second birthday, 'to meet my new English neighbours' and I had been very much taken by the sensual beauty of this lovely rose cheeked girl, whose long blonde hair cascaded down in ringlets to her shoulders and in whose bright blue eyes appeared a merry twinkle when she smiled. She had been wearing a figure hugging dress nipped in at the waist which accentuated not only her slender frame but also her pert, uptilted breasts which thrust saucily against an exquisitely fine silk blouse.

When, during the course of our conversation, I happened to mention that I was celebrating my birthday, she immediately invited me over to her house for a celebratory luncheon. At first I demurred, but she insisted, saying that her cook had just completed a *cordon bleu* course at Mrs Bickler's Academy of Domestic Science and that she would welcome the excuse to make a small party which would give her cook the chance to show off her newly learned prowess.

I rang the bell and my footman Edwards promptly appeared with a sheaf of letters on a silver salver. 'The second post has just arrived, sir,' he said, passing the tray to me. 'Thank you, Edwards, I'll read these in the library. Meanwhile, would you please telephone Harrods and ask them to deliver by noon a large bouquet of flowers suitable for a gentleman to take as a gift to a lady who has invited him for luncheon.'

'Certainly, sir,' said Edwards, bowing slightly. 'May I presume that the bouquet is for Miss Carrington at number forty-seven? If so, may I recommend chrysanthemums as the lady is particularly fond of them.'

It never fails to surprise me how servants glean their information but it is a fact that nothing went on at Albion Towers – our family home near the sleepy little Yorkshire village of Wharton – which was not known by Goldhill, our old butler, and his staff, and which was doubtless discussed in detail in the servants' hall! But in this case, as will shortly be shown, I soon found out how Edwards knew about Nancy Carrington's taste in flowers, it being the result of a romantic liaison my young footman had formed with Nancy's personal maid.

After telling Edwards that I would be dining at my club that evening, I went into the library to open the post. The first letter was from my tailor, Mr Rabinowitz, thanking me for the prompt payment I had made for my new suit and offering to make me an overcoat, at a very moderate cost, out of a beautiful eighteen ounce grey tweed cloth which he had bought directly from the mill. I filed the letter away for future reference and then opened the envelope postmarked Knaresborough which suggested that the letter inside came from my parents.

It was indeed a short note from my father, informing me that His Majesty King Edward VII would be visiting Yorkshire in three weeks time and that we had been invited to a reception in York on November 15 given in honour of the visit by the Deputy Lord Lieutenant of Yorkshire. Would I please let him know as soon as possible whether I wanted to attend? My mother had also scribbled a short note to add that our neighbours

Dr and Mrs Wigmore had also been invited and would attend as would their daughter Diana, the lovely girl who readers of my first book [*The Intimate Memoirs Of An Edwardian Dandy Volume One: Youthful Scandals* – Editor] will recall, was my guide and partner on that never to be forgotten summer's afternoon seven years before when I first sheathed my cock in a wet and welcoming cunney.

Whether wonderful or disastrous, one never forgets one's first fuck: I was a naïve schoolboy of fifteen and at first, frankly, bewildered by my maiden voyage along the highway of love; but I was fortunate enough to be shown the ropes by a sophisticated girl who took the trouble to explain how best I could please us both and thus cater for our joint needs. Diana is a talented artist and is working in Paris at present but whenever we see each other we usually end up in bed.

If for no other reason, this was a good enough bait to make me accept the invitation to go up to York, though I would probably have agreed to do so in any case, because I wanted to pay my respects to my old Uncle Humphrey who lived in Harrogate. It was Uncle Humphrey, my mother's eldest brother, who had persuaded my parents that I should spend a year sampling the delights of London after having gained (God knows how!) an upper second-class degree in law at Oxford University. [*For an explicit account of Rupert's hectic life at University read The Intimate Memoirs Of An Edwardian Dandy Volume Two: An Oxford Scholar* – Editor.]

He had taken me to one side at a family party

during the summer for what he called a man-to-man talk and from his opening remarks I gathered that during his youth he had been something of a young gay blade about town. After much clutching at the lapels of his dinner jacket and marching and countermarching across the drawing-room carpet, he confessed how he had conjoined, as he put it, with many attractive young ladies who may not have been thought suitable companions by his parents but whose company he very much enjoyed – especially during the wee, small hours, if I took his meaning!

'Marriage is an excellent and most proper institution, my boy,' Uncle Humphrey had intoned solemnly, 'and I trust that when your time comes to settle down, you have as satisfying and comfortable relationship as has been granted to me with your Aunt Maud. But let us not beat about the bush. Just as it is important for your bride to come to you unsullied, it is of equal import that you too gain experience in ah, "intimate relationships" between the sexes. The best place to do this is preferably far from one's home and in the anonymity of a big city. So if you agree, I propose that you spend the next twelve months in London. You can stay rent free at my old friend Colonel Wright's house in Bedford Square, Bloomsbury, where all your domestic needs will be looked after by Mrs Harrow, the housekeeper. There you will be able to entertain with total discretion any friends of the opposite sex. Furthermore, I will make you an annual allowance to enable you to live at a decent standard of comfort.'

He waved away my effusive words of gratitude.

'No thanks needed, my boy, it's my very real pleasure,' he continued, placing his hand on my shoulder. 'I've already settled fifty thousand pounds on both my daughters and your Aunt will never be able to spend what's left in the bank even if I kick the bucket tomorrow. And in any case, I'd far rather enjoy spending my money now whilst I'm alive than give the damned Government the satisfaction of mopping up thousands of pounds in death duties from my estate.'

It took a while for my parents to be won round to his freewheeling point of view, but in the end they consented, on the strict understanding that I would take up articles with Godfrey, Alan and Colin, the family firm of solicitors, immediately after the year was up.

So I owed a great deal to Uncle Humphrey and though I wrote to the old chap occasionally, I knew how much he thoroughly enjoyed the visits I paid him and Aunt Maud (especially as his two daughters had married and lived far away, cousin Beth in Cornwall and cousin Sarah in the Highlands of Scotland. So I sat down then and there and wrote back, first to my father, telling him that I would return home to Albion Towers two days before the party in York and secondly to Uncle Humphrey, asking him if it would be convenient if I came to see him in Harrogate whilst I was up in Yorkshire for a few days.

When I looked closely at the third and final letter Edwards had given me I saw that it had been posted in France. And yes, the name of the sender, Miss Diana Wigmore, was written on the back of the envelope – what a coincidence! I'll wager she's writing about this party for the King, I thought to myself, and sure enough that is what had made Diana put pen to paper. For the record, diary, I will copy her letter in your pages:

69 Rue General Olivier Norman, Paris

Darling Rupert,

My Mama has just written to me about a grand reception being given in honour of the King on November 15 in York. I gather that your people have also been invited and if you are going to accept then I will go back home as well for a few days. Write, or better still send me a telegram at the above address (trust me to find an apartment in a house numbered soixante-neuf!) as soon as possible to let me know your plans.

Have you been keeping well? I suppose your prick has been well-exercised since we last exchanged letters three months ago. You must either write and tell me all about what you have been doing with yourself or tell me all the juicy details if we are to meet back home next month.

Meanwhile, I have been enjoying myself too though I am working hard and not living the Sybaritic life of a lounge lizard like some I could mention! You remember I told you about my affair with Alain. Well, that fizzled out and for more than three weeks I was without a bed-mate for though I had many offers, including several from fellow artists and my landlord Monsieur Cantona, I am choosy as to whose cock I want sheathed in my cunt.

Relief came yesterday with the arrival of a new lodger, an American lad of about our age named Wilson who has come to stay for a month in Paris to perfect his French. He is a handsome young man with a craggy face, a strong nose, well-pronounced cheekbones, a firm mouth and a square jaw. We met on the stairway as I was carrying a kettle of hot water up to my room to make some coffee. I introduced myself to him and I was pleased by the feel of his firm handshake. 'Will you join me for a cup of coffee?' I asked and he thanked me warmly. 'Just let me put some papers in my desk before I forget and I'll be down in three minutes,' he said and I watched with appreciation his muscular, tight backside move quickly up the stairs.

In fact, I was so busy fantasising about Wilson's bum whilst I was preparing the coffee that I spilled some milk all over the front of my blouse. Hell's bells, I said to myself, and without giving it another thought, unbuttoned the garment and threw it in the direction of my laundry basket. There was a muffled cough behind me and there was Wilson, looking rather embarrassed as I turned round and faced him wearing only a thin transparent silk camisole.

'Oh – sorry – I – uh . . .' he stammered.

'No, please don't apologise,' I pleaded, as I watched a slight bulge form in the crotch of his trousers. 'I just spilled some milk over my blouse and had to change it.'

'I can't say I'm sorry,' he said wistfully and it struck me that the yearning expression on his face deserved to be captured on canvas. So I asked Wilson if he would sit for me and to my joy he agreed. 'You'll have to sit quite still for about an hour,' I warned him but he said he would be honoured to be sketched by such a talented artist.

'How do you know I'm talented?' I teased and he replied that the pictures on the wall testified to my

452

abilities. Well, Wilson proved to be a marvellous model, keeping stock still whilst I worked and when I had finished he came round and looked critically at my drawing. 'I only wish our roles could be reversed and that I could be the artist and you the model,' he commented.

'Why is that?' I asked, slightly puzzled by his remark.

'Because you have such a lovely figure, Diana. I can hardly take my eyes off your beautiful breasts,' he whispered hoarsely, running his hands up the sides of my arms, and I swiftly realised why I had so excited him. Of course, in my haste I had neglected to put on another blouse and all the while Wilson had been gazing intently at my breasts which were only covered by a transparent silk camisole. My titties fairly tingled with anticipation and I felt my nipples pucker with delight as he looked down my body. I took hold of his hands and boldly put them full on my heaving breasts and he sharply exhaled a long drawn out breath as he felt the rigid and upright titties against his palms.

I could see the bulge in his trousers getting bigger which made my pussey moisten and I started to walk backwards, pulling Wilson along with me. It took only three or four steps to reach my bed and we collapsed down upon the sheets as our mouths met in a burning, passionate kiss. His lips were very wet and soft and I could feel his tongue exploring every inch of my mouth whilst his hands roamed across my breasts, squeezing, nipping, and gently caressing the soft white globes, which drove me wild with desire for him. He unzipped my skirt and pulled it down as at the same time I pulled the camisole over my head so that I was now naked except for a pair of frilly white briefs and my stockings which were held up by two red garters.

'Now it's my turn to see more of you,' I said and I

quickly unbuttoned his cream flannels and plunged my hand inside his flies to free his bursting, erect cock as he hastily discarded his shoes and socks. His trousers and drawers soon followed and my eyes fastened upon his thick prick which was standing nicely to attention, a stiff staff up against his flat tummy. I grasped hold of the throbbing tube and ran my fingers down the blue vein which ran down the length of the smooth, warm shaft.

Wilson groaned and put his mouth on my titties, nibbling my nips which rose up like two red bullets. I lifted my bottom to allow him to pull down my knickers and a thrilling wave of pleasure flowed through me as his fingers massaged my hairy pussey and he slid his forefinger inside my oozing cunt whilst I played with his bare cock, slowly rubbing my clenched fingers up and down the hot, pulsing pole.

Our two nude bodies rolled in ecstacy on the bed. His hands were never still, and as he looked lovingly at each part of me, he stroked my breasts, my bottom and my pussey and whispered how gorgeous, how sensual and how desirable I was. 'Then fuck me, please, Wilson,' I murmured, and the dear lad was more than ready to oblige. He climbed on top of me and I spread my legs, eagerly awaiting the arrival of his cock which I still held tightly in my grasp. I guided his knob between my cunney lips and his rock hard prick filled my cunt as we wriggled round until we were both in the most comfortable position for some truly wonderful fucking. I wrapped my feet around his neck as he began to thrust his truncheon in and out of my juicy love channel and I quivered with delight as he began to pump faster and faster, his balls fairly banging against my bum.

'Deeper, Wilson, deeper,' I purred and he pressed his

buttocks together and rammed his tool into me as far as it would go. 'Aaah! Aaah! Keep going, you randy big-cocked boy!' I shrieked, and I shuddered with delight as his prick massaged my clitty and I could feel my cunney sucking at him and I squeezed every time he pulled his cock back for another huge thrust. Now I arched my back, willing the lovely lad on as I pushed my pussey up against him, forcing his cock even deeper inside me and I screamed out my joy as we came together, Wilson shooting a fierce fountain of creamy sperm inside my cunt as my own love juices flowed out of my sated honeypot. We threshed like wild animals, oblivious to everything except the breathtaking currents of the electric force which we had generated between us surging through our bodies.

He rolled off me and lay on his back, his chest heaving up and down as he sought to recover his senses, but his cock, which was glistening with a coating of my pussey juice, was still standing up stiffly and I leaned forward and crammed as much of the silky wet shaft into my mouth as possible. My head bobbed up and down as I greedily gobbled as much of his prick as I could, massaging the sensitive underside with my tongue. I could hear Wilson almost crying with pleasure. Soon I felt his prick go rigid and he spurted jets of sticky semen inside my mouth which I eagerly swallowed until I had milked every last drain of spunk from his trembling tool. His jism had a salty flavour, pleasant enough, but not as tasty as yours, Rupert, so there is no call for you to be jealous!

The grateful boy kissed my lips again and again and thanked me profusely for sucking him off, as, believe it or not, this was the first time he had ever enjoyed the delights of this grand sport. Unbelievably, the poor lad

455

had till now missed out completely on an activity which all men adore. I am sure you will agree that there is not a red-blooded man in the world who can control his excitement once a pair of female lips have fastened themselves upon his knob. But as far as Wilson was concerned, the very idea of girls and boys sucking each other off was alien to him. He had been brought up in a very strict environment and even the mechanics of oral sex were totally unknown to him until he was sixteen when his wise brother-in-law gave him a copy of Dr Nigel Andrews' excellent book Fucking For Beginners. Unfortunately, he was never given a chance to put into practice what he had learned from Dr Andrews' tome and if we had not been pressed for time I would have shown him how to eat pussey. Hopefully, I will give him his first lesson tomorrow.

But for now I could only stay for another hour or so as I had to leave for a seminar (you would be amazed at how well I can now converse in French) so we spent the next sixty minutes in fucking until poor Wilson was totally exhausted. Twice more he came inside me and twice I sucked his cock back up to a fine stiffness. We finished this torrid session of love-making by my swallowing the by now understandably diminished quantity of spermy essence from his trembling prick.

Rupert darling, I must close now — but I do hope you will be able to go to York next month. We should have some great fun if old Tum Tum [the lèse-majesté nickname for the corpulent Edward VII – Editor] is on form.

All my love,
Diana

I folded the sheets of this billet doux back in its envelope and resolved to keep it to copy into the pages of my journal at a later date. So I strode upstairs into my bedroom and locked the letter away in my escritoire. As I did so, I heard a slight noise coming from inside my bathroom. The door was slightly ajar and I peered inside to see that Mary, one of the prettiest maids in the house, was humming a tune whilst she was bending over the bath, polishing the enamel. Although she had her back to me I could tell it was Mary from the colour of her dark, almost black hair and the lissome shape of her body. I passed my tongue over my lips as I surveyed the contours of her ripe backside which, undisguised by a too-tight skirt, stuck out in an extremely provocative fashion.

Like my chum Frank Folkestone is fond of saying, I can resist anything except a pretty bum! I took two paces forward and pinched her glorious bum between my thumb and forefinger. 'Eddie! You randy bugger, stop that at once! Can't you wait till lunch-time?' Mary squealed as she shot up, but she clapped a hand to her mouth in horror when she whirled round and saw that it was the master of the house who had assaulted her. I smiled broadly to put the girl at her ease and said, 'Ah me, lucky Eddie, who I presume is my efficient young footman.'

She gulped with embarrassment and said, 'Yes sir, Eddie Edwards. I'm awfully sorry but I didn't expect you to come up behind me.'

'The fault is all mine and I had no right at all to startle you, but your delicious rounded bottom cheeks were simply too arousing as you bent over the bath. Please forgive me, Mary, it won't happen again,' I added, with as much sincerity as

457

I could muster, which was not a great deal, especially when even as I spoke, my cock began to swell up alarmingly, forming a noticeable bulge between my legs.

'Oh, that's quite all right, sir, I'm not cross with you – it was just being caught unawares which made me jump,' she said, turning back to finish her work.

I considered her cute arse again and placed a hand on each soft, rounded buttock. 'Oooh, you'd better not do that, sir. You really mustn't. Someone might come in.'

Amused and aroused now by this form of surrender I unbuttoned her skirt and pulled it to the floor. Then I tugged down her crisp white knickers and she stepped out of them before resuming her labours. I smoothed my hands along the creamy cool skin of her appetising bum cheeks and then slid my right hand between her legs. She neatly trapped it by squeezing her thighs together, leaving me to wrestle with my fly buttons with my left hand whilst I tickled the entrance to her honeypot with my imprisoned fingers.

My trousers and drawers now joined Mary's clothes on the floor and I begged her to release my hand so I could replace it with something more pleasing. She moved her head round and with shining eyes looked down at my hard, erect member. 'You'll have to go in by the tradesmen's entrance, sir, I can't risk letting you have my cunney till next week,' she said, and wriggled back so that her head and upper body were bent quite low over the bath as she pushed her glorious backside upwards and opened her legs to give me fair view of the tiny, puckered brown rosette. I knelt down and picked up a sponge and soaped my pulsating boner before parting her buttocks with my hands and pushing my uncapped helmet into the cleft between them.

'Yes, do go, sir. Go carefully though as you stick that nice thick length of cock up my bum,' she said excitedly.

I angled her legs a little further apart to afford an even better view of her winking little rear dimple and gently eased my knob forward. For a few seconds I encountered resistance but then her sphincter muscle relaxed and I slid my rigid rod in and out of her tight arse-hole, plunging in and out of the now widened rim as Mary reached back and spread her cheeks even further, jerking her bum in time to my rhythm as I wrapped one arm around her breasts, squeezing each of them in turn and snaking my other arm round her waist to frig her wet pussey as she whimpered with pleasure, squirming and wriggling about to such an extent that I had to work hard to keep my cock inside her.

Mary's bottom continued to respond gaily to every pistoning thrust as again and again I drove home, my balls bouncing against her soft buttocks. Then I shoved my shaft in to the hilt, corking her to the very limit. I stayed still for a moment and then jerked my hips slowly as I felt the first sweet stirrings of an approaching spend and with a strangled cry I shot a copious emission of gushing jism inside her bottom. As I spurted into her bum-hole, I continued to work my prick back and forth until, with an audible 'plop', I withdrew my shrinking organ from Mary's well-lathered nether orifice.

'Ooh, that was nice, sir. Could you suck my cunney now?' she asked.

Well, much as we would have both enjoyed a continuation of this frolic, *tempus fugit* – Mary had to finish her household chores and I had to compose myself for my luncheon with Nancy Carrington. I noticed a large blob of spunk had dripped down from Mary's bottom on to the marble floor which she wiped clean with a cloth.

'Just as well we didn't have that lovely bottom-fuck in the bedroom,' I commented as I hauled up my trousers. 'I wouldn't want to damage any of Colonel Wright's rare Persian carpets.'

This remark made Mary giggle and she said, 'Oh, spunk marks are no problem, sir. Whenever the Colonel has one of his special parties, we always manage to clean up without any trouble.'

'Special parties?' I queried and Mary put her finger to my lips. 'Please don't tell anyone I mentioned anything to you, sir. I thought you knew about the monthly reunions or I wouldn't have said a word about them.'

'Don't worry, my lips are sealed,' I said, intrigued by her concern. 'But I haven't had the pleasure of meeting the Colonel himself. He just happens to be a close friend of my Uncle Humphrey and agreed to rent the house to him whilst he is in India. I seem to recall my Uncle telling me that the Colonel was invited to join some government inquiry and will spend twelve months out East.'

Mary nodded and confirmed my vague memory

of the conversation with Uncle Humphrey. 'Colonel Wright's the deputy chairman of the Royal Commission on Native Education. The Prime Minister himself asked him to serve and so he felt he could not refuse. "I don't really want to go, Mary," he said to me before he left, "but the other day Mr Lloyd-George all but promised me a knighthood if I accept the job."

' "Never mind, sir," I said, as I squeezed his balls. "I'll bring my friend Sally round and we'll have that nice whoresome threesome you've always dreamed about." '

Was I dreaming or did this pretty young maid actually promise her former employer that she and another girl would share his bed? I looked at her in astonishment and burst out, 'You said *what*?'

She repeated her remark and I said incredulously, 'You were squeezing the Colonel's balls? That was rather forward behaviour, was it not?'

'Not really,' she replied, shrugging her shoulders. 'After all, he had his cock in my cunney at the time.'

I stared at her in amazement as she added, 'Don't look so surprised, sir. Cuthbert might be fifty-eight in February but I can tell you it's quite true that there's many a good tune played on an old fiddle. He takes longer to come than younger men but that's all to the good because so many boys of my age come too quickly.'

'Did he fuck you very often?' I wondered, and this question brought a satisfied smile to her lips.

'As often as I wanted,' she rejoined pertly. 'If I say so myself, I'm not short of a cock when I want one.'

'I'm sure you're not, Mary, you're a very attractive young lady. Frankly, I'm just rather curious as to how you two became involved.'

'Oh, that's easily explained,' she said lightly, picking up her box of cloths and polishes. 'I'll tell you how if you don't mind following me into the bedroom across the hall. I know it's not being used right now but Mr Bristow asked me to give it the once over every week in case we have a sudden guest coming to stay.'

Mr Bristow, I should mention here, was the butler I had inherited from Colonel Wright. Sadly, his aged father had died suddenly a few days previous to this conversation and naturally I had agreed at once to his request for a week's compassionate leave of absence. In the meantime, the estimable cook-housekeeper, Mrs Harrow, was taking charge of all matters below stairs.

'Certainly, I'll come along – you'll now have a witness if Mr Bristow alleges that you failed to carry out his instructions,' I joked as I followed Mary into the second bedroom. I sat on the bed whilst she told me of how she first became aware of Colonel Wright's attentions.

She told me, 'It all began about eighteen months ago just after I had joined the household. Although I was only seventeen, I had already sampled two or three cocks in my pussey before I came here. However, I hadn't been fucked for a good few weeks until a few days before this incident when I had let PC Shackleton thread me up against the back garden wall.

'Well, I went to bed well satisfied and, though I slept like a top, for once I woke before Mrs

462

Harrow knocked on my door and I remember snaking my arms above my head for a long stretch, thinking back with a smile about the little knee-trembler I had enjoyed with my randy copper, before kicking off the bedclothes and springing to my feet.

'Now I never wear anything in bed so I was stark naked as I padded over to the window, threw back the curtains and opened the window. As I gazed delightedly at the bright dawn sunshine my hand strayed down to my little nookie. I was twisting my curly pussey hair around my fingers and gently stroking myself around my crack when I heard what sounded like a sharp intake of breath from underneath my window. Was it a stray cat perhaps or was there some dirty beast down there spying on me?

'There was an easy way to find out – I withdrew for a moment and returned with my chamber pot which I had used during the night but I added the contents of my water jug to fill the pot almost to the brim. Then I raised the window sash to the highest level and leaned out, feeling the cool morning air tease my rosy nipples into little erect buds. I distinctly heard a low, furtive moan coming from down below which confirmed that it was indeed a Peeping Tom hiding in the dense foliage. So I withdrew for a moment and came back again, leaning out to tip the contents of the chamber pot out the window!

'An anguished yell told me that I had scored a direct hit on whoever had been spying on me – but to my horror, who should emerge wet headed, spluttering with rage, with his trousers round his knees and his hand round his bare cock but the Master himself!'

'The dirty old so-and-so! It served him right to be drenched in your you-know-what!' I exclaimed.

'Ah! But you've jumped to conclusions, sir, though of course I did the very same thing as well,' Mary remonstrated, touching my lips with her finger. 'The truth of the matter was that the Colonel, who has always suffered from insomnia, had woken with the dawn and had decided to potter around the garden. It was by pure coincidence that he happened to be outside my window when suddenly he had been caught short and rather than trudge back inside the house, he decided to relieve his bladder in the garden. He had just finished his piddle when he heard me open the window. He looked up and, well, I could hardly blame him for becoming speechless with astonished delight when he saw my naked body above him.'

Mary paused for breath and then continued with a grin, 'Well, poor old Cuthbert could hardly shout up anything to me or the other servants might have looked out to see what was going on. So he rushed inside, changed his clothes and came straight up to see me. I had already half a mind to start packing my bags but as soon as Cuthbert came into my room he began apologising for his rudeness and explained the circumstances which had inadvertently led him to the sorry situation in which he now found himself.

'And as for giving me the sack, nothing could be further from his thoughts. Instead, he insisted on presenting me with a gold sovereign to compensate, as he put it, for any distress I might have felt about the wretched incident which he hoped could now be forgotten.

'I thought this was more than generous and so I asked him to sit on the bed. "You deserve a proper view of what you only caught a glimpse of earlier," I said and tossing back my shimmering curls and running my tongue lewdly over my pouting lips, I unknotted the cord of the bathrobe I had hastily donned along with a pair of white cotton knickers when I realised that the Cuthbert was coming upstairs. I slid out of the robe, arching my spine and sucking in my breath to give Cuthbert a wonderful full frontal view of my big, luscious breasts. You haven't seen them yet, have you, sir? Well, take my word, I'm lucky enough to have two beauties and I don't mind admitting that I'm very proud of them.

'Anyway, I took my raspberry nipples between my fingers and tweaked them up till they blushed a deep red and grew stiffly erect. "By Gad!" said Cuthbert as I began to knead my firm, uptilted titties and then, planting my hands on my hips, shook my breasts at him energetically, trying hard not to giggle as I saw a huge swelling start to form in Cuthbert's lap.

'Then ever so slowly I began to pull down my knickers, wriggling round so that by the time I'd pulled them down I was facing the wall and he could see my bare bottom. "Oh my God, this is too much!" he cried out, and when I turned round, with my hand over my pussey, there was Cuthbert with his trousers ripped open, pulling out his thick, throbbing truncheon, the uncapped ruby dome bobbing gaily, as, panting with desire, he frenziedly frigged himself at a great pace.

'I thought that he would prefer me not to gawp at him whilst he brought himself off so I turned back and waggled my bum at him again. Then I gazed at him briefly over my shoulder and flashed him a smile as I parted my legs and bent forward with my arms dangling forward until my hands were almost touching the carpet. This way poor Cuthbert had an even more tantalising view of my firm, gleaming bum cheeks and the dark, secret cleft between them which even as he watched began to moisten with my tangy cunney juice.

'A strangled cry was enough to tell me that Cuthbert was shooting his load and sure enough I straightened up and looked back to see a tiny fountain of creamy white froth shoot out of the top of his twitching tool.

'I dropped to my knees to lap up his manly essence, as I adore the salty taste of hot, fresh jism but as I dived down a second burst of sperm jetted out of his cock straight into my right eye! "I would have preferred to have sucked you off," I said to Cuthbert, and he looked sadly down at his shrivelling shaft and said that he would be very grateful if I would meet him in the library any time after noon as these days he wouldn't be able to raise another stand till around lunch-time.'

This mention of luncheon reminded me that I had an appointment for which I was in grave danger of being late. I looked at my watch and asked Mary if we could continue this fascinating discussion in the library at around five o'clock. 'Oh yes, I'd love to, sir,' she replied promptly, picking up her box of cleaning materials. She then shot me a wicked little smile and added, 'That's on the understanding, of course, that we can have a nice snogging session as well.'

I replied that this was a condition I was more than happy to accept. Then, after a quick wash and brush up, I went downstairs and Edwards confirmed that Harrods had delivered the flowers. After helping me on with my hat and coat he gave me the large, colourful bouquet of chrysanthemums before opening the front door. 'I expect to return home around three o'clock,' I informed him, and set off to walk round to Nancy Carrington's house. Thankfully, the rain had stopped, though it was still quite cold and I was glad that I had worn one of Mr Rabinowitz's warm overcoats even for the short three minute journey to the far corner of Bedford Square.

Nancy Carrington's Negro butler must have seen me climb the short flight of steps for he opened the door before I had a chance to ring the bell. 'Good-afternoon, sir. It's Mr Mountjoy, isn't it?' he said in a deep American-accented drawl. 'May I take your hat and coat? Miss Carrington is receiving her guests in the drawing-room.'

I looked up at the tall, wide-shouldered man. He was a very handsome fellow of a light chocolate hue and, although his frizzy curly hair was jet black, his finely chiselled features suggested that he must have had at least one European grandparent. Presumably he is an old family retainer of Nancy's family, I thought to myself, as he opened the drawing-room door and announced my arrival to his mistress.

'Rupert, how super to see you – and what lovely flowers you've brought, you kind boy,' cried Nancy Carrington, who rose up from the sofa on which she had been sitting next to another extremely attractive, slightly older woman. 'I'm so pleased that you were able to join me for lunch today as I wanted you to meet a dear friend who I met in Paris earlier this year. Rupert, it is my great pleasure to introduce you to Countess Marussia of Samarkand. Marussia, this is my nice new neighbour Mr Rupert Mountjoy.

'Now I will have to ask the two of you to excuse me for a few moments as I have some last minute instructions for the kitchen staff.'

As Nancy bustled out of the room I walked over and, taking the Countess's hand in my own, raised her fingers to my lips. *'Enchanté, Comtesse,'* I murmured. By George, she was a stunning lady, nearer thirty than twenty perhaps, with long reddish hair, a pale face, and big brown eyes. She was beautifully formed with high breasts, a lithe, slender body and then and there I would have wagered a thousand pounds that her long legs, hidden under her skirt, were as stylish as I expected.

'I am delighted to make your acquaintance, Mr Mountjoy,' said this delicious creature in a sensual low voice. 'Nancy tells me that you have recently graduated from Oxford University. Did you ever come across my cousin Celestine Dushanbe there by any chance?'

Had I ever come across Celestine Dushanbe? How I wish I could have replied in the affirmative for Celestine was without doubt one of the prettiest, most desirable girls in the whole of Oxford and the surrounding county. Like many others, I had unsuccessfully sought her favours but these were only bestowed upon the Honourable Michael Bailey, the handsome captain of the University fencing team and (it was rumoured) the young Lord Arkleigh who travelled up to dine with her almost every weekend from his Hertfordshire estate.

'Alas, no,' I replied with a sad little smile. 'I know of her, of course, but she was always surrounded by a bevy of admirers.'

'I'm sure she was,' said Countess Marussia, returning my smile. 'Celestine threw herself into her work with great passion and like all dedicated students, she practised what she preached, though of course in Celestine's case she thoroughly enjoyed the experience.'

'Did she, Countess? Why, what was she studying?' I asked politely, but nearly fell over backwards when the Countess answered, 'Human sexuality. Dear Celestine was one of a small group of researchers working with Dr Trevor Tyler, the internationally noted specialist on masturbation, on his new book *The Facts Of Life*, a much needed book which will be published early next year by Messrs Dyott & Gradegate.'

'I must remember to order a copy from Hatchards,' I said, recovering my composure and adding (for I had decided that the Countess was obviously a fellow free spirit), 'although I would have thought that *Fucking For Beginners* by Nigel Andrews might have already covered this ground.'

'Not really,' said the Countess, shaking her head, 'because excellent as Dr Andrews' volume is for, say, newly married couples, it can only be bought *sub rosa* by enlightened people who have already shaken off the atmosphere of guilt, fear and ignorance about sex and subscribe to such journals as *The Oyster* or *The Jenny Everleigh Diaries*.

'Dr Tyler, on the other hand, is composing a manual for the complete relationship between the sexes, starting from the premise that though love-making is one of the few subjects in which we all have an interest, the understanding of many people of their bodies is frequently minimal. There is still a large body of opinion which treats sexual desire as a dangerous animal that has to be kept muzzled. At present, the few sex education books available prescribe abstinence and chastity – such hypocrisy when one considers the bedroom sport enjoyed by Society at country house parties and the *laissez-faire* attitude taken by your very own King Edward!'

As I nodded my agreement, I gnawed at my lower lip as I recalled the one opportunity I had missed of getting closer to Celestine Dushanbe. I had noticed a small advertisement in the University weekly newspaper for volunteers to take part in scientific research. I had expressed a vague interest to a friend but had hastily abandoned the thought of replying to the box number when he had opined that in all probability the advertiser was looking out for people to test their new medical pills and potions. I confessed this foolish blunder to the Countess who laughed and said, 'I must tell you that I remember Celestine writing to me about why she had placed that particular advertisement. She was discussing the "doggie position" with Dr Tyler who had told her that some people frowned upon it as being too animalistic although anatomically it is a most natural position of sexual congress.

'But look, you can read Celestine's report for yourself. One of the reasons I am here is that both Nancy and I have been asked by Dr Tyler to make any suggestions about his manuscript as we are both self-proclaimed liberated ladies. We were reading the section of his book which deals with Celestine's appreciation of being taken from behind.'

She got up and walked across to a paper strewn table, picked up a sheet and passed it to me, saying, 'Come and sit down and glance through this page. I would be most interested any comment you might have to make.'

I obeyed and read the following from an essay on sexual positions by Dr Tyler: '*My colleague Miss C.D. tried out rear entry with her boy friend and writes, in her own uncensored words: "I placed myself on my hands and knees, bending forward and throwing up my bottom cheeks as high as possible. My lover inserted his penis and began working it in and out of my love channel. He pressed heavily against me but there was no problem in supporting his weight. Perhaps this was because I was on my hands and knees with my back and thigh muscles (the strongest in the body) working.*

"The experience was thoroughly enjoyable as both his hands were free to fondle my breasts, legs and buttocks and he could bring his fingers round to my front and play with my clitoris which afforded an additional pleasure."'

'How very interesting,' I observed as I passed the sheet back to the Countess. '"Doggie fashion" happens to be one of my personal favourites although I am sure there are many sexual positions about which I am completely ignorant.'

'Oh, come now,' she said roguishly. 'I am sure that a good-looking young fellow like you has experimented widely in this field. Mind, the Indian *Kama Sutra* lists more than twenty major positions for fucking though Trevor Tyler insists that in practice there are really only six and all the others are simply variants.'

She patted my thigh and was about to say more when Nancy flounced back into the room carrying my chrysanthemums in a crystal bowl. 'There, don't flowers brighten up the room?' she said brightly. 'Now I hope you two are getting on famously.'

'Indeed we are,' I replied, struggling up from the deep cushions of the sofa. 'The Countess has just been telling me about the proofs you are checking of Dr Trevor Tyler's wonderfully interesting new book.'

'Ah yes, I'm so pleased you approve, Rupert. So many people have hidebound attitudes to an activity without which, let's face it, the human race would cease to exist! Anyhow, luncheon is served so you will have to escort both Marussia and myself into the dining-room.'

'That will be my pleasure,' I said with a bow. So I walked into the dining-room with a lovely girl on each arm. The marvellous meal we ate testified to the wisdom of household cooks attending a course at Mrs Bickler's Academy of Domestic Science. We dined sumptuously on *Terrine d'aubergines et poivres rouges aux saveurs de Provence* followed by a tasty *filet de flétan roti sur aromates au fumet de fin rouge* and as the main course succulent *côtelettes d'agneau roties à la chapelure provençale et legumes d'été* finished off with *assiette de fruits du moment au Sabayon de Kirsch et sorbet cassis.* [Aubergines, halibut in a red wine sauce, lamb cutlets, and a fresh fruit salad! – Editor]

We were attentively served by Hutchinson, the Negro butler, Standlake, and two housemaids and we drank at least two bottles of a very smooth Chablis as Hutchinson was always on hand to ensure that our glasses were never empty. Then we returned to the drawing-room for *petit fours* and (in honour of Marussia) *thé Russe avec citron.*

By this time we were all slightly flushed and feeling very well disposed to each other. Indeed, Nancy's shiny blonde hair, which she had been wearing in rather severe brushed curls, now hung in long, silky strands down to her shoulders. With Nancy in the middle we were all sitting on the luxuriously soft sofa when, after serving us glasses of hot lemon tea, Hutchinson left the room and closed the door behind him. Nancy squeezed both my hand and Marussia's and said, 'My dears, you must try some of the special thirty-year-old cognac I was given by Monsieur Istvan Tihanyi in Paris.'

'Not Monsieur Istvan Tihanyi who owns the dildo manufactory near Drancy?' said Marussia excitedly.

'Yes, the very same. Why, do you know him, Marussia?'

'Of course I do – Istvan has been a close friend for several years. Only last summer he fucked me beautifully after Senator Lipmann's Quatorze Juillet ball in Paris.

Nancy heaved herself up and walked to the sideboard and brought out the bottle and a silver tray with three balloon shaped brandy glasses placed upon it. She poured out generous measures of vintage cognac and Marussia suggested we drank a toast. 'To our charming hostess,' I suggested. Nancy thanked me and added, 'Coupled with the names of my two dear friends Marussia and Rupert.' We then drank a toast to Marussia's hero, Tamburlaine the Great, who in the fourteenth century had made Samarkand the chief economic and cultural centre of mid Asia. Then followed toasts to the United States of America, King Edward VII, Prince Adrian of the Netherlands (who often escorted the Countess on the Continent) and then to Monsieur Istvan Tihanyi's penis which the girls assured me was of heroic proportions.

'Nancy, how did you come to meet Istvan?' demanded Marussia. 'Did you meet him at his place of work?'

'Not at first,' answered Nancy. 'Our first meeting was at the Moulin Rouge where we were both guests at a party given by the American community in Paris to celebrate the fiftieth birthday of His Excellency, Mr Barry Gray, our new Ambassador to France. Istvan and I began talking and I must say I was fascinated when he informed me of his business.'

At this point I interrupted the conversation and said, 'Forgive me ladies, but I must confess ignorance of this gentleman and his work. Perhaps one of you could enlighten me.'

'Certainly, Rupert,' said Nancy cheerfully. 'Istvan Tihanyi owns an exclusive dildo factory patronised by the *crème de la crème* of European Society. His speciality is the production of ladies' comforters, individually made for clients based on the dimensions of the husband or lover as required.'

'How fascinating,' I commented, 'but I am rather surprised there is any demand for such artefacts. Surely there is a sufficiency of living male members to satisfy any need?'

Countess Marussia answered my question. 'Alas, no, for there are many women of the very highest standing in Society who are in great need of a good godemiches. To begin with, think of all the married women who cannot count on being regularly fucked by their husbands. For example, those married to men of business who have to be away from home, often for days on end. Then there are service wives who are often separated from their menfolk for months, and sometimes when these men return they are so fatigued from fighting that they are unable to resume their marital duties for a considerable while. Finally, one must never forget those unfortunate ladies whose husbands are no longer capable of performing their conjugals for other reasons such as over-indulgence in imbibing, and those, such as dear Lady Bertha Bumble, who have been tragically widowed at an early age, though in her case of course, she has been consoled more than adequately by her brother-in-law, Lord Radlett, who fucks her every other Thursday afternoon whilst his wife plays bridge at the local Constitutional Club.'

My hostess nodded her agreement and added, 'So you see, dear Rupert, there is a genuine and continuous demand for a discreet but effective substitute for a stiff, hard cock. Anyhow, many ladies commission a dildo of the same dimensions as a particularly well-loved prick and gentlemen being forced for one reason or another to leave their lovers, also contact him to produce a matching set of basin, ewer, soap dish and dildo for the boudoir.'

She stood up and went back to the sideboard from which she brought out a small silver box which she placed in my hands as she sat down again and said, 'After spending three nights of lusty abandon with Monsieur Tihanyi, I was thrilled to receive from him this charming momento of a glorious fuck.'

I opened the box and looked down upon a superbly fashioned ceramic cock nestling on a small, plump velvet cushion. It was painted in pale blue and further decorated in a complicated yet somehow familiar design of maroon and gold diamonds and hoops. Nancy must have read my mind for she commented, 'You may recognise the pattern, Rupert, for these are Monsieur

Tihanyi's racing colours.'

This remark jogged my memory and I now recalled wildly cheering on the jockey who was wearing these selfsame colours as he won the Portnoy Stakes on a game little filly called Lady Norma at Goodwood the previous summer. It had truly been a glorious Goodwood as far as I was concerned for although the weather had not been as fine as usual, I had placed ten pounds each way on Lady Norma at odds of seven to one and later in the afternoon I accepted the invitation to mount Mrs Chelmsford in a private tent whilst everyone else was watching the last race.

'It is certainly a very beautiful gift,' I murmured softly, as I handed the box back to Nancy. 'And if, as you say, this dildo is modelled on his prick, Monsieur Tihanyi is certainly an extremely well-endowed gentleman though I am sure that even a superb dildo cannot match the feel of the genuine article.'

She smiled sweetly and said with a naughty gleam in her eyes, 'Oh, Rupert, I think you would be surprised how many ladies actually prefer the substitute to even the thickest, real live cock. After all, a dildo doesn't shoot off and go limp too quickly and one can finely tune the speed and force of entry to one's personal taste. Perhaps you would like to see for yourself how easily it can be used? I am sure Marussia would have no objection in helping me with a little demonstration.'

'It would be my pleasure,' said the Countess, rising from the sofa. 'Come, let us adjourn to the bedroom.'

477

I followed the two women into Nancy's bedroom where I was invited to sit on a chair whilst they undressed. After kicking off their shoes they unbuttoned each other's blouses, and then, sitting on the bed, they unhinged their suspenders and peeled off their stockings, giggling merrily away as they saw my excited penis swell up to form a mountainous bulge in my lap.

Now they embraced each other and whilst kissing passionately on the lips they pulled off their camisoles and lay back, entwined in each other's arms, wearing nothing but flimsy silk knickers which appeared to be of identical design. Marussia noticed this as well and remarked, 'Ah, I see that you also patronise Madame Vazelina of Berwick Street, Soho for your underwear.'

'Yes, I am a regular patron,' replied Nancy, stroking her magnificently large creamy breasts which were tipped with delightfully rounded areolas and exquisitely fashioned nipples which were already pointing out so juicily that I longed to throw myself upon her and suck these gorgeous little red strawberries.

But Countess Marussia's hands were now upon them and Nancy placed her palms on the other girl's bare breasts which, though not of her size, also jutted out proudly and were capped by equally large tawney stalks which were brought up to full erection by Nancy tweaking them between her long fingers.

'Help us off with our knickers, Rupert, there's a dear lad,' said Nancy, and the girls raised their bottoms invitingly as I walked over rather awkwardly, trying to shield my raging hard-on as I pulled down their remaining garments, though the sight of their nude pussies almost made me 'cream my jeans', as my Yankee pal Paul Mallock would have put it, then and there. I would have given anything to have sunk my throbbing tool into either Nancy's notch, which was delicately covered by a curtain of frizzy golden hair, or Marussia's pussey, which was more thickly masked by a thatch of reddish curls, but for the moment it was obvious that the presence of my cock would have been considered *de trop*, so I sat on the edge of the bed and relaxed as I watched the girls enjoy themselves together.

Marussia's left hand continued to toy with Nancy's breast whilst her right hand slid down the American girl's snow white belly and into the mound of golden pussey hair through which I could now see the pouting lips of her cunney. I leaned forward to see Marussia's forefinger disappear between these lips and the girls exchanged a further series of voluptuous kisses until Marussia broke off the embrace to nuzzle her lips against one of Nancy's nipples, drawing it deep inside her eager mouth. Nancy gasped as Marussia, who was now firmly taking control of this tribadistic encounter, now had two of her fingers sliding in and out of Nancy's cunt, moving them so swiftly that they were almost vibrating. Her thumb skated rapidly back and forth over the protruding clitty and Nancy arched her back, squirming with delight as she jerked herself into a splendid little orgasm.

Now it was Nancy's turn to repay her pretty

bed-mate who turned her back on her, sliding her delicious bum cheeks on Nancy's dripping pussey. Nancy pushed her hips forward and the two rocked in rhythm as she caressed Marussia's breasts from behind, flicking up the large, tawny stalks to peak erection. Then she dipped a hand down to the Countess's bushy *mons veneris*, itself a shapely hillock of firm flesh, surmounted with its rich profusion of reddish curls. Her finger and thumb soon found the hardening clitty which popped out between Marussia's cunney lips and made her gasp, 'A-a-h-r-r-e! A-a-h-r-r-e! You clever girl, now please finish me off with your tongue and Monsieur Tihanyi's dildo, there's a dear.'

Nancy slid out from under her and as she knelt between the other girl's long legs, she said, 'Mmmm, I can smell your juicy cunt from here, Marussia.' She lowered her head between her legs and began kissing her full, gorgeous pussey. I craned my head forward to see Nancy run her tongue along the full length of Marussia's parted cunney lips, stopping at the hardened little ball of her clitty which she gave her best attention, nibbling from side to side, up and down, as the Countess threw back her head and writhed with passion.

'Yes, yes! You're so good, Nancy. Keep sucking! Eat my pussey! Oh, how I adore it!' she cried, as Nancy's right hand snaked out, searching for the dildo. I aided her by opening the box and placing the instrument in her hand and gazed with increasing interest as Nancy now nudged the tip of dildo between the yielding lips of Marussia's cunt. Then she began fucking her in earnest with the superbly-fashioned dildo, sliding the thick china shaft in and out of her dripping honeypot. 'Further! Harder! Faster!' yelled out the Countess, as, with a final wrenching shudder, she gained her release, yelping with happiness as waves of ecstasy coursed through her body.

They were both still so fired up from this fray that they squealed their approval as I began to tear off my clothes. As soon as I was stark naked I threw myself upon the bed, rolled the two squealing girls over on their sides so that their gorgeous bare bottoms were open to view.

But how was I to solve the ticklish situation of which girl to fuck first? As the snooker player said when presented with a choice of colours, I had to decide whether I should go for the pink or the brown! What a dilemma! I had no wish to cause offence so I was extremely relieved when Nancy called out, 'Marussia, as it was my idea to ask Rupert round this afternoon, I think this gives me the right to claim the first fuck.'

Well, that solved the problem well enough so I took my meaty cock in my hand and pushed my stiff shaft in the smooth valley between the rounded cheeks of Nancy's arse and attempted to force a passage between them.

'Aaah! What a thick prick! But please don't go up my bum, Rupert, I would really prefer that hard hot cock in my cunney!' panted my kind hostess.

I needed no further urging as Nancy lifted her bottom slightly to effect an easy lodgement for my pulsating prick which slid into her moist crack from behind with the utmost ease. I embedded my shaft almost up to the root until my belly was squeezed against her bum and lay still for a moment. At this juncture Marussia entered the fray and nestled her head on Nancy's bosom and began licking and lapping at her lovely erect titties whilst she frigged Nancy's clitty with one hand and her own clitty with the other. I now started to pump my trusty tool in and out of Nancy's squelchy love channel as Marussia continued to frig her from the front. It was all so exciting that I was spent far quicker than I would have liked, though I squirted so many jets of frothy white cream into Nancy's cunt that I could swear that I felt my balls lighten as the delicious thrills of my climax tingled throughout every inch of my perspiring body.

I lay back, heaving with exhaustion, as Marussia now lifted her head from Nancy's titties and said to her, 'Well, darling, as you've now had the first fuck, I'm surely entitled to the first taste of Rupert's succulent chopper.'

'Of course you are, my love,' said Nancy generously, and in a trice, Marussia's hands were clamped around my semi-stiff shaft. 'But do allow me to assist you.'

Nancy sat up and perched on my chest. I felt Marussia's lips envelop the tip of my cock as she began licking all round the edge of my knob. As she started to suck noisily on my now iron-hard stiffstander, Nancy moved up to place her pussey over my mouth so I could tongue her cunney. I sighed with delight as Marussia's wicked tongue now began to lap around the sensitive underside of my shaft, making it ache with unslaked lust. Now she sucked in my helmet, teasing my knob against the roof of her mouth with her tongue and in no time at all I felt the surge of a powerful spend making its way up from my ballsack.

Marussia sensed this and withdrew her skilful tongue for a moment or two before returning to the attack as I continued to slide my tongue through the damp, blonde pussey hairs of Nancy's cunt, letting the tip of my tongue burrow between her pouting pink cunney lips. But when Marussia squeezed her hand round the base of my cock, sucking me harder and harder, I simply could no longer contain myself. My lusty love truncheon pulsed in her mouth as I let out a small cry and jetted spurt after spurt of creamy spunk inside her mouth. She gulped down every drop of my masculine essence and murmured with satisfaction as she licked the last drains from round the head of my gleaming prick which was only slowly losing its stiffness.

All the while I was trying to stimulate Nancy into a spend by nibbling on her clitty and sliding my fingers in and out of her sopping slit. Alas, it was to no avail and the charming girl said regretfully, 'I don't think I can get there without a cock in my cunt.'

Marussia immediately offered to frig her with Monsieur Tihanyi's dildo but then I offered my own organ because, if she could wait ten minutes or so for me to regain my strength, I would be delighted to fuck her again.

'Could you really do it again so soon, Rupert? My, you must have a superb constitution,' Nancy said excitedly with her bright blue eyes shining with lewd anticipation of a second sheathing of my stalk in her cunney.

I swallowed hard and said with a small smile, 'Well, I can usually rise to the occasion three times without having to retire from the game. At school, when we used to play Mother Thumb and her Four Daughters in the dormitory, I could usually manage four spends with only a short break between them though Harry Barr, who is now the Rural Dean of Coketown, could sometimes come five or even six times virtually without stopping at all.'

'I would like to meet this gentleman,' said Marussia instantly, but I shook my head and said, 'No, I don't believe you would, Countess. Most unfortunately, poor Harry became a confirmed homosexualist whilst studying for the priesthood and I shudder to think where he puts his prick these days.'

'What a waste,' sighed Marussia, as she took hold of my dangling shaft and idly began to rub it up and down in her clenched fist. To Nancy's and my great joy, Marussia's frigging was all my shaft needed to begin swelling up to its former glorious state and when it was standing as proudly high as before, Marussia relinquished her grip in favour of Nancy, who clutched my cock in her hand as she pulled my face towards hers and sank her naughty little tongue in my mouth. I stroked her damp blonde bush of pussey hair as she lay back and relaxed, her head supported by her hands whilst I clambered upon her without delay. Immediately she parted her legs to allow me to

484

kneel in front of her open cunney and then Nancy took my rampant rod and guided it directly inside her wet, welcoming cunt.

Although I was admittedly tired from our previous exploits, I think this was the best fuck of all. How exquisitely her velvet cunney walls clung to my cock as she sinuously moved her hips whilst I pistoned my prick up and down, my balls smacking lewdly against her backside with every forward thrust. I pounded in and out of her pussey, my hands gripping her firm, fleshy bum cheeks as we bounced up and down on the soft mattress.

'Oh Rupert, you lovely big-cocked boy! Fuck my juicy cunt with your thick prick!' she gasped, as I thrust home, sliding my shaft home in and out of her marvellous muff. Several times I thought I would spend before her but somehow I managed to hold back till she was ready for me. Again and again, faster and faster, I fucked the sweet girl until with a hoarse wail she achieved a tremendous climax, writhing uncontrollably as a multiple series of spends racked their way through her.

As Nancy had orgasmed I pulled out my twitching tool and reared over her. I gripped my cock and gave it two or three convulsive jerks until a huge fountain of salty sperm spouted out, arcing out towards her breasts, splashing her nipples, streaming down towards her belly button and into her soaking golden thatch.

'Oh how wonderful!' breathed Marussia, who had naturally been watching avidly, frigging herself unashamedly as she saw me rub the spunk around Nancy's erect nipples and all over her tummy. I moved over and squatted over Marussia with my bottom against her face as I leaned down and caressed her palpitating pussey with my tongue, licking up her tangy love juice, as she lifted her head and took my ballsack into her mouth, nibbling my balls through the hairy, wrinkled skin whilst I continued to stimulate her cunt, flicking my tongue in and out of her juicy love channel.

Now Nancy slid her head between my thigh and Marussia's body and began to gobble greedily on my glistening shaft which had miraculously still retained its stiffness (perhaps because I had not shot my total sticky load over Nancy's nipples). She moved round so that she could take my cock in her mouth and she sucked hard upon it, moving her lips from tip to balls and back again, faster and faster, intoxicated like Marussia and myself by the sheer ecstasy of this grand, uninhibited three-way fuck. My prick pulsed against the back of her throat, releasing a further frothy flood of hot jism and she greedily swallowed all my creamy emission as Marussia also spent, filling my mouth with her aromatic love juices, which I also gulped down, as together the three of us ran the course to a complete and totally satisfying fulfilment.

We lay quietly for a few minutes and Marussia asked Nancy and myself if we had planned to go up to Scotland for the rest of the season. 'My companion Prince Adrian of the Netherlands has taken over a house in the Highlands,' she told us, 'and you'd both be very welcome to join us.

You'd be sure to flush out many a gamecock from its covert, Nancy, whilst you, Rupert, would certainly enjoy our rather eccentric version of the Highland Fling let alone the complex routines of our all-nude eightsome reel.'

'I'm sure I would love it,' I said politely, 'but alas, my engagement book is full until the New Year.'

She was about to reply when suddenly Marussia's body stiffened and she said in an urgent, worried voice, 'Hold on a moment, I am sure I heard someone coming.'

'It could be any one of us,' I said wittily.

'No, I mean I thought I heard someone enter the room,' she continued, with a startled look on her face.

Nancy looked across at her and kissed her engorged nipple. 'Don't worry, that will only be Standlake the butler. Whenever I take any guests into the bedroom, he usually comes in after an appropriate length of time to see whether his services are required – either for myself or any other girl who might fancy being fucked by his big black cock.'

'I think I'll pass up the opportunity at present,' said Marussia thoughtfully, 'though I must say that I have always wondered whether the tales I have heard about Negro prowess and the size of their equipment should be taken with a pinch of salt.'

'Well, I'm no expert on the subject,' replied Nancy, 'but those of my girl friends who have sampled the delights afforded by Standlake's dark, thick tool have been unanimous in their praise of both its dimensions and the way he uses it, which of course is far more important, for, as we say back home, it isn't the size of the ship that counts, it's the motion of the ocean.'

'Still, I would have been most interested to see Standlake in action,' mused Marussia. 'Is there no other way we could see him fuck? Surely he must have some admirers amongst your female staff?'

Nancy clapped her hands in delight. 'Yes, of course, that's the answer – unless Rupert here wishes to take part in a—'

Here I hastened to say that whilst, like the vast majority of public school chaps, I and my best chums Frank Folkestone and Prince Salman of Lockshenstan, had fiddled around with each other after 'lights out' in the dorm, these juvenile experiments were now way behind me. Also, I added, that whilst I had nothing against homosexuals who could do to each other whatever they wished in the privacy of their own homes, frankly, the mere thought of having any prick (let alone a big black one) rammed up my arse was utterly abhorrent to me.

'Don't worry, Rupert, I don't think Standlake is that way inclined either,' Nancy reassured me with a smile. 'Leave this affair to me.'

She called the butler on the house telephone and asked him if he would kindly arrange to fuck one of the maids in his bedroom whilst Countess Marussia and I watched. I could not hear his reply but Nancy nodded her head as she said, 'Yes? Very good, then, we'll go up to Lucy's room in ten minutes.'

Nancy provided us with white towelling robes

to slip on and the three of us made our way back to the drawing-room where we refreshed ourselves with tall glasses of ice cold lemonade which Standlake had thoughtfully left on the sideboard. Then, hardly able to contain our excitement, we went upstairs to Lucy's room which was directly above Nancy's bedroom. When we arrived on the top floor Nancy knocked at the door and her personal maid called out, 'Do come in, everyone, the door is open.'

Standlake and Lucy were already in bed, covered by a sheet but Lucy sat up as Nancy introduced Marussia and myself and we sat down on three chairs that Lucy had placed between the window and the foot of the bed. She was, I must record, a not unattractive girl of some twenty-five years, slightly on the plump side perhaps but blessed with extremely large breasts topped by equally large areoles and rich red nipples which were exposed as she jumped out of bed to greet us. Her mound was covered by a thick profusion of light brown curls and the swelling lips were already pouting most deliciously, the glowing red chink indicating that in all probability Standlake had been frigging her before we arrived.

'Are you ready for me, Philip?' she asked the handsome black man, who grinned, showing two even rows of sparkling white teeth, as he said, 'I should say so, you lucky girl,' and he pointed to the sheet covered peak between his legs. Lucy smacked her lips and threw back the sheet to reveal his naked torso to us. There was a momentary silence and then I heard Marussia gasp in awe at the sight of Standlake's

489

magnificent nude body and I could well understand her admiration for his superb physique. Standlake was, as aforesaid, a handsome fellow, and the muscles fairly rippled as he drew breath and expanded his broad chest. His torso narrowed down to a flat stomach and narrow hips and, as he turned to embrace Lucy, I had also to admire his lean muscular flanks. When he turned back I also gasped with wonder as we caught sight of his heavy, dangling cock which was of such a thickness that I do not believe I have seen before or since.

Marussia was similarly struck by the size of the black butler's boner for the Countess whispered to our hostess, 'My God, Nancy! What an enormous prick! Doesn't the very thought of sucking that huge penis make your mouth water?' And then turning to the girl on the bed whose hands were already encircling this fast-swelling monster, Marussia added, 'You *are* a lucky girl, Lucy. I just hope he doesn't stretch your cunney too much with that giant truncheon.'

'No fear of that, madam, it's only if I take too much of Philip's cock in my mouth that I have any problems, I just can't take it all in without gagging,' said Lucy cheerfully as she leaned over and prepared to begin the demonstration. She took the butler's pulsating dark knob between her lips, jamming down the foreskin and lashing her tongue around the rigid shaft. Then she sucked hard, and amazingly she was able to take about a third of Standlake's extraordinarily thick cock (which at a later date Nancy measured as having a five-and-a-half-inch girth and being fractionally over ten-and-quarter-inches in length) into her mouth whilst her hands toyed with his hanging, heavy balls.

The aroused girl now started to lick this giant dark lollipop, drawing her hot, wet tongue from his ballsack right up to the top of his shaft, fluttering briefly around the uncapped helmet. He clutched at her hair and emitted a low gutteral murmur as she circled her tongue all round the fleshy dome of his knob, paying particular attention, I noted, to the especially sensitive underside.

Then Lucy removed her hands and, clasping them behind her back, she sucked up almost the entire length of Standlake's black prick almost down to the root. This caused the well endowed, handsome Negro to writhe and jerk under this oral stimulation as Lucy sucked up and down his tremendous tadger with noisy abandon. And the clever way she managed to keep her head bobbing up and down without using her hands to steady his twitching tool brought a spontaneous round of applause from Nancy and Marussia, who were still marvelling at the dimensions of Standlake's glistening, veiny boner.

Lucy was obviously enjoying herself for now she transferred her hands back to the front, one clasped as far as her fingers would stretch around Standlake's cock and with the other she was busy diddling herself, rubbing her clitty as she continued to suck on the great stiff staff held lightly between her teeth.

By now we had all reached a fever pitch of

excitement and Nancy was now smoothing her left arm across Marussia's crotch whilst the Countess repaid the compliment by moving her own left hand across to stroke Nancy's breasts. At the same time Nancy reached out with her right hand and with a little help from yours truly, had managed to unbutton my trousers and taken out my own not inconsiderable shaft and her fingers were busying themselves sliding up and down my shiny staff.

Back on the bed, Standlake now had Lucy's head in his hands and was jamming her lips round his cock and I could see that very shortly she would be sucking up all the semen out of his tight, firm balls. In fact, it was only a matter of seconds before the tell-tale quivers and contractions began and Lucy pushed up her head for a moment to allow us to view a great wash of white jism come jetting out of the top of his cock. She slurped up this flood of spunk with evident enthusiasm but to my astonishment, Standlake's proud prick stood as stiff, hard and strong as before he had shot his load!

Indeed, the butler now took control and he leaned forward, his thick lips seeing and finding one of Lucy's engorged nipples, as she now spread herself flat on her back. Once the first tittie had been drawn out to stand up like a little red tap he sucked up the other to a quivering peak of rubbery flesh. Lucy trembled as Standlake moved over her and guided his throbbing tool towards her juicy honeypot and she opened her mouth to take his tongue deep between her moist lips as he now placed his knob at the entrance of her cunney and she pulled her pussey lips apart to widen the entrance for his enormous cock.

I gazed intently as he pushed his prick firmly forward and saw his gleaming pole disappear inch by inch inside Lucy's love channel. Then he began to move it in and out in full yet gentle thrusts as he again attacked her pert little nipples that were standing up, simply begging to be flicked by his long, tapering fingers. To my surprise, Standlake then pulled completely out of her cunney, his black pole gleaming with its coating of pussey juice. But the respite for Lucy's cunt was only temporary – first he lightly traced the open wet crack with his fingertips, flicking the erect clitty that was peeping out at the top, and then he thrust his knob back between those pink, pouting lips and Lucy moaned with delight as he propelled inch after inch of his thick chopper until his rough pubic curls and her muff of smoother pussey hair were matted together.

He pulled back until only his knob was inside her juicy love-channel and then drove the full length of his massive shaft full inside the trembling girl as she urged him on and he quickly established a powerful rhythm whilst Lucy closed her feet together at the small of his back to force even more of that huge stiffstander inside her.

Standlake was now panting with exertion as he rammed his cock in and out of her cunney, his lean black body rocking backwards and forwards between her creamy spread thighs. Lucy was spending as Standlake fucked her for she raked his back with her fingernails as she shuddered with the voluptuous sensations afforded by his thick prick in her voracious cunt. He pumped faster and faster and we three spectators were on our feet, with Nancy's hand still tightly gripped round my own throbbing tool, as we cheered him on. What made the finale even more exciting for us was that Lucy had not been able to find any linseed oil for her *douche* [This was a popular spermicide some hundred years ago though not as effective, of course, as a condom or better still the 'pill' – Editor] so at the very final stage he withdrew and shot a flood of creamy white spunk all over her belly just as Nancy's frigging brought me off and my cock ejaculated an arcing fountain of jism over Standlake's dimpled buttocks.

In fact, I was somewhat concerned, when the butler rolled off the sated girl and lay on his back to recover his senses, that some of my spunk stained the crisp, white sheet. However, when I pointed this out to Nancy she told me not to worry as the cotton was already soaked with Lucy's love juices as well as perspiration from both of the lovers. 'Anyhow, Rupert,' she remarked gaily, 'spunk stains cause no problem if a small amount of Mr Maxwell's Special Compound is used – it is guaranteed to remove all blemishes. We buy a large bottle every month for as you have seen, my friends and I are extremely fond of fucking.'

Countess Marussia looked at her jewel-encrusted pocket watch and said, 'Dear Nancy, I really must be going – I am already late for Lady Suffield's tea party. Thank you so much, my darling, for a divine lunch and a wonderful fuck – for which I must also thank you, Rupert. It was a pleasure meeting you and your nice cock.'

'The pleasure was mine, *simpatichnaya jenshina*,'
I replied, bowing low to kiss the Countess's
offered hand and using the few words of Russian
I remembered from the lessons given me by Dr
John O'Connor, the languages master at St
Lionel's, one of the most brilliant linguists in
England, who was fluent in French, German,
Polish, Russian, Turkish and Arabic. Indeed, if
Dr O'Connor had not been caught *in flagrante
delicto* with the twin eighteen-year-old daughters
of a senior Foreign Office official, he would
undoubtedly have enjoyed a distinguished career
in the diplomatic service instead of having to earn
his daily bread as a humble pedagogue at a minor
public school.

'You speak Russian, Rupert? Is there no end to
your accomplishments?' laughed Marussia. 'You
must take my card. Please call upon me at any
time, especially when my consort, Prince Adrian,
is back in Amsterdam performing his royal
duties.'

We thanked Standlake and Lucy for their
wonderful performance and made our way down
to the drawing-room. But I stopped at the foot of
the stairs and said, 'Nancy, would you object if I
popped back upstairs and presented your
servants with a small token or our appreciation?
After all, they did afford us some excellent sport.'

'By all means,' she replied. 'I am sure they will
be far from offended by such a generous gesture.'

'I climbed back up the stairs and as the door of
Lucy's room was slightly ajar, I simply strode in.
Standlake had already left to shower and change
in his own quarters, but Lucy was still lying

naked on the sheets, her hands under her head, with a blissful smile of contentment on her pretty face.

'Ah, Lucy, I wanted a quick word,' I said, shutting the door behind me and taking two gold sovereigns out of my pocket. 'On behalf of Countess Marussia and myself, I would like to give you and Standlake a well deserved little present.'

Her eyes lit up as I placed the coins on her bedside table. 'Thank you, sir,' she said, glancing across at the coins and when she saw the glint of gold her eyes sparkled and she sat up and exclaimed, 'Oh, that really is kind of you, sir! I'll give Philip his share later this afternoon.' [Rupert was indeed leaving a very generous gratuity ás a housemaid only earned about £30 a year! – Editor]

I was about to leave when the luscious nude girl called me back. 'Must you go, sir? I'd very much like to give you something in return for your generosity.'

Perhaps I was naïve but I honestly didn't know what she had in mind until she crooked her finger and motioned me back to sit next to her on the bed. 'Did you notice the enormous size of Philip's cock, sir?' she asked with a sly smile.

'Yes, I must say that I did, and like most men I was very envious of his tremendous tadger,' I said. This reply made Lucy hold up her hand and say, 'Ah, but honestly, size isn't everything, though I know that all boys would like bigger pricks just as all girls would like an extra few inches on our busts. Now I won't deny that Philip's big stiffie really fills my cunney up a treat but I've known men with much smaller cocks who can bring me off just as well. Lord Hammersmith, for example, is a wonderful lover even though I don't think his bell end is much more than half the size of Philip's – but he reams me out beautifully and his spunk has a fresher, less salty taste too.

'I saw the mistress wanking your cock whilst Philip was fucking me, sir, and I thought that your cock looked very nice. Would you mind if I had a closer look at it?'

'Not in the slightest,' I said, hastily unbuttoning my trousers and pulling out my dangling shaft, 'but as you can see, I am afraid that it's a little bit down in the dumps.'

Lucy clasped my stalk in her fingers and said softly, 'Dear me, we can't let Mr John Thomas stay in this sad state, that's for sure.' She moved herself across and leaned down to place her head on my thigh as I pulled down my trousers and drawers to my ankles. She eyed my cock critically and then moved her hand to pull down the foreskin and expose the naked red bulb of my knob. Her tongue flashed out and slicked across the smooth skin of my uncapped helmet which set my cock swelling up within seconds!

She continued to frig me as she wet her tongue against her lush red lips and then took my knob fully inside her mouth, sucking with gusto as my tool throbbed with pleasure. Sensing that this intense activity would make me spend too soon, she ceased sucking and instead dived her head down to plant a light series of tiny butterfly kisses up and down the stem, encompassing my balls and running beyond to that too often neglected area between the ballsack and arse-hole. She followed this delightful oral massage with some sharp licks on my now bursting shaft and then thrust my trusty tool in and out of her mouth in a quickening rhythm, deep into her throat and then out again with her pink tongue lapping my helmet at the end of each stroke, soaking up the drops of thick liquid which were already forming at the 'eye' on top of my knob. In vain I tried to prolong the delicious pleasure but Lucy's lasciv- ious sucking was simply too powerful to resist and I could not prevent the sperm that had boiled up inside my balls spurting up my stem and crashing out of my pulsating prick.

I pumped a thick, creamy emission of jism inside her mouth which she swallowed with evident delight, smacking her lips as she happily gulped down the last dregs of spunk from my fast-deflating cock. 'Was that nice?' she enquired somewhat unnecessarily. I nodded my head and panted my agreement, 'Lucy, that was a truly splendid sucking-off. Do you know, I've often wondered whether girls can learn how to suck a stiff cock or whether it is simply an inbred ability.'

'I don't really know,' she said, considering my question thoughtfully. 'Perhaps it's something to do with the first time a girl ever takes a cock in her mouth. I remember my introduction to, what's the posh word for it, sir?'

'Fellatio, Lucy,' I answered, as I stole a quick look at my watch.

She must have seen me do so for she continued, 'Oh, please don't go yet, sir. For a start, the mistress will be engaged with Standlake for at least another ten minutes and I'm sure she'd want to say good-bye to you before you leave.'

'Jolly good, then I'll gladly stay and listen to you.' I said, snuggling myself on the bed next to her as she lay with her head on my shoulder and her fingers still toying with my limp shaft.

'Well, it all began three years ago when I left school and took up service in Lord and Lady Jackson's house in Grosvenor Street. It was a very happy household but when her son Terence came back home from Cambridge University for the Christmas holidays, I was silly enough to become intimately involved with him.

'He was a nice, good-looking boy and from the moment he first saw me I could tell that he was as attracted to me as I was to him. Well, it all started one evening when the master and mistress were out at one of Sir Barry Gray's literary soirées in Chelsea. Terry's sister was also out so I knew that he would be alone in the sitting-room. So I marched in there after supper on the pretence of tidying up the newspapers and changing the ashtrays as Lord Jackson smokes those big Cuban cigars. Terry was sitting in an armchair reading the evening paper but I could see him eyeing me over the top of the page as I leaned down in front of him to see if the ashtray on the side table needed emptying. I was wearing a frilly white blouse and I had purposely undone the top two buttons so that the swell of my breasts must have been visible to him. I knew that he would have loved to feel them but, being a polite young gentleman, needed some sign of encouragement before even speaking to me.

'So I deliberately emptied a few grains of cigar ash on his trousers! "Oh, I am sorry, Master Terence, here, I'll brush it off for you," I said, and started to flick away the ash which had landed on his thigh.

'We began to talk and one thing led to another and after about ten minutes I found myself sitting on his lap with my head resting lightly on his shoulder. I was still unsure how to react but then Terry suddenly turned my face up to his and kissed me passionately on the lips.

'I felt a sudden tingling rush of excitement surge through me. There was something so special about his kiss that it made it impossible for me not to respond. His hand slipped down from my shoulder to down underneath my arm and then I felt his fingers close gently over my breast whilst at the same time his tongue sank inside my mouth and his other hand began stroking my thigh under the hem of my skirt.

'Now everything was happening so fast that I didn't even consider trying to resist these unexpected advances. I just sat cuddling him, soaking up the lovely sensations of his kisses and his touches.

'His hand soon reached the top of my legs and his thumb began a delicious stroking of my pussey as I pressed my lips even more firmly against his and his fingers now probed downwards and rubbed against my dampening crack. He then started to tug at my knickers and I lifted my bum off his thighs to allow him to pull them right off. Then I felt my whole body vibrate with pleasure as his thumb rubbed against my clitty and I held on to him as tightly as I could. At that moment, I think we both knew for sure that we wanted to fuck, but as I said, Terry Jackson was a real gentleman because he whispered, "Lucy, before we reach the point of no return, are you certain that you want to make this journey?"

'He need have had no fear for I would have been glad and willing to let him do anything he wanted with my curvy young body. So I simply whimpered when Terry stopped fondling my titties but began undoing the rest of the buttons on my blouse. He slipped it off me completely and then unhooked my chemise and I raised my arms so that he could pull it up and over my shoulders. Now his hands ran firmly over my bare breasts, tracing circles around my stiffening nipples with the tips of his fingers. Then he lowered his head and took one of my erect titties in his mouth and the wet friction of his tongue made it tingle with delight as he sucked it firm and deep between his lips.

'My skirt was next to come off and I was now naked except for my stockings which were held up by two frilly garters. I trembled with desire as he passed a hand over my hairy muff and my cunney was fairly aching for more attention. Yet he still did not attempt to proceed further and it suddenly struck me that Terry might be concerned that I was a virgin! So I nibbled his ear and whispered, "Don't be worried about deflowering me, Master Terry, because in South London where I come from, I don't think there's a girl over sixteen who hasn't had a cock in her cunney at some time or another."

'This did the trick and I helped him undress until he stood naked in front of me with his thick, stiff cock standing high against his tummy. He stretched me out on the big settee and knelt alongside, kissing my breasts and belly and running his hands up and down my thighs. My excitement grew stronger and stronger and I lovingly clutched at his head of curly brown hair, moaning my approval as he now pressed his mouth onto my bushy mound.

'The sensation of his moist lips felt truly heavenly and when I felt his tongue starting to wash its way around my clitty, I almost fainted away with the sheer ecstasy of the wonderful waves of pleasure which emanated from my cunt and coursed their way through my body. I pushed my pussey up against Terry's face and parted my legs as he now licked even harder at my clitty and at the same time began to prise open my cunney lips with his fingers. He sank his forefinger slowly into my sopping slit, making me gasp as he eased a second and then a third digit deeper and deeper inside my love channel.

'Although I'd been fucked by Mr Hollingberry, our next door neighbour, and by Charlie Haynes and Tim Hutchinson, two boys who lived in the next street, Terry Jackson's wicked tongue and clever fingers were thrilling me like I'd never been thrilled before. My clitty was buzzing with a marvellous feeling which I never before experienced. He twisted his fingers round as he now thrust four fingers in and out of my dripping cunney which made the buzz feel more and more wonderful as he finger fucked me up towards a spend. He realised that my climax was approaching when I began to quiver because he licked harder than ever at my clitty and his fingers raced faster and faster out of my sopping honeypot. When I felt myself on the verge of spending my body jerked wildly but he held his head firmly against my cunney whilst I squeezed my nipples and drummed my feet against the cushions.

'The fabulous pressure of Terry's tongue and fingers kept me at the peak of pleasure for what seemed an incredibly long time – and even when my orgasm finally subsided, I was still feeling very fruity and eager to continue. More than anything, though, I wanted to repay Terry for the gorgeous time he had given me.

'So I urged him to change places and to lie on his back on the settee and I knelt between his legs. His throbbing cock stood up like a flagpole between his thighs and I grasped it with the intention of spitting myself upon the smooth, pink mushroomed knob. But then I remembered that it was not the most propitious time of the month for fucking and anyway I had nothing in my room with which to douche. With a crestfallen look on my face I told him that perhaps I shouldn't let him fuck me after all – this was a terrible thing to have to say for after what had just gone on it was like leading a man dying of thirst in the desert to an oasis and then as he was about to drink warning him that the water was poisoned!

'But Terry did not show any great irritation

with me. He simply stroked my hair and said, "Don't worry, Lucy, I'll be just as happy if you'll suck my cock instead."

'"Of course I will," I said, not wanting to let him know that I had never taken a prick in my mouth before this time. But I'd heard all about how men love being brought off this way and my friend Nellie had told me about how nice it was to lick and lap at a thick prick and how clean and fresh spunk tasted. "It can't get your belly up either, my girl," she had also told me, which was certainly an added attraction as far as I was concerned.

'Nevertheless, the question was whether I would be able to do it well enough for Terry. Now of course, I knew how men liked to be tossed off, and my boy friends had all said that I was very good at giving them hand-jobs, if you'll forgive the expression, sir.

'Anyway, I decided to have a go, and I held the thick base of Terry's prick with one hand and rubbed his shaft up and down with the other as I leaned down and nervously flicked my tongue over the smooth dome of his uncapped helmet. He groaned and lay back with his eyes tightly closed as I repeated this sensual experiment. I must say that I found the sensation of licking his cock much nicer than I'd expected and I could tell from his throbbing tool and his heavy breathing that I must be doing it well.

'Now I gradually eased the crown of his cock into my mouth, nibbling the hot, smooth pole and sucking harder as I moved my hand which had been clutching his shaft downwards to caress his hairy ballsack. I pushed in as much of his thick, rigid rod as I could and for the very first time, sucked and slurped at this lewd lollipop. Terry stretched out his arm and began to frig my cunney as his prick began to twitch and I guessed that the spunk would soon be spouting out. Then with a cry he filled my mouth with a gorgeous spray of frothy warm jism and his shaft bucked wildly as I gulped down all the creamy liquor, which tasted slightly salty but was as pleasant and refreshing to drink as Nellie had told me. I gobbled his jerking prick, rather noisily sucking out every last milky drop of sperm, as Terry's fingers now helped bring me to another voluptuous spend.

"'Was that good for you?" I enquired anxiously, and he smiled up at me. "Lucy, that was truly wonderful," he murmured softly, and would have undoubtedly said more when we heard a ring on the front door bell. I grabbed my clothes and rushed out into the hall and fled upstairs to my room. In fact, the unexpected visitor was only Arthur Barker, an old chum·of Terry's who undoubtedly would have loved to have looked on or better still joined in the canoodling. I did come down later at Terry's request and we did enjoy a romp with Arthur along with Jemima, the scullery maid. But that is another story.'

I looked at my watch again and said, 'Lucy, thank you very much for your entertaining little anecdote, but I really must be leaving. Do you think Miss Carrington has finished with Standlake yet?'

505

'I would imagine so, sir, for as Miss Nancy told me recently, she finds his oversized shaft uncomfortable if it stays too long in her cunney.'

'That doesn't surprise me,' I declared as I began to dress. 'Another time perhaps, you will be able to demonstrate your skills as a *fellatrice* to me.'

Her eyes sparkled as she nodded her head and said, 'I'd love to, Mr Mountjoy. Bring a friend along and I'll show you how I can suck two cocks at once – so long as your friend doesn't have such a giant prick as Standlake!'

I made a mental note of her promise and chuckled as I realised that her *caveat* would rule out my oldest chum Frank Folkestone of whom I had frankly always been a mite jealous as his chopper was by far the biggest amongst all the boys at St Lionel's Academy for the Sons of Gentlefolk [see *The Intimate Memoirs Of An Edwardian Dandy Volume One: Youthful Scandals* and *Volume Two: An Oxford Scholar* – Editor]. It would be an admittedly malicious pleasure to call Frank and tell him sadly that his tool was too large to be sucked off along with my own by this randy young minx.

I bid Lucy good-afternoon and met Nancy at the foot of the stairs. Her face was flushed, her chest was heaving and her clothes were somewhat dishevelled, but she smiled broadly at me and gasped, 'Ah, Rupert, you're just the man I need. Would you allow me to lean on your shoulder as we walk to the drawing-room? I've been really well fucked by Standlake, but I need to lie down for half an hour.'

'Of course,' I said, proferring my arm which

506

she took in her hands. 'I have also been entertained very nicely by Lucy although I was frankly *hors de combat*. But though I didn't fuck her she told me a lively tale which I will set down in my diary as soon as I get home.

'Nancy, thank you once again for a delicious luncheon and for our post-prandial fun and games. I will telephone you this evening once I have checked my diary and I do hope that you will allow me to return your hospitality.'

We reached the drawing-room and I helped her onto the sofa. 'Phew, that's better,' she exclaimed with a heavy sigh. 'I'll be walking bandy-legged this evening, but I will have no-one but myself to blame. I know I really shouldn't take in Standlake's huge tool after being fucked by another man but my blood was up and as Oscar Wilde said, I can resist anything except temptation!

'Rupert, my dear, I look forward to your call. I am dining with Mr Horne of The Grove Gallery this evening at Romano's so would you telephone before seven o'clock?'

'Yes, I'll call in an hour or so. But how strange you should be meeting Mr Horne tonight. I happened to meet him only last week at my Club where he gave a talk on these new French painters, the post-impressionists, he called them, who have been creating quite a stir on the Continent. Are you in the market for some pictures, Nancy?'

'In a manner of speaking,' she answered, settling herself down on the sofa. 'My father is a keen collector and he has telegraphed five thousand dollars to my bank account in London so I should be able to buy anything that I think he would like.'

'No wonder Garry Horne is taking you out to dinner!' I laughed, as Standlake now appeared with my hat and coat. 'But if you really are looking for some worthwhile paintings, Nancy, I would very much like to show you some work by a very good friend of mine, who used to live very near my own Yorkshire home.'

Then I explained to her about my involvement with Diana Wigmore. I finished by saying that Diana was coming back to England shortly for the important reception given by the local big wigs for the King. Then I had a brainwave and I said, 'Nancy, why not come to York with me and meet Diana for yourself? She has a wide selection of her work at her parents' home and I will telegraph her and tell her to bring some of her latest pictures back with her from Paris.

'You'll stay at Albion Towers, our family seat, of course, and there will be no problem arranging an invitation for you to the party to meet His Majesty. My father is an old chum of the Deputy Lord Lieutenant of the County who is in charge of the whole affair.'

Like all Americans, Nancy was fascinated by royalty and she clapped her hands in delight. 'Gosh, you mean I might meet King Edward himself?' she said excitedly. 'Sure, I'd love to go up to York with you – but I insist on buying the train tickets, especially if I'm to stay at your house. No, Rupert, I won't have it any other way. You have to live on the allowance your Uncle

Humphrey has generously set aside for you whilst I have more money than I know what to do with. Anyhow, Papa can probably use the receipts to offset against his income tax. So when you telephone me in about an hour, give me all the details of the trip.'

I kissed her good-bye and slipped on my hat and coat which Standlake had been patiently holding in his hands. I walked briskly across the Square and as soon as I was home I wrote out a telegraph to Diana telling her that I would definitely be going to York and that I was also writing to her about my plans. Then I scrawled a letter to my father to say that I would come up for the party and that I would be bringing a guest, Miss Nancy Carrington, with me, falsely adding that the relationship between us was strictly platonic because I did not want my Mama to start hearing marriage bells.

Edwards came into the drawing room with a copy of the evening newspaper and I gave him instructions to telegraph my message to Diana immediately and to post my letter to my father. I settled down to read my newspaper but was interrupted by a knock on the door. 'Come in,' I called, and Mary, the pretty maid I had bum-fucked before luncheon, came in and said in a timid voice, 'I'm sorry to trouble you, sir, but I wondered if you would like to have me again this evening. It's my night off and I've nothing to do and nowhere to go.'

'Dear, dear, that's a sorry state of affairs,' I said, folding the paper, and looking up at the demure girl who was standing with her eyes cast down modestly to the floor. 'Though I must say, Mary, how surprised I am that an attractive girl like you hasn't any followers.'

Her face coloured a pretty shade of pink as she said, 'To be honest, Mr Mountjoy, I was going to the music hall with PC Shackleton, but he's been told he has to work an extra shift as three constables at his station are ill with influenza.'

'A policeman's lot is not a happy one,' I said sympathetically, as I hummed the eponymous chorus from the Gilbert and Sullivan opera. 'Still, his loss is my gain. I'd be happy to take you to the music hall, Mary. Where did you want to go?'

'The Alhambra Theatre. Fred Karno's topping the bill,' she said, her face brightening up and her eyes sparkling as she added, 'Oh, you *are* a kind gentleman, sir.'

It was my turn to blush, for my motives were hardly as pure as the driven snow! Although I had already enjoyed what some may call a surfeit of fucking that day, I was never one to turn down the chance of a further frolic. So I said to her, 'It might be a little awkward if we leave the house together, Mary. Why don't we meet at the corner of Gower Street at six o'clock. We'll take in the first house and then we'll have a bite of supper at my Club. But not a word about this to Mrs Harrow or any of the other staff – it'll be our little secret.'

'I won't say a word to anyone, cross my heart,' promised Mary, and she gave me a quick kiss on the cheek before happily scurrying out back to her room. I grinned as I scoured the sports page of the newspaper. To my great joy I read that Fairbridge's Organ had skated home at eight to one in the two o'clock race at Doncaster. Old Goldhill, our family servant back at Albion Towers, who was a keen follower of the sport of kings, had written to me about this horse which was running today in preparation for the Royal Hunt Cup. I had staked a fiver with my Club's head porter who acted as our unofficial bookmaker, so my evening out with Mary would now be doubly pleasing: I could pick up my winnings when we dined at the Jim Jam after the theatre. A seraphic smile creased my lips as it occurred to me that I could fairly claim, after my fol-de-rols with Countess Marussia, a place to ride in the Royal Hunt Cup!

Anyway, I managed to take a quick nap before Edwards brought me tea and sandwiches and after refreshing myself (fucking always gives me an appetite – despite the ample luncheon I was still able to scoff a couple of sandwiches and a pastry), I telephoned Nancy Carrington and we finalised arrangements to go up to York. I also invited her to dine with me next Wednesday evening along with Michael Reynolds, one of my favourite cousins, who being a year older than myself, was already beavering away in his third year as a medical student at the Royal Free Hospital up in Hampstead. Michael was a lusty lad who would appreciate Nancy's liking for free love and I was sure that the girl he was bringing along – a most attractive petite Portugese girl named Shella de Souza, whose soft feminine curves and flashing, lustrous eyes turned men's heads as she walked down the street – would be similarly broad-minded.

There was barely time to shave, shower and change my clothes but at six o'clock on the dot, I carefully descended the front door steps and walked purposefully towards the corner of Bedford Square and Gower Street where I could see Mary was already waiting for me.

Suddenly, the stern words uttered by my father in a private man-to-man talk shortly after my sixteenth birthday crossed my mind. One must never be too intimate with the servants, he had admonished me after seeing Polly the chambermaid leaving my room looking flustered and breathing hard as if she had been running a race – as well she might, incidentally, because the lusty young lass had just ridden a vigorous St George on my stiff cock till I had ejaculated a copious emission of jism up her clinging cunney! My father had gone on to warn me that my behaviour would be bound to lead to problems when the relationship ended, and to be fair, the pater's advice was sensible enough. After all, though I would never simply turn out a girl who became troublesome (especially if she was *enceinte*), on the other hand, as my Indian pal, Prince Salman, used to say, why make problems for yourself in your own home?

But when I caught sight of Mary's pretty face, all thoughts of caution were thrown to the wind. Taking a deep breath, I marched on, and she ran towards me and lifted up her face to be kissed. Arm in arm, we walked down towards Great Russell Street where I hailed a taxi-cab and told

the driver to speed us post haste to the Alhambra
Theatre.

CHAPTER TWO

On The Town

MARY AND I ARRIVED IN good time for the first house at the Alhambra. Truthfully, I always preferred the second house which was usually noisier and jollier, but this evening, even the first house was crowded, though I did manage to buy two good seats in the fourth row of the *fauteuils* as the front stalls were grandly known.

'I've never sat in the posh half a crown seats before,' said Mary, as she looked up admiringly at the plush velvet curtains which would soon be raised for the first of the evening performances. [These 'posh' seats cost twelve and a half pence each! And even in the Alhambra, one of the smartest of the London halls, a place in the gallery would only cost sixpence. For their hard-earned money, Edwardian music hall audiences were treated to two hours of variety plus a few minutes of jerky Bioscope film 'reproducing the latest events from all parts of the world' – Editor]

We both enjoyed the deft juggling of the talented David Kent (though I inadvertently made Mary choke with giggling when I whispered, 'How on earth does he keep his balls in the

514

air like that?') and we 'oohed' and 'aahed' in amazement at the clever conjuring of the Continental illusionist Simon Barber who produced rabbits out of a hat and white doves out of his inside jacket pockets.

Yet whilst I appreciated the surprisingly clear voice of Seamus O'Toole, a bibulous Irish tenor whose staggering gait convinced me of my initial impression that he was definitely performing in a semi-drunken state, the cloying sentimentality of his songs about lost sweethearts and poor old mothers way back home bored me. But I did perk up after the interval when a twinkling little 'naughty but nice' soubrette named Suzanne Moserre came on and sang *Roly Poly For Mr Moley* and *You Can't Give Mother Any Cockles* and I joined in the choruses with gusto. Fred Karno's troupe acted out a hilariously funny series of sketches and Mary and I laughed till the tears ran down our faces.

After we applauded the company off the stage, I suggested to Mary that we skip the Bioscope and leave before the crush. She agreed and we walked the short distance up through Piccadilly Circus to the Jim Jam Club in Great Windmill Street [a notorious semi-secret rendezvous for Society rakes which is featured in several late Victorian and Edwardian 'underground' journals such as *The Oyster* and *The Memoirs Of Dame Jenny Everleigh*. In his younger days as Prince of Wales, King Edward VII, is known to have attended the extremely raunchy entertainments offered, including dance routines by naked chorus girls and the Club's best-known speciality, the infamous Victor Pudendum contests, about which Rupert will shortly explain – Editor]

I signed Mary in as my guest at the Jim Jam, though I could not help thinking to myself that bringing a girl to the Jim Jam was like bringing coals to Newcastle, for a chap who could not find a female companion at the Club had to be soft in the head – and for good measure, soft in the cock as well! But the reason why I wanted to take Mary to the Jim Jam – though I still feel slightly ashamed about it – was that despite its *louche* reputation, the Club had a strick code of conduct by which its patrons had to abide. For example, all male members who wore a red pocket handker-chief in the top pocket of their jackets or female members who wore a red rose on their dress or in their hair, signified their wish to remain totally *incognito* and would thus not be acknowledged or approached even by their best friends. Needless to say, I was sporting a handkerchief of the brightest red!

'Shall we dine in the restaurant or shall we have supper in one of the private dining-rooms?' I asked Mary, and she immediately plumped for taking our meal in one of the *salles privée*. I ordered whitebait, mulligatawny soup, roast chicken and the chef's fruit compote and whilst we waited for our room to be prepared, we drank glasses of ice-cold white wine. Mary revelled in seeing in person such 'toffs' as Sir Roger Tagholm, Bernard Osborne-Stott, Louis Highgate and all the other men-about-town about whom she had read in the weekly illustrated magazines. 'Do the men only come here to play cards or billiards? They are all walking about unaccompanied,' she remarked, but even before I could answer, her face broke into a sweet, dimpled grin and she said, 'I suppose this is a place where they can meet their sweethearts and make mad passionate love in the upstairs bedrooms.'

I returned her laugh and said, 'You may not be far from the truth, Mary but how did you know there are bedrooms at the Jim Jam?'

'I just guessed as much,' she retorted gaily, 'and Sir Roger Tagholm looks as if he will need one unless the lady he is talking to so intently is a known cock-teaser.'

Looking across the hall I saw Sir Roger engaged in deep conversation with Lady Elizabeth Stompson who was wearing a blue dress with one of the most daring decolletage I have ever seen. Sir Roger, who was a foot taller than Lady Elizabeth, was peering down at the ripe swell of her breasts with undisguised lust as he whispered something in her ear which made her shriek with laughter.

'This is a really ritzy place, Rupert,' said Mary (I had earlier asked her only to address me as 'sir' in the house). 'But what goes on at the Victor Pudendum contest I see advertised on the noticeboard?'

After she had promised not to reveal what I was about to tell her, I explained to Mary that the Victor Pudendum is a contest of elegant fucking that is held monthly in aid of a deserving cause. In this current year, all monies raised would be donated for the Society for Providing Comforts for Poor Families in the East End of London and the total could be quite a substantial sum, the highest being in 1906 when the Club collected £12,500 to send hundreds of slum children to the seaside for a summer holiday.

Quite simply, entrants (who are restricted to Club members or nominated guests at the discretion of the Victor Pudendum Committee) are required to fuck their lovers in front of a specially invited audience. An entrance fee of one hundred guineas per pair was payable together with an extra twenty five guineas if a gentleman preferred to partner a *demimonde* from Mrs Wickley's establishment in Macclesfield Street or Mr Baum's bar just off Soho Square.

The couples were awarded marks for style, grace and originality by a distinguished panel of judges and a gold cup and a purse of two hundred gold sovereigns was presented to the winner of each monthly contest. The entrance fee to watch (which included a bottle of champagne and light refreshments) was twenty pounds for a double ticket and reservations usually had to be made at least two months in advance to ensure getting a table.

'How wonderful,' breathed Mary, who had listened with ever widening eyes to my explanation. 'If you ever fancy entering, do let me be your partner. I'm sure we would do very well and I could certainly make good use of the money if we won!'

A uniformed flunkey sidled up and murmured to me that our room was ready so I escorted Mary up the stairs, nodding to the Prince of Mitten-

Derinen who had beaten me in the second round of the Club lawn tennis tournament held at Hurlingham in July, but who was now coming downstairs with his arm linked with that of a young, buxom blonde who I recognised from the *Daily Mirror* as the winner of the recent national swimming contests held at the Crystal Palace.

The room was tastefully furnished with a table and chairs and also in the darkened corner was a bed with beckoning fluffed up pillows and the sheet invitingly turned back.

But we were now quite hungry and we ate a tasty meal washed down with the fashionable new Buck's Fizz [champagne and orange juice – Editor]. After the waiter had cleared the table, set down a bubbling pot of coffee under a spirit lamp and finally retired, Mary stood up and said, 'Thank you for my lovely supper, Rupert. I've had a splendid time. The only slight problem is that I'm feeling rather warm – would it bother you very much if I took off some of my clothes?'

'Not in the slightest, my dear,' I said, also rising to walk across to the door and lock it. 'As it so happens, I'm also feeling very hot, so if you don't mind I think I'll join you.'

We swiftly stripped to our underclothes and I was clad only in my underpants when, dressed only in her knickers and a slip, Mary sat down next to me on the side of the bed. 'I do hope that Miss Carrington didn't tire you out at lunch-time,' she giggled as she slid her hand in the slit of my drawers to bring out my fast-stiffening cock. 'I've heard what goes on at that house what with the black man and his gigantic prick. Is it really as huge as they say?'

It has always been a source of wonderment to me how one's staff pick up all the gossip which circulates around one's friends and acquaintances. I rather suspect that much of the material one reads about in the columns of the popular newspapers is furnished from paid informants in some of the wealthiest and influential houses [nothing changes! – Editor] – but heaven forbid, if a change in fortune meant that I had to wait upon some of the nincompoops who treat their servants like a lower species of *homo sapiens*.

Nevertheless, I chose my words carefully as I did not want to spread any rumours about Nancy Carrington. 'I did hear that the chap does possess a tremendous whanger,' I said carelessly, 'but size isn't everything, you know.'

'Oh I do agree,' said Mary, running her fingers up and down my now rampant rod which was sticking up like a flagpole out of my undershorts. 'Within reason, my cunney has no problem adjusting to any thickness so long as the cock concerned is hard and stiff. But you men all think that a great big prick will make a girl weak at the knees – and honestly, it ain't necessarily so.'

She cradled my cock in her hand and added, 'Now look at your tadger, Rupert. It isn't the biggest I've ever seen but it's got a nice shape and I like the way it cheekily curves slightly to the left. Mmm, let's see if you've any spunk left in your balls since your lunch, because, despite what you may say, I'm sure that you had a jolly good fuck at Miss Carrington's!'

Her directness acted as a spur and we threw off

our remaining clothes in an ecstasy of abandonment. Our lips met in a passionate kiss which shook us both by its probing, violent tonguing as we explored each other's mouths. Then suddenly she wrenched her lips away and pulled me by my cock onto the bed. Obediently I lay down and then, with a quick smile, Mary's head was between my legs and her hands were clenched around the root of my straining staff. She kissed my knob and washed around it with long swirls of her pink tongue and then the sensual girl brought her mouth down and ran the length of her tongue along the width and length of my shaft, salaciously sucking my throbbing tool, sending waves of sheer, ecstatic pleasure throughout my entire body.

Mary sucked my cock with great relish, cleverly moving her pretty head so that the thrilling sensations ran throughout every last inch of my palpitating prick. At the same time, she smoothed her hand gently underneath my ballsack, lightly grazing the wrinkled, hairy skin with her fingernails. These movements were so exciting that very soon I was trembling with the approach of a searing wave of pleasure which was building up inexorably inside me and my shaft started to shiver uncontrollably as the sweet girl's warm, wet lips continued to encircle my swollen stiffstander.

'I'm coming, Mary, I'm going to shoot my sticky spunk down your throat,' I cried out hoarsely, and this lewd warning seemed to make her suck even more frantically on my quivering cock. The fire flared in my loins and globs of frothy jism spurted out into her receptive mouth. She licked and lapped up my spend, gobbling down my copious emission until I was milked dry.

To our joint delight, my trusty tool was still semi-stiff as I kissed Mary, sinking my tongue inside her mouth and tasting the salty tang of my own spend. I now stroked her cool thighs and she continued to manipulate my shaft which shot back up into a smart erection, pulsating with pleasure at her soft, sensual touch. Now my fingers strayed through her thick auburn curls, tracing their way down the length of her moist crack as she pressed her wet lips even more firmly against mine, clinging to me as tightly as she could, sighing with delight as she soaked up the electric thrills as our melting kisses stimulated us to a fresh round of fucking.

I let my tongue wash over her lips and trace a wet path down to her breasts which I suckled in turn until her rosy nipples were as hard as little red bullets. Mary moaned as we lay writhing naked on the bed and she parted her legs to allow me to run the palm of my hand over the crisp wetness of her open, naked pussey. I raised myself above her and she positioned my cock with her hand, guiding the knob in between the welcoming folds of her cunt.

But then I suddenly remembered what she had told me earlier in the bathroom about this being a bad day for fucking and asking me to go up her bum instead. 'Mary, wait a minute, don't you recall that you said I shouldn't fuck you today?' I gasped, willing myself not to slide my knob home between her cunney lips.

'Yes, but don't worry, when I checked the

calender, I found I had added up the days wrongly. Now's a good time and in any case, I've brought my linseed oil douche with me.' [Linseed oil was a favoured spermicide though not nearly as effective as a condom or 'the pill' – Editor]

Her reply put my mind to rest and so I plunged forward until my cock was embedded to the root in her tingling love sheath. All my senses were now in thrall to her passionate pussey as I pounded my proud prick in and out of her juicy cunt, pushing my cock in as Mary lifted her rear to receive her injection and my ballsack fairly cracked against her arse. She wriggled from side to side as my prick jerked inside her, stimulating every minute part of her tight little honeypot and I could see from the seraphic smile on her face how much she was enjoying this glorious fuck as we rocked furiously towards nirvana.

'Oooh! Oooh! I'm ready, Rupert! I'm ready for your sticky spunk. Fill me up, I want it all!' she hissed through clenched teeth. I jerked my hips as I crashed my cock inside her wonderful cunt one last time before shooting wad after wad of creamy white sperm deep inside her. As my jism splashed against the walls of her womb, Mary's fingernails clawed my back as she spent simultaneously with me and our bodies slapped together as she met each of my violent thrusts with an equally convulsive one of her own and we both screamed aloud with joy as we swam in our mutual love juices, our bodies threshing around wildly until the flow finally slowed and my chastened, shrinking shaft slipped out from the sopping embrace of Mary's love channel.

Gad, what a truly wonderful fuck, though as Mary had to get back to the house before midnight, we had to finish our frolicking after a short rest to recover our composure. However, I shall never forget that hour of lovemaking which, short but sweet, was one of the most passionate I have ever enjoyed.

Before we left the Club I collected my winnings from Bob Cripps, the head porter, who said to me admiringly, 'How on earth did you pick out Fairbridge's Organ, Mr Mountjoy? Did you have some inside information from the stable? I know that Captain Webb in *The Sporting Life* said he was a game little stayer but at best I would only have had a couple of bob each way on a rank outsider in such a strong field. Do you think he's worth backing for the Royal Hunt Cup? Here's your winnings, sir, forty quid exactly. Oh, and when I went round the bookie's to collect, Mr Applebaum asked me to present his compliments and say if you ever wanted to take your business elsewhere, he won't be in the least offended!'

I shrugged my shoulders as I passed the porter five shillings [twenty-five pence – Editor] for his trouble and grinned, 'Hymie Applebaum can't really grumble, Bob, can he? Look how we all came a cropper on Shortbread Biscuit, your friend's tip for the Derby. Remember how Sir Harold Brown had five hundred pounds on the nose and that he had the deuce of a job afterwards placating Mrs Archway and Lady Dyott when it came in one from last because he couldn't afford to take them to Paris for a week which he promised if they'd spend a night in a threesome with him at the Club.

'But as for Fairbridge's Organ, I thought it would be worth having a flutter because I was told the jockey would be trying, Bob, and that's half the battle won in my book. I'm not so sure about the big race, though. It was our old butler back home who tipped me off about the horse so when I see him next month I'll ask his opinion. He knows what he's talking about when it comes to horse-racing and I've often thought that old Goldhill could do much better than Captain Webb and all those other newspaper tipsters. I don't bet very often as you know and one of the reasons is that the horse can't tell me if he fancies his chances. But at least with one of Goldhill's tips, you're not as handicapped as all the other mugs who give their hard-earned money to the bookies.'

'Thank you, sir,' said Cripps, as he saluted me and pocketed his gratuity. 'You're quite right, of course, it is a mug's game. But so long as you don't lose what you really can't afford, I don't think any great harm is done. Mind, some of these idiots who chase their losses by doubling up their bets are crazy and almost deserve to be ruined.'

And with these words of wisdom, the porter hailed a taxi-cab for us and in just ten minutes Mary and I were tip-toeing upstairs to bed. 'You will come into my room when you've finished undressing, won't you?' Mary enquired, and I nodded my assent. 'I should say so, but give me twenty minutes or so as I want to have a shower first,' I said, as I gave her a little kiss, before retiring to my own second floor suite, whilst Mary climbed up to the attic.

I took off my clothes and used the privy before

taking a shower so it was nearer half an hour than twenty minutes before I crept upstairs to Mary's room. There was a soft light flooding out under the door so I knew she was not asleep and indeed I could hear little moans of passion coming from behind her door. Perhaps she was playing with a dildo, I thought, as I opened the door – but in fact, the sounds I had heard had not been coming from Mary but from the throat of young Edwards, the footman, who was sitting on the pretty girl's bed, his head thrown back and his eyes tightly closed and his stiff cock was standing up out of his opened trousers whilst Mary, who was stark naked, was busying herself palating his pulsating prick, running her pink tongue up and down the not inconsiderable shaft.

When she lifted her eyes and saw me standing there she lifted her head and murmured, 'Eddie, Mr Rupert's arrived, we can begin our fun in earnest now,' and then the bold miss looked up to me and said, 'I thought you'd like something a little different to end the evening. To start with, would you like to see Eddie fuck me? Perhaps you could tell us if we're good enough to enter this Victor Pudendum contest at the Jim Jam Club you were telling me about. It would be great fun and absolutely marvellous if we actually won – Eddie needs some more money to help his brother who is an apprentice carpenter and doesn't earn very much and God knows, my family are always broke.'

Frankly I was none too pleased at her little speech because Mary knew full well that I did not want any news of our evening out to filter through to the other servants. But she must have read my mind because she added, 'Oh, I know you wanted everything kept secret, sir, but don't worry. I wouldn't have mentioned a word to Eddie if I didn't know he could keep mum. I mean to say, he wouldn't get a reference if he ever split, would he, and I wouldn't ever let him in my cunney again.'

'She's right, sir,' said Edwards, nodding his head. 'Honestly, I'll be as silent as the grave. Colonel Wright knew I could be trusted and often asked me to poke one of the ladies he brought home if they were feeling randy and he was too tired to oblige.'

Well, at first I wasn't very keen at the prospect of sharing Mary with anybody, let alone a lowly footman, though this unworthy sentiment (for I am sure that the chap who cleans out the public conveniences at Oxford Circus is probably a more considerate bed-mate than some aristocratic toffee-nosed chump like Lord Slough whose unspeakable behaviour towards Miss Nellie Colchester led to his expulsion from the Jim Jam Club) soon passed, as I've always enjoyed an erotic exhibition – especially when I know that I will have an opportunity to join in if I so desire, and so I pulled up a chair and told the couple to proceed. If nothing else, it would be interesting to compare them to Standlake, Nancy Carrington's big-cocked black butler, and Lucy, her attractive and articulate maid.

Mary began by feeling for Edwards' prick which had shrivelled up and sunk back inside his drawers. She moved her hand up and down, giving his shaft a few vigorous rubs and then brought out his now stiffened shaft. Then she lowered her lips to kiss the uncapped knob but after a quick lick or two she lifted her head and said, 'Eddie, I think we'll do far better if you undress first.'

He swiftly shed his clothes and stood up as Mary ran her hands across his broad, hairy chest and then slid them down to grasp his thick, hard cock which was standing up to attention almost flat up against his belly. She then knelt down to take his cock inside her mouth, pushing out the cheeks of her bum to afford me a truly excellent view of both her cunt and arse-hole. This exciting sight made my own cock swell up to a throbbing stiffness and I could barely restrain myself from tearing open my trousers and frigging off then and there.

Mother Nature never ceases to amaze, for somehow Mary managed to take the whole of Edwards' bursting shaft between her lips. Then the libidinous little minx started to suck this giant pink lollipop, moving her head to and fro so that his cock moved smoothly back and forth though she took care that his knob was always engulfed inside her wet, warm mouth. Meanwhile, she juggled his balls gently through their hairy, wrinkled covering until she opened her mouth and whispered to him to lie down on the bed. He obeyed without demur and lay flat on his back, his rampant stiffstander sticking up as firmly as an iron bar under Mary's deft handling.

She then rose up, still clenching his cock in her hand and turned her peachy bum cheeks to me as she straddled him and inserted his knob between her pussey lips which I could see pouting out amidst her curly muff. Slowly she lowered herself upon his veiny shaft until she was sitting on his upper thighs with every last inch of cock crammed inside her dripping honeypot They stayed motionless for a few moments as in a *tableau vivant*, enjoying to the full the mutual sensations of repletion and possession, so delightful to each of the players of this most glorious sport afforded us by our beneficient Creator.

Soon it was time, however, to commence those soul-stirring movements which lead inexorably to the grand finale of frenetic fucking. I wriggled in my chair as I heard the squelchy sound of Mary's cunney sliding up and down Edwards' thick shaft and I licked my lips as I saw the gorgeous girl rub her titties as she drove down hard with a delighted squeal, spearing herself on his glistening tool until the lusty pair melted into a delicious state of ecstasy. They came together with great cries of release as Edwards shot a great gushing stream of spunk up her cunt mingling with Mary's own love juices which were running out of her love channel and soaking Edwards' pubic bush.

The footman swung himself out from under her gleaming, ripe young body and he was so intoxicated by the force of his spend that he rolled over too quickly and went crashing down onto the floor. Mary giggled as she looked over the bed and Edwards groaned but luckily he was unhurt though naturally a little shocked by his fall. She threw him a pillow which he tucked under his head as he gasped, 'Phew, what a great fuck! But you must both forgive me – I'm absolutely done in and I just must grab forty winks.'

'Don't worry about it, Edwards, we'll wake you up when we need you,' I cried and within a few seconds I could see his eyes close and his chest heave up and down as he sank directly into the arms of Morpheus. Of course, I was more than happy at his being *hors de combat* as, despite what my father disparagingly calls my egalitarian notions, I had no desire whatsoever to fuck in front of my well-endowed footman. Anyhow, I tore off my clothes and Mary jumped out of bed and stood stark naked in front of me as we embraced, standing belly to belly, with nothing between us except my thick, throbbing tool which was being delightfully squeezed between our tummies.

She grabbed hold of my prick and inspected my cock closely. 'You are lucky to have such a nice-looking cock, Rupert,' she said admiringly. 'It fits so nicely in my cunt, I really couldn't ask for more. It's one of the thickest I've had for some time too.'

'You're just saying that to flatter me,' I laughed, but she shook her mop of dark shiny hair. 'No, I mean it, really I do,' she insisted. 'Why, it's thicker than Eddie's for a start.'

I looked at her in disbelief but she squeezed my shaft again and said, 'It is, honest it is! You know, the trouble is that you can only see your cock when you look straight down at it whereas when, say, you see another gentleman's prick in the changing room, you're seeing it from a different angle which makes it look bigger.

'I heard Colonel Wright say that at a dinner party after the ladies had retired and I was helping Eddie clear the table,' she said with some satisfaction. 'It's so obvious when you stop and think about it.'

I couldn't help laughing as I hugged her tightly and then inclined her backwards until we fell upon the bed and we lay at full length, side by side but with my head by her calves, both of us as eager as could be to enjoy a good *soixante-neuf* to start the ball rolling. I began the programme by burying my head between her thighs and I inserted the tip of my tongue into her inviting little crack, sucking up the remains of her previous spend, making Mary writhe with passion as she pulled her face up to my prick and murmured, 'Let me honour His Highness with a twenty lick tonguing,' as she slipped my ruby knob inside her mouth. She worked on my helmet for a while and then bobbed her head in rhythm as she lapped at my trembling tool with great long licks from the base to the top which almost drove me insane with desire.

I was so aroused that I stopped nibbling at her erect little clitty and panted, 'Careful now, Mary, or I'll come too quickly, and that will never do.' She heeded my warning and scrambled round to lie flat on her back with her legs wide open. Naturally, I took my cue from her blatant posture and grasped my cock, giving it a quick rub before feeding into her juicy cunt. Without undue haste, I slid my knob between her pink pussey lips and inched my shaft inside her willing cunney. Then, once I was fully embedded, I started to fuck her with long, smooth strokes and we laughed merrily as I hovered above her, supporting myself on my arms. My balls slapped in slow cadence on her buttocks as I moved down, up and down again, increasing the pace as I thrust in with intensity until the voluptuous girl was squealing with joy.

As I approached the heights, I changed the tempo of my fucking to one of swift, short jabs. Mary rotated her bum cheeks as I pulsed in and out of her squelchy cunt. I climaxed first, my quivering cock squirting out jets of creamy jism and very soon afterwards Mary followed me over the top to a huge, shuddering orgasm. Luckily, my cock remained stiff for Mary's blood was on fire and she immediately wriggled over and thrust out her proud curvey backside at me. Nothing loath, I now proceeded to fuck her doggie-fashion, gripping her hips and sliding my still rampant rod between her bum cheeks and into her pussey. I fucked away with all the energy I could muster, the throbbing and contraction of her cunney muscles on my enraptured cock spurred me to even greater efforts until with a cry of triumph I pumped a second stream of boiling spunk inside her. This exhausting exercise made me dizzy with fatigue and I collapsed down beside her in an untidy heap whilst Mary rolled over and kissed my cheek with a warm smile of satisfaction on her lips.

By the time I had recovered, Edwards had woken up from his intense slumber and at Mary's invitation, had squeezed himself onto the bed. There wasn't enough room to lie down so we sat on the side of the mattress with Mary in between us. By Jiminy! This randy girl was really insatiable! In no time at all she had taken our two naked cocks in her sweet grasp and following her directions, Edwards held one taut tittie and I held the other and we squeezed and rubbed them as she squirmed with pleasure, holding on to our pricks all the while as she frigged our tools delightfully.

Mary was so aroused by this lewd scenario that she climaxed before either Edwards or I had squirted our spunk and so we waited impatiently to take our further orders from this lusty mistress of ceremonies. She took little time in deciding what she wanted, sliding back onto the pillow and demanding that Edwards tittie fuck her. He clambered over her and she cushioned his cock in the valley between her ample bosoms. The footman began sliding his shaft between them as she called out for me to pay homage to her cunney. So I knelt down between her legs and she wrapped her thighs around my neck as I buried my face in her curly thatch of black pussey hair. I kissed her salivating cunney lips and started by licking her slit in long lascivious swipes. The vermilion love lips soon turned red and parted and between them I felt for her stiff little clitty which I rolled around in my mouth.

'Ohhh! Ooooh! OOOH!' she yelped as I nibbled the edges of her clitty with my teeth. 'Suck harder, Rupert, suck harder and make me come!'

How could I disobey such a sweet command? I

sucked and slurped with renewed vigour, rolling my tongue round and round her love button, lapping up the aromatic love juice which was now flowing freely from Mary's juicy honeypot. Her whole body stiffened as she felt an oncoming orgasm and then her hips bucked violently, her back rippled and from her cunney there spurted a fine creamy emission, which flooded my mouth with its milky essence, that I swallowed down until Mary shuddered into limpness as her delicious crises melted away.

Meanwhile, Edwards' cock was still being massaged between the soft globes of Mary's breasts. The sight of his throbbing boner slewing its way back and forth stimulated her so much that she pulled his bottom cheeks towards her until his prick was above her face and she popped the hot staff inside her mouth. I could see her tongue work up and down, licking the entire length of his tadger, taking playful little nips at the sensitive tube of cockflesh, and when she realised that he was about to spend, her hands flew up to his balls and, smoothing her hands over them, she gulped down the copious emission of jism which poured out from the young footman's twitching tool.

I dived down to kiss her pussey once again and instinctively she opened her legs to make the swollen love lips more accessible. My tongue moved, delving, probing, sliding from the top of her sopping crack to the base of her cunney-hole, my tongue lapping up the tangy cunt juice which was cascading out of her pussey.

Then I stiffened the tip of my tongue and

started to lick the soft, puffy inner lips and I eagerly inhaled the fresh zephyr of feminine aroma which arose from her and I made her moan with ecstasy as I pushed the tip of my tongue deep into Mary's love channel. Her hips were gyrating wildly as I stroked my tongue in and out of her and I licked her rhythmically up and down, delighting in the feel of the swollen flesh pulsing in eager response. Her clitty grew harder each time my tongue flicked across it, jerking and rising up to meet my wicked little laps. I moved my head up to concentrate on her clitty and I must say how much I loved the way it grew like an excited miniature penis as I tickled it with my tongue. I continued to tease it, driving her wild with slow, firm strokes until she fairly screamed out, 'Fuck me, Rupert, please fuck me! I must have your big cock inside my cunt!'

I gave her cunney a final *au revoir* kiss and flipped the quivering girl over to fuck her doggie-style. This greatly appealed to her for she stuck her rounded backside high in the air and reached back to fondle my balls as I parted her bum cheeks and pushed my prick into her drenched, welcoming cunney. Holding on to her delicious bottom I began pounding in and out of her cunt with long, deep strokes, raising the tempo from *lento* to *andante* and building up to an inevitable *furioso*. She squealed delightedly and yelled out, 'Now! Now! Shoot your spunk up my pussey, you randy rascal!'

I was ready to oblige as I could already feel the first pulsations of an oncoming spend as the jism started to boil up in my balls though I hung on for as long as possible, drawing out the joust to a thumping climax. My sinewy cock slewed a passage through her tingling cunney and Mary was tearing at the sheets and moaning into the pillow as with a final heave I coated her cunt with a fine spurt of sticky sperm as together, we rode the wind . . .

The three of us licked and lapped, sucked and fucked until the first rays of the morning sun lit up Mary's bedroom. I hastily threw on my clothes and said to the two servants, 'Mary, tell Mrs Harrow that you are suffering from a severe headache. Edwards, you'll have to rise up at the usual time, I'm afraid, but don't come in and wake me. Now I will be going out after breakfast and I won't need your services until I return this evening. You can also tell Mrs Harrow that you feel unwell and that you will also have to retire to bed. The good lady will assume that you and Mary have both caught the same germ and will not question either of you too closely.

'However, to be fair to the rest of the staff, I would suggest that you both get up by about two o'clock to help out with any remaining domestic duties.'

They thanked me for proposing this kind stratagem and quietly I made my way back to my room and fell into a deep sleep from which I did not wake until almost ten o'clock. As I washed and shaved it occured to me that I had really been foolish to fuck with my footman and chambermaid. I might be able to trust Mary but as the old saying goes, no man is a hero to his valet, though it would be shockingly unfair to dismiss

Edwards who had done nothing dishonourable.

Well, it would all depend on his behaviour when I sat down to breakfast. Would he be arch? Would he be familiar? Or would he put on airs? Perhaps he wouldn't even come in with the newspaper and the post. But thank goodness, all my worries were unfounded, for Edwards greeted me with his usual deferential 'good morning, sir,' as he passed me the *Daily News* and the single letter which had arrived earlier in the morning.

A lucky escape, nevertheless, I mused, and resolved never to repeat the mistake as I read the short note addressed to me by Henry Bascombe-Thomas, an old chum from St Lionel's Academy, who I had not seen for a year – since after leaving Cambridge University, he had decided to cross the Atlantic and spend a year in America, studying modern art under Professor Sidney Cohen of New York University.

Henry was an artistic cove, much given to writing occasionally good verse, painting some rather rum pictures and wearing his hair far too long for our headmaster, Dr Keeleigh's taste. Some foolish fellows at St Lionel's wrongly assumed that Henry was a woofter [homosexual – Editor] and soon found out that though of an eminently peaceful disposition, if pushed too far, Henry could also deliver an uppercut to the jaw, though like myself, he abhorred physical violence and refused (again like myself) to be considered for the school boxing team.

I should add that like a surprising number of very clever chaps, Henry was terribly absent-minded – which explained why his letter to me arrived a full two days after he had posted it from Southampton as he had addressed it to Bedford Street instead of Bedford Square. However, no harm had come from the delay as you will see, dear reader, from this copy of his message which I had deciphered with no little difficulty from his unreadable scrawl. It read as follows:

Dear Rupert,

I returned to England last week on the SS Shmockle, the flagship of the Hanseatic Line owned by Count Gewirtz of Galicia who happened to be on board. The weather was inclement for the first two days but all in all I had a most enjoyable journey which I'll tell you about when we meet.

Could we lunch on October 29 at the Jim Jam? I'm on my way to Chichester this afternoon to see my parents but I'll be coming up to town tomorrow evening and staying at the Jim Jam for a week till I find myself some rooms. Unless I hear from you (you can telegraph me at The Old Vicarage, Mackswell Avenue, Kendall, Near Chichester), I'll assume you can make it. Shall we say one o'clock in the first floor bar?

Looking forward immensely to seeing you again,
Henry

Now I had planned a semi-artistic kind of day myself. This would have started with a brisk stroll down to Holywell Street to see the new prints from Paris at the Birmingham Gallery where Mr Malcolm Campbell owns the largest selection of erotic pictures in the country, kept under lock and key away from the general public and shown only for viewing by selected customers. Afterwards, I would have hailed a cab to Pall Mall to take luncheon followed by an afternoon snooze at The National Reform, one of my more respectable clubs.

However, even though I had spent some time at the Jim Jam the previous evening with Mary, I wanted to see Henry again and hear all his news. So I decided to postpone my visit to the Birmingham Gallery to another day and instead I thought I would spend a quiet morning browsing amongst Colonel Wright's bookshelves as my landlord was an avid reader and collector of first editions. There was little of interest in the newspaper, so after demolishing a bowl of porridge, a full plate of bacon, eggs, sausages and five slices of buttered toast, I took my third cup of tea into the library and scoured the shelves for something interesting to read.

By pure chance I pulled out a book titled *Modern Women* and opening it to the title page I read that this leather bound tome was of 'conversations with various girls in Belgravia and Mayfair' by a Mr Oliver Dunstable, an author whose writing was hitherto unknown to me. There was, however, a preface written by none other than Sir Rodney Burbeck, one of the gayest Lotharios in London. He had written: *'This fresh and original book gives us an excellent verbal picture of what today's men and women are thinking and what they want from their counterparts. There is a perception and a sense of humour in his writing which makes Mr Dunstable not only delightful to read but well worth thinking about afterwards. The illustrations consist of portraits which will be recognised at once by anyone familiar with current members of Society.'*

539

This was praise indeed! And from such a source as Sir Rodney, it surely heralded some gallant writing, which always afforded me the greatest enjoyment. So I settled down with a glow of anticipation on my face as I read Mr Dunstable's account of his interview with Melissa Rotherwick, perhaps the prettiest of all the debutantes who 'came out' in 1905, who I remembered meeting at Lord Bresslaw's Autumn Ball last year. She was one of the most beautiful young women one could wish to see, with gold-dusted light-brown hair, expressive large eyes, rich ruby lips and pearly white teeth.

Mr Dunstable had had the good fortune to meet her at the splendid country mansion of Stockleigh Hall, her family country seat down in Kent and she talked openly of her belief that further education should be given to young people about matters appertaining to *l'art de faire l'amour*.

As this book was printed privately, I doubt if many readers will be acquainted with Melissa's frank account of how she and her schoolfriends were forced to kidnap, if this is not too strong a term, a willing young man, so as to find out for themselves the joys of a good fuck. Therefore I propose to bring her words to a wider audience by reproducing them here. The uninhibited young girl was telling Mr Dunstable of her years spent at Mrs Bartholomew's Boarding School For Young Ladies not far from Redstock at the foot of the Mendip Hills.

Melissa Rotherwick told Mr Dunstable: *It will be readily understood, I am sure, that being all of the same sex, we found it most frustrating to be shut up in a*

540

friendly but strictly enclosed establishment in the heart of Somerset without a single member of the male species to be found anywhere on the premises with the exception of our chaplain, Reverend Jonathan Crawford, a nice old gentleman of seventy-three who conducted services every Sunday morning in the school chapel.

As may be readily imagined, we were forced to explore amongst ourselves, so to speak, for our private pleasures and it was hardly surprising that there were many close, emotional ties which flourished between the young ladies.

However by the time my pals and I had reached the dizzy heights of the sixth form, such juvenile 'pashes', as we called these intra-feminine love affairs, had palled and we were ripe for plucking by any lucky young man who might come our way. But we were so strictly chaperoned away from anything masculine (even the school cat was a plump ginger tabby!) that it seemed we would never be able to sample the fruits of sensual passion until we had left Mrs Bartholomew's custody.

Yet despite these restrictions, as the old saw has it, love laughs at locksmiths, and in the course of time a day dawned when some of us were able to put the theoretical knowledge we had gained from the copy of Dr Nigel Andrews' Fucking For Beginners, which my friend Annabel had smuggled into school after borrowing the copy she found in her brother's room during a Christmas vacation, to a most pleasant practical use.

This event happened by a series of fortunate circumstances and involved George Cox, the aptly named young nephew of Reverend Crawford, who was spending a few days down in Somerset visiting his elderly relation. But first I had better explain that at Mrs Bartholomew's, one of the benefits of seniority was that on Wednesday afternoons members of the upper sixth form were allowed out of bounds to stroll unaccompanied along the path, through Farmer Trippett's meadow, down to the banks of the small stream which ran between his fields.

Well, one fine spring afternoon, during my penultimate term at the school, my friends Annabel and Sheena accompanied me for a walk along this path and we were discussing some abstruse mathematical problem which had been set that morning by Mrs Bartholomew herself. I must give my old head teacher due credit at this point and record the fact that science and mathematics played major roles in our curriculum, unlike the majority of similar academies for young ladies where only the arts are studied in any serious way. Anyway, we were deeply engrossed in this rather learned conversation when Annabel suddenly stopped talking and I saw her jaw drop and her mouth hang open as she stood stock still, staring across to the far bank of the stream.

Sheena and I followed her gaze and we were also struck dumb by what we saw – for lying flat on his back, fast asleep, was none other than George Cox, who had obviously taken a dip in the river and followed it by a luncheon of sandwiches and the best part of a bottle of white wine which lay beside in an ice-box. This in itself would not have been such an extraordinary sight but for the fact that George had divested himself of his clothes for his swim and had not bothered to put them back on again afterwards, thinking no doubt that as he was on private land, no-one would be coming by! So there he lay, naked as nature intended, and for the first time in our lives, we three girls were given the opportunity to look at a full-sized genuine penis.

Frankly, at first sight, this squashed up tube of flesh which protruded out of a growth of mossy pubic hair and lay limp over George's thigh did not impress us.

'It doesn't seem nearly as big as the pricks shown in *Fucking for Beginners*,' commented Sheena, and Annabel agreed with her, saying that the dildo she had purloined from her sister was also of a greater length and girth.

'Wait a moment though, girls,' I said to them. 'Surely we must only compare like with like and so we mustn't pass judgement upon George's cock until we've actually seen it standing up to attention. You may recall that Dr Andrews wrote in Chapter Three about the vast majority of cocks all swelling up to about the same size even though some look bigger than others when simply dangling between men's legs.'

Annabel nodded sagely and said, 'Yes, I think you are absolutely right, Melissa, but *experientia docet*, as Miss Bartholomew would doubtless say. I suggest that we find out exactly what a stiff prick actually looks like for ourselves. I'm sure that George won't mind. He's fast asleep anyhow and if we keep very quiet, we might be able to play with his cock without waking him up.'

This sounded like an extremely sensible course of action to me and Sheena also agreed to take part in this voyage of sensual discovery. So we slipped quietly over the ramshackle wooden bridge and sat ourselves carefully round George who was still apparently fast asleep. Boldly, Annabel took hold of his soft shaft whilst I tenderly lay my palm underneath the hairy, wrinkled ballsack underneath it.

Thanks to our careful perusal of Dr Andrews'

valuable tome, we were not too alarmed when George's tool stirred as Annabel clutched it in her fist and began to swell and thicken. Sheena now entered the fray by drawing back the skin at the top to reveal a smooth pink mushroom shaped knob. I withdrew my hand from George's ballsack which had tightened up as his prick had begun to grow and ran my fingers round it as well. I was fascinated by the feel of this, my first naked cock, which felt like an ivory column covered in warm velvet.

'It looks far better now,' Annabel commented with all the satisfaction of having been proved right. With a glint in her eyes Sheena said, 'George has a very pretty prick indeed and the way it throbs when I touch it is making me tingle all over.'

Her words made me aware that I was also experiencing a buzz of excitement throughout my body. My titties were as hard as two little rubbery nuts, my legs were trembling and my pussey was throbbing with the same kind of urgency I experienced when playing with myself, only stronger and more insistent. A novel thought then entered my head and I said to my companions, 'I wonder whether this cock tastes as good as it looks,' and I kissed the very tip of the smooth dome of the uncapped helmet. Remembering what I had read in Dr Andrews' book, I licked round the knob and then I opened my lips and inch by inch, took the throbbing tool in my mouth. As my lips gently slipped further and further down its length, I sucked and pulled at the hot, hard shaft with my lips and I noticed that Annabel had now slipped her hands under George's ballsack and was very carefully caressing his testes.

It was at this stage that George's eyes began to flutter open and he looked on in amazement as I continued to palate his prick whilst Annabel now busied herself by licking his balls. 'I must be dreaming,' he muttered and struck himself a sharp blow on the cheek.

'No, I'm awake all right,' he said aloud, trying to reassure himself that he had not taken leave of his senses. 'This is really happening. To the best of my knowledge I'm not simply the victim of a delicious hallucination. It's still Wednesday afternoon and I have just woken up after falling asleep after lunch and now I find I'm being sucked off by two beautiful girls from Mrs Bartholomew's school.'

Poor George may have been dreadfully puzzled but he was no fool and with a contented sigh he decided not to tempt providence by asking further questions and simply laid back to enjoy the exquisite sensations of the soft, wet lips and tongues running over his cock and balls. 'A-a-a-h!' he gasped and he shot a jet of frothy creamy essence into my mouth. Instinctively I swallowed his sticky emission and though a tad too salty for my taste, I knew it would not harm me, for as our mentor Dr Andrews noted, fresh semen is highly nutritive. [Indeed it is, as it contains substantial amounts of vitamins and some traces of zinc and nickel – Editor]

However, as the good doctor also said, the tang may vary from man to man, which made me resolve to have another suck, preferably of another meaty specimen, for whilst I much enjoyed milking George's member, I wanted to try out the flavour of other suitable young men, for as Dr Andrews commented, the flavour of spunk is an acquired taste which often takes a little time to appreciate.

But meanwhile Sheena now demanded a turn to gobble George's prick and the dear lad kindly proferred his limp shaft without hesitation saying only that he would appreciate a few minutes' recuperation from the prodigious spend of seed caused by my own superb sucking of his cock.

To help revive his crestfallen member I told George to get up on his knees in front of me as I lay back and parted my legs to give him a wonderful view of my furry thatch and pink cunney lips. I took his hand and placed it on my already dampening mound. 'Oh my what a truly beautiful cunt,' he breathed, as the fingers of his left hand splayed my outer lips and the fingers of his right ran up and down the length of my love slit. Gently, he inserted his forefinger between my pussey lips and my hips rose up to greet the welcome visitor.

He finger-fucked me for a little while but soon his head dived down between my thighs and I was in raptures as he found my excitable little clitty and my pussey started to spend freely under the voluptuous titillations of the randy youth's velvety tongue. I clasped my legs around his head as he licked and lapped on my tingling cunney and I screamed with joy as I quickly reached the pinnacle of sensual delights.

I released George's head from between my crossed legs and Annabel and Sheena pushed him flat on his back and he obeyed with alacrity their command to lie quite still. Sheena smoothed her hand over his flat stomach and let her fingers wander into his thick growth of pubic curls. She licked her lips with gusto as she gazed down upon his thickening shaft that was not yet fully erect but which had a lovely, heavy look about it. She grasped the swelling staff in her hand and gently squeezed it – and immediately George's cock stood up in full, glorious erection, his rosy helmet now bared as Sheena helped snap back the covering foreskin. Her lips now swooped down and she began to kiss and lick the

*red mushroomed knob, dwelling around the ridged edge
and moving slowly up and down the underside before
sucking in as much of the shaft as possible into her
mouth. She frigged his prick firmly with her fingers,
licking and lapping, as she clamped her lips over his
cock, sucking furiously until she was forced to release it
as she felt she was in imminent danger of choking.*

*Whilst this was taking place, I was fingering myself,
opening up my pussey even further and, when George
withdrew from Sheena's mouth, I reached up and pulled
his glistening, wet cock towards my aching cunt. Then,
as if I had been doing this all my life, I raised my legs
and grasped him round the waist and for the first time
savoured the indescribably delicious feeling of my cunt
being filled with a real live prick slewing a path
backwards and forwards as he began to fuck me in
earnest.*

*Of course, my hymen had long ago been broken by a
combination of horse-riding and frigging with friends
and the aid of a dildo, so there was no pain but only a
most delightful pleasure as George's cock pistoned deep
inside my cunney and then slid back to repeat the effort.
Also, I could lie back and enjoy my first fuck without
worry as my monthies were due within forty eight
hours.* [Hardly infallible reasoning but certainly
this is a most unlikely time in the cycle for any
unwanted consequences – Editor]

*By now my body was responding as if by instinct and
I was thrusting my hips up to meet him time and time
again. I responded with vigour, now carried away
totally as he rubbed my titties whilst his sinewy rod
crashed its way through my sopping love channel. Then
my back arched and I realised in one unforgettable
instant that for the first time in my life I was spending*

547

with a man's cock inside me . . .

Suffice it to say that I came and I came and I came and when at last George's prick quivered and spurted a sticky libation of spunk inside me I was so overcome that I almost swooned with ecstatic joy. George too was similarly overcome and collapsed on top of me as I lay heaving and panting whilst the last waves of this gigantic spend washed over me.

So ended my first fuck. Annabel and Sheena kindly helped me dress and we arranged to smuggle George into our dormitory that very evening for some further fun and games. Annabel also had the brilliant idea of asking George to bring a friend with him if he possibly could, as even such a stout hearted and well-endowed cocksman as he could not hope to satisfy six lusty young maidens. As luck would have it, his old school chum, Clive Hampstead (who later became renowned for his abilities to perform cunnilingus, until his marriage to a wealthy American heiress led him to settle in Chicago), lived not five miles away and was happy to join us in a riotous night of sucking and fucking about which I cannot tell you as at least one of the girls concerned is now the wife of a very important personage indeed and she would be horrified if her participation in this orgy of sensuality was ever made public.

I closed the book and stood up with a raging hard-on as I thought about how divine it would be to fuck the gorgeous Melissa Rotherwick who, as one could gauge from this graphic account of her first fuck, was obviously a generous and free-spirited girl. I made a mental note to check if by any chance her name appeared on the members' list of the Jim Jam Club before I met

Henry Bascombe-Thomas there for luncheon.

Reluctantly I decided against summoning Mary to be fucked or at least to frig or suck off my uncomfortably stiff cock. It was not only my earlier resolve to cease fucking servant girls which kept my thumb away from the bell, but also the thought that it would be sensible to give my prick a rest in case Henry and I were offered invitations to one of the wild private parties which certain ladies had taken to holding at the Club on weekday afternoons.

So I walked slowly round the room three times, emptying my mind of everything, except the question of how many books might be stacked on the shelves of this well-stocked library. In time, my attempt to solve this problem by assessing the approximate number of books on one average shelf and multiplying this figure by the number of shelves did the trick and my rampant stiffstander slowly subsided. I went into the hall and called Edwards to say that I would probably return around five o'clock but in the unlikely case of needing to speak to me urgently, he could contact me at the Jim Jam Club whose telephone number I scribbled on a sheet of paper and pressed into his hand.

Now as the rain which had pattered down earlier in the morning had subsided and enough patches of blue were visible through the clouds, I had planned to walk down to Great Windmill Street – but just as I strode away from the front door, a carriage drawn by two smartly attired black horses pulled up alongside me and a familiar voice called out to me. 'Hello there, young Rupert, can I give you a lift?'

I looked round to see the occupant of the carriage throw open the door. I walked across and squinted inside to see if I had correctly identified the owner of the rather fruity tones. And yes, I was right, for leaning against the expensive kid leather upholstery was the portly figure of Colonel Stanley Gooner formerly of the Ninth Punjab Rifles, a former comrade-in-arms of my father and one of my parents' oldest friends.

The Colonel, in his early days, had won an award for gallantry whilst serving on the North West frontier in an incident that made headlines in the popular newspapers. After his patrol had been ambushed by the Pathans, he escaped, but returned dressed in the clothes of a native woman and in an audacious single-handed operation, he managed to rescue two captured colleagues whose pricks were about to be amputated (without even the benefit of anaesthetic) by a mob of angry Afghans. I am hazy as to exactly how he managed to place a pistol against the balls of the much-feared enemy commander, a bandit notorious for his brutality, but the stratagem worked and the then Captain Gooner was able to bargain successfully for the freedom of the prisoners and himself.

Yet Colonel Gooner could never be described as a typical Army officer. He was a man of progressive political views and championed the rights of the indigenous people in a book about his time in India, published after he had left the services. I had always known him as a jolly, amiable old buffer, far removed, one must add,

550

from those many retired Indian Army officers whose brains have perhaps been affected by the heat and dust of the sub-continent. Perhaps readers have come across these poor chaps themselves, the ones who spend their days writing obscure tracts on the Egyptian Pyramids in the reading rooms of public libraries, or travelling to meetings to propound some fanciful idea about a secret international conspiracy of one-legged freemasons or about the Welsh race being descended from one of the lost ten tribes of ancient Israel.

'Where are you off to, my boy?' enquired the Colonel genially.

'I have a luncheon appointment with a friend who I am meeting near Piccadilly Circus,' I said, a statement which, if not false, was certainly economical with the truth as I doubted whether Colonel Gooner would approve of the raffish Jim Jam Club.

'Climb aboard then, I'm going that way myself and it's no trouble whatsoever to drop you off wherever you want,' he said, and not wishing to offend, I complied with his instruction. The Colonel disliked the motor car and owned one of the few horse-driven carriages still to be seen around the West End of London. We lurched forward and then as I sank back against the soft, comfortable seat, one of the horses broke wind with a quite astonishing ferocity.

'Oh, pardon me,' said the Colonel, and though I should have contained myself, I replied, 'That's quite all right, sir. If you hadn't spoken I would have assumed it was the horse.'

But all was well for Colonel Gooner laughed loudly and said, 'Good one, old boy, very good indeed! I must remember to recount your witty riposte at my Club. So how have you been spending your time off in old London town? Enjoying yourself to the full, I'll be bound, and why not for heaven's sake, you're only young once. Tell me though, you must have heard about this grand reception back home for His Majesty in which your father has been involved. I'll be there myself, as my wife's brother is a local landowner near Boroughbridge and he's also on the organising committee for the royal visit.'

He was most pleased when I told him that I was of course going back home for this important event. 'Excellent! Mrs Gooner and I will look forward to seeing you there. We live in the country ourselves as you know, but so many of my old friends live in London that I must spend a couple of weeks here every so often to keep in touch with them.'

We were clipping our way briskly down Shaftesbury Avenue when I called upon the driver to halt. 'I'll get off here, sir, if I may,' I said, shaking hands with the Colonel, 'and I look forward to seeing you again in York.' Little did I realise just how soon I would see him again – far, far sooner than I could have expected!

I crossed the road and bought a button-hole from an itinerant flower seller. My sixpence was received with the usual blessings upon my head and I made my way up Great Windmill Street to the discreet entrance of the Jim Jam Club. Cripps was on duty and was eager to pick up any racing tips, but alas, I had heard nothing further from old Goldhill and was forced to disappoint the porter, who nevertheless passed to me the name of a horse Sir Harold Brown had given him as a good each-way bet in the two o'clock race at Chepstow that afternoon. 'It's a fast filly called Big Brenda, Mr Mountjoy, and I reckon the odds won't be less than twelve to one. What do you think?' he asked me.

'Well now, Cripps,' I said carefully, 'you must be familiar with the old saying, "He who decides to bet each way/Lives to bet another day!"

'Sir Harold's gone through a lean patch lately and it's about time he picked a winner, so I'll risk a pound each way on Big Brenda. Will you place the bet with Hymie Applebaum for me?'

I gave Cripps two pound notes and sauntered upstairs to the bar. Although it was almost ten past one, there was no sign of Henry Bascombe-Thomas. I sat down and ordered a whisky and soda from a passing waiter and hoped that my absent-minded chum had not forgotten the appointment which he himself had asked me to keep with him.

In fact my worry was unfounded for I had time only to pour the soda into my Scotch when I looked up to see Henry striding towards me. I stood up and greeted him. 'Hello, stranger, how nice to see you again,' I said warmly as we shook hands.

'A pleasure to see you, Rupert,' he responded, pumping my hand. 'I'm so pleased you were free for luncheon. It's been a long time since we broke bread together. To be exact, it would be a couple of days before I sailed for New York when you, Frank Folkestone and Prince Salman laid on a splendid farewell dinner for me at Romano's. So what's the news with you, Rupert? Neither of us wrote to each other as often as we should have done. But Frank Folkestone did mention in one of his letters that your Uncle Humphrey has provided you with the wherewithal for a year off doing very little indeed except fuck pretty girls, you lucky so-and-so! Or has some clever beauty managed to get you to put a ring on her finger?'

I grinned and replied, 'No, though I've fingered quite a few rings since we last met! Still, whilst it's true that I'm taking a break from my studies, you've been to America, which is something I'd love to do. Have you had a rewarding time, Henry? Have you painted much yourself? And what brings you back to Britain?'

'I'll answer your questions in reverse order,' he said with a smile, as we rose and walked into the dining-room where we were seated at one of the best tables overlooking the busy street below. 'I came back simply because my course with Professor Sidney Cohen ended and there was no further need for me to stay in New York.

'And I do still paint, but only for my own pleasure. I now know and accept my limitations, Rupert, which are – well, those of a talented amateur and not a gifted professional. That's how Professor Cohen delivered his verdict on my work and I wasn't too disappointed because the truth is that it wasn't very different to my tutor's back here in Britain.'

The head waiter came up to us and after we

ordered our meal Henry continued, 'His verdict doesn't mean that I can't be involved in the world of art. I've written some critiques for the New York papers and I'd like to do the same in London. I feel I have something to say after spending a year away. God, it was refreshing to leave that dreadful insular resistance to modern painting which one finds here in England. People have told me that third-rate British pictures are still preferred to the new, exciting paintings shown in Paris, Rome and Madrid. I want to help change this head-in-the-sand attitude.

'What's really exciting though, Rupert, is that Professor Cohen, whose influence is very substantial in the New York art world, generously gave my name to Clive Labovitch, the wealthy owner of a leading gallery on Fifth Avenue who wants to set up an exhibition of the most promising, exciting young artists from all over the world. The Professor suggested that I act as his agent in England when I return to London. After discussing the project with me, Mr Labovitch agreed to the proposal, and has transferred five thousand dollars to a bank account over here to be spent on buying for this event which will be staged in New York next Spring.'

Well, naturally, even before Henry had finished speaking I was wondering whether this information would be of use to the lovely Diana Wigmore. I explained to Henry how my closest girl friend was a talented artist who was living in Paris but who would be coming to Britain shortly. An idea struck me – if I could only persuade Henry to come up to York for the grand Royal reception, he would be able to meet Diana and see some of her pictures there, as she was bringing a selection over from France so that Nancy Carrington could have the opportunity to purchase a painting or two for her father's collection.

The only problem was how to interest Henry enough in Diana's work to travel up North so soon after returning to London. Surprisingly, for he showed little interest in politics except to support the radical Liberals, Henry was a staunch Republican and unlike Nancy Carrington, for instance, had no desire whatsoever to hob-nob with the King, so partying with all the swells would have no appeal for him.

But the promise of a good fuck – now that was another matter! I leaned across the table and told him all about Diana, Nancy and the whole business of my going up to see my folks and attending the reception for the King. I invited him to join Nancy and myself and stay a few days with my family at Albion Towers.

'You really must come up with us,' I urged him. 'My parents would be delighted to see you again and you know how interested my mother is in art. She would so enjoy hearing all your news about any up and coming American artists. And talking of up and coming, old boy, Nancy Carrington is a very attractive young lady who simply adores fucking, as does Diana, who particularly liked taking part in a whoresome foursome. I guarantee that you'd be dipping your brush into a fresh pot of paint every night if you take up my invitation.'

Henry's eyes lit up and he said, 'Gosh, you certainly make the trip sound extremely tempting.

But I really have a tremendous amount of work to do in London and I hadn't planned on spending any time out of town. On the other hand, all work and no play makes Jack a dull boy, eh? When do you plan to go?'

'In just over a couple of weeks time,' I replied promptly. 'The big party is on November 15 so Nancy and I thought we'd go up on the previous day. We hadn't decided exactly when we'd go back, but I might stay a few days and visit my Uncle Humphrey and look up some old friends.'

'And you say that I might get the chance to look up some new ones?' Henry quipped wittily. 'I don't think I can pass up such an opportunity, Rupert, so I'll take up your invitation with grateful thanks. I don't mind telling you that I'm in desperate need of a good fuck. Whilst I can't grumble too much about the availability of willing girls in New York, though they are probably a little more inhibited than in London, I've been forced to live like a monk for the month or so. Both the girls I was fucking in Manhattan were unavailable during the last three weeks of my stay and to make matters worse there were no available women on board ship on my journey home.'

'Poor you,' I sympathised, as I refilled his glass with the excellent Club claret. 'Yet I was given to understand that on Atlantic crossings, except during the winter months, there are always a number of unattached females on board eager for masculine company.'

'Maybe, but I was unlucky enough to be a passenger on a ship which was an exception to the rule. The only consolation was that I struck up a friendship with a girl named Jenny Cameron, the Scottish governess of an American family coming to live in London for six months whilst the *pater familias* travelled around Europe on business.

'Jenny was very happy to be coming home to her native Scotland after working for a year in Washington. She was a bonny Scottish lass of twenty-two whose light freckled skin and long reddish hair set off her well-made young body. Perhaps her best attributes were her large breasts which jutted out proudly like two firm spheres.

'Well, on the fourth evening, I engaged her in conversation after dinner and we talked over a lemon squash in one of the lounges (for she was tee-total and I had already put away a bottle of wine during the evening meal). I gazed longingly at these two beauties as we walked back along the deck to our cabins which happened to be very close to each other. Naturally, she slept in the same first class suite as the two children in her charge. After formally shaking hands and parting company at her cabin door, I wished Jenny good-night and I walked back alone very disconsolately to my own quarters.

'I undressed quickly and as it was rather warm in the cabin I lay on the bed naked as I reached over to thumb my way through a copy of *The Oyster*, a "horn" magazine which Frank Folkestone had posted to me every so often. As I thumbed my way through the magazine, the randy stories soon made my shaft stiffen up and demand to be exercised. I took my rock-hard cock in my hand and slowly rubbed it up and down as I closed my eyes and fantasised about running my hands across Jenny's magnificent breasts, of handling her delicious, ripe titties and then placing my hot, throbbing prick in her cunt . . .

'I was on the very verge of spunking when my reverie was disturbed by a gentle knock on my door. I jumped up and called out, "Who's that?" and my heart began to pound when I heard the soft reply, "It's me, Jenny Cameron. Henry, can I come in for a moment?"

'I slipped on a dressing gown and rushed across to open the door where Jenny stood clad in a blue silk night-robe. "Hello, Henry, I hope I haven't disturbed you," she said with a slightly worried look.

' "Not in the slightest, it's lovely to see you again so soon. Is all well though? Are the children all right?"

' "Oh yes, they're sound asleep and won't wake up till morning, so I thought I might join you in a wee night-cap," she said, and then impishly added as she looked slightly down-wards, "but I think you had something else on your mind when I knocked on the door."

'I followed her amused gaze downwards and with horror saw that my still erect truncheon was poking out between the folds of my dressing gown. I was so flustered that I sat down heavily on the side of the bed, my face burning and my cock quickly shrank back into its normal flaccid state.

'But to my overwhelming relief, Jenny had not been offended at all by the unintentional exposure of my stiff cock. Far from it, for the sweet girl giggled, sat down next to me and said in her pleasing Midlothian burr, "Dear oh dear, I didn't mean to upset your poor little cockie. Let's bring the shy fellow out again and have a proper look at him."

' "By all means," I said, opening my robe and she reached out and clasped my shrunken shaft in her fingers. As if by magic, it began to swell up again, rapidly returning to its former length and strength as the lovely lass slowly tossed me off, squeezing and rubbing my prick so deliciously that I was almost ready to spend within seconds.

'Then she let her fist stay still as she murmured, "If I let you fuck me, will you promise not to tell anyone? I've only had two or three romps with the children's tutor since leaving home and I'm feeling even more randy than usual after playing with your nice cock. But I must make sure that Mr and Mrs Barbach give me a reference."

' "I swear I won't tell a soul," I panted, and to back up my word I told her of the oath we take at the Jim Jam Club never to reveal the names of lovers. She listened carefully, then smiled and said gaily, "Very well then, you've convinced me, you smooth-talking rogue!"

'Trembling with excitement, I tore off my robe as the delicious girl pulled her night robe over her head and stood stark naked in front of me. I stood up and she walked the few steps towards me, her firm, uptilted breasts jiggling and her strawberry nipples looking up pertly as our mouths met and I clasped her thrilling young body to me.

'We fell backwards on to the bed and my hands

ran over her hard, engorged nipples and her own hand slid down to clasp my pulsating prick which bucked uncontrollably in her sweet grasp. As we threshed around, writhing in each other's arms, my fingers played around the silky strands of red-gold hair which formed a light veil across her pouting little slit. Jenny was justly proud of her pussey for her thighs were full and proportionally formed and my cock leaped and pranced in her hand as it sought access into her dampening cunney. So it was with great excitement that I scrambled to my knees when Jenny wriggled out of my arms and lay flat on her back with her legs apart. Quivering with anticipation I positioned myself between her thighs and gently lowered myself on top of her soft body and a low moan escaped from my throat as she took hold of my truncheon and guided it firmly between her cunney lips into her juicy, wet quim.

'I thrust my yearning cock inside her cunt and when I was fully embedded by the luscious love channel I stayed quite still for a few moments, revelling in the exquisite sensations afforded by her clinging cunney muscles. Then I started to fuck her slowly, pistoning in until our pubic hairs were entwined and then withdrawing all but the tip of my knob before plunging in again to the limit.

'This rich, deep fucking had the desired effect upon Jenny whose rounded bottom cheeks began to roll around as she arched her back, cleverly working her cunt back and forth against the ramming of my thick, hard prick, until I hoarsely groaned that I could no longer hold back the boiling spunk which was shooting up from my tight ballsack.

'Jenny grabbed my arse cheeks and pulled me forward so that every last fraction of my cock was encased in her cunt and our pubic bones mashed together as she started to move her hips up and down. With her hands still on my bum I matched her movements and now my glistening shaft was sliding in and out of her cunney at an even faster pace. With a cry I exploded into her, showering the walls of her love channel with sticky jism. I ejaculated copiously inside her willing pussey and this brought about her own orgasm: her body stiffened and I rubbed her clitty as her cunney was flooded with fresh rivulets of love juice whilst she shuddered in ecstasy as the force of her orgasm swept through her.

'After we had recovered I fucked her from behind as she stood with her feet on the floor, leaning forward with her arms held straight out, the palms of her hands flat against the sheets and her rounded backside pushed out towards me. I slid my shaft between her chubby buttocks and gloried in the sublime sensation as my cock slewed its way into her dripping cunt doggie-style. As before, young Jenny worked her hips in rhythm with my eager thrusts, letting my shaft sink all the way inside her juicy honeypot which I left there momentarily before easing back to piston forward again through the crevice between her bum cheeks.

'This time Jenny was the first to reach journey's end and she cried out, "Go on, Henry! Keep plunging forward! You're coming, aren't you? I can feel your cock shuddering inside my cunt! A-h-r-e! A-h-r-e!" A huge flow of her love juice soaked my shaft and I gasped, "I'm going to spend, Jenny! Yes, yes, I can't hold back any longer!" and I made one last lunge forward, my balls cracking against her bottom as I sent a stream of hot spunk hurtling into her sopping snatch as we collapsed down together on the bed. I'm not sure I could have obliged Jenny with a third bout but fortunately I did not have to try as she looked at my watch and decided she had better go back to her own bed in case one of the children woke up.

'However, after breakfast we exchanged addresses so after staying with you in Yorkshire I might journey on up to Edinburgh as she will be on holiday in mid-November, visiting her parents.'

I sipped my coffee and said, 'Well now, Henry, has the telling of that lascivious anecdote drained you or is your cock still available if required? Since you left our shores for the New World, certain ladies of quality, such as the wives of Army officers serving abroad, have taken to holding discreet little afternoon parties. Entry to these gatherings is not open to all and sundry, however, and to ensure privacy, the ladies leave the names of those members they wish to invite with Cripps and his underlings who pass them on verbally to the lucky chaps chosen to enjoy a wild afternoon's fucking.'

'It looks as though we may be in luck,' commented Henry. 'Look, Cripps has just walked into the restaurant and it looks as though he's coming our way.'

The head porter did indeed make his way to our table but though his message was of good cheer, it was not the news Henry wanted! 'Hope I'm not interrupting you, Mr Mountjoy, but I thought you might like to know that Big Brenda came in second. She was only beaten by a short head but at least you win two pounds.'

'Is that all? I thought you said the horse would be a twelve to one shot,' I said rather disappointedly.

'So it was, sir,' the Club head porter explained patiently, 'but you only get a quarter of the odds for the place and so you win three pounds, but as you lose one of the two pounds of the each-way bet, I'm afraid that you only win a couple of quid. Still, that's better than poor old Sir Harold Brown has done: he had fifty pounds to win on Big Brenda and only had ten pounds each way as a saver.' [British bookmakers are even less generous these days, only offering one fifth of the odds on most each-way bets unless there are more than sixteen runners in the race – Editor]

'Oh well, it's still always better to come out on top,' I said with a sigh, as Cripps handed me my winnings. The crafty porter always made sure that all members' winning bets were paid out with lots of coins which almost always ensured a generous gratuity. As it was Cripps himself who had given me the tip for Big Brenda, I gave him three half-crowns [forty-two and a half pence! – Editor] which naturally put a large smile on his face.

'No afternoon parties today, then?' I enquired or him. He shook his head. 'Not as far as I know, sir,' he replied. 'Though I understand that General Gooner is having a private party with a

564

couple of girls from Swan and Edgar's ladies' underwear department in room nine on the third floor. But please don't say I told you about it, sir.'

I waited till Cripps had left us and then I said to Henry, 'My God! Did you hear that? I never knew General Gooner was a member of the Jim Jam.' And I told Henry how the General had seen me before lunch and had given me a lift in his carriage. I laughed and said, 'To think I fibbed and said I was meeting a friend nearby because I was worried that the old boy might know about this place and would report my coming here to my father! Come on, my dear chap, let's go upstairs and see if the General is still firing his artillery.'

Before we went upstairs Henry insisted on signing the bill for our meal and urged me to hurry as I said that I first wished to visit the cloakroom. When we finally reached the door of room nine, to no great surprise, we found it was locked. 'Damn and blast!' cursed Henry, but I put a restraining hand on his arm and withdrew a silver key from my jacket pocket.

'Do you remember when Count Gewirtz of Galicia paid for the Club to be totally redecorated about five years ago?' I said, grinning at the look of frustration on Henry's face. 'Well, mixed in with the altruistic motive behind the Count's generous gesture was the rather darker desire to own a set of skeleton keys to the private rooms and he paid for a secret set to be made for him. These keys weren't simply used to embarrass other people, although you know how the Count enjoys a good practical joke and one afternoon he used his key to burst in to a room dressed as a policeman just as Lady Pachnos was about to sit upon Mr George Bernard Shaw's quivering naked stiffstander.

'But what the Count actually wanted was to be able to nip into a room without even having to book it with the staff, so nobody, but nobody knew he was there. This facility was not really necessary as far as he was concerned, but it was of great importance for high-ranking personages. They even say his friend Mr Tum Tum [London Society's nickname for the portly King Edward VII – Editor] has used this facility to bring Mrs Keppel and Mrs Quentonne here for a quick fuck.

'However, be that as it may, Cripps somehow found out about the Count's little game and bribed a locksmith to make him a similar set of keys and he sells copies of them at a vast profit to selected Club members.

'Frankly, I wasn't in the market for such items but I happen to have the key to the third floor rooms as I won it from Tubby Meredith at a baccarat evening a few months ago. Now so long as the General hasn't bolted the door, I don't think we'll have too much trouble in joining his little party.'

Henry was very impressed and he rubbed his hands in glee. 'Here's hoping,' he said, as I turned the key and gently pushed against the door which yielded to my weight. 'Hey presto,' I said softly, as I slowly opened it and we popped our heads round to see exactly what military manoeuvre was being attempted by General Gooner, whose heavy breathing we could hear before we saw for ourselves what was taking place.

Well, whilst I did not expect to see the General standing in front of a blackboard, lecturing on lessons to be learned from the Boer War, I was still taken aback at the sight which greeted our eyes. For there on the bed, stark naked and flat on his back the gallant veteran lay with his hands clasped behind his neck. His chest was covered with matted grey hair and without the restrictions imposed by a belt, his corpulent belly sagged all over the place. But his gnarled old penis was standing up smartly enough, a thick, twitching love truncheon which was being manipulated by the buxom Maisie, one of the Jim Jam's barmaids, who was dressed, or more accurately half-undressed, in her black Club uniform. She was kneeling on the bed beside him and was still wearing her skirt but, in all probability assisted by General Gooner, she had taken off her blouse and chemise and her large, bare breasts looked mouth-wateringly ripe for a touch of masculine lips or fingers.

We stood silently at the door, watching with growing interest as Maisie squealed, 'Stanley, please undo the buttons of my skirt so I can take it off before you fuck me.'

'Certainly, my dear, I'll do my level best but I don't know whether my old John Thomas is up to much today,' said the General doubtfully. However, he helped unbutton Maisie's skirt and she stopped frigging his prick in order to peel off her knickers and stockings. When she was naked she took hold of his cock in both hands but I could see that his tool had now wilted and despite some vigorous frigging and tonguing, Maisie seemed unable to coax it back up to an erection.

'Maybe this will help your old soldier stand to attention,' Maisie suggested, as she knelt in front of him, facing the curtained bay window. She stuck out her sumptuous backside and the General placed his hands on her rich, rounded bum cheeks and parted them to give himself a close-up view of her hairy pussey pouch and her wrinkled little bum-hole, whilst at the door Henry and I were also treated to a tantalising glimpse of the fur lined lips of her cunt.

Maisie raised her buttocks and the General spread them open even further, showing her to be wet and open and she turned her head towards him and said, 'I'm ready and waiting for inspection, sir.' But he shook his head and looked sadly down at his flaccid shaft which flapped feebly against his thigh. 'Sorry, m'dear, it looks as though I shall be forced to run up the white flag even before battle commences. Gad, if I were only ten years younger, I would have had a massive boner by now! But lately, my treacherous old plonker has been playing the most diabolical games with me.

'Strange to think that when I was a young lad I had only to think fleetingly of a juicy cunt and it would swell up in an instant. All the working girls who serviced the cadets at Sandhurst used to say that Stanley Gooner's cock was the thickest and hardest of them all,' he added gloomily. 'Nowadays though, merely striving for a stiffie is enough to put paid to all hope of my achieving one.'

568

'Never mind, dear,' said Maisie comfortingly. 'I'll tell you what, why don't I lie down and you can bring me off with your fingers instead?'

She settled herself down next to him and began to squeeze her own engorged nipples. 'Now then, Stanley, rub my clitty, there's a good boy,' she ordered, as she continued to massage her horned up teats. 'Ah, that's very nice, and slide your fingers in my cunney whenever you like, I'm getting really moist. Mmm, keep going, you'll have me going off in no time at all.'

The General turned to the side and their mouths met in a passionate kiss. Then he bent his head down and while Maisie rolled one rubbery nipple between her thumb and forefinger, he sucked deeply on the other tawny tittie. Soon he was sliding three fingers up to the hilt inside her sopping slit and she threshed around wildly, her feet drumming a tattoo on the sheets as she tried to work herself off.

Alas, it was obvious to Henry and I that she was having as little success as her partner, whose penis still lay obstinately limp despite all the action around it. 'Don't you think we should help out?' muttered Henry, who had already taken off his jacket and was unbuckling his belt.

'Oh yes, most certainly we should,' I said with a grin as I loosened my cravat. 'I would even go so far as to say that it is our bounden duty as Jim Jammers [as Club members were known – Editor] to aid Maisie reach her climax.'

It took only a few short moments before we too were as naked as babes and we padded briskly up to the bed, our two stiff cocks standing almost up against our bellies. Our footsteps were heard by Maisie who sat up and gaped at us. 'What the hell—'

'It's the cavalry, Maisie, arriving just in time to ensure you enjoy a good spend! Seriously, don't worry, it's only me, Rupert Mountjoy and Henry Bascombe-Thomas. He's a Club member too but he's been away for some time so you might not recognise him.'

She grinned lewdly at us. 'Who says I don't? His face has changed especially now he's shaved off his moustache, but I'd recognise Henry's roundheaded cock anywhere.'

I looked down at Henry's bulging boner and sure enough, Maisie's memory was absolutely spot-on, for like the handful of Jewish boys at St Lionel's and my close chum Prince Salman, who was a Mohammedan, Henry's slightly curved pecker was bereft of its foreskin.

'I'm truly honoured that you remember the shape of my tadger, Maisie,' said Henry politely. 'Though I'm damned if I can think where on earth you might have seen it before.'

'Dear, oh dear, still the absent professor, aren't you? Just before you went away – to America, if I'm not mistaken – the Club committee gave you a farewell supper followed by a presentation by one of the girls from Mrs Wickley's place in Macclesfield Street. I can't believe you'd forget *that*!'

Henry gave a loud chuckle as he stroked his throbbing tool. 'No, of course not – who could forget such a grand send-off! I thought the girl was going to present me with a wallet, a

570

picture-frame or some momento of the Club. Much to my delight, she presented me with her pussey and I seem to recall that I fucked her on the dining-room table in the Harcourt Suite.'

'Quite right, and I was serving behind the bar and happened to notice how the knob of your love trunk had been bared, presumably when it was only a tiny sapling!'

'How observant of you! Yes, my parents took the advice of the learned Doctor Aigin of Harley Street who recommended the operation when as a very small boy I had an irritating rash on the skin round my helmet. I hardly remember the operation – which perhaps is just as well!'

At this point General Gooner, who had understandably been very quiet during these exchanges, snorted loudly and thundered, 'Come now, gentlemen, enough of this idle chatter. For heaven's sake do your duty and fuck this poor girl without further delay. God knows she's been kept waiting long enough for a thick, stiff prick of whatever shape or size.'

'Thank you, Stanley,' she said with a giggle. She took each of our two rampant rods in her soft hands and began to frig our stiff shafts. 'Well now boys, I can hardly fuck you both together, so who's going to be the first to cram his cock inside my juicy cunney?'

'After you, Henry,' I said generously. 'You were bemoaning the fact that your prick hasn't seen too much action lately.'

'That's dashed kind of you, Rupert,' he said with gratitude, as General Gooner heaved himself up to sit on a nearby easy chair and Maisie lay back and opened her legs, exposing her damp pussey to Henry. Without further ado he crawled between her spread thighs and immediately parted her serrated cunney lips with the tip of his cock.

'Go on, shove it right up as far as you can,' she panted, and, nothing loath, he rammed his veiny pole deep inside her clinging cunney. The General and I watched Henry's gleaming cock slide its squelchy path in and out until Maisie whispered a few words to Henry who grinned – and without missing a stroke, rolled over so that he was now on his back and Maisie was sitting astride him. She pivoted happily on his shaft, rhythmically rocking to and fro as he thrust upwards, plunging his pulsing prick up inside her warm wetness. His back arched upwards as Maisie worked her soft, moist flesh against his iron-hard staff and as they spent simultaneously their surging cries of fulfilment echoing around the room as her cunt milked the manly essence out of his shuddering penis until he withdrew his sated, shrinking shaft from her love channel.

The happy pair lay panting with the effort of their joust but General Gooner cleared his throat and broke the silence. 'Now then, don't just stand there like a lemon, young Mountjoy, what the deuce are you waiting for?' he cried, like a demented sergeant-major. 'You young fellows don't seem to know you're born! Isn't it obvious that Maisie needs a second seeing-to? Damn it all, when I was your age I would have been up and at her as soon as you could say Jack Robinson.'

'I am right, aren't I, m'dear?' he asked Maisie,

who reached out and pulled my twitching tool towards her as she replied, 'Well, I wouldn't say no, that's for sure, especially with such a nice-looking young cock ready and waiting to ream out my tingling pussey.'

I climbed onto the bed next to Henry with Maisie still clutching my cock. She leaned forward and brought her lips to my knob, rolling her tongue around the purple dome and giving me playful little nips with her pearly white teeth. My prick began to pulse furiously in her mouth as she greedily gobbled my throbbing tool and her eyes smouldered with passion as I sat up and cupped her full breasts with my hands, deftly flicking her nipples with my nails.

She now began to give me sharp little licks on my swollen shaft, followed by a series of quick kisses up and down the stem, encompassing my hairy ballsack and she ran her lips down to my perineum, the so-sensitive zone between the balls and arse-hole, which sent waves of pleasure floating through my body. Then she thrust my cock in and out of her mouth, deep into her throat and she tongued me at the end of every stroke, lapping up the pearly of creamy white fluid which was already beginning to seep out of the 'eye' on the tip of my helmet.

My arse began to undulate as she grasped the base of my shaft and sucked hard on my bulbous knob, but as soon as she felt I was on the verge of spending, she made ready to swallow my spunk. I thrust my hips upwards and my cock shuddered violently between her lips as with a long spasm I released my sperm, first in a few early shoots and then in crashing dollops of frothy hot jism which filled her mouth and oozed out from between her lips. Maisie let the sticky white love juice flow down her throat as she gently teased my spongy knob with her tongue as very gradually I allowed the wet shaft to slide free.

I thought that this little orgy would now end but General Gooner was standing up, holding his now rampant cock as he cried out happily, 'Well done, Maisie, that was a splendid sucking off. Just watching you at work has finally done the trick and given me a cockstand.'

'Quick, come over here and fuck me,' she laughed. 'I had a good little spend whilst I was sucking Rupert's prick so my cunney's wet and waiting for your thick, fat shaft.'

'Strike whilst the iron's hot, eh?' he grunted, as he clambered on top of her and Henry and I scrambled up and stood by the side of the bed, watching the game old boy mount Maisie and guide home his ramrod between her yielding cunney lips.

Once he was fully embedded in her, Maisie trapped his cock inside her cunt by lacing her feet together behind his back. The General could hardly pump in and out of her pussey because her cunney muscles were gripping him so tightly, so instead he slid his hand under her and inserted the tip of his forefinger inside her bum-hole which sent such powerful sensations running through her that she squealed and wriggled in an ecstasy of passion. This also made her shift her legs and the General was now able to piston in and out, fucking at a surprisingly high speed, bringing Maisie off time and again as the fierce momentum sent fresh thrilling spasms of pleasure out from her drenched pussey.

Maisie knew that it would be unfair to ask the General to over-exert himself and so she brought her legs up against the small of his broad back, humping the lower half of her body upwards to meet the violent strokes of his raging rod. But as he bore down on her yet again, she grabbed his balls in her hand and tenderly squeezed their hairy sack. This had the desired effect of hastening his spend and seconds later his body tensed and with a hoarse cry of 'Steady the Buffs!' he crashed down upon her, his cock jetting its jism inside her sopping slit as she clenched her thighs together until she had extracted every last drain of cream from his spurting shaft.

I applauded the General on his prowess as a veteran cocksman. 'Well done, sir, I'm sure neither Henry nor myself could have bettered you for technique,' I said with total sincerity, although the gallant old soldier would accept no praise and waved aside my congratulations.

'Thank 'ee, my boy, but you should have seen me in my prime. Then I could have brought Maisie to the boil, cooled her down, and brought her up again at least five times before shooting my load. But gone are those roistering years back with the regiment when I could fuck all night with the lovely Gita, the beautiful dark-skinned daughter of the Maharajah of Bangitin, who was a true expert in eastern erotic arts, and then take part in the special short-arm parade of the officers of Ninth Punjabi Rifles organised by our

Colonel's lady wife, whose favourite breakfast consisted of mouthfuls of fresh spunk obtained by sucking off the cocks of her three favourite young subalterns, Brandon Smith, Charles Farnes-Barnes and myself.'

'How very interesting, General,' said Henry with a puzzled look. 'My uncle Eric was for many years Governor of Bangitin and he never mentioned the Ninth Punjabis to me, nor is there any mention of them in his memoirs.'

Oh-ho, I thought, so the old goat might be guilty of embroidering his tale. But at St Lionel's, it was firmly dinned into the pupils that it is the height of bad manners to question the accuracy of another gentleman's story, especially if it were entertaining, so I held my peace. Nevertheless, I filed the incident away in my memory in the unlikely event of ever having to persuade General Gooner not to tell my father about my escapades at the Jim Jam Club – but as he could hardly do this without seriously compromising himself, I was not unduly concerned about details of my secret life finding their way to the ears of my parents!

General Gooner himself confirmed this belief whilst we helped ourselves liberally to the sandwiches, fresh fruits and chilled white wine which he had ordered to be on hand before (as he had mistakenly thought) he had locked himself and Maisie away from any prying eyes!

'Er, gentlemen, I don't think there is any need to mention details of this afternoon's activities to a living soul,' he said, tapping his fingers nervously on the arm of his chair. 'Don't you agree that the three of us promise to keep silent about our fun and games – for Maisie's sake, if nothing else.'

'Yes, of course,' I said gravely, giving Henry a broad wink. 'I'm sure that none of us would want to compromise her reputation as one of the Club's most valued employees.'

'Good, that's settled then,' said the General with obvious relief. 'I'm truly glad you chaps happened to be passing and helped the party go with a swing, though I'm still puzzled as to why you wanted to come into room nine this afternoon, let alone how you managed to open the door, for I would have sworn on a stack of bibles that I had locked it after Maisie and I slipped upstairs after luncheon.'

'Maybe you turned the key the wrong way, sir,' said Henry disingenuously. 'I've done that myself occasionally. But the reason why we came in here was that we understood that Lord Searle had booked the room for a showing of the new naughty films he brought back from Paris last week.'

'Oh, that's not till six o'clock,' said Maisie, who probably knew full well that one of us had purchased one of Cripps' skeleton keys, but who had enjoyed the afternoon's sport and was more than satisfied with General Gooner's little present of five pounds for her participation. 'You must have misread the notice pinned up on the Forthcoming Attractions board.'

I offered our apologies for this mistake but, as the General said, everything turned out for the best so we parted friends.

As we went downstairs, I suggested a game of snooker but Henry looked at his watch and said regretfully that he must be going as his Aunt Clare was expecting him to take tea with her. We shook hands and he said, 'Rupert, I so enjoyed seeing you again. Will you confirm all the arrangements for our trip up to York? I'm staying at the Club until I find a decent apartment, so if need be you can always leave a message with Cripps.'

After he took his leave I went into the writing-room and dashed off a letter to my parents. I told them that I had bumped into General Gooner in Bedford Square (though I omitted to mention the later meeting!) and that in addition to Nancy Carrington, I had now invited Henry Bascombe-Thomas to stay with us and hoped that this would not be an inconvenience. I added that if an invitation to the party could be wangled for Henry, so much the better, but this was not of prime importance for the main purpose of his visit was to assess the worth of Diana Wigmore's pictures.

I handed the letter in to the desk to be posted and went back into the lounge for a snooze. As I dozed off, the thought passed through my mind that whilst I have never suffered from insomnia, the noted Society physician, Doctor Aigin of Harley Street, has always maintained that fucking is by far the best cure in the world for this troublesome complaint. I would go further and add that the activity is efficacious for many other complaints as well, except perhaps for the common cold, a cure for which has so far eluded the medical profession. However, in my experience, a small whisky to soothe the throat followed by a rattling good fuck will at least temporarily banish the miseries of a feverish chill.

CHAPTER THREE

Art for Art's Sake

FOR THE SAKE OF BREVITY I will mention only briefly the events which took place between my reunion with Henry Bascombe-Thomas at the Jim Jam Club and the brisk November morning just over a fortnight later when Henry met Nancy Carrington and myself at King's Cross Station for our journey up to Albion Towers, our family's estate, which lies on the edge of the Forest of Knaresborough, some six miles or so outside Harrogate.

By a supreme effort of will, I fucked Mary the maid just one more time during this period, to be precise, on the evening of my departure to Yorkshire, and that was at her insistence. I, perhaps foolishly, asked her what she would like as a small present for taking on, so cheerfully, many extra duties when my housekeeper, Mrs Harrow, was laid low with a nasty bout of influenza.

Otherwise, I had no further erotic adventures of note, except of course those which took place during the wild evening enjoyed with Nancy Carrington which I had arranged, as mentioned earlier in this narrative, when I reciprocated her invitation for the wonderful luncheon party and the splendid orgy with Countess Marussia of Samarkand. Nancy came over to dine with myself and my cousin, Michael Reynolds, a lusty young medical student though unfortunately his current *amour*, the pretty little Shella de Souza who I also earlier mentioned *en passant*, was at the last minute prevented from joining us by the onset of the same indisposition which had affected Mrs Harrow.

However, Lady Knuckleberry, my next door neighbour, returned to town that very afternoon from a few days at Sir Michael Bailey's country house in West Sussex, and very kindly agreed to make up the numbers at my dinner party. Furthermore, she turned out to be a willing participant when later in the evening Nancy suggested a game of 'Blind Man's Cock' in which Edwards and Mary were also invited to take part, and she thoroughly enjoyed her reward of being fucked by both Michael Reynolds and Edwards as I tongued Nancy's hairy cunt whilst Mary sucked my rampant prick.

Naturally, on the day of our journey up North, Nancy accepted my offer of transport to King's Cross and so as not to risk being late because of an absence of taxis, I ordered a Prestoncrest chauffeur and motor car for the short journey to the station. We were in good time to meet Henry who had already arrived from his new apartment in Philimore Gardens, Kensington. I introduced my old friend to Nancy Carrington, saying that I hoped they would both wish to buy Diana

Wigmore's works and bid against each other in auction. I spoke only half in jest as Diana did need a substantial sum to continue living in France because her parents wanted her to come home and meet more suitable young men than she was mixing with on the Left Bank in Paris.

Whilst our luggage was being loaded onto the train, I was curious to see Henry walk over to the station bookstall and whisper a few words as he passed over some coins to a sales assistant, who then reached down under the counter and gave Henry a large sealed brown envelope in which I assumed was a magazine which he slipped under his arm. I said nothing at the time but as soon as we were settled in our first-class compartment – and to our great satisfaction we were not burdened by the company of other passengers – I asked Henry what publication he had bought at King's Cross to read on the journey.

'Oh, just something light to while away the time,' he said carelessly, as, spot on time, the locomotive pulling our train hissed loudly and began to slowly chug its way out of the station. Henry did not further enlighten me as to the nature of his purchase but neatly changed the subject saying, 'I've brought some writing paper with me if either of you wish to catch up on any correspondence. After all, even though this service runs non-stop to Leeds, we still have nearly three hours to kill until we change trains there.'

'Thank you, but I can think of better things to do in a railway carriage, Mr Bascombe-Thomas,' said Nancy saucily, putting her hand on Henry's knee.

582

I queried her statement and asked, 'Better things to do? Such as what?'

'Fucking, of course, you silly boy,' she said brightly. 'Especially during the day, I don't think that a railway carriage can be beaten when it comes to finding a suitable place to indulge oneself.'

Henry looked at her blankly at first and then his lips broadened out slowly into a lascivious smile. 'Really, Miss Carrington? I don't think I have ever had the pleasure of testing your interesting hypothesis although I can well imagine the excitement of bucking one's hips in rhythm with the clickity clack of the wheels passing over the rails. Yes, the words of Thomas Grey come to mind, "No speed with this, can fleetest horse compare,/No weight like this, canal or Vessel bear."

'And I recall reading a thrilling little tale in *The Oys*—, ah, a magazine to which I subscribe, about a young couple making love on the London-Manchester express. The boy came at Crewe, the girl climaxed at Stoke and they both spent together at Rugby and Watford.'

'They were fortunate not to have been interrupted,' I commented. Henry nodded his head. 'They were fortunate indeed,' he agreed with a smile. 'But the ticket collector was a good sport and a sovereign bought his compliance to wait until the train was approaching Euston before inspecting their tickets and the ripe, nubile nakedness of the girl concerned.'

'Have you ever fucked a nice juicy pussey on a train, Rupert?' asked Nancy, and I was forced to admit that this was a pleasure I had yet to experience. But I added, 'Mind you, I'll never forget a fine time I had on a train with a randy girl when I was in my last term at St Lionel's.'

'Did you, Rupert?' said Henry, raising his eyebrows. 'I don't recall your ever mentioning it to me.'

'I didn't tell anybody, not even Frank Folkestone who had shared my study for the previous two years. You see, the girl concerned was the daughter of an employee of the school and I was concerned about her reputation as well as the fact that if news of the incident had reached the bursar's ears, he might have dismissed her father.'

Nancy's eyes shone with emotion as she moved up closer to me on the seat and said, 'That did you great credit, Rupert, and shows that even in your youth you acted like a true English gentleman. However, four years have now passed and perhaps now you feel able to reveal exactly what occurred.'

I thought for a moment and then said, 'Yes, I see no reason why I should keep the secret any longer.

'It happened when the First Eleven went to Winchester to play cricket. Normally, I would never have been in the side for I am no great lover of the game and have never been more than average with either bat or ball. But a couple of chaps had to cry off for one reason or another and I found myself included as twelfth man. I could have declined the invitation but being the reserve was no hardship as I didn't really want a game and on a fine day there are many worse things to do than watch your friends running around from the comfort of a deckchair with a glass of iced lemonade in one hand and a good book in the other.

'Well, one of my few duties consisted of bringing on a tray of cold drinks to the team during a short break in play whilst we were out in the field. I managed to perform this hardly onerous chore but walking back briskly to the pavilion, I caught my right foot in a small pothole and severely wrenched it. I was in great pain and at first it was thought I might have broken a bone. However, although the foot ballooned out, the pain slowly subsided, but the Winchester matron advised me to keep my foot from the ground for as long as possible.

'The match ended quite early as for some reason St Lionel's has never had a good cricket side since the old days of James St John thirty years ago. We were skittled out for only eighty-three runs and Mr Dexter, the master in charge of our party, decided that the team could catch the five forty-five train back to Chichester. "It might be a good idea for you to stay and take a later train, Mountjoy," he suggested, and the Winchester chaps made me most welcome, carrying me into the sixth form common-room and standing me a slap-up high tea.

'By seven o'clock, the swelling on my foot was going down and the bruise was beginning to come out. As it was unlikely that I had inflicted any lasting damage, I decided to ask for a lift to the station and catch the seven twenty train. Mr

Dexter had left me some cash with a train ticket so in the unlikely event of there being no taxis at Chichester, I could always telephone the school and ask for a cart to be sent for me.

'I was given a walking stick and driven to Winchester station in the school porter's pony and trap and I managed to hobble on to the train without too much difficulty. The carriage was empty except for a girl whose pretty face I vaguely recognised sitting in the "ladies only" compartment of the carriage [recently there has been talk of reintroducing these compartments for the comfort of modern female travellers – Editor] reading a newspaper and I placed myself out of her field of vision as one of the Winchester chaps had passed me a copy of *Cremorne Gardens* and I was dying to read this horny book.'

I turned my head to look at Nancy, who was now snuggled up beside me with her hand on my thigh, and continued, 'No-one else entered the carriage at Winchester nor at the first few stations. Then the train slowed to a halt in the middle of nowhere and the guard came through to tell us that we would be delayed twenty minutes because of a buckled rail further down the line. Well, this was the ideal opportunity to take out my book and I avidly read the saucy tale about the randy romps of Penny and Katie, the two pretty daughters of Sir Paul and Lady Arkley.

'Their naughty escapades with the gardener's boy soon made my prick swell up though I made no effort to hide the bulge in my lap which pushed hard against the material of my flannels. Idly, my fingers strayed down to caress my cock but I was rudely shaken out of my erotic reverie by the sound of a muffled girlish giggle. I looked up and to my horror saw that the girl I had seen sitting in the far corner of the carriage had, unnoticed by me, moved out of her compartment and moved into mine via the corridor.

'As you may well imagine, I gasped with embarrassment and my cheeks flamed bright red as I crossed my legs in a vain attempt to hide my tumescent crotch. Then I foolishly tried to blurt out an apology but I struggled hard to find the right words. After all, I could hardly say, "Please pardon my prick," and just continue reading as if nothing had happened. But as it turned out I was in luck, for the attractive young miss burst out laughing and said, "Please don't apologise, for that's not the first time I've seen a man with his shaft straining to be freed from his trousers. Anyway, it was rude of me to disturb you when you were so engrossed in your book. May I see what you were reading? I'm sure that it must be a jollier read than the newspaper I bought at Winchester Station."

'She stretched out her hand to take the book in question which I was weakly holding over my cock which was still sticking up in my lap. "Gosh, this really is hot stuff!" she said, as she flicked through the pages. "Where did you get it from, Rupert? I suppose you'll give it to Frank Folkestone or Prince Salman when you've finished it because I'll bet that *Cremorne Gardens* can't be found in the library at St Lionel's! However, you never know, perhaps Dr Keeleigh keeps his own private copy under lock and key in the headmaster's study, away from the prying eyes of his scholars."

' "I somehow doubt it," I replied, now feeling more at ease despite being quite perplexed by her knowledge of my name and of my school. "But you seem to know a great deal about me, even though we've never met. And I'm certain we haven't met, by the way, as I would certainly have remembered such a pretty face as yours if I had ever been honoured by the pleasure of an introduction to you."

'She brushed back a lock of golden blonde hair which had fallen over her face and two charming dimples appeared at the corners of her mouth as she smiled and said, "Thank you for the compliment, kind sir. Well, it's true that we haven't exactly been formally introduced but surely you must have noticed me walking around the school playing fields whilst you were practising at the nets."

' "The playing fields?" I repeated, for I was puzzled by her remark. "No, I can't say that I have ever seen you there, but then I'm not a frequent visitor there as frankly, I'm not all that keen on games. If you are to be found walking nearby, though, I'll change my ways immediately and go to cricket practice every evening. But in return do please tell me how you seem to know all about me."

'This made her laugh and she said, "You are such a smooth talker, Rupert Mountjoy! Well, I'll give you a big clue which should solve the mystery for you. My name is Pauline Hollingsworth. There now, doesn't that information help everything fall into place for you?"

' "Hollingsworth, did you say?" I ruminated and then the penny dropped. "Oh, then you must be one of old Mr Hollingsworth's daughters."

'She clapped her hands to applaud my deduction. "Absolutely right, Rupert, my father, old Mr Hollingsworth as you call him, has been the head groundsman at St Lionel's for the past twelve years and my mother is one of the school cooks. My sisters and I grew up here but now we've all left home. My two sisters are in service near Brighton at Lord and Lady Newman's and I won a scholarship to study at the Chelsea School of Art in London. But I do come back to St Lionel's occasionally and I've heard an awful lot about you and your friends from my friend Melanie the laundrymaid." [See *The Intimate Memoirs Of An Edwardian Dandy Volume One: Youthful Scandals* – Editor]

'I had the grace to blush but Pauline stroked my arm and then let her hand fall to my thigh. "Do you know what Melanie and the other servant girls told me about you, Frank Folkestone and Prince Salman? They said that Frank was hung like a horse, Prince Salman's prick had no foreskin and slipped in very easily – but they judged that out of the three of you, Rupert, you were the best fuck, instinctively knowing how to excite a girl with your tongue and fingers as well as your big cock.

' "I'd love to find out for myself whether they were right," she murmured, letting her hand slide across my lap and squeeze my still semi-erect shaft, before beginning to deftly unbutton my flies.

'I could hardly believe my ears and my whole body began to shake with barely suppressed excitement. I tried to speak but the words just refused to come out as Pauline moved her head closer to mine and whispered, "Now then, Rupert Mountjoy, let me look at the evidence for myself," as she now unbuckled my belt and I lifted my bottom off the seat to allow Pauline to pull down my white flannels. She plunged her fingers inside my undershorts and I let out a little gasp as her warm, soft hand grasped my now rigid tadger and I raised my hips a second time to let my drawers join my trousers around my ankles and to leave my cock and balls in a proud state of nudity.

'Just then there was a loud whistle from the engine, the train lurched forward and we slowly began to move along through the thankfully deserted countryside. "Blast, there won't be time for a fuck but that looks like a splendid meaty cock – and what a large ballsack you have for a boy of your age. Oh, Rupert, I must draw out some spunk and see how spicy your spunk tastes!" I looked at her glassily, not believing I could have heard her uninhibited remark correctly, but without further ado she took a firm grip around my pulsating prick and bending down, swirled her tongue around my bulbous purple knob. She sucked lustily, noisily gobbling upon my throbbing tool which twitched and bucked in her mouth as her moist pink tongue travelled up and down the length of my pulsing shaft.

'This delicious stimulation soon brought me to the brink of a spend and then with an immense shudder, my creamy emission gushed out of my cock and flowed down her throat. Pauline skilfully sucked up the last drops of sperm and then she fell away from me, licking her rich, full lips with evident enjoyment. "Mmm, that was quite delicious," she commented, as she recovered her senses. "Your jism isn't as salty as my boy friend's or that of Dr Brooke, my college lecturer."

' "Your college lecturer?" I said in surprise, as I pulled up my drawers and trousers and began buttoning myself up.

' "All the girls in my class have sucked his prick at one time or another – and none of us ever fails to gain passes on his courses!" she replied, as the train picked up speed and we rattled along towards our destination. Of course, I would have preferred to fuck the sweet girl but as she had rightly remarked, there would not have been adequate time as the driver did his best to make up for the lost time and the only thing worse than a hurried fuck is no fuck at all!

'Anyway, we were only ten minutes late in reaching Chichester and we commandeered a hansom to take us back to St Lionel's. But Pauline only stayed a brief while with her parents before going off again to London and I have never seen her since that glorious afternoon.'

I closed my eyes and sighed as I recalled that blissful journey and my mind had been so filled with the pleasant remembrance of this lively interlude that I had not noticed how my saucy anecdote had affected Nancy, who had raised her skirt, pulled down her knickers and was busy frigging herself by gently rubbing her fingers against the lips of her moistening cunney. Looking back on this scenario, I am certain that it was not only my graphic storytelling which made the lovely lass feel so randy, but also the gentle rocking of the carriage which many ladies have confessed to me makes them highly conducive to voluptuous ideas.

'Let's re-enact Rupert's lascivious story,' suggested Henry, whose stiff cock had formed a Himalayan peak in the elegant new trousers he had picked up from Mr Rabinowitz's workshop only the night before.

'A splendid idea,' Nancy enthused, ceasing her frigging to begin unbuttoning her blouse. 'Rupert, be a dear and lock the door, please.'

I stood up and performed this simple favour whilst my fellow travellers started to tear off their clothes in an ever increasing frenzy. When they were naked, Nancy and Henry moved into a passionate clinch and they fell back upon the seat with Nancy's soft hands smoothing over his slim body, sending my friend into a rapture of sensual delight. Then moving quickly, she scrambled over him and bent her head down to engage his lips in a burning kiss. They moved their thighs together until their pubic muffs rubbed roughly against each other as they now rolled over into the more usual position with Nancy flat on her back and Henry between her parted legs, his slightly tanned body fairly trembling with excitement. I could see Henry's thick, hard shaft throbbing with a powerful intensity as his circumcised cock probed the entrance to her exquisite loveslit and I aided the lewd pair by taking Henry's cock between my fingers and guiding his helmet between Nancy's pouting cunney lips. They cried out their joint thanks as his pulsing boner slid home, massaging her clitty as he embedded his proud prick inside the juicy love channel which so lovingly welcomed it.

Watching this storm of passion sent my own cock sky high and for the sake of comfort I was forced to unbutton my trousers and bring out my swollen shaft which stood stiffly to attention as I watched Henry's prick slew in and out of Nancy's sopping cunt. My trusty right hand flew to my cock and began frigging as Henry arched his back upwards and then crashed down upon Nancy's soft curves. We all came together and the wonderful feeling shuddered through every pore as I pumped spurt after spurt of sticky spunk over the entwined lovers, who were writhing in their own paroxyms of pleasure.

Alas, as I coated the couple with sperm, Henry turned his head towards me and received a great glob of jism in his left eye which brought the proceedings to a somewhat inglorious end and after wiping ourselves down with a towel from my travelling case, we dressed ourselves and I unlocked the door of the compartment.

It was just as well that we did not continue this frenetic frolic, because within only a few minutes an inspector appeared to clip our tickets and to announce that luncheon would shortly be served in the restaurant car. We trooped in to the dining car and I should mention that I was agreeably surprised by the quality of our luncheon which consisted of an excellent clear soup, after which came a generous slice of turbot with anchovy sauce, followed by a main offering of tender duckling with new potatoes and green peas. The dessert of a gooseberry tart and cream was also first class, as was the Stilton cheese with which we concluded the meal. The service was cheerful and attentive and I was impressed with the care which had been taken to ensure that the silver service really sparkled in the sunlight which was surprisingly strong for a late autumnal day. All in all we thought the luncheon very good value even at the relatively high price of four shillings and sixpence. [Only twenty-two and a half pence, which shows how inflation has robbed us of our currency during the twentieth century! – Editor] As I had paid for the bottle of Chardonnay we drank with our food, Henry insisted on paying for our meal and he was thanked effusively for the handsome gratuity by the two waiters.

After coffee, we sauntered back to our compartment and Nancy said to me with genuine regret in her voice, 'I'm dreadfully sorry, Rupert, but would you mind waiting till this evening when perhaps we can make love before dinner? I know how frustrated you must feel after seeing Henry fuck me just now but frankly, I'm feeling so tired after that delicious lunch that I'd rather close my eyes for half an hour or so.'

'Please don't give it another thought,' I replied truthfully. 'I'd also appreciate forty winks and I'm pretty sure that Henry will be pleased to follow suit.'

'I will indeed,' said Henry, taking off his jacket and settling himself down for a nice little nap. 'Wake me up when we get near Leeds.'

In less than five minutes both my companions were fast asleep, worn out too, no doubt, by their brief but intense bout of pre-prandial fucking. Although I was also feeling tired I was not actually sleepy so I decided to read for a while. Then on the seat next to Henry, my eye caught sight of the mysterious brown envelope which had been passed to him at the King's Cross bookstall. The flap was open so I carefully pulled the envelope towards me and took out the magazine which had been stuffed inside. My face crinkled into a broad smile as I saw that Henry had bought a copy of *The Latest Letters and Verses of Jenny Everleigh*. I eagerly thumbed through the pages, as the Everleigh horn books were highly prized both at St Lionel's and at Oxford University where even second-hand copies were sold for as much as two shillings each. [Several volumes of Jenny Everleigh's erotic diaries have recently been republished in paperback form, though most of her correspondence and poetry has been lost – Editor]

It took a minute to two to fully appreciate the following verse:

Come Teddy dear, lay your body down
Upon your lover's naked belly white,
Now raptures soon shall our embraces crown;
This is the path to sheer delight.

I know the lessons I have learned from you,
Sweet teachings in the flowery path of love,
Sure I'll remember all I must do,
When I am under and you are above!
Each day upon my cunt your burning kisses fall,
Each movement of your tongue gives me such bliss,
Till no longer for your cock I can forbear to call!

And at this point I rumbled that this poem was a clever if rude acrostic and possibly written – as Jenny had certainly been fucked by His Gracious Majesty King Edward VII during his wild years as Prince of Wales – for the King. My suspicions were confirmed on the very next page on which was printed a love letter from Jenny to A – E –, surely Prince Albert Edward himself. As we were soon to meet the great man, I read this epistle to him with especial interest . . .

My Dearest,

If your duties allow you, come round to my Aunt Portia's house, number sixty-nine, Exhibition Road (a felicitous address in the circumstances, don't you think?) around midday on Thursday and I'll suck your noble prick whilst you are bringing me off with your tongue and then you'll fuck me with your big cock all afternoon!

How I missed you last night at the soirée Lady Linda Brighton gave for Signor Marchiano, the new Italian ambassador. Not only was I bored but I had to fend off the unwanted attentions of Sir Oswald Holland and his friend Colonel Grahame – even the amusing charms of Dr Jonathan Letchmore who rescued me from the randy pair could not fill the void in my heart.

What would I give to have your hands freely roaming

across my nude body as they did that night after Lord Zane's ball! But I shall have to make do with my imagination and the beautiful dildo made by Monsieur Tihanyi, fashioned upon your own royal measurements. I am sitting on my bed quite naked and I am looking in the mirror at the silky blonde pussey hair which curls around my crack. Now I am moving my hands slowly across my breasts, cupping the firm globes and rolling my palms over the upright red stalky nipples which have risen up to greet them.

Darling, I am whispering your name softly as I close my eyes and slowly slip one hand downwards to rub my fingers against my pouting cunney lips. With the other I am fondling my breasts and, aaah, my fingertip has just entered my love channel but how much nicer it would be if it were you who was parting the soft folds of skin.

My hands are now busy, forming circles over my aroused clitty, pressing my blonde bush until I can feel the thrilling flow of an approaching spend. Now my left thumb is slipping inside my moist slit, though it is a poor substitute for your majestic member, and I am pushing two fingers in my cunney to make it nice and wet. It is time now to grasp hold of your gift of the finely crafted comforter based exactly upon your noble stiffstander. Aaah, I am slowly nudging the helmet between my separated cunney lips and in the mirror I can see to the very depths inside my damp, tight honeypot.

Yet as I push this ivory cock further inside my pussey, I can only think of how you dipped your prick into me gently at first and then moved harder and faster just as I am now moving my comforter, rubbing it across my erect little clitty which now throbs and *tingles and my cuntal juices are already dripping out onto the sheet. I'm lifting my titties and pressing my breasts together so I can lick my hard little nips and now I'm fucking myself with the dildo at great speed . . . Oh! Oh! Oh! I am coming! Yes! I'm there! Aaah! Aaah! A-h-r-e! Oooh, that was nice, very nice and I'm licking the creamy cum from the dildo which I am pretending is your live, quivering cock . . .*

I won't pretend I didn't enjoy this frigging, but believe me, my dearest, nothing in the world can compare with making love to you, lying back on rumpled sheets with a soft pillow underneath my head and being thrilled to the core by the voluptuous sensations aroused by your gorgeous thick cock reaming out my juicy cunney.

Unless I hear otherwise, I will expect to see you on Thursday. I am feeling so randy that I shall make you forgo your usual lobster salad at lunchtime and feed you half a dozen oysters instead!

All my love,
Jenny

Naturally, reading this racy narrative made my cock rise up again but I resisted the temptation to pull out my prick and administer manual relief to my swollen shaft by a quick five knuckle shuffle because I knew that a great deal of serious fucking awaited us all later this evening and in all probability during the next few days. So I closed my eyes and soon I joined Nancy and Henry in the Land of Nod but we woke up well in time to collect our possessions and alight at Leeds where porters took off our luggage and guided us to the platform where the local Harrogate line train had just arrived. There was only a brief wait of about ten minutes before we were on our way again and in half an hour we had arrived at our destination of Knaresborough.

At the station, Crabtree, our chauffeur, was waiting for us with my father's large Lanchester motor car and old Goldhill was also on hand to meet the party and to supervise the loading of our luggage into one of the estate's carts, with the aid of Frederick, a handsome young footman. I could see that Frederick's powerful physique, shown as he heaved the cases into the cart, had caught Nancy's attention.

On our way to Albion Towers, the seat of the Mountjoys since the sixteenth century, we passed through the high road via Starbeck and, like the American cinematographer Frederick Nolan [see *The Intimate Memoirs of An Edwardian Dandy Volume One: Youthful Scandals* for a graphic description of how Rupert assisted in the production of perhaps the first blue flim made in Britain – Editor], my guests marvelled at the superb view of the luxuriant woods, the venerable cottages, the ruined castle and the old church which make up a superb vista.

'Diana Wigmore is one of many artists who have brought out their easels and painted scenes of Knaresborough from the Castle Hill,' I commented, as we trundled down the hill towards the sleepy village of Wharton. 'If we have time, I'll gladly show you round what's left of the castle which has an interesting history. It was to here that the knights fled after murdering Archbishop Becket, and John of Gaunt is believed to have built the Keep. Incidentally, given half a chance, my father will show you the secret passage he discovered twenty years ago leading from the castle yard to the moat.'

'Such a pity it was demolished,' said Nancy sadly. 'When did that happen?'

'In the seventeenth century, during the Civil War when it was in the hands of the Cavaliers, until Fairfax successfully besieged it after the battle of Marston Moor. Four years later it was reduced to ruins by the Roundheads,' I informed her, and Nancy murmured, 'My, that would be ancient history as far as New Yorkers are concerned.'

'Oh, but part of the Parish Church goes back to the twelfth century, the nave to the fifteenth and the tower was built in 1774, just before your Declaration of Independence,' I added, which impressed Nancy even more. Henry, who had stayed with me several times and knew Knaresborough well, chipped in, 'I'll escort you to the Church one morning if we have time, Nancy. Even an atheist like myself can appreciate the naïve beauty of the two full length paintings on wood of Moses and Aaron in the vestry which date from around the middle of the fifteenth century.'

'I may well take up your offer,' mused Nancy thoughtfully, as Crabtree swung into our drive for the half mile run up to our house. My father, Colonel Harold Elton Fortescue Mountjoy, late of the Sixth Bengal Lancers, was standing by the front steps waiting to greet us.

'Hello everyone, welcome to Albion Towers.

Ah, it's Bascombe-Thomas, good to see you again, young man,' he boomed, shaking hands with Henry as we climbed out of the car. 'Now Rupert, you must introduce me to this charming girl who hails from America, does she not?'

'Yes, Father, this is Miss Nancy Carrington of Fifth Avenue, New York City, Nancy, this is Colonel Mountjoy, my father.'

'A pleasure to meet you, my dear young lady. Ah, here comes my wife who has been busying herself all morning with some dashed political meeting about votes for women. Well, being an American, at least you can't be a blooming suffragette, Miss Carrington,' sighed my father, who, though a decent old stick, was still in many ways a crusty old buffer and was genuinely astonished by the 'wild women' who had the temerity to demand equal rights and even more puzzled when two years ago my mother announced that she had joined Mrs Pankhurst's Women's Social and Political Organisation and would be actively canvassing on its behalf around the county.

'No, I don't need to be; in my country women have already secured the vote,' said Nancy, a smile playing around her lips. 'But I must warn you, Colonel Mountjoy, that the British suffragettes have my total support and I did in fact join their march to Trafalgar Square last September.'

'Oh Lord,' he groaned, though in fact he was not that put out by Nancy's declaration of support for my mother's cause, for despite his innate conservatism, if pressed by my mother, my father was forced to admit that there was no logical reason to bar women from having their say as to how the country should be run.

The stones crunched under my feet as I walked across to meet Mama who embraced me warmly and I introduced Nancy to her. 'How nice to meet you, Miss Carrington. And I'm so pleased that I have a further ally to support me if the subject of female suffrage comes up in conversation. Although my husband would not gainsay me in company, his support is at best lukewarm and I have had to rely solely upon Rupert to back me up when reactionaries like our vicar, Reverend Forsyth and Mr Archer, the squire of Wharton, insist on arguing against me on the grounds that women are inherently inferior to men.'

'How perfectly ridiculous, but then can one really expect more from the stupid sex?' said Nancy, which caused Henry to protest, 'I say, steady on Nancy. There are plenty of men who back the idea of sexual equality. Rupert and I do, for a start and there are many more besides.'

'Yes, I suppose we mustn't tar you all with the same brush, though it would be hard indeed to find more silly fools than Messrs Archer and Forsyth,' said my mater with a little chuckle. 'But don't let's stand here, come inside the house and have some tea. Don't worry about your luggage. I have left instructions with Polly so that when Goldhill and Frederick arrive they will know into which rooms they should put the various suitcases.'

'Polly, did you say, Mama? But isn't she just a scullery maid? What's happened to Sally?' I asked anxiously, for though I had fucked both girls, I was especially fond of Sally Tomlinson whose ripe, generous curves were admired by a great many male visitors to Albion Towers from our local medical practitioner Doctor Attenborough to my Uncle Algy (Lord Trippett) who always gave the girl a five pound note for services rendered during his frequent stays with us.

'Sally Tomlinson left us after announcing her engagement to Farmer Harrington's youngest son, Edmund, whom she met whilst he was on leave from his ship,' explained my mother patiently. 'Do you remember Edmund, dear? He joined the merchant navy after deciding that the agricultural life was too staid for his taste,' explained my mother. 'So Sally is staying with her parents in Ripley until his next leave early next month when the marriage ceremony will take place.'

'Gosh, that's a step up the social scale for her, isn't it?' I remarked mischievously. 'Though I don't suppose the Harringtons were exactly overjoyed at the match. Good luck to her, she's a sprightly girl and I'm sure she'll be able to cope with her new position as a naval officer's wife. So meanwhile, I presume that Polly has been promoted to the exalted rank of parlour maid.'

As we walked through into the hall my father looked at me through narrowed eyes and muttered, 'I didn't realise how interested you were in the running of the household, my lad. Mmph, I think it's just as well Sally's left Albion Towers or both you and she might have found yourselves in a spot of bother.'

'I'm sure I don't know what you mean, father,' I

said innocently, but the pater waved away my protestations. 'Don't give me any of that nonsense,' he growled angrily as we followed the others into the drawing room. 'I'm damned sure your Uncle Algy was poking her and I wouldn't put it past you ignoring my advice to keep your hands off the servants.'

Wisely, I did not attempt a denial and was careful not to appear to be over familiar with Polly, the pert girl who now proudly wore a smart housemaid's uniform instead of the drab clothes of a scullery maid. I answered Polly politely when she said, 'Good-afternoon, Mister Rupert, I hope you are keeping well.' However, despite my vow to heed my father's warning about the perils of being too intimate with the servants, I simply could not resist pinching her luscious bottom as she brushed past me carrying a tray of sandwiches. She gave a tiny squeal but thankfully held on to her tray which she offered to Nancy Carrington. When she came to me, she leaned forward and though her loose black uniform prevented a look at her firm breasts, she winked at me and whispered, 'Wait till after dinner, you naughty boy, I'll come up to your room at eleven o'clock.'

There was no opportunity to speak further with Polly so I nodded briefly although I was now in the happy position of having, if anything, an over-abundance of girls laying claim to my cock during these few days at home. Even as I mulled over the situation, my father informed me that Diana Wigmore and her parents would be dining with us tonight. There was also Nancy Carrington to consider, of course, who during the train journey had already extended an invitation to share her bed later in the day and now Polly Aysgarth had as good as demanded to be fucked after dinner!

Then, would you believe it, Goldhill entered the room, and, after announcing that our luggage was all safely in our bedrooms and was being unpacked by Polly and Alison, another new addition to our household who I had not yet seen, our faithful old retainer turned to me and said, 'There is a telephone call for you, sir. Miss Cecily Cardew is on the line.'

'Thank you, Goldhill, I'll take the call straightaway. Please excuse me, everybody,' I said as I hurried into the hall. Cecily, as readers of my first book of uncensored memoirs [*Youthful Scandals* – Editor] will recall, was Diana Wigmore's closest friend, who joyfully helped my best friend Frank Folkestone through his first ever rite-of-passage on a wonderfully sensual afternoon in the old barn near our freshly laid lawn tennis court.

I picked up the telephone and said, 'Hello, Cecily, are you there? Rupert Mountjoy here. How are you keeping?'

'Rupert, hello, how nice to hear your voice. We haven't seen each other since Christmas, have we?'

'No, not since Diana's Old Year's Night party,' I said, and then I almost bit my tongue, for I remembered that to be absolutely exact, the last time I saw Cecily, she was kneeling on the floor of the Wigmore's dining-room (fortunately Diana's parents had decided to stay out until midnight with my folks at Albion Towers), and she was lustily sucking the veiny shaft of Reverend Campbell Armstrong, the curate of Farnham whilst being fucked doggie-style by young Brindleigh Pearce, the seventeen-year-old son of a nearby landowner, whose shining eyes and speed of spending suggested that Cecily had just taken another young man's unwanted virginity.

However, my recollection did not trouble Cecily who carried on, 'Diana has told me all about what you're doing to sell her paintings. You are a good chap, Rupert, let's hope something comes out of all your efforts. And the reason I'm calling is I understand that Henry Bascombe-Thomas is staying with you at Albion Towers. Just before he went to America, Henry and I met at Maureen Waller's coming-out ball and we struck up an immediate friendship although we did not manage to seal our relationship with more than a quick good-night kiss. My parents are away until tomorrow afternoon and I wondered if there was any chance of meeting him tonight?'

'Of course you can, Cecily. Why don't you dine with us? No, really, my parents are always pleased to see you. Anyhow, Diana and her parents are coming over this evening so you could come with them. Will you fix the arrangements with Diana? Good, I look forward to seeing you tonight and I'll tell Henry that he has a pleasant surprise in store. Au revoir till tonight.'

So now there would be a fourth girl who would probably be calling for my cock as Cecily was renowned for enjoying a threesome with her close friends. However, even though I was renowned as a lusty, libidinous fellow who could wield a pulsing prick from dusk to dawn, I was very glad that I would be able to call upon Henry's sturdy stiffstander to help ensure that none of the four girls concerned would have cause to complain of a shortage of stiff cockshaft!

I went back into the drawing-room, but before I could sit down Nancy said to my mother, 'Mrs Mountjoy, would you mind if I went upstairs? I'd like to take a short rest before getting ready for dinner.'

'Of course not, my dear,' replied my mother. 'Please feel quite free to do so. Rupert, perhaps you would kindly escort Miss Carrington to her room.'

'With pleasure, Mama,' I said, little thinking that Nancy had any ulterior motive for wishing to leave the company. After all, I could hardly stay very long with her considering that my parents and Henry were downstairs and it would be very bad form for Nancy and I to be away more than a few minutes together, especially when the others knew that we were in her bedroom.

Therefore I took Nancy upstairs without any trepidation that my prick might be called upon to perform. Now I have no wish to appear blasé, as I've always been game for a good fuck at any time of the day or night, but I honestly wanted to conserve my strength for what I knew would be a strenuous evening ahead. On the other hand, what was I to do when as I stood at the entrance of her bedroom, Nancy bundled me inside and swiftly locked the door? It would have been most impolite to my guest to refuse her the use of my stiffening shaft which she was squeezing deliciously as our lips met in a warm, passionate embrace, especially as I could hardly tell her that she was going to be one of four girls whose cunnies would be competing for my cock in a very short space of time.

In the circumstances, I felt it best to let Nature take its course and made no effort to move away as, quick as a flash, Nancy pulled off her blouse and chemise and knelt bare breasted before me as she hungrily unbuttoned my trousers. The sight of her two snow white spheres tipped with their delicious engorged nipples sent my shaft rising high and my rod was rigid when she opened her mouth and began sucking and licking my uncapped knob.

Nevertheless, I felt it incumbent upon me to warn the dear girl that I could only stay with her a short while. For answer, she held my throbbing tool in both hands and washed my bell-end with her tongue. Then, filling her mouth with saliva, she plunged my prick inside her, withdrew her head back and then bobbed her head forward and backwards, forwards and backwards in a wonderfully sensual manner. Within a minute, the pressure built up in the base of my cock and with a cry I held her head as I heaved my hips forwards, filling her mouth with a fierce fountain of sticky spunk as my shaft shuddered out a copious emission of jism.

Nancy sighed and pouted, 'A short but sweet sucking off like that should be the hors d'oeuvres to an entrée of a jolly good stint of fucking. So I hope you won't let me down, Rupert, and you'll give me your word that after dinner my cunney will be the first to be filled by your lovely thick penis.'

I looked blankly at her and she wagged her finger at me, saying, 'Oh come on, Rupert, I wasn't born yesterday, as we say in New York. I could see you had an eye for Polly, the maid who served us tea, and I'm sure your best chum Diana Wigmore will also be after her share of stiff cockshaft, won't she?'

Well, what could I say to this perpicacious girl? My old headmaster, Dr Keeleigh always advised us in awkward situations 'to tell the truth and shame the devil'. So I decided. 'That is very possible as I haven't seen Diana for some months,' I admitted with a grin as I pushed my still wet semi-stiff prick back into my trousers. 'But on the other hand, I am a firm believer in the maxim of first come, first served so I promise upon my honour as an English gentleman that I will fuck you before anyone else tonight.'

'Anyone else?' she echoed, clapping a hand to her mouth. 'Oh, I suppose you are thinking that Polly will expect to be brought off too.'

In for a penny, in for a pound, I thought, and I said, 'Yes, and in all probability, so will another young lady who you have not yet met who is also dining with us this evening.' And I then told Nancy about the telephone call from Cecily Cardew, hoping that she would not take umbrage at the situation which had now developed.

'Cecily also enjoys a gambol with other girls and I don't think Polly would object to taking part

609

in such encounters either,' I concluded, which made Nancy smile and say, 'In that case, you had better go back downstairs, Rupert, and I'll take a rest so as to be fit for the fray.

'Just do me one small favour, Rupert, don't indulge yourself too much at dinner tonight, especially as far as alcohol is concerned, and please ask Henry to be similarly abstemious when it comes to passing the port after the ladies have left the table. Remember what the Bard of Avon had to say about drinking – it makes and mars, sets you on and takes you off, persuades and disheartens, and provokes the desire but takes away the performance!'

'Don't worry yourself on that score,' I assured the lovely Yankee miss. 'Henry and I would far rather get laid than get drunk,' I assured her. 'We usually dine at eight so why don't we meet in the lounge at seven o'clock for a pre-dinner drink?

'I'll have fresh apple juice which Mrs Randall our cook always has on hand,' I added hastily, as I kissed her proferred cheek and went out onto the landing where Polly passed by me carrying a pile of clean towels.

'Hello, Rupert,' she said softly, as she brushed her hip against my groin. 'Don't forget now that I'll be in your room at eleven o'clock and I might have a nice little surprise for you. But don't worry, I've already taken off my knickers and I'm looking forward to milking your thick prick all night. Just as well it's my day off tomorrow so I don't have to get up too early.'

I gave the frisky girl a glassy smile before running downstairs and just as I was about to open the door of the drawing-room, old Goldhill called out to me from across the hall. 'Just one minute, sir, if you please, I must speak to you.'

His tone sounded urgent so I said with slight irritation, 'What is it, Goldhill? Can't it possibly wait till later? I'm in a bit of a hurry just now.'

'Sorry, Mister Rupert, I won't keep you long but it is a rather important matter,' said the butler, as he hurried across to me and lowered his voice. 'Look, sir, I think you should know that Alison, our new housemaid, celebrates her eighteenth birthday tomorrow. She has taken a great shine to you and she has told me that the nicest present of all would be being fucked by Mister Rupert whenever he has a spare hour or two.'

Another honeypot to be sampled! Now whilst I was flattered to be fancied by a girl who I had not yet even clapped eyes upon, the forthcoming evening was threatening to get out of control! I steeled myself to tell Goldhill that Alison would have to wait her turn when a mop of bright blonde hair appeared around the corner of the door leading to the kitchen and scullery. The owner of this tousled mass then showed her face for a couple of moments and Goldhill called out, 'Very well, Alison, I'll be with you very shortly.'

All thoughts of postponing my prick's appointment with the new maid fled rapidly from my brain for Alison was quite stunningly pretty with cornflower blue eyes, a tiny nose but with generously wide red lips and I caught a glimpse of her smile which showed off two pearly white rows of teeth. So I said to Goldhill, 'I'll try to fit Alison in after dinner tonight. Please tell her to come to my room just before midnight. But I've never even met the girl and she can only have seen me for a few moments this afternoon, so I'm rather puzzled as to why she has been so attracted to me.'

The silver-haired servant scratched his head and said, 'To be truthful, sir, I didn't ask, but my guess is that her appetite has been whetted by Polly who never tires of talking in some detail about the uproarious night with you and Master Frank Folkestone some years ago when she was a mere slip of a girl.'

A slow smile crept over his face and I also chuckled as I said, 'Well, she may have only been sweet sixteen but by Jove, she was far more experienced than either of us. In fact, if my memory serves me right, we first encountered Polly Aysgarth when she was bending over the scullery table with your John Thomas pressed between her luscious bum cheeks.'

'Very true, sir, Polly adores fucking although I have never had the pleasure of conjoining with her again as she is well-served by some lusty young bucks in the village. Actually, soon after the event you have just mentioned, she went down to London to serve in Lord Borehamwood's town house in Belgravia. But she did not enjoy the experience and your mother was kind enough to take her back about six months later.'

'Oh yes, of course, Mama did mention it in a letter whilst I was up in Oxford. I was surprised when I heard the news because Polly always wanted to go to London. Do you know why she came back here?'

Goldhill cleared his throat and murmured, 'I understand that his lordship has somewhat strange tastes when it comes to intimate affairs. Apparently most of his loves are of the homosexualist variety, although he did occasionally take a girl to bed. But his demands were very odd – the only way he could achieve an erection was if Polly dressed up like a schoolboy and caned his bare behind. Even then, all he wanted was for her to suck him. He never fucked her all the time she was in his service.'

'What very odd behaviour,' I agreed as I pushed open the drawing-room door, 'especially when there's an eager, willing wench like Polly on hand. Anyhow, Goldhill, don't forget to tell Alison to come for her birthday present just before midnight and she'll see that at Albion Towers we don't have such nonsense as poor Polly had to put up with in London.'

'Ah, there you are, Rupert,' said my father crossly as I entered the drawing-room. 'Your mother was about to send out a search party.'

'Sorry to have been so long but I was just giving Nancy the usual lecture on the more interesting aspects of local history,' I said, making for the whisky which stood on a silver salver on the sideboard.

'An oral lesson, eh? I wonder who was the teacher and who was the pupil,' muttered Henry, who was standing by me.

'Don't fret, Henry, you'll find out for yourself later on,' I advised him cheerfully. 'Can I offer anyone a drink?'

'No, thank you dear,' said my mother, rising to

her feet. 'I suggest you drink only soda or you can ask Polly to bring you some more tea. We'll dine at the usual time and your father has favoured us with the best bottles in the cellar to complement Mrs Randall's excellent cooking, haven't you, dear?'

My father grunted, 'Well, I've done my best to provide something worth drinking. We'll start with champagne, and, for those who prefer to change to a non-sparkling wine for the fish course, there'll be a 1902 Pinot Blanc – I've already told Goldhill to chill half a dozen bottles in the ice-box. I'm putting out the last of the chateau bottled Beaune from Count Gewirtz's vineyards which will go splendidly with the beef and there'll be a sweet wine, of course, afterwards for the desserts. We'll serve that 1903 Chateau d'Yquem I bought last time we were in Bordeaux.

'So it would be foolish to begin imbibing heavily before dinner,' he said meaningfully with a disapproving look in my direction.

I accepted the implied rebuke and splashed some plain soda into a glass as my mother said to me, 'By the way, dear, I forgot to mention that your Aunt Penelope will also be joining us for dinner. Unfortunately, as Uncle Stephen has been called to London on business, she will come alone and stay the night here. And that reminds me, I'd better make sure her bedroom is ready.'

My father looked less than ecstatic at the news and after my parents left the room, Henry said, 'Your father gave the impression that he was hardly overjoyed at the news of an extra guest, although you looked far more pleased to hear

614

than an old aunt was dining with you.'

'Ah well, for a start, Aunt Penelope isn't old. She's a very attractive woman in her mid-forties and about ten years younger than her husband, Uncle Stephen. And she's not an aunt in the strict sense of the word. Penelope and Stephen Trelford-Neil are perhaps my parents' closest friends and I grew up with Alicia and Georgina, their twin daughters, although I haven't seen the girls since they went to Italy last year for an extended stay with Uncle Stephen's brother who is the commercial attaché at our embassy in Rome.

'Aunt Penelope is a keen amateur artist and I suppose my mother thought that she would be interested to meet you and Nancy. I like her very much and I'm sure you'll also enjoy her company. My father has always admired Aunt Penelope (in fact I think he harbours naughty ideas about her) but since she has also become a keen member of the women's suffrage movement, he and Uncle Stephen tend to drown their sorrows together whilst my mother and Aunt Penelope go round the county drumming up support for votes for women.'

'She sounds a feisty lady and I look forward to meeting her,' said Henry and, after I had swallowed down my soda, we went upstairs to prepare for dinner.

'You've never mentioned your Aunt's twin daughters,' said Henry suddenly, pausing at the entrance of his bedroom. 'Have you been keeping some wicked secrets from me as far as they are concerned? Having a pretty set of twins together is one of my unfulfilled fantasies.'

615

I laughed and said, 'In that case you would be even more frustrated if you ever met Alicia and Georgina. They are only nineteen years old and although not identical twins, they do look very much alike.'

'And are the two girls both attractive?' he asked.

'Absolutely ravishing, old boy, but I've never had the opportunity to progress further than a kiss under the mistletoe at Christmas parties,' I said regretfully, as it had been my ambition to bed the heavenly twins.

On this wistful note I left Henry and went to my own bedroom where the young footman, Frederick, whose duties also included basic valeting for my father and any male guests, had unpacked my cases, hung up some clothes in the wardrobe and had laid out my best evening suit which Mr Rabinowitz made for me when I came down from Oxford. The black barathea cloth was almost as smooth as the silk collar and lapels. It would set off the sparkling new stiff shirt and cuff links I had been given by Mama for my birthday which I would wear for the first time tonight.

I ran a bath and enjoyed a luxurious soak before drying myself off in front of the mirror, feeling refreshed and pleased with life. As I passed the towel between my legs I thought of the grand festival of fucking that awaited my pleasure after dinner and I idly imagined how nice it would have been to have started the affair by being sucked off by Alicia and Georgina Trelford-Neil.

These lewd thoughts combined with the pressure of the towel on my cock caused my shaft to spring to life and in a trice it was standing rigidly to attention up against my belly. Now, perhaps I had not heard a knock on the bedroom door because of the swirling gurgle of the bath-water disappearing down the plug hole, but as I was lightly stroking my proud prick, I was startled to hear a discreet little cough from the bathroom doorway – and when I looked up to see who was there, I was only partially relieved to see that it was only Polly standing there, for whilst she would be pleased rather than scandalised to see my erect naked prick, on the other hand, I honestly wanted to conserve my strength for later. Though from the gleam in Polly's eyes, I could tell that her blood was up and it would be difficult to deny her a taste of her favourite lollipop!

It was then with a resigned pleasure that I dropped the towel and stood with my legs slightly apart as Polly dropped to her knees and clasped her warm, soft fingers around my prick. She cupped my ballsack with her other hand as if weighing the contents in her palm whilst she frigged my swollen shaft.

'Do you like having me play with your cock and balls, Mister Rupert?' she whispered and all I could do was to nod my head as by now my heart was pounding and my whole body was thrilling to the sensations afforded by Polly's skilful fingers.

'Well, if that's the case, let's see what you think of this,' she said decisively and leaned right forward to take my throbbing cock and encase my knob inside her hot, wet mouth. Her darting tongue moved to and fro along my shaft and, as she sucked on her cocksweet, I felt my balls begin to swell and fill with sperm. Frenziedly, I thrust forwards and backwards between her lips and I must have transmitted my urgency to Polly because she began to suck harder and harder, letting my prick slide thickly against her tongue whilst she squeezed my balls.

I groaned as a rush of creamy spunk sped along my stem and jetted out into her mouth. She gulped down as much of my jism as she could but Polly simply could not contend with the tremendous gush I produced. My copious emission dripped down her chin and onto her blouse and after finally milking my cock of the final drains of sticky sperm, she kissed my now flaccid staff, wiped the jism off her blouse and sucked her fingers clean.

'Goodness, my blouse is damp and I'm soaking wet between my legs,' she said. 'Look for yourself, I told you as you were leaving Miss Carrington's room that I've already taken off my knickers.' And she immediately proved the truth of this remark by pulling down her skirt and lifting her blouse and chemise to reveal the dark patch of pubic hair adorning her sweet little cunt.

The sight of Polly's pussey coupled with thoughts of anticipation of what was scheduled to occur after dinner made my tadger tingle and it began to swell up again. Heroically, I passed up the opportunity for a quick knee-trembler, and I picked up the towel and wrapped it around my waist.

'Polly, there just isn't time to fuck you right now,' I said firmly. 'Please be a good girl and come back here around eleven o'clock. Then, as I've told you, I will have more time to pay your lovely cunney the close attention it richly deserves.'

This little speech seemed to mollify Polly and she put her skirt back on, saying, 'Yes, we certainly don't want to rush things. After all, as Goldhill's already told you, you also have to keep Alison satisfied all night and she's a very passionate girl.'

I hurried her to the door and when she closed it behind her I sank down upon the bed for a brief snooze. But I found it hard to sleep because I was very worried as to how I would be able to do my duty by Nancy, Polly, and Alison – as well as by Diana and Cecily who would soon be arriving downstairs! Henry would put his trusty tool at my disposal but I reckoned that I still needed one more cock to ensure that none of the girls was disappointed by the arrangements for their entertainment.

In the end, I did manage forty winks before it was time to change for dinner. I walked downstairs at about half past seven to find Nancy and my parents already engaged in conversation with Diana's parents, Charles and Helene Wigmore.

'Good-evening, Rupert,' said Mrs Wigmore, as I entered the drawing-room. 'How nice to see you again. Are you enjoying your sabbatical year in London?'

'I'll say he is, Helene,' interrupted Dr Wigmore

with a short laugh. 'After all, he has nothing else to do with himself, has he?'

'You're just jealous, sir,' I smiled, accepting a cup of punch from Frederick who was serving my Mama's excellent recipe from a large silver bowl.

'You're quite right, Rupert, I admit it,' cried our neighbour and family medical practitioner, pointing towards Nancy. 'Especially when I'm told you have this charming young lady as your neighbour.'

'Well, Rupert and I are almost neighbours, I suppose, as we both live in Bedford Square,' said Nancy, coming over to us. 'But I'm also fortunate in having such a friendly gentleman living nearby.'

'Ah, my daughter has just come in,' said Dr Wigmore, as Diana and Cecily Cardew made their entrance. As always, the girls looked simply stunning together: the blonde Diana's cool, lissome beauty was exquisitely complemented by the equally pretty Cecily's wavy brown hair, rosy cheeks, large dark eyes and rich red lips.

Dr Wigmore was about to introduce the girls to Nancy when Henry suddenly appeared, so I took on the job for him. Just as I had finished, Goldhill sonorously announced the arrival of Mrs Trelford-Neil and this time my mother came across to perform a similar function for Aunt Penelope although, as my mother remarked, only Henry and Nancy were strangers to her.

'I dislike that word, Veronica,' said Aunt Penelope. 'As the Irish poet says, there are no strangers in the world, there are only new friends I have yet to meet.'

Aunt Penelope was one of those people whom hostesses loved, for without hogging the limelight herself, she was often the life and soul of a party. She was adept at finding subjects of interest for lively conversation as well as for drawing out shy guests and ensuring that they were not left out in the cold.

So, very soon, she had elicited the fact that both Henry and Nancy were in the market for paintings and she said to them, 'I suppose I should offer you a selection of my water-colours. My husband would probably faint clean away if I informed him that I'd actually sold one of my studies of Knaresborough Castle! But seriously, I paint solely for my own pleasure, whilst Diana here is a talented young professional artist who has a great future in front of her.'

'Mrs Trelford-Neil is one of my staunchest fans,' explained Diana, who had glided gracefully towards us. 'In all fairness, I must tell you that her opinion of my work is hopelessly biased.'

'Nonsense,' Aunt Penelope declared. 'I confidently predict that your portrait of my husband will one day be hung in the Royal Academy.' [This prophecy was fulfilled in 1912 when Diana Wigmore's portrait of Sir Stephen Trelford-Neil (he was ennobled in 1913) was shown at the Academy's Summer Exhibition. Alas, many of Diana Wigmore's works were lost when enemy action destroyed the Allendale Gallery during the London Blitz of 1940 – Editor]

Goldhill called us in to the dining-room and during the meal much of the conversation around my corner of the room revolved around twentieth-century art. I was glad to see that Nancy and Henry were obviously impressed by Diana's knowledge and enthusiasm which boded well for the time when they would cast critical eyes on her own canvases.

'I have just had a splendid idea,' Henry announced excitedly. 'Rupert, why don't you help Diana and myself organise an exhibition in London of the French impressionists – a mix, let us say, of famous fellows like Matisse, Van Gogh and Gaugin with equally talented artists who are not as well-known over in England. As Diana is based in Paris, we would have someone on the spot to choose paintings for us from the new avant-garde.'

'That's quite an undertaking,' I said doubtfully. 'The cost would be considerable and it would take a great deal of time to organise.'

'Well, you're not doing very much these days,' called out my father, who had caught the drift of this conversation, 'so you've enough time to lend a hand.'

'Finance wouldn't necessarily present a problem,' said Henry. 'I don't believe it would cost a fortune to hire a gallery early next Spring and we would pay Rupert his travelling expenses as a nominal honorarium.'

Now whilst I would stoutly defend myself against any accusation of being a Philistine regarding artistic affairs, initially the idea of spending my precious free months working on setting up an exhibition of modern paintings was hardly of great appeal. But then I realised that such a position would give me ample opportunity to visit Diana in Paris – and my trip would be paid for, in the bargain!

My eyes brightened even further when Diana said, 'What a wonderful idea, Henry. I know that you and Rupert would judge potential exhibitors solely upon the quality of their work for there are several girls I know who are held back simply because their sex precludes them from being shown at the best commercial galleries.'

'Don't begin talking about downtrodden women again, Diana,' said Dr Wigmore teasingly. 'I am sure that Colonel Mountjoy agrees with me that this subject is becoming tiresome through constant repetition.'

Diana smiled but my mother took the bait and bristled, 'Charles, the subject will need constant repetition. Only last week I came across a small but pertinent example of blatent sexual discrimination. You may know that Mrs Anna Kempster, who has supervised the Yorkshire School Boards for many years, retired this year. Her co-chairman, Mr Spencer Arbuthnot, has received an OBE in the King's Birthday Honours list, whilst Anna's name was conspicuous by its absence.'

'Actually, that's not a good example, Veronica,' said my father. 'Arbuthnot didn't get his gong for his work on the School Boards. His gift of five thousand pounds to Conservative Party funds earned him his medal.'

'How disgraceful,' remarked Cecily Cardew, who was sitting next to me but had said little during the meal. 'Such sordid horse-trading makes the list a parody of honour and an insult to those members of the community who truly merit recognition.'

'Well, whilst I can't reasonably defend the system, my dear,' my father said, 'you must admit it keeps Civil Servants happy and loyal to the government of the day and hopefully some decent chaps do get their just rewards for selfless service. As for politics, it's a dirty business but party funds need replenishing and I suppose selling baubles is as good a way as any to top up the accounts.'

'Maybe so, but it is indefensible that membership of the House of Lords should be decided by accident of birth,' said Cecily, a sentiment which earned a murmur of approval from all but my father and Dr Wigmore who shrugged their shoulders and muttered something about the need for an officer class in society.

When the ladies left the table and Frederick came in with the port and cognac, the two old codgers continued their objections to twentieth-century standards and the passing of the old ways. Henry and I listened in silence, giving each other an occasional conspiratorial wink. After all, there was little point trying to change their views, although when Dr Wigmore opined that what this country needed was 'a few people to give the orders and the rest to obey them pretty smartish!' Henry mouthed a muttered suggestion as to where Dr Wigmore should next stick his stethescope!

Anyhow, our minds were concentrated upon more immediate matters to hand and when my father suggested that we rose and joined the ladies, we took up his remark with alacrity. When we rejoined the girls, Diana said to me, 'Rupert, would you and Cecily like to accompany Henry, Nancy and myself to the library? Your mother has my portrait of her hanging there and has kindly agreed that I should show it to our guests.'

I looked enquiringly at my mother who said, 'By all means, Rupert, and then do feel free to adjourn to the games room. Perhaps you young people might enjoy a game of billiards or table tennis whilst we old fogies sit down to a game of bridge.'

We thanked Mama for her considerate thought and trouped out towards the library. But in the hallway, Cecily laid her hand on my arm and said, 'Rupert, why don't we leave Diana to show Nancy and Henry the painting by herself? They can talk amongst themselves about the pre-Raphaelites, the post-impressionists and whatever artistic gossip they choose without worrying about us.'

'What a good idea,' said Henry approvingly. 'We'll meet you later in the games-room.'

'Or if we don't find you there, Diana, Henry and I will make tracks for your bedroom and come straight in without knocking on the door,' warned Nancy jokingly, although I knew that she was totally serious about taking such a drastic course of action!

Anyhow, we agreed to split up and when the library doors closed upon the three artistic aficionados, Cecily rubbed the palm of her hand suggestively against my prick and said, 'You know, Rupert, I do believe that Nancy meant what she said about flinging open your bedroom door, so why don't we adjourn there now. That way we might actually be able to meet them in the games-room later!'

I looked at my watch and saw it was almost twenty minutes to eleven and it occurred to me that not only would it be delicious to make love to this gorgeous girl but if Cecily Cardew's love channel was the first to be crammed full of my cock, this would solve a tricky problem which had been bothering me. For even though fucking Cecily first meant I would be breaking my promise to Nancy and Diana, both of them knew of each other's desire to have me fuck them, but this way, by first favouring Cecily's neutral pussey, so to speak, neither Polly nor Diana would have cause to feel any jealousy towards one another.

Perhaps I might abandon law and try my hand at diplomacy, I thought to myself as I opened the door to my bedroom for Cecily. I was swiftly shaken out of any smugness, however, because as I closed and was about to lock the door, it became apparent that someone had filched the key!

Which girl had taken it? Probably Nancy, I reasoned, as I responded to Cecily's advances and kissed her on the lips, although I would not have put it past Polly to have slipped the key into her pocket when she left me just before dinner.

Unfortunately, it became obvious to Cecily that something was on my mind for she said reproachfully, 'Rupert, what's the matter with you?'

'Nothing, nothing at all,' I reassured her and swept her into my arms. But the nagging question still ran through my mind and Cecily broke away from me and began to undress until she stood naked in front of me. 'Now then, Rupert Mountjoy,' she said crossly, as she pirouetted round in a circle, 'do you like the merchandise or would you prefer to have it wrapped up and sent back to the shop?'

I gazed upon her soft, white body, now totally nude and of such ravishing beauty that almost unconsciously I licked my lips in anticipation. Cecily was a real corker and when she unpinned her hair and let the silky strands fall over her shoulders onto her large breasts, I would have challenged any red-blooded man in the world not to have had his cock standing stiffly in salute. I looked down and smiled as she ran her fingers across the curly brown bush between her legs and pulled open the pouting love lips to reveal the pink chink of her cunney.

'Certainly not, I wish to make a purchase,' I croaked as she took three paces forward and helped me off with my jacket.

'You will?' she cooed happily, transferring her attentions to my fly buttons. 'I hope you won't change your mind and look elsewhere half-way through the transaction.'

'No I won't,' I panted heavily as I sat down on the bed and Cecily assisted me to remove my shoes. 'Though if necessary I promise that I'll leave a deposit and come back later to complete the sale.'

Within a very short space of time I was also naked and all extraneous matters like the missing key and who might come in whilst Cecily and I were enjoying our naked romp fled from my mind. Cecily opened her legs and I buried my face in the damp patch of curly cunney moss. 'Make love to my cunt, Rupert,' she whispered, and, nothing loath, I began to kiss her salivating pussey lips and started to lick her hairy crack in long lascivious swipes of my tongue. The vermilion lips parted and between them I felt her stiffened clitty which I rolled around in my mouth.

'Oooh! Oooh! A-h-r-e!' she cried out, her body threshing from side to side as she rolled her thighs around my neck. 'Suck me off, darling, make me come with your wicked little tongue!'

I sucked away at an ever-increasing speed, rolling my tongue round and round her clitty, nipping it occasionally with my teeth which made her squeal with ecstasy and I licked up Cecily's tangy love juices in great gulps as she began to spend. Her entire frame was caught up into a giant shudder and then a fine creamy emission spurted from her cunney, flooding my mouth with a salty essence, which I lapped up until she shivered into limpness as the delicious crisis melted away.

'Please fuck me now,' she breathed and naturally I was happy to fulfil her demand, moving my body upwards so our lips met as my swollen knob slipped in between the portals of her rubbery pussey lips, straight into her sopping cunt. I moved my head downwards to suck on her firm, tawny nipples which made her gasp with delight and I fucked Cecily with great ardour, plunging my prick in and out of her sopping pussey, my balls banging against her backside as my shaft slid all the way inside her and our pubic hairs mingled damply together.

By Jove, Cecily was a grand fuck! How tightly her pussey clasped my rampant cock and how luscious was the suction created by the folds of her juicy cunt as my trusty tool embedded itself inside her slippery sheath. How voluptuously she met my thrusts with the most energetic heaves as we gave ourselves up to an all-enveloping feast of lascivious delights.

Then it struck me that I must ration my fucking if I were ever to get through the night, so I made no attempt to hold back the ultimate pleasure when I felt the spunk boiling up in my balls. With a groan I exploded into a huge climactic release as I shot my load of hot, sticky spunk deep into the lovely girl's cunney which I could feel throb as my cock spurted jet after jet of jism inside her, lubricating her love channel as we went off together. For some moments neither of us moved. We lay there huffing and panting in each other's arms, luxuriating in the utter bliss of it all.

About five minutes later, Cecily turned to me and said, 'Now I know you must want to fuck Diana and she had already told me how much she wants your big boner between her legs. Now I would be the first to admit that as Diana is your closest girl friend, she is entitled to first claim on your darling cock – but she's not here yet, although she did take the precaution of coming upstairs and popping your bedroom key in her handbag when we left you men to pass the port.

So it was Diana who had taken my key! I made a mental apology to Nancy and Polly as I heard

Cecily continue, 'On the other hand, speaking as one of her oldest friends, I can also say that she would have no objection whatsoever to you fucking me again in her absence.'

Without waiting for my reply, the insatiable girl took hold of my limp shaft and in seconds had frigged it up to another bursting erection. Then she rolled over on her elbows and knees with her head on the pillow and her white, rounded bum cheeks stuck high in the air. I climbed up and parted the soft globes with my hands though I hesitated a moment before plunging my prick in the crevice between the fleshy spheres. Cecily guessed what was in my mind and turned her head round and panted, 'Yes, yes, Rupert, do go on. I have a great fancy for a bottom fuck but please go carefully.'

As she wriggled her bum to an even higher angle and opened her legs still wider, I placed my knob, which was still wet from our previous encounter, at the rim of the puckered little rosette. I angled her legs to afford a better view and then gently eased my knob forward and mounted her, sliding my shaft in and out of her rear dimple whilst I squeezed her tits in my hands. I didn't manage to reach another climax myself (which in the circumstances didn't bother me too much) but thankfully Cecily began gasping and moaning as I finished her off by tickling her pussey with my fingers.

I withdrew my cock carefully from her puckered bum-hole and we lay together on the bed and I cuddled Cecily tightly in my arms. Frankly, we were now both ready for a short rest

– remember, we'd consumed a delicious dinner not all that long before – but just as we were sliding into the arms of Morpheus, who should sidle quietly into the room but Polly and Alison, who both wore dressing gowns with, as I correctly guessed, nothing on underneath.

'Hello Mister Rupert, who's that with you? Oh, it's Miss Cecily, isn't it? Goodness me, young sir,' she said saucily, in the kind of stately deferential tone beloved of butlers like old Goldhill. 'Do Miss Diana and that nice American lady, Miss Carrington, know you've already started shafting? I last saw them half an hour ago when they were being fucked by Mr Henry in the library but I'm sure I heard one of them say that she wanted to be fucked by you later on. But you did tell me that you would give Alison a special eighteenth birthday present, and come to think of it, I was promised a fuck as well.'

'Is this right, Rupert? Did you promise to fuck these girls?' demanded Cecily, sitting up but making no attempt to hide her luscious naked body.

I nodded miserably, but to my great relief, the sweet girl was not annoyed. 'In that case, you must stick to your word,' she said as an amused smile played around her lips. '*Noblesse oblige*, you know. Whilst you three are occupied, I'll run a bath.'

She swung her legs over the side of the bed and smiling at Polly and Alison, said, 'I hope you're not too disappointed at finding that Rupert has already fucked me.'

'Not at all, Miss Cecily, first come, first served,'

said Polly politely and Cecily added, 'Well, I must admit that I'm glad I was first in the queue but I'm sure Rupert has lots of spunk left in his balls for you and Alison.'

'Thank you, Miss Cecily, you're a real lady to give up a nice thick prick to two servant girls,' said Polly, and she and Alison both curtsied as Cecily heaved herself up and walked across the room into the bathroom, closing the door behind her.

Polly slipped off her robe and as I had guessed, the dressing-gown was her only clothing and the pert parlour maid now stood stark naked in front of me. I feasted my eyes and drank in the sensual beauty of her proud, uptilted breasts, flat white belly and the trimmed tuft of dark pubic hair through which peeped her pink cunney lips.

Yet despite this stirring sight, my prick failed to stand fully to attention, stirring only slightly against my thigh. I leaned forward to take it in my hand and frig my cock up to its full majestic height but Polly removed my fingers which had already closed around my semi-erect shaft.

'Mister Rupert, your cock would prefer to wait a few more minutes before charging back into action,' she said wisely. 'Alison and I are in no rush. Why don't you just move over and we'll amuse ourselves until you're fully ready for us.'

This was sensible advice so I wriggled over and Polly sat down next to me as she motioned Alison to come forward and stand beside her. She then tugged at the sash of Alison's robe, which opened and the gorgeous young girl stepped out of her gown in all her naked glory like a glorious statue come magically to life.

What a truly delectable, enchanting sight! Her creamy white skin showed off her full curvy breasts to their best advantage and her well-rounded shoulders tapered down to a small waist; her dainty feet expanded upwards into fine calves and her marble thighs were beautifully proportioned, whilst hanging between them was a golden veil of curly blonde hairs over a pouting crack which simply begged to be kissed, sucked and fucked.

Not surprisingly, the sight of this cute little cunney made my prick shoot up back to bursting point and I would certainly have replied in the affirmative when Alison spoke for the first time and in a sweet little voice said: 'What a nice, big stiffstander, sir. Did I make your prick swell? I can hardly wait to have you slide it inside my pussey, but would you mind if Polly and I get ourselves warmed-up first?'

'No, not at all, Alison, please carry on,' I croaked and Polly drew the trembling girl down onto the bed between the two of us and parted her thighs. 'You lucky girl, you're going to be fucked very shortly,' she said softly. 'Mister Rupert, look closely at this lovely creature. Just look at her flushed, aroused face, her stiff tawny titties and her luscious cunney. Isn't she simply divine?'

The two girls embraced and slipped their arms around each other's waists in a loose, almost casual hug which quickly tightened and brought their breasts and bellies fiercely into contact. Alison tilted her head and raised her mouth to Polly's lips and closed her eyes expectantly. Her hands quivered as they pressed hotly into the base of Polly's back and the more experienced girl looked down on the lovely, breathless girl, studying the intense desire which was etched upon Alison's face as she yielded to her natural instincts.

At first they kissed like sisters, their red lips meeting in a tentative brushing which gradually deepened into a far more urgent, passionate pressure as their bodies rubbed sensually together. Polly's mouth opened and she probed with the tip of her tongue, sliding it slowly but insistently between Alison's teeth in an inquisitive caress around her gums. This delicious oral stimulation aroused Alison to a sudden, overwhelming passion and her hands slid feverishly up and down Polly's back. This sensuous massage set Polly off and she shuddered violently, thrusting her breasts and pussey forward as she darted her tongue backwards and forwards inside Alison's mouth.

Now Polly cleverly arranged the younger girl's position, making her lie partly on her right side facing me. Her right leg was pushed out almost straight and her left one was drawn up with the heel of her foot being hooked behind Polly's neck as she pressed her face against Alison's wonderful blonde fringed pussey and taking a deep breath, she inhaled the pungent pussey odour. Polly rested her left cheek on Alison's thigh as she slid her left arm under her waist, leaving her right hand to toy with Alison's nut brown pointed nipples. Then when both had settled into the most comfortable position, Polly pressed the gentlest of kisses on Alison's cunney, now and then letting the very tip of her tongue glide between the moistening love lips.

I now scrambled onto my knees and peered down at the thrilling scenario. The serrated lips of Alison's exquisite cunney parted as Polly now thrust her tongue more sharply between them and tongued along the sopping slit whilst now Alison's clitty popped out, as big as a boy's thumb. Polly passed her tongue lasciviously over the rounded ball and nipped at it playfully with her teeth. This made Alison cry out with joy as she tore wildly at the sheets, dragging her body across the bed as Polly stayed with her, her mouth glued tenaciously to Alison's juicy cunt.

This lewd orgiastic display sent me frantic with unslaked desire and I moved quickly behind Polly and slid my shaft in the crevice between her rounded buttocks straight into her own well-oiled honeypot. My hips jerked back and forth whilst I fucked the delicious girl doggie-style, and as my prick slicked in and out of Polly's pussey, I frigged her swollen, erect nipples between my fingers.

But Alison had seen me get behind Polly and she cried out, 'Oh, sir, you did promise that you'd fuck me first!'

Polly lifted her head from Alison's pussey and said thickly, 'Alison's right, Mister Rupert, you had better go on and take my place, but hurry as she's almost ready to spend.'

She rolled off Alison and quick as a flash I took her place, kissing the quivering young girl as I said, 'Happy birthday, Alison, I hope you enjoy your present.' For reply she slipped her hands around my bum cheeks and gripped them as she pushed her glorious breasts up against my chin and manoeuvred one up to my lips. Naturally I bent down and sucked it up inside my mouth as her hands now roamed all over my body, setting my skin on fire. I moved my tongue downwards, drawing circles across her belly even further downwards to her soft blonde nest of cunney hair. Dipping my face close, I licked my fingers and separated the folds, sniffing up the tangy cuntal aroma and lapping up the love juice which Polly's ministrations had already caused to flow. Spreading her cunney lips with my tongue, I explored for a moment, gauging her responses. Then, sliding my arms round her thighs I adjusted my position and tongued her in long flowing licks, flicking her engorged clitty, pushing against the hood.

My tongue moved quickly along her crack as I licked and lapped the tasty juices which now filled my mouth and she let out yelps of delight as she reached the pinnacle of erotic ecstasy.

'Oooh! Oooh! Oooh!' she squealed as I lifted my head and raised myself over her, holding my painfully stiff prick as I guided the knob towards its juicy haven and I delighted in an exquisite pleasure when my helmet parted her cunney lips and I slowly but firmly inserted my throbbing tool inside her slippery sheath. I slid my shaft forward until I was buried up to my balls in Alison's cunt and at first I lay quite still, savouring the feel of the velvety walls of her love channel, as she began to move her hips sinuously, discovering that she could work her cunt up and down my cock with ease as I began to pump up and down and my balls smacked a fine dance against her bottom with every thrust. I pounded to and fro into her squishy cunney, my hands gripping her luscious bum cheeks, as now, at the urging of Polly, I lifted my legs so she could snuggle under my thighs with her head on the sheet and begin sucking my balls whilst she reached down to frig her cunney with her fingers.

Of course, this extra icing on the cake soon sent the surge of spunk shooting up my stem, but by great effort I managed to delay the exquisite moment as the clinging muscles of Alison's cunt continued to sleek back and forth along my sated shaft. However, I would challenge even Sir Clive Bull, perhaps the most noted cocksman south of the Border, to have held back any longer – I certainly could not for more than a few seconds and with a mighty groan I flooded Alison's love hole with a torrent of creamy jism as the sticky essence poured out of my prick, completely filling her cunney and trickling down her inner thighs whilst she screamed out in joy as a huge orgasm shuddered through her delicious body.

'Congratulations, Rupert! Well fucked, sir!' came a familiar female voice from the side of the bed and I looked up to see that the speaker was none other than Diana who had quietly entered the bedroom with Henry and Nancy whilst I had been in the throes of the above described threesome with Alison and Polly.

'Oh Rupert, you did promise me to fuck me first tonight,' said Nancy reproachfully. 'I suppose it's my own fault for getting too carried away with Henry, though I'm sure you will not cavil at my being fucked by your old friend.'

'Not in the slightest, Nancy,' I replied with genuine relief. 'I'm only too pleased that you have been enjoying yourself – but what about you, Diana? I hope that you haven't been left out in the cold.'

'Certainly not,' Henry interrupted indignantly. 'What kind of chap do you take me for? Any man worth his salt would give his right arm for a chance to fuck a beautiful girl like Diana.'

Diana gave a little mock-curtsey and said, 'Thank you, Henry, how sweet of you to say so. You were pretty good in bed yourself and I'm not just saying that because you bought three of my paintings for your proposed New York exhibition of young artists.'

This was good news indeed and there was even better to come. 'Yes, and I purchased Diana's portrait of Sir Louis Segal and also two of her landscapes of Knaresborough Castle,' Nancy chipped in, 'so I think Diana is a very happy young lady.'

'And she certainly deserves to be,' came Cecily's voice from behind the group which slightly startled them. 'Oh, I'm sorry, I didn't mean to make you jump ... There's just one thing wrong here, though,' she added with a twinkle in her eye. 'Why are you three dressed whilst the rest of us are naked?'

'That's good thinking, darling,' said Diana, hastily unbuttoning her dress. 'Move over, Rupert, I think that Cecily would like to congratulate me in her very own special way.

It took only moments for Diana to undress and everyone in the room thrilled at the sight of her superb lissome nakedness. Diana looked the very acme of feminine perfection, and when she raised her arms to pin up her tresses of light ash blonde hair around her graceful neck, the sight of her proud, firm breasts sent my cock shooting up, and Polly reached over and grabbed my thick stalk, manipulating my foreskin to uncap my swollen knob.

She looked invitingly at Diana as if to ask whether she should keep my prick in a state of stiffness for Diana's use but Cecily took command of the situation and issued some crisp orders for us all, 'Polly, please would you keep Rupert's cock stiff for Nancy as he has yet to fulfil his promise to fuck her – as for you Henry, you should also take off your clothes and attend to the needs of young Alison who is lying there very demurely, although I can see from the lascivious look on her face that she would love to play with your circumcised cock especially as she probably hasn't seen one before.

'As for me, as Diana just said, I'm going to congratulate her in my own special way,' she added, pulling the eiderdown off the bed and spreading it on the floor next to the bed. Then she let the towel which was draped round her hips fall to the ground, and she moved across to smooth her hands sensuously over Diana's equally nude body. The two girls embraced and kissed lovingly, their tongues fluttering together as their hands roamed around the soft curves of each other's pretty rose tipped breasts. They sank down onto the eiderdown and I threw a pillow down against which Diana could rest her head as she lay back and parted her legs for Cecily's hand to insinuate itself between them.

'Oooh, what a lovely blonde pussey you have, Diana,' Cecily sighed as she cupped her hand around the exquisite blonde bush. 'Open your thighs a little wider, darling, bend your knees and then you can rub yourself off against my hand.'

Diana sighed with contentment as her delicious breasts jiggled from side to side as she worked her cunney lips backwards and forwards against the heel of Cecily's palm.

'Isn't that nice,' cooed Cecily rhetorically, as she raised her thumb to caress Diana's clitty with each upward thrusting of the blonde girl's hips. This exciting sensation made Diana moan petulantly and work her bottom faster whilst Cecily increased the pressure by cleverly swirling her thumb around the little unhooded ball which had popped out like a tiny prick from Diana's pussey.

Cecily muttered, 'Ah, darling, you have such a sensitive clitty, I can feel it bouncing against my fingers. Now let me finger fuck you – mmm, how hot it feels inside your cunney. How it sucks in my finger so easily! If only I possessed a prick I would love to slide it in and out of your honeypot.'

The lewd girl now kissed Diana's erect red nipples which had flared up into two hard little points and then swept downwards towards her sopping crack where she slid her tongue through the pouting lips deep into the cleft, prodding her clitty as she worked her tongue deeper and deeper into Diana's soaking quim, which was now creamed liberally with the pungent love juice which was running down her thighs.

Cecily's glorious young backside was now high in the air and at Polly's whispered instruction, Alison clasped hold of Henry's cock, which she had been licking and lapping up to a huge erection, and pulled my friend by his prick behind Cecily. When she saw him, she pulled her bum cheeks apart and slightly parted her legs and gasped, 'Don't go up my bum because Rupert's been there already, but you can fuck me doggie-style if you like.'

Cecily reached back and directed Henry's wide purple knob between her love lips as she bent down again and continued to suck on Diana's juicy cunt with renewed relish. The sight of this erotic tableau had sent my own tadger high in the air and Nancy, who had by now also thrown off her clothes, pulled me down on the bed and on her knees began lustily sucking my shaft, taking great gulps of cock as her head bobbed up and down, whilst Polly slid her hand between Nancy's legs and started to tickle her pussey. This so fired Alison that she lay beside me playing with her breasts whilst Nancy stretched out a hand to frig the young girl's gorgeous golden haired cunt.

I was lying on the edge of the bed and so could look down on what was happening down on the eiderdown. It was easy to tell from Diana's high-pitched squeals that she was thoroughly enjoying being licked out by Cecily, who herself was very happy at having Henry plunge his prick inside her whilst his hands came round to play with her succulent large nipples. Indeed, just as I glanced at the lascivious trio, Henry gave a deep growl and jerked back and forth in a short, convulsive movement as he creamed Cecily's cunney with a liberal coating of frothy white jism which jetted out of his twitching tool.

'A-h-r-e! A-h-r-e! A-h-r-e!' gasped Cecily as her body was racked by a thrilling all-over orgasm. She was forced to suspend her tonguing of Diana's cunt and roll out from between her legs which made the poor girl wail, 'Oh no, I haven't come yet! Henry, will you please finish me off?'

'I'll do my level best,' said Henry, taking his glistening semi-hard shaft in his hand and rubbing it furiously until it swelled back up to its fullest height.

Diana clambered up and with a gleam in her blue eyes, grasped hold of Henry's circumcised cock, 'You really must be a little tired after fucking Cecily. Lie back on this pillow and shut your eyes whilst I sit on your nice wet cock which you'll feel become embedded in my tight little wet cunney.'

He was only too pleased to fall in with such a plan and, as he stretched himself out, Diana straddled Henry's heaving frame with a quick jump and sat herself down on his thick flagpole which slid effortlessly into her sopping love box. She pivoted gracefully, swivelling on his tingling tool and bouncing up and down as he moulded her superbly firm breasts with his hands, arching his back to catch her rhythm and they moved in time, their interlocking respective cock and cunney totally oblivious to everything except their joyous mutual thrusting.

By now, Nancy was more than ready to be fucked and she lifted her lips away from my cock and gently moved her fingers away from Alison's cunt. She lay back, opened her legs and lifted her bottom as I carefully pushed my gleaming knob between her yielding cunney lips. She writhed and twisted in ecstasy in answer to my urgent pumping, her legs curled around my waist. We were both so fired up that very soon she screamed, 'I'm going to spend! I'm going to spend! Give it to me, Rupert! Come deep into me! Do it! Do it!'

I pushed forward again a few more times, but on the last delicious stroke I held my throbbing tool inside her honeypot for some fifteen seconds before pulling out my shaft completely and then with one almighty shove, I thrust in one final time and spunked great gushes of sticky jism into her welcoming love channel.

Meanwhile, a loud cry from Diana proclaimed the news that Henry's thick boner had ejaculated a copious emission of manly essence inside her pussey which left poor Polly and Alison totally cockless for neither Henry nor myself were in any state to continue this sport and both of us needed time to rejuvenate our overworked pricks and balls.

But I had not credited Polly Aysgarth with the resourcefulness which she now showed, for she rummaged underneath her dress which was lying nearby and with a flourish produced a leather box which she must have brought in my bedroom with her.

643

'Would you be so kind as to move up and let me snuggle up to Alison?' she enquired. Naturally, Nancy and I complied with this reasonable request. Polly thanked us and slipped in besides Alison, who murmured, 'Have you brought Herr Schnickelbaum's marvellous comforter?'

'Of course I have, you silly goose, I knew it would come in useful tonight,' said Polly, climbing on top of the trembling young girl so that their two naked bodies rubbed together cheek by jowl, or more accurately in this case, nipple to nipple and pussey to pussey. Alison threw back her head and Polly began to fondle her waiting high pointed breasts, swirling the hardened nipples in her mouth, making her shiver with lustful anticipation whilst Polly now moved her hands across the girl's white, flat belly and down into the corn-coloured silky moss of hair which lightly covered the pink, pouting pussey lips, around which Polly drew tiny, hard triangles until Alison was squirming with pleasure and then dipped her finger delicately inside Alison's yielding cunney lips.

'Oh, Polly! That's simply wonderful!' she whispered, as Polly now kissed her titties and tummy and then moved down to lap at her sopping crack. Then suddenly Polly lifted her head and asked me to pass the small leather box to her.

I did so and we all looked on with added interest as Polly opened it up and with a flourish brought out a superbly formed rubber dildo of the two headed variety – moulded by Herr Schnickelbaum of Vienna, as Polly informed us afterwards, upon the elephantine organs of Baron Lothar von Ober-gurgel and Count Gewirtz of Galicia.

644

Then she also took out of the box a bottle of orange flavoured oil and liberally poured the contents over both heads of the dildo, letting the last drains run down on to Alison's pussey which she now started to kiss again but this time, pressing the dildo to the entrance of her cunt, working it in slowly until Alison gasped out that her cunney was now crammed with this imitation prick.

Polly pulled herself up until she was sitting astride Alison's thighs, fingering herself with one hand whilst with the other she continued to fuck the younger girl's sopping pussey with the rubber cock. When her own cunt was juiced up, she carefully slid the other exposed head of the dildo into her honeypot and reached forward to pull Alison closer to her so that the two tribades were pressed together, tittie to tittie, cunt to cunt. Alison wrapped her legs as tightly as she could round Polly's back, who did the same and the two girls rocked back and forth, achieving a rhythm which was sending pulses of pleasure to every nerve centre in their bodies, and as their excitement grew, their motions became more and more frenzied.

'Aaaah! Aaaah! Polly, what a wonderful fuck! Aaaah! Aaah! Don't stop, don't stop!' screamed Alison. Polly gasped, 'I won't, I won't! How scrumptious! Do it more, that's the way!' as they fucked themselves beautifully on their magical dildo which prodded through their love channels, nipping its way through the velvety grooves of their cunts as they arched their bodies in ecstasy.

'I don't think either of them are missing our

stiff cocks at all,' Henry commented, as the two girls began to shudder and their heads thrashed about as they spent together, swimming in a sea of love juice and almost swooning clean away with the ecstatic enjoyment afforded by their efforts.

Polly and Alison lay there for some moments, heaving and panting with their cunnies still pressed together by the dildo, of which only a fraction of an inch was visible. Nancy used her long tapering fingers to manipulate it out of them, first from Alison's squelchy love channel and then from Polly's well-oiled pussey.

Watching this sensual display had excited me so much that my prick had forgotten how tired it had been and was now as hard and stiff as it had been when I had woken up back in Bedford Square at seven o'clock that morning. 'It's time to pay homage to your lovely cunt, Nancy,' I said forcefully, giving my shaft a few quick rubs to bring it up to its fullest dimensions.

'Come on then, you big cocked boy, show me what you can do!' enthused the American girl who opened her thighs as I rolled across on top of her. My hands moved over her aroused body with practised ease. I squeezed her large, firm breasts and rubbed the big, dark nipples against my palms which made them rise up into little red stalks. I kissed her forehead and worked downwards via her cheeks, lips, breasts and tummy to her open, wet cunney which smelled really nice, with a spicy tang that had my mouth watering. I slurped around Nancy's cunt and prised open her pussey lips with my fingers, sinking them slowly into her sopping slit which was already dribbling with love juice. She squeezed her breasts as I gently heaved myself upwards and when I was on top of her she wrapped her arms and legs around me as I guided my cock into her glistening little nookie and at once we fell into a completely abandoned bout of wild, uninhibited fucking.

Nancy managed to contract her cunney muscles so that her honeypot took hold of my prick like a delicate, soft hand as I pumped my raging shaft in and out of her sodden pussey. She urged me to thrust deeper as she raised her legs to rest them on my shoulders and her juices dripped against my balls as they banged against her arse. Cupped now in my palms, her tight bum cheeks rotated almost savagely as my lusty cock drove home, and her kisses rained upon my neck as the friction in her love channel reached new heights and the sensual girl reached climax after climax as my throbbing tool slewed back and forth.

'Go on, Rupert, spunk into me,' she gasped, and I plunged down as hard as I could, crushing her luscious breasts beneath me as her cunt squeezed my cock even more tightly and this voluptuous pressure was too great for me to bear. I sensed the creamy jism rising from my balls and seconds later, with a tremendous woosh, it surged out of me, spurting from my knob inside her in a huge spend which seemed to last and last as I ejaculated what seemed like gallons of sticky spunk into Nancy's juicy, dark warmth, whilst she gripped my bottom and pushed me ever deeper inside her as we shouted with joy in our mutual orgasm.

She squeezed my balls as I withdrew and the last drains of my emission trickled down her thigh as we lay back exhausted though we had enough energy to raise a smile when our audience spontaneously broke into a round of applause.

'That was a very well-executed fuck, if I might be so bold as to say so,' commented Polly, and Diana agreed, saying, 'There's a lot to be said for the good old-fashioned missionary position.'

'Very true,' said Cecily thoughtfully. 'Although I am very fond of the Eastern position much favoured by Sir Clive Bull where the man sits down with his feet crossed and you sit on his cock with your feet round his back. You only have to rock backwards and forwards for your clitty to be wonderfully stimulated.'

Diana nodded her head and said, 'I'm also keen on that position, especially with such a thick prick as Sir Clive's in my cunt, but have you tried the Lotus variation which I think is even better? One of my lecturers at the Sorbonne taught this to me – the boy lies supine whilst you sit on top of him with your back turned to his face whilst you fold your legs into the classic Oriental position with each foot placed on the opposite thigh. His cock enters you from the rear which I always enjoy and uses his arms to steady you. I just close my eyes and lose myself in self absorbed contemplation as I bounce up and down on his throbbing cock.'

'I've never tried fucking that way,' said Alison shyly, 'but then I do like to thresh around and grab hold of my boy friend's cock and play with his balls whilst we are fucking, just like you did, Miss Diana, with Mr Henry's prick.'

'Well, I must say that I do prefer looking at my partner,' declared Henry, as Diana gave his prick a few loving rubs and it rose majestically to attention from the curly black mass of hair at the base of his belly, 'otherwise the whole act becomes too impersonal for my liking, and as far as I'm concerned, the cleft position for fucking takes a lot of beating as it allows you to look at each other although there is a degree of detachment for either party if they want it.

'It's not difficult to get into either – this is how I love to do it. I kneel, leaning backwards from the waist with my left hand behind me on the bed for support. The girl sits astride in basically the same position with her arms extended behind her. We're able to look at one another but from some way away as we both now lean backwards. However, as she's sitting on my thighs above me with only my hand on her backside, it's up to her to control the pace of the fuck.'

This little lecture seemed to spur Diana who bent down in front of Henry as she frigged his sinewy shaft and then opened her lips and took his hairy ballsack into her mouth, sucking slowly first one ball and then the other. The sight of this erotic play stirred my own prick which swelled up to attention as I jumped off the bed, positioned myself behind Diana's delicious bum cheeks, and pulled aside the soft globes to edge my knob towards her pouting cunt.

She reached behind for my cock and guided my

649

tool towards its chosen port of call and with one vigorous shove I buried my shaft in to the hilt and my balls flopped against her heaving bum cheeks. This scene so excited Cecily that she slid herself between my legs and began to copy what Diana was doing to Henry, licking and lapping my balls and gobbling them each in turn inside her wet mouth and coating them with her saliva from her wet tongue.

I thrust my cock back and forth as I flicked my fingers around Diana's hard, red nipples in an ecstasy of enjoyment and the other girls now joined this stimulating fucking chain by joining Nancy on the bed. Whilst Diana continued to frig his cock and suck his balls, Henry took the dildo in his hand and leaning forward, slid it into Polly's waiting honeypot whilst the lewd girl, who was lying between Nancy and Alison, used her hands to finger fuck each of the other girls' pussies whilst they sucked her titties. Henry and I changed positions to ensure that every girl was afforded the pleasure of having a thick throbbing length of prick in their cunney and we manfully managed to give each of them satisfaction before we all collapsed into a sweaty, naked heap of bodies on my bed.

However, at around two o'clock in the morning I woke up with a start. It suddenly occurred to me that what now seemed ages ago before our lustful orgy, Cecily and I had left my parents, Aunt Penelope and the Wigmores to their bridge and had not returned even to say good-night! I gnawed on my bottom lip as I wondered whether the others had also rushed up to my room without going back to see the older members of the household.

Polly stirred and asked what was the matter, but when I told her she whispered, 'Don't worry, Rupert, your Aunt Penelope is a real sport. She guessed what was going to happen tonight and before Alison and I came up here, your Aunt told me that she would make apologies on your behalf and tell your parents that the young guests were all rather tired and had gone upstairs for an early night. She knew the others wouldn't mind as they were all keen bridge players which let her off the hook and she was also able to slip away upstairs for a nice fuck.'

'Three cheers for Aunt Penelope! But what are you talking about her slipping away for a nice fuck?'

'Oh dear, I'm sorry, I shouldn't have said anything, Mister Rupert, but I thought you knew about your Aunt and Mr Goldhill,' she said apologetically.

'Goldhill?' I echoed blankly. 'Are you telling me that our butler has been fucking my Aunt?'

'Well, yes, I'm surprised you never knew. I've a shrewd suspicion that your mother has guessed what's been going on over the last couple of years.'

She yawned and snuggled back down against the small of Henry's back. 'Come on, let's get back to sleep,' she muttered, but my curiosity was aroused. I slipped out of bed, put on a dressing gown and tip-toed upstairs to the servants' quarters. Was old Goldhill really slewing his gnarled old truncheon in and out of my Aunt's juicy pussey? I scoffed at the thought, but seeing is believing. When silently I opened his bedroom door, with my own eyes I saw our faithful old retainer and Aunt Penelope together in each other's arms, with her hand clasped round his cock even though they were both fast asleep.

I closed the door as silently as I had opened it and made my way back to my own room. At first I was irritated by the fact that our servant had fucked an honorary member of the Mountjoy family but I soon came to realise that this was an unworthy thought. After all, Aunt Penelope must have wanted the liaison, so in fact our butler had only been doing his duty! Why, it would serve Uncle Stephen right for leaving her alone so often – I remember my mother saying once that she was certain that he could cut down his trips to our capital city if he so wished. 'I can't think why he wants to go to London so often,' she had said to my father, 'and why doesn't he ever take Penelope with him? For instance, he only went to a meeting at his club last week.'

As my more radical female friends are wont to say these days, what's sauce for the goose is sauce for the gander, which would explain why even if she had guessed what was going on, my mother had decided that it served Stephen right if his wife was forced to look elsewhere for her intimate needs.

With that in mind, I settled down to go back to sleep. But Polly had other ideas and she grabbed hold of my prick as soon as I returned to bed. 'Now you've woken me up, I can't get back to sleep,' she complained, stroking my shaft so sensuously that it immediately swelled and bounded in her hand.

'Polly, you've got to be up at six o'clock as usual,' I warned her but she pouted her lips and continued to frig my cock and begged me to thread her juicy cunney. 'It's my day off tomorrow so I'd love a quick little fuck,' she pleaded as she kissed my uncapped knob, 'then I'll be able to fall asleep.'

Well, how caddish it would be to refuse a request from a damsel in distress? I followed her as she slipped out of bed and lay on the carpet, leaning back and raising her knees, spreading them invitingly as I moved across her and planted her legs on top of my shoulders.

'We must be quiet and not disturb the others,' I said softly as I rubbed the tip of my cock against her soaking crack and slowly sank my shaft inside her wet cunt. I pulled out and re-entered, and her slick love channel clasped my cock lovingly with each long, slow stroke. Although this was as enjoyable as ever, the hour was too late for a prolonged bout and as soon as my balls began rhythmically to slap against her backside, I let myself go and unleashed a flood of hot spunk inside her luscious love nest which caused her to shiver all over and spend profusely. Polly was as good as her word for almost as soon as we had climbed back into bed, she snuggled down again and was asleep within minutes.

But I lay awake for a while musing on the morrow. This coming day we were all travelling to York for the evening reception for His Gracious Majesty King Edward VII. I was looking forward to meeting the Merry Monarch who was, from all accounts, a man after my own heart, who enjoyed life to the full. I would go to York with a sore cock after this wild night's fucking, which was not yet over, for the girls would doubtless demand that Henry and I perform again when they woke up. But I would also have a light heart as the main mission – to help Diana Wigmore's career progress – had been accomplished and brewing in the back of my mind was a happy intuition that in the next few days I would be taking part in some further lusty bedroom adventures.

Was I to be proved right? I will tell all, dear reader, in frank, uncensored detail, in the next volume of my memoirs.

TO BE CONTINUED . . .

VICTORIAN EROTIC CLASSICS
AVAILABLE FROM CARROLL & GRAF

☐ Anonymous / Altar of Venus	4.50
☐ Anonymous / Autobiography of a Flea & Other Tart Tales	5.95
☐ Anonymous / Black Magic	6.95
☐ Anonymous / Careless Passion	5.95
☐ Anonymous / Confessions of an English Maid & Other Delights	5.95
☐ Anonymous / The Consummate Eveline	4.95
☐ Anonymous / Court of Venus	3.95
☐ Anonymous/ Best of Erotic Reader	6.95
☐ Anonymous / Eroticon	4.95
☐ Anonymous / Eroticon II	4.95
☐ Anonymous / Eroticon III	4.50
☐ Anonymous / Fallen Woman	4.50
☐ Anonymous / Harem Nights	4.95
☐ Anonymous / The Intimate Memoirs of an Edwardian Dandy	4.95
☐ Anonymous / The Intimate Memoirs of an Edwardian Dandy, Vol. II	4.95
☐ Anonymous / The Intimate Memoirs of an Edwardian Dandy, Vol. III	4.95
☐ Anonymous / Lay of the Land	4.50
☐ Anonymous / The Libertines	4.50
☐ Anonymous / Maid and Mistress	4.50
☐ Anonymous / A Man with a Maid	5.95
☐ Anonymous / Memoirs of Josephine	4.50
☐ Anonymous / The Merry Menage	4.50
☐ Anonymous / The Oyster	4.50
☐ Anonymous / The Oyster II	3.95
☐ Anonymous / The Oyster III	4.50
☐ Anonymous / The Oyster V	4.50
☐ Anonymous / Pagan Delights	5.95
☐ Anonymous / The Pearl	6.95
☐ Anonymous / Pleasures and Follies	3.95
☐ Anonymous / Romance of Lust	5.95

☐ Anonymous / Rosa Fielding: Victim of Lust	3.95
☐ Anonymous/ Sharing Sisters	4.95
☐ Anonymous / Secret Lives	3.95
☐ Anonymous / Sensual Secrets	4.50
☐ Anonymous / Sweet Confessions	4.50
☐ Anonymous / Sweet Tales	4.50
☐ Anonymous / Tropic of Lust	4.50
☐ Anonymous / Venus Butterfly	3.95
☐ Anonymous / Venus Delights	3.95
☐ Anonymous / Venus Disposes	3.95
☐ Anonymous / Venus in India	3.95
☐ Anonymous / Victorian Fancies	4.50
☐ Anonymous / The Wantons	4.50
☐ Anonymous / White Thighs	4.50
☐ Anonymous / Youthful Indiscretions	4.50
☐ Cleland, John / Fanny Hill	4.95
☐ van Heller, Marcus / Adam and Eve	3.95
☐ van Heller, Marcus / Lusts of the Borgias	4.95
☐ van Heller, Marcus / Seduced	5.95
☐ van Heller, Marcus / Unbound	5.95
☐ van Heller, Marcus / Venus in Lace	3.95
☐ Villefranche, Anne-Marie / Passion d'Amour	5.95
☐ Villefranche, Anne-Marie / Scandale d'Amour	5.95
☐ Villefranche, Anne-Marie / Secrets d'Amour	4.50
☐ Villefranche, Anne-Marie / Souvenir d'Amour	4.50
☐ von Falkensee, Margarete / Blue Angel Confessions	6.95
☐ "Walter"/ My Secret Life	7.95